Lightbringer

A novel by
Mike Bara

ACKNOWLEDGEMENTS

I would like to acknowledge the following beings for their participation in the creation of this book.

First, my brother Dave, who showed me that it was possible. Second, Scott Miller at Trident Media for being the best agent for this work that anyone could have. As always, Indy, Aurora, Miss Fluffy-Muffy and Seabass for all the lap time while I worked on it. Aviva Layton for the superb job of professional editing she did to get the manuscript in shape. And finally to Richard Hoagland, whose work gave me the idea.

1.

Dr. Xian Tsien didn't know it yet, but he had less than five minutes to live.

He stumbled through the darkness, his head throbbing from the blow he'd taken when the dark SUV had run his car off the road and into a tree. He stopped briefly, his hand going to the wound on his forehead and coming back with warm, wet blood on it. Luckily, he hadn't lost consciousness, but his mind was foggy and he found it hard to focus. He wondered if he had suffered a mild concussion. He consoled himself with the thought that it didn't really matter much. They were after him, and if he didn't get away into the foothills, he was sure he'd have a great deal more to worry about than a headache.

He started to move again, shuffling through the scrub brush as best he could. He struggled to maintain his balance as he went downhill, grabbing tree branches as he slid across the hard, dusty ground.

Then he heard a sound behind him. It was not the awkward sounds he'd been making, but swift rushes of air as his pursuers moved lithely from place to place. There had been three dark-clothed men in the SUV. They were getting closer now, and he worried that they could see him in the dim moonlight that illuminated the Pasadena hills. The darkness might be his only advantage— if he remembered enough of his youthful military training back on Taiwan to use it.

He pushed himself close to a thick pine tree, clutching the trunk for support as the world spun about him. The moment of wooziness passed and he tried to control his hard breathing, to be as silent as he could. As he checked over his shoulder, he could see the lights of the Jet Propulsion Laboratory in the distance below. At that moment, those lights meant safety. Even though he was sure his work at JPL was the source of his present predicament, it still seemed like a much friendlier place than the dark, dusty hillside he was clinging to now.

He caught a glimpse of a silhouette against the lights of the lab. The figure seemed to be wearing a black body suit with a stocking cap or hood over it. *They sure as hell aren't JPL security,* he thought. And even though he had no idea who his pursuers were, he knew exactly what they were after.

His hand went instinctively to the flash drive in his coat pocket. It was a new tan canvas jacket. He'd just bought it. Now it was torn and matted with dirt and blood. He refocused; it was difficult, but he managed to stay almost completely still as he watched the dark figure move past him and continue down the hillside. His tactic had bought him some time, but how much?

After a few more moments of silence passed, Tsien risked moving. He made his way back up the hill as quietly and swiftly as he could go.

Crawling up through the brush, he found himself back on the dirt road. He considered making a run for it down the road toward the lab, but he had to assume his pursuers were faster than he was and would cut him off before he could get to safety. Looking up the road, he saw the lights of a Forest Service shack at the top of the mountain. He prayed that the shack was occupied, it was fire season after all— and that his years of jogging these hills would pay off.

It would be a tough climb, maybe another five hundred feet up and around a twisting road in the dark and heat of an Indian summer, but he was in reasonably good shape for his age. Besides, it was his only chance.

He took off running.

After thirty seconds he began to wonder if he'd lost them. At the one-minute mark, he was panting hard, straining against the exertion his body was unprepared for. Then he heard it, the unmistakable sound of footsteps behind him, running him down.

At most he'd made it maybe a hundred feet up the mountain. His right hip throbbed. It must have been injured when his car hit the tree. As he wheezed against the pain, his lungs straining for air, the idea of just giving up and dropping to his knees became very seductive. They were closing now, and he wondered if he could bargain for what they were after, offer it to them in return for his life. He didn't look back.

And then, they were on him.

One of the men struck him in the right leg with a club and continued past him. He crumpled to the gravel road, scraping his hands along the rough, rocky surface. A sharp pain radiated through his injured leg, and he cried out as a second man ran past him and struck him in the knee. A third man, like the others just a black blur against the dimly starred sky, swung at him with another club. His arms went up to instinctively cover his face, and the club struck him on the left forearm, shattering the bone.

He screamed out in agony as he collapsed on his back, writhing, his right kneecap broken, his left forearm shattered, and his right hip and head throbbing. He grasped his knee in a reflexive attempt to ease the pain as the three men began tearing at his clothes, ripping off the jacket and cutting his left shirtsleeve off with the swift slash of a knife. He screamed again while the third black figure worked at his feet, pulling off his shoes and socks. As the right sock was yanked off and thrown away, he prayed that they would not find the second flash drive he had secured there.

They lifted him to one knee, forcing him to kneel on the broken right cap. The pain was excruciating, and he found himself longing for unconsciousness. As they had lifted him, one of the men rolled up his left pant leg. Another of the men in black took a rope and fashioned a noose loosely around his neck.

Tsien knew at that moment that they meant to kill him. There was no idle lesson to be taught here, no message to be sent. They were going to end his life in some strange, ritualistic way, and his only hope was to find a way to bargain with them, to give them something they wanted more than his life.

"I . . ." he blurted out, barely able to speak through the pain, "I have the flash drive. Please! I have what you want! It's in the jacket! Take it and leave me!" He could see the eyes of the man in black standing directly over him. They were dark, soulless eyes. There was no mercy in them.

The first man signaled to the others, and they went to the jacket and rifled through it. Soon one of them held up the flash drive for the others to see. The man standing over him tightened the grip on his metal club and then reached out and pulled the noose tighter around Tsien's neck. Tsien closed his own eyes, eyes that were warm and human, and waited for the end of his life.

Abruptly the darkness was pierced by a blinding light. A split second later, Tsien heard the sound of tires spinning on the gravel road. He turned his head to the right and opened his eyes. A large white truck with its high beams glaring in the night was rounding the corner and coming up the road. In that brief moment of hope, Tsien allowed himself to believe he might yet escape, might still survive this night. He thought that the approaching headlights were the most beautiful thing he had ever seen. . .

Then, Tsien's world went forever black.

2.

FBI Special Agent Lori Pars looked down at the green light blinking on her cell phone. The smartphone sat precariously on the control panel of the treadmill she was using, vibrating as it blinked and threatening to pop right off the machine as she ran. The phone's ID panel indicated that it was her L.A. division lead, Ron Harmon calling.

Any business that could warrant a call from him at 2:00 A.M. probably couldn't wait for her to finish her run, but instead of stopping for the call, she increased her pace. Although she liked her boss, he wasn't someone she was anxious to talk with in the middle of the night. Sweat ran down her taut, athletic stomach as she pushed to the end of her run. Looking down, she saw the light blinking again.

Second ring.

For a brief moment, she considered letting the phone ring to her voicemail. No one could rightly expect her to be awake at this hour, much less in a position to reach her phone before the customary four rings. The light blinked relentlessly at her again.

Third ring.

She gathered herself as she slowed the treadmill to a crawl, pulling the white headphones out of her ears and wiping her face with a towel. As much as she would have liked to, she couldn't ignore the call any longer and she picked up the phone just as the fourth ring started and hit the talk button. "Special Agent Pars," she said, her manner as professional as it could be considering she was still slightly out of breath.

"Jesus Christ, Lori," said Harmon, "it's two in the morning! Are you in the gym? Don't you ever sleep?" He could obviously hear the treadmill winding down and the background music over the club's speaker system.

She balanced the phone on one shoulder and wiped more sweat from her strawberry-blonde, ponytailed hair. Harmon was a gruff and traditional cop from the Chicago streets, and he rarely disguised what he was thinking at any given moment. He was also prone to being overly friendly with his female subordinates. She decided it was none of his business what she was doing in the gym.

"What can I do for you at this hour, Chief?"

"Well, you're not gonna like it," he said, not commenting on how much he hated being called "Chief."

"Try me."

"We have a murder up in the Pasadena hills. I need you to handle it. The L.A. County Sheriff's on the scene right now, but they're waiting for you to get up there."

Lori's brow furrowed as she tried to make sense of what Harmon had just told her. For one thing, the local Pasadena PD should be handling the case, unless there was some reason they had called the county sheriff's department in on it. Even then, there would be no need for the FBI to be involved. "I'm sorry, but if the county sheriff is on the scene, why do I need to go up there? They've got jurisdiction."

"Yeah, they usually do. But this involves an employee of the Jet Propulsion Laboratory."

"I still don't see . . ."

He cut her off immediately. "Look, I may as well tell you now because you're gonna find out anyway. This wasn't my call. It came directly from AD Ruby's office. He specifically requested you."

"*Eric* Ruby?"

"Oh good, you've heard of him," Harmon said sarcastically.

Ruby had been one of her instructors at Quantico eight years before, and they'd had a fling that felt more like a serious love affair to her at the time. It was a view he had never shared.

She shut off the treadmill now and stood with the towel at her hip, still breathing a bit heavily from her run. The thought of dealing directly with Ruby again made her skin crawl.

"I'm not in homicide," she said firmly. "I'm in the National Security Branch. My expertise is in counterterrorism; you know that. Why don't you send Donovan? He's good."

"Donovan's on vacation. And besides, this *is* your area of expertise anyway."

"I don't see how."

"Because the assistant director in charge said it was, that's how," Harmon said sharply. He didn't like being questioned by his agents on anything. "You've been assigned temporarily by the AD to assist the Criminal Investigations Branch."

Lori was silent for a moment as she contemplated that piece of information. Harmon seemed bothered by the pause in their conversation. "Look, I know you weren't thrilled to be transferred to this command in the first place," he added more sympathetically.

"Not thrilled is putting it mildly, Chief."

Harmon cleared his throat before continuing. "But if the AD believed in you enough to request you from the Seattle office, he must know something about you that makes him think you can handle this case."

If you only knew, Lori thought.

"The dead man is an employee of the Jet Propulsion Laboratory who also happens to have a Level Three DARPA security clearance. That's why the Bureau has been called in on this."

"DARPA?" Lori knew what a Level Three clearance was—Top Secret. She, like all special agents, was required to have such a clearance herself. But she wasn't up on the alphabet soup of federal agency acronyms.

"The Defense Advanced Research Projects Agency," Harmon informed her. "I've ordered the area sealed and the suspect held until you can get up there."

"There's a suspect in custody?"

"Yeah. The AD doesn't want those bozos from the county sheriff screwing up this investigation, and I agree with him. This one goes way up, Lori, eyes on it all the way to the top of the Bureau. Get up there and report back to me as soon as you've made an initial inquiry."

"Yes, sir," she said, her manner all business.

"I'll send the GPS coordinates to your cell phone," he told her. Then he hung up abruptly. A few seconds later, the location arrived in a text message on her cell phone. She noted it, called up a map for directions, and stored it on her phone. It was at least a forty-five minute drive, even at this hour. She looked around the empty gym, wondering for a moment just what she *was* doing there at two in the morning, then grabbed her gym bag and headed for the shower.

Andrea Tully rolled over and tried to snuggle up with the man she knew only as "Trevor," but he was having none of it. He brushed her hand away and got out of bed, his skin still glistening from the exertion of their tryst. She smiled as she watched him walk across her bedroom and begin dressing, starting with his black boxer briefs. The coral-colored sodium streetlights coming through the partially opened blinds in her apartment accented his tall, masculine form like light and dark stripes on a tiger. Even though he was older than she, there was no gray in his thick, brown hair, and he still had an admirable, athletic physique.

"Where is it?" he said to her, fastening up his trousers.

It was always like this with Trevor, quick and rough, just the way she liked it, then on to business. Her bottom still stung from him slapping her, and her scalp was tingling from the forceful way he had yanked her by her long, dark hair.

"Where it always is," she said back to him with an adolescent tone to her voice.

He looked up from the chair where he was slipping on his expensive Bruno Magli shoes. "Aren't we a bit bratty today," he said, amused at her audacity. She liked that he spoke to her in a formal, educated British accent that was very different from the street lingo her young boyfriends tried to impress her with.

She slid down to the end of the bed and posed for him on her stomach, her still reddened rear end slightly elevated. "Maybe I need a spanking."

He stood and clamped on his Rolex watch. "*Another* spanking, my dear?" He smirked at her and then went to her closet. Standing on a stepstool, he pushed aside the attic panel and pulled down a brushed-titanium Apple laptop from the opening. After starting the computer and examining the contents in silence, he attached a flash drive to the USB port and began copying files to it.

As she watched him work, Andrea wondered what it would be like to be his girlfriend. She knew he had money; that much was obvious from the way he dressed and the silver-gray Maserati he always drove up in. But more than that, he was sophisticated, mysterious and interesting, with an agenda she could only guess at. She wondered if he was some kind of spy or private detective, but in her youthful naïveté, it never occurred to her that he might bring trouble into her life. All of this intrigue was only enhanced by the fact that after three months of seeing him at least once a week, she didn't even know if Trevor was his real name.

She understood the need for that kind of anonymity from her own experiences as a dancer in a strip club. She was always giving customers her dancer name and sometimes even a fake "real" name. She kept a separate cell phone just for calls and text messages from regulars who thought they were getting her personal number.

"Hey," she said after watching him for a few minutes, "why don't we hang out together this weekend?"

He looked up from whatever task he was performing on the laptop. "You mean go to the movies or have dinner at Koi?"

She broke into a big smile. "Yeah! That's exactly what I mean."

"I thought you were busy dancing for your customers on the weekends. And don't you have a live-in boyfriend?"

"Sort of," she said, rolling over and smacking herself on the hip. "But none of them treat me as well as you do."

"You mean as rough as I do."

"Yeah."

He finished up his task, pulled the flash drive out, closed the laptop, and restored it to its hiding place in her closet attic. Then he crossed the room to her dresser, took five one-hundred dollar bills from his wallet, and came to the bed to sprinkle them over her naked backside.

"I'm sorry, my dear, but you know my rules," he said, leaning down to kiss her on her rump. "No pleasure without business."

He put his wallet away, grabbed his car keys, and opened the door to her bedroom, stepping over the little black Scottie terrier that was waiting dutifully outside. He said nothing more and didn't look back until he was out the door. As she heard the deep, throaty sounds of his car engine revving, the terrier pattered over to the bed and barked a soft, questioning house bark at her.

Still lying on her stomach, she reached down and petted him with a few gentle strokes. "No, Brutus," she said in a soothing tone, "I don't think he loves us at all."

Three men huddled around a computer terminal in the Mission Control Center of the Jet Propulsion Laboratory. The room was dark and empty except for them, illuminated only by the dim blinking lights of dozens of other computers. The shades over the windows, where the public could watch the activity in the room during the daylight visiting hours, had been drawn. It was late at night, and normally no one was even in the MCC at this hour. A heavy-set mustachioed technician sat motionless at his computer terminal, intently watching the data stream on a nearby flat-panel monitor. The other two men stood behind him, their eyes transfixed by the three huge projection screens that dominated the far wall of the center. One of the men was tall, wavy haired, and dressed casually in jeans and an open-collared brown shirt. The other man was dressed in an impeccable charcoal-colored suit, sipping from a Starbucks coffee cup. His face was far more wrinkled than it should have been for a man of his age.

"Any second now," the taller man said. The technician made a few adjustments to his keyboard inputs.

"How much of a lag is there in the signal transfer, Dr. Saunders?" the craggy-faced man asked.

"Forty-three point three minutes," the taller man answered.

"Like he said, any second now," the technician added, still focused on his screen. He could not see the sour look the craggy-faced man gave him. A few seconds later, and the leftmost of the three screens, labeled HST, flickered to life and began to draw an image, line by line.

"Here we go," Saunders said, tension in his voice.

The image slowly formed, top to bottom, one line at a time. When it was complete, it showed a blurry red, spherical object, not even distinguishable as a planet.

"You fools," the man in the charcoal suit said angrily. "You haven't compensated properly for the relative motion. We can't tell a thing from this."

"Just wait," Saunders assured him. "The software will correct for it automatically."

As they watched, a second and then a third image formed on the successive two screens, each more clear and familiar than the last. Then the process started over again. After ten minutes, they had a crystal-clear, color-corrected, wide-angle image of the planet Jupiter.

"Enhance eleven by one-fifteen," Saunders instructed the technician. He dutifully did so. After a few minutes, a new close-up image of Jupiter's equatorial region appeared on the overhead screens. In the center of the image was a massive pitch-black spot, blotting out the surrounding bands of colorful clouds.

"We did it!" Saunders declared, a relieved smile crossing his face. The technician banged his fist on the console in front of him and turned to high-five the scientist. The craggy-faced man watched impassively.

"Be sure and quarantine these, as per the protocol," he reminded them. Saunders calmed a bit, the broad smile fading from his face. The technician turned back to his screen and typed in some codes. The large screens went back to displaying their usual telemetry and spacecraft status simulations.

"Done, sir," the technician said, turning around. "We're back to nominal on all the systems."

"Excellent," the older man said, sipping from his cup and putting his hand on the technician's shoulder. The big man jumped as if he'd been pricked with a sharp needle. "Hey!" he said, "what the fuck was that?"

As the other two men watched, the color drained from the technician's face and his hands went to his throat. Saunders took a few steps backward, watching in horror, but the craggy-faced man just sipped from his paper coffee cup once again. The big man tried to stand and reach out for Saunders, panic on his face, but his legs were already dying and wouldn't support his weight any longer. In a moment it was over, and the technician lurched forward and crashed to his console face-first, knocking his own coffee cup to the floor as his eyes stared sightlessly into space.

Saunders stepped back and immediately broke out in a cold sweat. His eyes darted back and forth between the dead technician and the gray skinned monster that had so indifferently killed him. His craggy face contorted into a tight, almost disgusted expression. "What did you think, doctor? This was all just some academic exercise? You knew from the beginning that this job would have a price. If you couldn't pay it perhaps you shouldn't have asked for places for you and your family."

Saunders felt a sick emptiness in the pit of his stomach. "No," he said cautiously. "I'm grateful for my place in this project."

The charcoal suited man brushed the spilled coffee off his suit pants and looked back over his shoulder at the technicians still body as he did so. "Shame for such a young man to die of a heart attack," he said casually. "Good thing you have such excellent death benefits for your employees. Mrs. Oberg is going to need them."

"Yeah," Saunders replied nervously, "we'll have to reconsider our workplace rules about letting anybody work graveyard shifts alone."

"I should think so."

The craggy-faced man walked past Saunders, brushing very close, then turned and extended his hand, the same one that he had touched the technician with. "Congratulations doctor," he said to Saunders.

The frightened scientist did not take his offered hand, and sweat began to bead up on his forehead.

"Relax, doctor," he said, a phony smile creasing his face. "We still have quite a ways to go yet." He stared Saunders down for a few more seconds and then withdrew his hand and headed for the main double doors. "And you have a great deal to do."

Saunders stood motionless, looking down at the lifeless body of the technician, resisting the temptation to vomit.

The craggy-faced man left his coffee cup on an empty console ledge as he pushed through the doors. "I'll let myself out," he called back casually.

Saunders waited without moving for another two minutes, flop sweat pouring down his torso. Then, satisfied that the other man was gone, he gathered his notes and got out the door as quickly as his feet would take him.

3.

As she drove up the I-210 toward Pasadena, Lori's mind raced. Why had Eric Ruby picked her for this case, given their history? What could there be about her that would be of such interest—or use—to him?

She did not by any stretch of the imagination have the best case closure rate in the office, and she had never even worked a homicide case before. At thirty-two, she'd had eight solid but unspectacular years on the job, mostly in counterterrorism. Jim Donovan or Connie Balver had a lot more experience with murder scenes. She doubted very much that Harmon would have assigned this case to her if the decision had been his.

Maybe, given the heat coming through the political channels—the "eyes" Ron Harmon had mentioned—Ruby had gone to her because he knew her well, or at least thought he did, and knew what he'd be getting in her. He'd been Assistant Director of the L.A. office for only nine months and hadn't had much time to review the personnel.

But that scenario assumed two things that were highly unlikely; first that he truly knew her well enough to count on her in what was sure to be a high-profile case, and second that she was sufficiently professional not to let their romantic history interfere with her performance.

All this reminded her that while Ruby might be a ruthless bastard with serious political ambitions, he wasn't stupid. When it came to his career, he'd taken a lot of risks to get what he wanted, but they were always well calculated. Since there was no way he could view Lori as anything but a wildcard in this case, that implied that Ruby hadn't chosen her for it at all. Somebody else, somebody above even him, must have handpicked her out of all the available agents.

As she tried to change lanes to the right toward the freeway exit, she was very aware of the high-speed traffic whizzing by. The Hollywood bars had closed up less than an hour before, and the customers, many of whom were likely to have been drinking too much, were powering home to the wealthy areas of Pasadena in their Porsches, Mercedes and BMWs. The last thing she needed was an accident to add to her worries.

She wasn't long off the freeway when she could see the lights of JPL in the distance, enclosed in an area once called the Devil's Canyon. Soon her car was snaking up the dirt road marked NF-2N70 in the hills above the lab. She took it easy as the road was twisty and very dark. Just as the thought crossed her mind that this would be a dangerous road to drive at high speed, she rounded a corner and came upon a crash scene. There were red and blue police and fire department strobe lights, and a tow truck was lifting a white Volvo from the hillside below. She pulled out her ID as she approached the roadblock, and the officer in charge waved her through.

Just about half a mile farther up, she came upon what she took to be the crime scene. There were two county police vehicles and a coroner's wagon parked in the middle of the road, their strobes lighting up the night sky. Off to one side, a white truck with a Forest Department insignia was parked with the driver's door open. A man sat on the sill of the truck with his head in his hands, guarded by two sheriff's deputies. Lori pulled over and got out of her car, and she was met by a sergeant from the sheriff's department as she approached the scene. He was a potbellied, gray-haired man in his early 50s with a slightly receding hairline. He wore a trim mustache and a no-nonsense attitude. He clearly didn't want Lori there.

"You must be the Fed," he said disdainfully. "I'm Jim Ellis." Lori flashed him her badge and walked past him to survey the scene. The coroner was standing over a figure that was lying facedown on the road while another member of his team took photos. There was a puddle of drying blood staining the dirt around the head of the victim. As she watched, a tarp was laid over the body. Several deputies were milling about and searching off the road and down the hillside. Lori turned to Ellis. "Special Agent Lori Pars. What have we got here?"

He seemed amused at her question. "Well, ma'am, judging by the dead body, I'd say we've got a homicide case."

She gave him a pointed look, and he continued more seriously. "Looks like we have a dead Asian male, approximately thirty-five years old and formerly employed down the road at the Jet Propulsion Laboratory. From the looks of him, he's been dead about two hours. You'll have to ask the coroner for a preliminary cause of death, but I'd say it was pretty obvious."

She waited for him to continue, but he just stared at her. "OK, I'll bite," Lori impatiently.

Ellis pointed toward the body. "Somebody bashed his skull in."

Lori nodded and then turned away. "What are they doing?" she asked, pointing out the deputies who were searching down the hillside.

Ellis grunted. "Looking for the footprints of the perps."

"I gather you think they're wasting their time?"

"Now that you're here it doesn't matter much what I think, does it lady?"

Lori tried to ignore the resentment she felt flowing from him and stick to business. "My report said you had a suspect in custody . . .?"

Ellis pointed to the man sitting on the door sill of the truck. "This is the guy who called it in. Said he saw who did it and they took off down the hill where my boys are searching. Claims there were three of 'em."

"And what do you think?" Lori asked, trying not to aggravate his obvious displeasure at her presence.

This time, Ellis smiled at her and crossed his arms. "I think he hit the poor bastard with his truck and is trying to get out of it."

Her one quick look at the body had told her that idea was ridiculous. "Well, then it wouldn't be a homicide, would it, Officer Ellis?"

He cracked a quick smile, but she could tell he was not really amused. He was just trying to get under her skin.

Humoring him in the interest of jurisdictional cooperation, Lori reached out for his flashlight, and they went to do a walk around the truck. She highlighted all the bumpers and panels, but there was no sign of an impact. Ellis smiled slyly at her. He clearly hadn't expected her to find any evidence to support his assertion. Handing him his flashlight, she approached the coroner. He was a tall, thin man with thick-rimmed black glasses and was speaking into a dictation recorder. His skin seemed oily, and there was a passionless grayness about him, something almost disturbing. She flashed him her badge. He stopped the recording and reached out his hand.

"Armando Sandoval, County Coroner's office."

Lori wasn't in the mood for pleasantries, even before meeting Ellis, and she disregarded his introduction. "What can you tell me about the body?" He withdrew his hand, clearly miffed that Lori had ignored his offering. For a moment she had sympathy for him. He probably didn't meet too many women in his profession. . . not live ones anyway.

"Well, I can say that the preliminary COD is a skull fracture, caused by multiple blows to the head with a blunt instrument, probably a club of some kind. Judging from the condition of the skull, I'd say he got hit from three directions simultaneously."

"So that implies three assailants?" Lori asked.

"Obviously," Sandoval responded.

She shot a glance toward Ellis. "And there's no chance his injuries were caused by a truck or car hitting him in the head?"

Sandoval shook his head. "Not unless he got hit from three directions at the same time. I don't see any tracks that indicate three vehicles. Do you? And that doesn't account for the wardrobe malfunction either."

Lori gave him a quizzical look and bent down to remove the tarp from the body. At first, she had to fight the urge to vomit. The man's skull was broken into pieces and brain matter and blood soaked the dirt around his head. But his clothing was bizarre. Someone had torn off his jacket and discarded it and had also cut off his left shirtsleeve. He was barefoot, his shoes and socks tossed away, and his left pant leg had been rolled up. A makeshift rope noose hung loosely around his neck.

"What the hell is that all about?" She said it aloud even though didn't mean to.

Sandoval pointed to Tsien's right knee and arm. "He also appears to have a fractured kneecap and a broken arm. Neither injury seems likely to have been caused by the car wreck back there, although it was probably a pretty hard hit. I'd say it's likely they took their time with him. Beat him up a bit first before they killed him."

Ellis audibly snorted. "You don't take the time to play dress-up and beat somebody up that good if you're out to kill them."

Lori turned to him. "You do if you're trying to get information out of him first." Ellis reacted with a look that indicated he hadn't thought of that, and she thoroughly enjoyed the moment. She moved to step around the body. "You've taken all the crime scene photos you need?" she asked Sandoval. He nodded but then seemed to realize she might not have seen the gesture in the darkness. "Yes," he finally said.

Lori bent down over the body and lifted the shoes with a pair of heavy tweezers she pulled from her pocket.

"Hey," Ellis said. "My guys have already gone over the scene."

She didn't look up at him. "Yeah, but I haven't."

She shook the shoes—nothing—then the first discarded sock—nothing. Then she lifted the second sock and turned it upside down. Out of it slid a tiny computer flash drive.

"What's that?" Ellis asked.

"A clue," Lori said simply. She lifted the drive and placed it in a plastic bag, then put it in her coat pocket. She smiled in the dark as she walked past Ellis and over to the white truck. The driver still sat on the door sill, head in his hands.

"Excuse me, Mr. . . ." Lori drifted off and motioned for one of the sheriff's deputies. He held out the man's driver's license and put the beam of his flashlight on it. "Dolfinger. Mr. Dolfinger, I'm Special Agent Lori Pars with the FBI. I'd like to ask you a few questions."

The man lifted his head and gazed straight ahead. "I'll tell you the story again, but I doubt you'll believe me either."

"Just tell me what you saw, sir," Lori said soothingly. It was obvious the man was distraught, but that didn't make him guilty of anything.

"Horrible, it was horrible," Dolfinger said. Lori put her hand on his shoulder. "I was just coming up the road, headed for the fire shack at the top of the butte, overlooking Mount Wilson. It's my shift at midnight. . ." He trailed off, clearly not wanting to remember.

"It's OK, sir," Lori reassured him.

He nodded and took a deep breath. "I come 'round this corner here, and I see these three guys, dressed all in black, standing over this little fella. When they saw my truck, they all just blasted him. Swung these sticks at him and the poor guy's head just exploded! I've. . . I've never seen so much blood in my life!" He covered his eyes again.

Lori stayed stoic. "Mr. Dolfinger, I know this isn't easy, but I need you to tell me what happened next."

Dolfinger nodded. "Anyway. . . the poor little guy. . . he was kneeling on one knee, he just falls over in a heap. I knew he was dead right away. By the time I look up, these three guys are tearing out of here. They ran up the ridge and over the cliff so fast, they were like cheetahs or something. I've never seen anything move so fast!"

"Where did they go?" Lori asked again to be sure.

He pointed to where the sheriff's deputies were still searching. "Right over that ridge."

Lori got up and walked to the edge of the road where Dolfinger had pointed. It was a dizzying sight. The cliff was about seventy-five feet almost straight down before it began to taper at a more reasonable angle. She went back over to Dolfinger.

"Sir," she began, "that's almost a seventy-five-foot sheer drop before there's anything that a person could scale downward. Are you sure that's where they went?"

Dolfinger nodded his head. "Yes, ma'am."

She wanted to doubt him, but his tone was firm. Maybe he'd missed something. "These three men, can you describe them?"

"Like I said, they were all dressed in black, head to toe, with ski masks or something over their heads. One of 'em was facing me. All I could see were his eyes."

"Do you remember anything else about them?"

He took a moment. "No."

"Mr. Dolfinger, what did you do when you saw the men run away? Did you get out of your truck to help Mr. . . . ?" She looked up at Ellis, realizing she didn't even know the victim's name.

"Xian Tsien," Ellis interjected. He pronounced it "Zy-anne Sen" and flashed her a displeased look. He clearly didn't believe a word of Dolfinger's story.

"Mr. Tsien," Lori finished. "Did you try and help him?"

"No way," Dolfinger said quickly. "Not the way those guys moved. It was creepy. Scariest thing I ever saw. I stayed in my truck and dialed nine-one-one on my cell. I didn't get out until the police got here."

Lori had heard enough. She thanked him and signaled to Ellis as she moved away. Ellis followed her to a spot about twenty-five feet from Dolfinger's truck.

"You're not buying any of this shit, are you, lady?" His tone was even more dismissive than his words.

"What's your explanation?" Lori snapped back. "He somehow hit the guy in the head with his truck from three sides at once, leaving no tracks and with no blood on his truck? Come on."

Ellis looked back at Dolfinger. "It's not that I think he necessarily did it; I just don't believe a word of that story. I mean, what are we supposed to do, put out an APB for three ninjas? That's what these guys sound like."

"Has he been drinking?" Lori asked.

"Blew a dead zero."

"Well, then I don't think we have any choice but to take this man's story seriously."

Ellis scoffed. "You've got to be kidding me! I got my men out here in the middle of the night looking for three ghosts dressed in black that can't possibly have jumped over that cliff over there. This guy's got to be lying."

Lori took another look at Dolfinger. "I don't think so."

"I realize you're the detective here lady, but what the hell do you base that conclusion on? Women's intuition?"

"No, I just can't find another plausible scenario. Even you don't have one."

He grunted. "That's for sure." He pointed her to a squad car. "Well, if you want to put out an APB on three ninjas, be my guest. But I ain't doin' it."

She noted his tendency to slip into a slight southern drawl and made a mental note to check his file and see if he'd ever lived outside the L.A. basin. She walked over to the car, resigned to her task, and activated the police radio, calling up the dispatcher.

"This is Special Agent Lori Pars of the FBI, badge number 194733. I need to put out an all points bulletin on three murder suspects."

"Description?" the female dispatcher asked after a slight delay.

"Three men, height and weight unknown, dressed in black body suits or black tops and pants, also wearing black hats or ski masks. They have been observed to be extremely agile and quick on their feet. They should be considered armed and dangerous."

The dispatcher took her time coming back. "Can you describe the type of weapon, Special Agent?"

"Clubs or thick sticks of some kind."

"Were they nunchucks, Special Agent?" This time the dispatcher could not contain herself and started giggling. In the background, Lori could hear the cackles of other officers who were obviously listening in. Clearly, Ellis had forewarned them about Dolfinger's story. Lori just let them laugh until they were done making fun of the big, bad, FBI girl.

"Have you got it?" Lori asked.

"Yes, ma'am. An APB on three ninjas. Going right out."

Lori didn't wait to sit through the rest of the laughter. She cut the radio and went back over to Sandoval. "I'll need your report first thing in the morning."

"Naturally," he said. She tried not to notice the contempt with which he answered her. She would have preferred to be nicer to him, but he was just too creepy. This whole night was too creepy, for that matter. She pulled her cell phone from her pocket and started to head for her car when Ellis's voice held her up.

"Hey, Special Agent," he called out. She turned.

"Be sure and Google 'Dolfinger' when you get home."

She opened her mouth to ask a question in response, but then decided if it came from Ellis, she'd probably rather not know.

It was past four-thirty A.M. when Lori started to head home. She lived a good distance away, in Torrance, but she really felt she needed to get some sleep. Normally she slept only three to four hours a night, as she had a really tough time shutting down her mind. This had been a handy characteristic in school, enabling her to study longer and be sharper for early-morning classes, but as she graduated to adulthood, she often wished she could just relax and empty her head, give up all her concerns and obsessions. But before she could even try to get to bed, she had a call to make.

She activated her Bluetooth earpiece and scrolled to the number on her smartphone. It rang through to voicemail, but she called a second time. This time, a very tired voice answered on the fourth ring. "Masters," was all the voice said in greeting.

"Marshall? It's Lori."

"Lori who?"

"Come on, Marshall. I need you to get into the office and help me with something."

"It's four-thirty in the morning. Why are you doing this to me?"

"Because I can," she said sweetly into the phone, "you can't resist me."

"You'd be surprised at what I can resist at four-thirty in the morning," he said wearily.

She pretended to be offended. "But I'm a beautiful blonde!"

"Yeah, there's a real short supply of girls like that in L.A."

Lori was well aware that Marshall had a strong crush on her because Connie Balver had told her about it once over drinks. He evidently had a picture of the two of them together at an office party she didn't even remember, and Connie said he kept it in his wallet. She was pretty sure he'd come close to professing his affection to her at least once on a road trip to an FBI conference, but she didn't have time to talk to him and they hadn't sat down alone together since.

She felt bad for Marshall. He was a sweet and smart man, but short, a little chunky and with a prematurely receding hairline that she noticed way too often. There was just no way anything romantic was ever going to happen between them. She tried not to take advantage of his adolescent fantasies about her, but he was the best analyst in the L.A. office and one of the sharpest computer geeks in the FBI. And besides, this time she really needed his help.

"Pleeeese," she said in her best girly voice, "I really need this favor from you."

He groaned in resignation. "What is it?"

"I need you to get into the office and run everything you can find on a JPL scientist named Dr. Xian Tsien. And I need it today by ten A.M."

"That's all?" he asked sarcastically.

"I know you can do it. You're the best."

"Yes, I am. That's why you're calling me at four-thirty in the morning."

"Will you do it?"

"You want me to get out of bed *now* and go do this for you?"

"Yes please, Marshall."

"Hmm. . ." his voice trailed off for a moment. "With that name he sounds like a foreign national. That's a lot more work. What will you be doing while I spend hours pulling immigration files and reading visa applications?"

"Sleeping."

"Ah," he said knowingly, "so this is one of your generous and unselfish proposals?"

"Don't you want to help me catch some bad guys?"

"Of course," he said quickly, "but it will cost you."

She sighed very dramatically into the phone. "What is it this time?"

"Well, I'm thinking," he began.

"Yes?"

"Halloween is coming up in just a few weeks."

"I noticed the spider decorations at Target last week," she deadpanned.

"And I've suggested this before. . ."

"No." Her tone was firm.

"OK, going back to bed now."

"No, Marshall, wait!" she said urgently. "Fine. You win. I'll do it."

"You will?" His excitement was obvious from the rise in the pitch of his voice.

"Yes, but only at the costume party. I'm not wearing it to work."

"Deal," he said quickly. "Do you still have it?"

"Yeah. It's in my closet. Hanging. Unused."

"Excellent!"

She'd always known it would come to this, that someday she'd have to wear the Star Trek Halloween costume he bought her back when she was still oblivious to his crush on her. One night, out of boredom, she'd actually tried it on and could barely squeeze into the thing. But she'd dropped a few pounds in the intervening months, and the tight, space-age miniskirt looked damn good on her even then. "So now that you've got what you want, can I assume you're on your way into the office?"

"Are you kidding?" he said. "I'm not even going to bother with a shower."

"Yes, you most certainly are!"

He sighed, resigned. "Sure. See you at eleven."

"Ten," she reminded him.

"Right. Ten."

"Bye, Marshall."

She hung up the phone and picked up her speed, wondering just how much weirder the coming day was going to get.

4.

Richard Garvin found himself in an all-too-familiar situation, finishing up another appearance on *Nationwide AM,* the number one overnight radio talk program. As he had done so many times before, he and the host, George Kalb—an old ally in the overnight paranormal wars—were taking calls in the last hour of the show. As usual, the program's habit of not screening their calls had led to a parade of UFO stories and abductee experiences. It mildly amused Garvin that no matter how many times he said, "We don't do UFOs," invariably the questions went in that direction when the show went to the call-in lines. Sometimes he wondered if the guys back at the network really did handpick the calls just to drive him nuts.

As he waited for the show to come out of a commercial break, he pondered how he'd ended up in this time and place. Since the days when he'd walked proudly amongst the inner circles of academia and called people such as Sagan, Asimov, and Clarke his friends, he'd been fascinated by the anomalies, the pieces that didn't fit. His paper on the "thing in the rings," a point source in the rings of Saturn emitting eerie, regular radio pulses, had caused quite a stir among his friends and colleagues when he suggested it might be artificial. But that was nothing compared to the firestorm he'd created when he took on an even more taboo subject—the idea that certain features on Mars, in a region called Cydonia, might be artificial.

Somehow in his insatiable curiosity and dissatisfaction with NASA's pat answers about the objects imaged at Cydonia, including the famous "Face," he'd gravitated from best buddy to the stars of science to the "Face on Mars" man. Once, his rogue research group had been welcomed, even in the hallowed halls of NASA headquarters. Now the mere mention of his name inside NASA usually evoked a reaction akin to showing a cross to a vampire.

Even now, in his distinguished, silver-haired early sixties, surrounded by the stacks of papers in his cluttered office and basking in the light from a dozen scented candles, Garvin wondered what had shifted internally at the agency.

Even though Sagan and most of his friends were gone, he continued to hold out hope that somehow, someday, he'd get "the disk" he always suspected they had held for him.

Then he heard George's voice coming over the phone again as the bumper music faded. "Welcome back now to *Nationwide AM,*" he said in his deep, baritone voice. "Final segment now with the one and only Richard Garvin. You all know who he is if you listen to this program at all. Richard, shall we go back to the phone lines?"

Garvin leaned forward in his chair. "Absolutely, George," he said brightly.

"All right, west of the Rockies, you're on the air."

"Hello?" an uncertain male voice stammered into the phone. "Am I on the air?"

"Yes you are, sir. Go ahead," Kalb said, adding a soothing tone to his voice.

"Oh, well. . ." the caller began, sounding very nervous, "I. . . I live in North Hollywood, and I have a police radio I like to listen to sometimes. Well, tonight I was listening to a report, and they said that somebody had been murdered at JPL. Have either of you heard any reports on this?"

Garvin's ears pricked up. Kalb interceded quickly. "I just checked the wires during the break, sir, and I saw nothing on this. How certain are you of what you heard? You're sure they said a murder *inside* the Jet Propulsion Laboratory?"

"Well, maybe not inside the lab itself but near there. They said the FBI was being called in."

"Really?" Garvin was on the scent now, his instincts honed by years of catching NASA in one lie after another. "Sir, do you have any way of recording what comes over your police radio?"

"Sure," the caller answered quickly.

"Then here's what I want you to do. I want you, and anybody else out there in the audience who has a police radio in the Los Angeles area, to record anything further you hear on this tonight and send it to me in the morning."

"OK."

"You can get my contact information off my web site."

"OK, I'll do that. George? Can I ask one more question?" the caller asked.

"Certainly, sir, but hurry. We're up against the clock here," Kalb told him.

"Well, I wanted to ask Dr. Garvin—"

"It's not 'doctor,' sir, but thank you for the endorsement," Garvin interjected, trying to keep the mood light.

"Uh, well, OK. Um, I think I have one of those alien implants in my ear lobe, and I was wondering if you could tell me the name of that doctor who removes them."

Garvin rolled his eyes, thanking the stars that he didn't have a webcam. Kalb jumped into the conversation.

"You mean Dr. Roger Leir, sir," he said. Just Google his name and I'm sure he could arrange to meet with you about this."

"Oh. All right. Thank you."

"Thank you, sir." Kalb turned his attention back to Garvin as the bumper music started to rise in the background. "Well, Richard, another outstanding show, my friend," he said to Garvin.

"Yes it was, George," Saunders responded. "Pretty intriguing last caller there. That JPL story is one that bears watching."

"Indeed it does, my friend. Indeed it does." The phone line cut off as Kalb went into his closing shtick, and Garvin hung up the phone and immediately began to search the news wires for any reports on the JPL murder story. After finding nothing, he decided to check his e-mail one last time before turning in. In his inbox were a series of e-mails from "Honey," all sent in the last few hours. Assuming they were junk mail trying to sell him an online Viagra prescription or penis enlargement products, Garvin selected them all and relegated them to his spam folder. There was only one unread e-mail left in his inbox. It was from a contact he called Deep Space, one of his more intermittent and secretive sources.

Deep Space made a habit of dropping in and out of Garvin's life for months at a time. Sometimes he would be nearly omnipresent, calling and e-mailing at all hours of the night with interesting and sometimes vital inside information. Garvin knew almost nothing about his background, other than he was apparently British, judging by his accent. But he did know that his information was very reliable.

As he considered the unread e-mail, Garvin wondered just what juicy new inside info it might contain. Perhaps it was some confirmation of the caller's JPL murder story. He clicked on it, and to his disappointment all it contained was a single .pdf file. As he waited for the PDF to download, he stood up from his desk to stretch and turned around, trying to catch a glimpse of Sirius or Orion out of his picture window. He loved this time of night, in the deep black of the New Mexico desert with only his dim candles and the stars to keep him company. As he raised a coffee mug full of hot tea to his lips, he noticed a brief, all-too-quick red glint just as the cup passed his chest. It took him a moment to realize what the red glint was.

It was a laser pointer beam, just like the one he used to torment his two cats, Roswell and Isis, as they chased it around the house. Only this one wasn't pointing along the walls or up and down the curtains. It was dead still, and right in the center of his chest. Garvin stood frozen for a moment, wondering if the annoying teenager from next door was playing another prank on him. Then he looked up, and saw a dark silhouette against the starry New Mexico sky.

He had just enough time to figure out what the red laser sight really was before his chest exploded.

The bullet shattered the coffee mug, and the tea mixed with blood and body fluids in a spray that covered the furniture in front of him. The force of the projectile spun him around to his left and backward, and his body toppled with a great force onto the desk. Barely alive, his heart all but blown apart, Garvin crashed to the floor along with a pile of papers, manila file folders, and two of the candles. The hot wax and flame spilled across the papers and they ignited. Soon the hardwood floor was ablaze, followed quickly by his oak desk, the fabric couch nearby, and then the curtains.

The black figure carefully unscrewed the silencer from his short-barrel SG-551 rifle while he watched and waited until the entire house was fully engulfed. Then he slinked away to a waiting SUV, so stealthily that not even the next door neighbors' Border collie heard him.

5.

It was starting as it always did.

Lori, in the netherworld between sleep and consciousness, felt herself lifting off the bed. Her cat Cleo, sensing her mommy leaving her, put her forepaws on Lori's tummy to try to hold her down, but it did no good. Soon Lori saw herself from above, as if she were standing or hovering over her own slumbering body. She could see the rhythmic movements of her chest up and down, even feel the gentle vibrations of Cleo's purring on her stomach, but she was somewhere else, somewhere disconnected from her physical being.

Then it began to happen. She saw the light, a glittering, brilliant tingle of energy touching her in a thousand places along her spine all at once. She felt the warmth, the comforting touch of God on her back, and she turned from her bedroom. Slowly, not even feeling the soft carpet below her bare feet, she crossed her living room, now filled with the brilliant light of a billion Christmases, and went to her apartment door and opened it. The hallway, as she was used to seeing it, with its red and gold–patterned carpet and the black elevator doors, wasn't there. Instead, she was stepping out into a meadow with flowers and birds and white, billowy clouds and the most beautiful sunrise she'd ever seen. Cottages and tree houses dotted the rolling green hills in the distance. She knew instinctively where she was and that she was dreaming—a dream within a dream.

Then her sister was standing next to her, her curly brown hair still flowing down to her shoulders, her face still the innocent fifteen years she'd been when God had taken her. They both knew in their hearts that He hadn't really done it, but they didn't ever discuss the vile man who had. Melissa's murder had shattered both their worlds when Melissa was fifteen and Lori only twelve.

Melissa smiled at her as she always did and reached out and hugged her sister. Lori could feel the solid, three-dimensional reality of her embrace, and she often thought in her waking hours that it was the most real and true thing in her life. Then they went to Melissa's car, the same rusted green Buick Skylark that their father had bought for her to learn to drive in. Melissa had never gotten her driver's license in life, but she explained, as she always did, in a way that wasn't really quite speaking, that she'd learned to drive here. They drove the short distance to Melissa's cottage, the warm breeze flowing through their hair. Lori could smell the grass, and here it never made her sneeze. She liked that about this place. Here she never felt any pain, worried about any problems, or doubted her sister's eternal love for her.

A few moments later, they were in Melissa's cottage. It was a small white brick structure with a rose garden like the one their mother had at home. The stone birdbath, as always, was occupied by a few chirping robins. They got out of the car and Melissa showed her all of her things, her dolls and teddy bears, the easel where she worked on her paintings, and the big, fluffy bed where she would lie and read from her library of books. Lori heard a rustle and looked over to see Peeve, the tuxedo tomcat they'd had to put down when Lori was eight, come bouncing in the window. In all the times she'd visited Melissa in this way, Peeve had never been there.

He came right up to Lori and rubbed himself around her ankles, purring loudly and flirting with her in his feline way. Lori reached down and lifted him, surprised that he'd let her do it since picking him up and petting him was something he'd never tolerated in life. "How's my pet Peeve?" she asked, seeing Melissa smile broadly as they shared their favorite joke. Lori never thought to wonder if Peeve liked his name, but he responded to the sound of it by rubbing his head on her palms and marking her with his scent glands. He felt so solid and soft in her hands, it was hard for Lori to believe she wasn't really holding him; that this was all just a dream.

Then it began. She felt it before she heard it, a high-pitched, resonant humming sound that seemed to be coming from the far distance over the horizon and up through her feet at the same time. As the waves of light and sound passed through her body, she felt herself begin to vibrate and tingle, and a sense of joy and love seemed to emanate from her at the same time that it passed through her and drew her spirit upward. She thought that she was rising again, but she could still feel Peeve in her arms and see that she was still inside Melissa's cottage.

She turned, and Melissa was watching her and smiling at her with a perfect, fifteen-year-old smile. "What's that?" she asked her sister.

"That's the angels singing," Melissa told her, this time in her speaking voice. "They sing twenty-three hours a day. One hour a day, they stay quiet so we can play whatever music we like."

Lori smiled as she felt the vibrations surging through her. She'd never been here when the angels were singing before. All she wanted in that moment was to stay here forever with Melissa.

Then Lori got the sense that it was time to go. She knew without asking or being told that Melissa had brought her here to let her know she was OK, she was happy, and that Lori didn't need to keep worrying about her.

Then they were back in the car and driving back to the meadow where Lori had first seen her. They had somehow gotten ahead of the wave of sound that the singing of the angels had generated, but Lori could hear it in the distance, coming closer. She wanted more than anything to be back in its embrace, to stay here where it was warm and safe and always beautiful.

She found herself standing back in the meadow, in the place where Melissa always met her. She was looking back toward the cottage, hoping that the sound of the angels would catch up to them before she left, but she knew it was not for her. It was not her time to be with Them.

She felt Melissa's hand touch her arm.

"Lori, I have something more to tell you," she said. Lori saw Melissa's lips move, and she heard a sound, but she couldn't make out a single word or understand a single gesture.

Then it was morning, and Lori's eyes were open and she could see the light of the California day coming through her window. Her right arm was asleep from Cleo laying on it, and she carefully extracted her arm from under her cat's warm body and rolled over to a different position as it tingled back to life. Cleo was unhappy at being dislodged and let Lori know about it with grumpy prrt. Lori tried to stay in the hopeful place she found in the dream, but the more time passed, the less she could feel it and the heavier her heart was. She wished she knew what Melissa was trying to tell her, but she had long since given up on that.

She'd had the dream, or something like it, many times before. She took no comfort from it, but she was glad she still had it, even if it often left her feeling lonely and a little depressed. As she got out of bed and readied herself for work, she accepted that whatever her dream place was, it wasn't a mindset she could stay in and still function in the real world.

An hour later Lori had left her apartment and began the drive in, her thoughts turning back to the events of the night before. The fact that Eric Ruby himself had assigned her to this case kept gnawing at her. The more she thought about it, the more she was convinced that the whole scenario had the stink of a setup. Her lack of experience with murder cases made it likely she'd make a crucial mistake somewhere along the line. It might be better for her long term career ambitions to refuse the assignment and face a reprimand for it rather than fail in a spectacular and public way. If she wasn't careful, she knew she could end up suspended or even transferred to an unappealing locale like North Dakota. Having become accustomed to the cultural benefits of living in Los Angeles, she had no desire to trade the big-city life for Small Town, USA.

As she pulled into the lush greenbelt campus of the Wilshire field office, she still wasn't decided on the best way to deal with Ruby or even if she should play such a game of career roulette at all. She figured the events of the next few hours would help her to sort it all out.

She arrived at her cube on the eighth floor a few minutes later and logged into her computer. Sandoval had already e-mailed her his preliminary coroner's report, and there was a message from Marshall to drop by his desk as soon as she got in. She got up, straightened her tan skirt, and headed over to the analysis bay. Marshall was there with Connie Balver, who was sitting on the desk next to him as he worked at his computer.

Connie was by far Lori's best friend at the agency, probably because they were close in age. Lori was thirty-two and Connie was twenty-nine. She was a very pretty brunette with shoulder-length hair; dark, sharp eyebrows and striking green eyes. She looked up as Lori entered the analysis bay, flashing a perfect white smile and beautiful teeth that had cost her parents a fortune when she was a teenager.

"Hey, girl," Connie said. "I hear you've got a hot case. Congratulations."

Hearing the greeting, Marshall turned and also smiled at Lori. Lori waved silently at him and leaned over to embrace Connie.

"Air kiss!" Connie said playfully, smooching the air next to Lori's cheek.

Lori stepped back and tried to get a look at Marshall's screen, but he covered it up with his hands. "No way! Not till I have everything organized," he protested.

"Fine." Lori knew how temperamental Marshall could be about sharing his analyses.

Marshall turned to Connie. "Did you hear about Lori's costume for the Halloween party?" Connie shrugged. "A red-dress girl from *Star Trek*," he said, giving a thumbs-up sign to Connie.

"I'm all tingly!" she said.

"Marshall," Lori said sternly. "Remember what I told you about girls and surprises?" Realizing he'd broken one of Lori's edicts, Marshall cringed just a bit. "OK then, let's just keep that tidbit of information to ourselves until the party, shall we?" Marshall nodded sullenly.

Lori was anxious to change the subject. "When am I going to get to see what you've got for me?"

"It's almost ready, just a few more minutes. Did you get some sleep?"

"Yes I did Marshall. Connie and I are going to go get some coffee. When we come back, I want to see what you have."

Connie got up from the desk and accompanied Lori to the hallway break room. "I can't wait to find out what he did for you to deserve that," she whispered to Lori.

"Yeah, you never will."

A few minutes later, they were back at Marshall's desk, peering over the screen. "Let's see it," Lori said, her tone more demanding this time.

Marshall dutifully brought up Tsien's JPL personnel file. "OK," he said, flicking his mouse back and forth across the screen. "Your dead guy is Dr. Xian Tsien, thirty-five years of age, a processing analyst at the Jet Propulsion Laboratory."

"That much I knew," Lori cut in.

Marshall smirked at her. "Oh, really," he said, "then I guess you can tell me what a 'processing analyst' does at JPL?"

Lori frowned.

"That's what I thought," Marshall said. "Shall I go on?"

"Please," Lori said, choking down a sip of coffee.

"OK," Marshall continued. "So this guy's job at the lab was to process and enhance images coming from the Mars Global Surveyor and Mars Reconnaissance Orbiter cameras. The Surveyor went dead a couple years ago, but there was still a backlog of images from that mission that he worked on. When the MRO probe arrived in orbit, he was switched over to that program and has been processing those images ever since."

"Pretend I don't know anything about NASA satellites," Lori said.

"OK. Well, the MRO camera is an order of magnitude better than the one on the Surveyor. I mean, this thing is so good that it could easily see us sitting in this cube from orbit, if there weren't walls all around us."

"NSQ, then?"

"Near Spy Quality, yes, Lori." Marshall smiled at her. He was always making up acronyms for everything, and Lori and Connie had started to use them fairly regularly. "As you might have guessed," Marshall went on, "Tsien's not an American by birth. He was born on Taiwan and raised there until his parents emigrated when he was fourteen. They put him in a series of private Catholic schools, and he graduated from high school a year early. He then went to Stanford, where he got a bachelor's in computer science, also a year early, and then a master's in computer science and a doctorate as well. His thesis was on a new way of processing old Surveyor images to bring them up to near-MRO quality. He finished school in 2002 and became an American citizen the same year. After his doctoral thesis was published, JPL offered him a position and bought the rights to his software process."

"So he's been at the lab for eight years, give or take," Lori said. "When did he get hooked up with DARPA?"

"Well, they won't let us have his personnel file from over there, but according to his JPL file, he first got a DARPA e-mail address when he was assigned to the Information Awareness Office right after he was hired," Marshall said.

"What the hell is the Information Awareness Office?" Connie asked.

Marshall smiled an 'I'm-glad-you-asked-me-that' smile. Lori liked it when he was more self-assured and lost his inherent shyness around women. "It's a division of DARPA set up after the 9/11 attacks. Its stated purpose was to predict 'asymmetric threats,' whatever that is, and to achieve 'total information awareness.' The whole thing was defunded in '03 because some in Congress thought it was consolidating too much power in one small organization."

"Anything else?" Lori asked.

"Not much," Marshall said. "The flash drive you gave me was encrypted. It'll take me a few more hours to crack it. Maybe we can just ask the JPL guys for the encryption code? I assume it's one of theirs anyway."

"Nope," Lori said quickly.

"Why not?"

"Because," Connie interjected. "What if somebody he worked with is the one who killed him? We'd be alerting the killer that we had the drive."

"But wait," Marshall said, feigning ignorance, "I thought three ninjas killed him?"

"Not funny," Lori said to him. "Get on it. I assume that whatever is on that drive is what he was protecting. And what his killer"—she shot Marshall a firm look—"or *killers*, were after."

"Fine. At least I know what I'm doing all afternoon," Marshall said dejectedly.

A young intern in a shirt and tie stopped by the cube and knocked on the plastic frame. "Special Agent Pars? Assistant Director Ruby asked me to tell you to stop by his office right away."

"Thanks," Lori said, her eyes meeting Connie's.

"Game on," Connie said, her smile masking her concern.

6.

As Lori rode the elevator up to the top floor of the building where the executive offices were located, she inwardly cringed as her thoughts invariably drifted back to her affair with Ruby.

As a student at the FBI Academy at Quantico, she had been quite taken with his darkly handsome looks and his quick, impressive intellect. He was on the fast track at the Bureau, all the students could see that, and she had fallen for him fast and hard when he made a play for her. She'd always assumed that their relationship would continue beyond the end of her training program, but by the time her graduation approached, he was losing interest. He never actually ended the relationship; he just stopped calling and one night she'd found out why when she caught a younger girl from his new class leaving his house after two A.M. She never confronted him, but instead obsessively stalked him for months after that, staking out his house night after night. She sat alone in her car and watched while a seemingly endless parade of comely FBI hopefuls entered and left his house at all hours.

She couldn't bring herself to be mad at the girls. They were her just a few short months before, hoping that his praise and approval meant they were something special. One night after too many drinks, she drunk-dialed him and threatened to go to the Bureau about his unethical behavior. He soberly reminded her that she was a grown-up and equally responsible for their inappropriate relationship. He pointed out to her that any charges she leveled would be a matter of public record and that no choice field office would be interested in a special agent who could be so easily convinced to break the rules against fraternization. That exchange stopped her in her tracks. Her father was an Episcopal preacher, and the mere thought of having to face him after such a public exposure flushed her with shame. She'd found out years later that Ruby always made sure he picked girls like her, with strong family ties and from conservative backgrounds; girls who would be more easily embarrassed by a public disclosure of their habits in bed.

She'd always told her girlfriends that he did not start the romantic entanglement between them, that their inappropriate relationship was a product of her own ambition. In reality, he had played her and used her as he wished, and she loathed him for it.

Even now, eight years later, she felt revulsion when she thought about him and the prospect of having to face him again.

She pushed all this to the back of her mind as she exited the elevator into the plush, expansive offices they all called "mahogany row" and presented herself to Ruby's secretary. She was a young attractive redhead, and Lori couldn't help but notice that his tastes hadn't changed much. The secretary buzzed Ruby and sent her through to his office.

She was surprised when she entered to see the Assistant Director in deep conversation with another man sitting next to him behind the enormous cherry wood desk he used. The other man looked to be in his early fifties, wearing a charcoal-gray suit and sipping from a Starbucks coffee cup as he exchanged words with Ruby. Neither man acknowledged her for a few moments as they continued their quiet, almost whispered conversation. Lori calculated that this was intended to intimidate or diminish her, so she simply stood in the middle of the office and waited for them to finish. Finally, Ruby nodded and turned to her from his seat behind the desk.

"Special Agent Pars," he started formally. "Do you have a report on the case for us?"

"Yes sir, I'm prepared to give an update," she said, pausing to make eye contact with the other man. "To my superiors."

The man's face broke into a wrinkled, arrogant smile. "You can speak freely in front of me, Special Agent," he said in a deep, raspy voice that sounded heavy with too many years of addiction to alcohol.

"And who are you, sir?" Lori asked, not smiling back.

This time he smiled more broadly and naturally, taking another sip from the paper coffee cup. "I'm Prescott Dansby," he said, smiling again at her. "I'm over from DARPA, strictly as an observer. We're obviously very interested how this case is concluded."

Dansby had a wrinkled, ragged face and a great deal of gray interspersed with his dark hair. His complexion was gray and pale, and his body seemed almost impossibly skinny and frail beneath the meticulously tailored suit. He looked like a piece of cigarette ash that Lori could shatter just by flicking him with her finger. She noted that he specifically said he was interested only in *how* the case was wrapped up, not if or when it was actually solved.

Ruby interceded. "Fill us in on what you know so far."

Lori stiffened her back and shifted her feet. She could see that this man made Ruby uncomfortable, and she wanted to enjoy that moment for a bit.

"Well," she began, "I investigated the crime scene this morning, and we have ruled it a wrongful death. The man"—she shot a look to Dansby—"Dr. Tsien, his skull was crushed by multiple blows to the head. There were also clear indications of injuries which were inflicted prior to his death. Then there are the somewhat strange aspects as to the placement of the clothing and the body."

"Explain that," Ruby snapped.

"Well, sir, the left shirtsleeve was removed, the shoes and socks were removed, and one pant leg rolled up, and a rope noose was wrapped loosely around the neck."

Ruby shared a look with Dansby. "And you have no clue as to the meaning of this?"

Lori shook her head. "No, sir. It could be some new kind of gang initiation ritual. A witness reported that all the three assailants were dressed identically."

"I thought you had a suspect, Agent Pars," Ruby barked.

"No, sir. He turned out to be a witness. We've pretty much ruled him out as a suspect."

"I see." Ruby rocked back in his big, leather chair. "So you are treating this as an Asian gang killing at the moment? A random event?"

"I never said anything about an Asian gang, sir."

"But the way they were dressed—"

"I didn't mention how they were dressed, sir, merely that they were all dressed alike." She looked back and forth between Ruby and Dansby. What was he doing? Trying to warn her that her own case files were not secure? "A random gang killing is just one possibility, sir," she said.

Ruby nodded. "Did you find anything else at the crime scene?"

Lori realized she was on shaky ground now. He clearly knew about the flash drive, but just as clearly, he had no procedural business prying into her case to that degree when it was at such an early stage. If she lied, he'd know it but really couldn't do anything about it, at least not officially. She calculated that he must be anxious to keep Dansby from finding out too much about the case.

"Nothing of any great significance, sir. We're still running forensics on the clothing and personal effects." Lori figured that would just about cover her without exactly lying.

"Very well. Keep me posted." Ruby was almost too quick to dismiss her, and she realized again just how uncomfortable he was with the man beside him. She nodded and turned toward the door.

Dansby's gravelly voice stopped her. "Special Agent?" he said.

Lori turned back. "Yes?"

"What do you intend to do next?"

"I'm heading over to JPL to interview some of Dr. Tsien's co-workers."

"Excellent!" Dansby said, his voice sprinkled with a mocking tone. "If you have any problems over there, be sure and give me call. I can help." He stood and handed her a business card. She took it, thanked him, and opened the door.

They both held their positions, staring at her without moving a muscle as she slowly closed the door in their faces, their oddly phony expressions not changing at all.

Once she got past the receptionist and into the elevator, she let out a big breath. At least she had an answer to her earlier concern; this day was going to be *really* weird.

Lori was back at her desk when Connie approached her cautiously from behind. "Hey," she said in greeting. "Wanna talk about it?"

Lori didn't turn from her e-mail. "No."

Ever loyal, Connie just stayed at the entrance to her cube, staring at Lori's back, and waited. Lori knew she had to tell her friend something. She searched for the right words. "It just bothers me. . . that seeing him still bothers me."

Connie said nothing in response but Lori knew she would be there for her if she needed to talk more about it. An awkward silence hung over them for the next few moments.

"I'd like to bring you in as a consultant on this case," Lori said at last. "It's case number B-263-54. You can charge to the support AIC number."

"Sure," Connie responded softly.

"And Connie, this case is pretty weird so far. First priority is to get that flash drive decoded while I'm over at JPL."

"Right."

"And don't tell anyone we have it. Find out from Marshall if he's told anyone else about it. Keep a lid on it. It could be critical to the case."

"You got it," Connie said, her manner fully professional.

"Thank you," Lori said, her tone dismissing Connie. She could sense that Connie had left the cube without even looking up from the e-mail she was still typing.

She finished the e-mail and then leaned back in her chair, stretching. As she did so, her eyes scanned the desk in front of her. Something was out of place. She saw an image on thick photographic paper slipped in between a couple of file folders in her inbox. She reached out and pulled it from the pile. It was a glossy black-and-white image from the crime scene, showing Tsien's body uncovered and lying facedown in the pool of blood. It was undeniably an official crime scene photo.

Already wound-up from her meeting with Ruby, Lori grew livid. Red faced and furious, she got on her desk phone and dialed Sandoval's office number. After a few rings, he picked up.

"Sandoval," he said, his voice flat and emotionless.

"Mr. Coroner, this is Special Agent Pars," she said quickly. Before he could utter even a cursory "hello," Lori lit into him. "What the hell are you doing leaving crime scene photos lying around in the open? You know this is a priority case."

"What are you talking about? I haven't left any crime scene photos over there."

"I'm holding one in my hand!"

"Not from my office, madam." His tone told Lori he was being sincere.

"Are you saying that no one from your office dropped this on my desk?"

"That's exactly what I'm saying, Special Agent. Nobody from my office has been over there today. My preliminary report hasn't even been officially released yet. I e-mailed you an advance copy as a professional courtesy."

Now Lori's concern was growing. "So you categorically did not leave a crime scene photo on my desk?"

"No."

"Then who did?"

"How should I know? We haven't even issued hard copies of the approved images yet."

Lori mind raced. She dismissed him with a perfunctory, "Thank you," and hung up. Then she stood and went over to Marshall's cube with the photograph in hand.

"Did you leave this on my desk?" she demanded.

Marshall and Connie turned from his computer screen. "Hey, cool down!" Marshall said, cracking a smile. Lori grabbed him by the collar and shoved the picture in his face. When he saw what was on it, a look of disgust crossed his face. "Eww, no," he said.

"Are you sure?"

"Of course. What is it?"

Before he could even finish his question, Lori was headed back to her desk at a dead run. Several people in nearby cubes had heard the commotion and popped their heads up, like gophers out of holes, to see what was up. Marshall straightened his shirt and addressed Connie, who was watching her friend closely as she headed back to her desk. "What the hell was that all about?" he asked her. Connie just shrugged as she headed out to follow Lori. "Girl's got issues," she said.

Connie got to Lori's cubicle just as she was rifling again through the papers on her desk. "What's going on?" she asked.

Lori held up the picture. "It's a crime scene photo from last night."

"But the coroner's office hasn't sent the scene package over yet."

"I'm aware of that. So where did this come from?"

Connie took the picture from Lori and flipped it over. "Maybe this will tell us," she said as she showed her the back side of the photo. On it, written in black marker, were two capitalized words: *Entered Apprentice.*

A look of dread crossed Lori's face. She picked up her desk phone and dialed the office emergency code. "We've got a security breach," she told Connie.

7.

Lori, Connie, and the building security officer stared intently at the security camera footage from Lori's floor. Lori had never been in the sixth floor security office before, and it looked to her more like something out of the space program than a police facility. With its darkened workspaces, low ceiling, multiple computer terminals and one-way glass walls, it looked more like how she imagined the situation room at the White House must appear.

The security officer in charge was a very polite black man in his early sixties. Lori had waved to him just about every working day in the past eight months as she passed through the security checkpoint at the field office entrance, but it occurred to her she'd never bothered to learn his name. His badge identified him Marvin McWilliams, and then she remembered one of the other security officers once calling him "Mac."

Although he did work for the FBI's Security Division, McWilliams was not a special agent, and his job focused entirely on maintaining the internal security for the Wilshire field office. As the local officer in charge, he had godlike authority over anything relating to building security and also had access to all the security cameras at any given moment. Lori had never really seriously considered what that meant until they started looking for footage of an intruder. As she looked around the rows and rows of computer consoles and multiple camera feeds, she was reminded that she and the rest of her co-workers were always potentially under surveillance—even in the bathroom. She tried not to think about what that actually meant in terms of her privacy, even as she watched them scroll through the various cameras. Finally McWilliams found and settled on the camera overlooking Lori's workspace on the fourth floor. He then rolled the tape back an hour and then fast-forwarded it at double speed.

It was quite nondescript at first. Various people coming and going. Lori arriving and checking her e-mail, and then heading over to Marshall's desk. They watched the next several minutes with the footage from Marshall's desk side by side, as Marshall ran Lori and Connie through Tsien's background and the intern arrived at Marshall's cube and told Lori that Ruby wanted to see her. They switched cameras until Lori was in the elevator heading to Ruby's office. Within thirty seconds, a figure appeared in the area of Lori's desk and slipped a piece of paper—obviously the photograph—into a stack on her desk.

He was a dark-haired man over six feet tall, wearing a dark business suit and what looked like a special agent ID badge on his left suit pocket, as was the custom in the office environment. No one took any notice of him as he walked up, placed the photo on her desk, and headed for the elevator. He seemed calm and completely at ease among the various FBI workers and agents, quite a feat for someone who wasn't, theoretically at least, an agent himself. Lori watched his movements carefully as she was trained to do, and he belied no nervousness or discomfort; nothing that would give him away as an intruder. The camera view was wide and meant to catch as much of the office as possible, but when he made his way back to the bank of elevators and got in for the ride down along with several other people, they had chance to get a good look at his face. As the doors shut and the elevator began descending, the man turned his head up and looked right into the camera, giving them an excellent chance to capture all of his facial features. He was handsome and rugged looking, probably about forty with a mild five o'clock shadow, a slightly cleft chin; and dark, wavy hair that was kept fairly closely cut. It was obvious he was aware of the camera and wanted, or at least didn't mind, it catching a good view of his face.

"That's weird," Connie said aloud. "It's like he wanted to make sure we got a good look at him."

"Yeah," Lori agreed. "He did."

"Well, then," McWilliams said, "Let's run him through the face ID database and find out who he is." He hit a button, took a screen capture of the image, and pasted it into an e-mail.

"Give it to Marshall Masters," Lori suggested. "He's the best analyst in the office."

"I'm gonna give it to one of my guys," McWilliams said curtly. Since he was on the hook for the incursion, it sounded like he was damn well going to make sure his team made a contribution toward catching the man.

"Officer McWilliams, I understand you have the authority here, but Agent Masters is the best computer man in this office. He has several programs that enhance the recognition code to the point that it's almost twice as fast as the base FBI facial recognition code."

He ignored her and kept typing up the e-mail. "That's nice, Special Agent, but as you pointed out, I have the authority here."

Lori realized she was going to have to be diplomatic, but it frustrated her to no end. "Officer—Mac. Look, Marshall is really good. I'd like him to have a shot at it."

McWilliams noted the use of his nickname with a scowl and turned back to his e-mail. "I met your boy last year in a Six-Sigma class. Can't say I was too impressed with him. He fell asleep in a lecture."

"This is still technically part of my case."

He slid the wire-framed glasses off his nose, turned, and stood straight up, looking down at her. "Don't you go and try to rank me, young lady. I'll handle this the way I see fit."

Before Lori could respond, the door buzzer went off and Marshall was admitted. He came in and crossed the low-ceilinged room to where they were grouped over the security terminal. He kept looking out through the one-way smoked glass walls, seemingly fascinated by them. "That's so cool," he said, ducking his head down to look past them at the office workers and agents beyond.

"Do you have anything?" Lori asked him.

"Oh, yeah. It's what Connie thought. Entered Apprentice is the first degree of Freemasonry. I cross-confirmed the FBI database with stuff from Google. Apparently it's standard custom to dress the initiate in this way when he takes the first degree."

Lori took the paper from him and skimmed it. "And?" she said, knowing Marshall well enough to know when he wasn't finished.

"Well, it's also the way they dress a victim when the Freemasons want to kill him for violating the secrets of the order. It's a way to send a message."

"Hmm. Mission accomplished," Connie said.

"Yeah," Marshall looked down to see the intruder's face on the screen. "Is that the guy?"

"Yeah, it looks that way," Connie told him.

Lori took the opportunity. "Marshall, how fast can you have an ID on him?"

"If he's in the database? Probably an hour or two. If he's not American, maybe four."

"Four hours?" McWilliams cut in. "To run the entire FBI database? Foreign and domestic? That's crap. You can't do that in less than a day."

Marshall didn't seem to notice the intensity of McWilliams's denial. "Sure I can," he said. "I improved the facial recognition code a lot."

"Six hundred percent? I doubt that."

"No, he did," Lori said confidently. "Just ask him."

McWilliams started to protest again, but Lori stopped him with a gesture. "Officer McWilliams? Humor me on this, please."

"That's just not possible," he insisted.

Lori interceded. "Marshall, tell Officer McWilliams how you did it."

"Oh," Marshall said, finally seeming to grasp the power dynamic that was taking place in the room. "Well, I modified the biometrics algorithm using a hidden Markov model to constrain the Bayesian probabilities range. Then I applied a neuronal model using wavelet transformations to enhance the dynamic link matching and compensate for the lighting and camera angles. Then all I had to do was add a skin texture analysis component, and I got a major improvement in pattern matching dynamics as well. It saves tons of time."

McWilliams just stared at Marshall. Lori exchanged a look with Connie and then leaned in and added Marshall to the e-mail's "send-to" list. McWilliams did not protest. "OK, Marshall. Do me a favor and get right on it." She clicked the send button with the mouse.

Marshall looked back and forth to Lori and McWilliams. "All right. Is that it?"

"Yes," Lori said. "Thank you."

"Sure," Marshall said back to her, not quite sure what he had said that had impressed McWilliams so much.

After he left, Lori turned back to McWilliams. "Trust me," she said, "he's good."

"I don't doubt it," McWilliams said wonderingly.

Lori smiled. "Can you continue to review the tapes to make sure he's gone?"

"Yeah," McWilliams said. "And I'll need your report by COB today."

"Sure," Lori told him, having no intention of following through on her paperwork for the day. She gathered up Connie, and they headed out of the room and made for the elevator. Once inside, they went down a floor and another agent got off, leaving just the two of them.

"What are you going to do now?" Connie asked her as soon as they were alone.

"Head over to JPL, like I planned."

"Pretty weird about the Mason thing," Connie said.

"Yeah. I'm not sure what the Freemasons have to do with NASA. But we should find out. Can you check the local lodges around Pasadena and see if Tsien was a member of one?"

"Sure," Connie said. "But it seems like a long shot. There aren't many foreign members of those things most of the time."

"Check anyway," Lori said, her voice short.

Connie noted the tone of Lori's voice with a quick lift of her eyebrow. "Well," she said mischievously, "I guess this means we could be facing a crime wave by roving bands of Ninja-Masons in Pasadena."

The humor was lost on Lori and she didn't crack a smile. Then she saw Connie's face drop and knew she was being too hard on her. "Sorry," she said to her sympathetically. "But this isn't a joke. A man is dead, and it's my responsibility to catch whoever did it."

"Forget it Lori," Connie said to her friend. "This case worries me too. It's pretty weird."

"You don't know the half of it," Lori said, thinking about Prescott Dansby. "You have no idea."

8.

Lori's black Honda wound carefully through the hilly Pasadena campus of the Jet Propulsion Laboratory. She was looking for the E9 building, the one the guard had told her contained the offices that housed the Mars Reconnaissance Orbiter program. She quickly found it and parked in a designated visitors spot. The building was classic 1970s architecture, right down to the hideous, orange-brown artistic rendering of some of JPL's most famous robotic spacecraft in the lobby. After checking in with the guard in the lobby she was directed to the office of Dr. Steven Saunders, the program director and Dr. Tsien's nominal boss. She made her way up the elevator to the fifth floor and announced herself to the receptionist.

Dr. Saunders quickly emerged from behind a dark wood door and invited her into his office. "Please come in, Special Agent. Can I offer you some coffee?" He sounded more pleasant than he needed to be.

"No thank you, doctor. If you don't mind, I just have a couple of quick questions."

He smiled stiffly. "Yes, of course. I've been expecting you. I've taken precautions to preserve Dr. Tsien's computer and desk just the way he left it. I can take you right down there if you like."

Lori nodded. "That's excellent. But if you don't mind, I'd like to ask you the questions first."

"OK." Saunders resumed his seat and Lori sat in a guest chair opposite him and took out her notepad and voice recorder.

She decided to start with the basics. "When was the last time Dr. Tsien was at the lab?"

"According to security, he passed through the badge reader in his area about twelve A.M. last night."

"And does he have to scan his badge again on the way out?"

Saunders shook his head. "No, he wasn't in a strictly secured area. He only worked on our open projects."

"By 'open projects' you mean unclassified? Non-military?"

"Correct. He was part of a group that was responsible for processing Mars Reconnaissance Orbiter images for us."

Lori looked up from her notes. "I thought MRO was a University of Arizona project?"

"The HiRISE camera, yes. But we do a great deal of the actual image processing here."

"Oh, really? Why is that?" Lori tried to seem causal, but she could tell he was getting uncomfortable with the direction the questions were taking.

He cleared his throat. "Well, we have some of the best image processing experts in the world here—people like Dr. Tsien—and we help with the workload because they couldn't possibly handle all the data themselves in a small university lab."

That seemed plausible enough. "Dr. Saunders, are you aware that Dr. Tsien was working for DARPA?"

He shifted slightly in his seat. "DARPA? No, I wasn't aware of that, but many of us here at JPL do such work. I have a DARPA e-mail and security clearance myself."

"Would you have any idea if he was doing any work for DARPA recently?"

The answer was curt. "No, I wouldn't."

"Because of security clearances?"

"Correct."

"Was Dr. Tsien working on any other projects here at the lab lately?" she asked.

"Not that I'm aware of."

Lori scribbled in her notebook. "So he hasn't charged any time to anything other than the MRO project recently?" She figured just the mention of timekeeping records would be enough to worry him if he really had something to hide.

Saunders touched his neck, a sure sign that he wasn't being completely honest with his next answer. "No. Not that I know of."

"And since he's been at the lab?"

He cleared his throat a second time. "He's worked on MRO for the last several years."

Lori nodded. "So if you don't mind my asking, why does he have a DARPA clearance at all? I mean, there isn't anything classified about *Mars. . .* is there?" She let the last few syllables linger in the air to extend his discomfort. She could tell he wasn't a person who was used to having to answer to anyone.

"No, there isn't."

She maintained eye contact for a few beats longer before moving on. "Dr. Saunders, you mentioned that you've secured Dr. Tsien's computer. Can you explain that process to me?"

"Well, we have secured the work area. By that I mean we put it under guard, and the guys he shared a cube with have been asked not to touch their own computers until told by you that it's OK."

"So neither you nor your staff has touched the hardware at all?"

"Well, we did a scan right away when we heard about the murder from the sheriff's department this morning."

Lori raised an eyebrow. "A scan? What does that involve?"

"It's a strictly passive process. We log into his machine remotely and scan the hard drive for any changes or security problems. It's completely nondestructive."

"And what did you find?"

He cleared his throat yet again. "I'm afraid he managed to wipe his entire hard drive. Somehow he figured out how to bypass our admin locks and wipe it out."

"Can you restore it from backup?"

"Yes, but it will be several weeks old, I'm afraid. We only do daily backups of the network drives. The local hard drives are only backed up periodically."

Lori tried to hide her displeasure. "That seems very sloppy, sir."

"It's a calculated risk. It's very expensive to back up all the hard drive content every day."

"All right," Lori said carefully, not really letting him off the hook. "What about his e-mails?"

Saunders nodded. "We have those. They're backed up on a separate server. We can provide a transcript of all his e-mails going in and out for you today, and we should be able to transcribe the actual archive to a hard drive by tomorrow."

Lori wasn't particularly pleased with his answer, but what could she do? "All right, then. Have you assembled his co-workers?"

She could almost see the tension drain from his body. "Yes, they're down on the second floor in the science lab."

"Good. I'd like to speak to them next."

"Of course, I'll take you."

As they stood up to leave the room, Saunders went to the door but held up. "Special Agent, you don't have any idea who did this, do you?"

Lori considered him dispassionately. She could tell he was hiding something or was at least nervous about what she might dig into, but treating him like a suspect wouldn't help her case at this point. "No, but it seems to be a random act of violence. Our working assumption is that it's most probably some kind of gang initiation." She tried to make her tone conversational and sympathetic.

He shook his head back and forth, trying a bit too much to seem upset. "That's so very sad. Dr. Tsien loved this country. And Pasadena. It's such a shame he should fall victim to such a pointless act of violence."

"Don't worry, Dr. Saunders. I'll find out who did this and bring them to justice."

He sighed, almost a theatrical gesture. "I assure you we'll assist you in any way we can."

Now Lori put on her best poker face: "I'm sure you will."

Saunders escorted Lori down to the second floor science lab, where Tsien had worked until the day before. It was a standard, compartmentalized office space, with blue-gray cubicles and large, open walkways between them. It looked remarkably similar to Lori's own workspace at the FBI field office. Tsien shared a spacious workspace with two other scientists, who where dutifully waiting for her at their desks, seated but not logged in to their computers. Saunders introduced them.

"This is Patrick Timbol and Dr. Jared Aiken. They've been sharing a cube with Dr. Tsien for over a year." Saunders motioned for her to sit in Tsien's seat and then left them.

Physically, the pair could not have been more mismatched. Timbol was shorter – probably under five-eight, and had a very small frame. He was well dressed, meticulously groomed, and had a pair of white earphones around his neck that seemed as if they had always been there. From his complexion, Lori guessed that he was either Vietnamese or Filipino, and he had fine, almost delicate features and virtually no facial hair. He had numerous Photoshopped gag pictures posted around his cubicle, showing him and his co-workers as various pop-culture icons ranging from the cast of the original Star Trek series to eighties pop super group Duran Duran.

Aiken, by contrast, was tall and lanky and had a sloppy quality to him that exuded disinterest in the protocols of either his profession or society in general. He wore a faded short-sleeved plaid shirt over a white T-shirt, what looked like jeans from Costco or Sears, and a pair of beat-up green Converse tennis shoes. Evoking a style that her college girlfriends used to call "standard engineer issue," his hair was a curly mop-like mess, and even though he was clean shaven and relatively presentable, Lori detected an undertone of a somewhat negative sexual vibe.

Ignoring the weird way that Aiken was staring at her, as if she were a steak he was about to devour, Lori went to her notebook. "So," she began, matching Aiken's unblinking stare, "How long have you both known Dr. Tsien?"

Timbol was the first to answer. "About two years. But they only moved us into this workspace with him last year."

"Yeah, about a year ago. I didn't know him before," Aiken agreed.

Lori decided to see if she could unease them a bit. "So neither of you has any idea who'd want to kill him?"

They both reacted physically to her question. Timbol shifted in his seat and seemed to have lost some of his air of confidence, and Aiken stiffened up visibly, as if he just realized this was a serious inquiry. "No," Timbol offered cautiously, "everybody liked Specs."

"Specs?"

"That was his nickname around here," Aiken stated. "We all have nicknames."

"I see." Lori could not think of anything she wanted to know less than Aiken's nickname.

"Had you noticed anything different about him lately? Did he seem nervous or anxious about anything recently?"

They both shook their heads. "No, things were pretty normal. Tsien was kind of a humorless guy. He took everything pretty seriously," Timbol said.

"So you don't think he was having any personal problems? Issues with a girlfriend or anything like that?"

"No," Aiken offered. "I think he was still living with his sister. She was working on her master's in astronomy at Caltech. I don't think he exactly had a booming social life."

"So both of you do the same kind of work that Dr. Tsien did? Image processing on the MRO program?

Timbol nodded. "Correct," he said simply. Aiken also nodded.

Lori decided to shift the direction of the conversation on them. "Do either of you know anything about Dr. Tsien's work for DARPA?"

Once again, they both tightened up visibly. Aiken exchanged glances with Timbol. "No, we don't know anything about that," Aiken said, as if he were answering for them both.

Lori could see there was something more they weren't saying. She decided to up the pressure a bit. "And do either of you have a DARPA clearance yourselves?"

They answered quickly and in unison, "No."

Lori waited a moment, looking back and forth between them. "All right, gentlemen, one more question. Since you all worked exclusively on Mars Reconnaissance Orbiter images of Mars, can you think of any reason why any of that work would be classified?"

They quickly exchanged glances. "No," Aiken said, once again speaking for them both.

Lori stared right into his eyes and waited a beat. "Me either," she said. As Aiken shifted uncomfortably, Saunders arrived with a stack of paper printouts and handed them to Lori. He moved to stand between Lori and his two employees.

"These are the e-mail transcripts you asked for," he told her.

She took them and began to read through them. There wasn't much unusual except that he had sent several messages over the past month with file attachments to an AOL address. As she stood, she pointed out the filenames listed to Saunders. "What are these?" she asked him.

He placed his hand on her arm and began to lead her out of the cubicle. Obviously, he wanted her away from Aiken and Timbol. "Those look like MRO image numbers. I assume he was sharing his work with someone outside the lab."

"Is that unusual?

"No, we share our work with colleagues all the time."

"Uh-huh." She continued to read through the transcripts, then stopped and pulled out her smart phone. She got Marshall on the line and asked him to run the AOL e-mail address.

"The thing is," she said to Saunders, still holding the phone up to her ear, "this isn't a university or government e-mail address."

"Maybe he was sending the files to a colleague at his home address?" Saunders offered.

"Why would that be preferable to sending it to a work address? I doubt most of you have as much computing horsepower on your home computers as you do here at the lab."

Before Saunders could answer, Marshall was back on the line. She made certain not to let Saunders hear what he said. She thanked Marshall and hung up.

"So, Dr. Saunders, do you have a Richard Garvin working here at the lab or on the MRO program?" she asked.

"Why no," Saunders said, sounding puzzled. "I don't know that name."

"So you have no idea why Dr. Tsien would be sending image files to a person who was not on the program?"

"No, unless he worked for our public website developer. He could have been sending images for them to post on the public HiRISE site."

Lori considered that for a moment, then spun away from Saunders and went back to Timbol and Aiken in the cubicle. "Do either of you guys know somebody named Richard Garvin?"

Timbol smiled and laughed slightly, and Aiken had a look of dread cross his face involuntarily. Realizing he'd overreacted and they couldn't really dodge this question, Aiken spoke first.

"He's an overnight radio guy. He's always on this UFO radio program accusing us—NASA—of covering up evidence of ETs and stuff like that."

"Yeah," Timbol chimed in. "I think it's called *Nationwide AM* or something like that. He's a total conspiracy theorist. A real nut-job."

"A crackpot," Aiken added with a nod.

Lori considered them both carefully. "So. . . if he's such a crackpot, can either of you think of any reason why Dr. Tsien would be sending MRO images to his e-mail address?"

They exchanged a look once again. Aiken shrugged. "Maybe he was having some fun. Playing a joke on him or something."

Lori looked first at the gag pictures on Timbol's desk, then at Tsien's desk. It was filled with printouts of scientific papers, data charts, and a color image of Mars. She met Aiken's stare squarely: "Yeah, he seemed like he was a real prankster."

Neither of them had anything to add. Lori thanked them and left with Saunders. "Your employees seemed to know who Mr. Saunders was," she said to him as they walked down the stairs to the first floor.

"Yes, but I've never heard of him. I don't listen to late-night radio. I'm too busy."

As they walked to the glass doors in the lobby, Lori turned back to Saunders, putting her sunglasses on casually. "One last thing, Dr. Saunders: Can you think of a reason that Dr. Tsien would be sending image files to this Mr. Garvin?"

Saunders shook his head. "No, I can't. But Dr. Tsien was a very sober guy. Perhaps he was trying to talk him out of some of his stranger beliefs, show him that we weren't hiding anything on Mars. No ET cities or anything like that."

There was something about Saunders's demeanor, a sort of forced nonchalance, which bothered Lori. Did Saunders know more about this Richard Garvin than he was letting on?

Keeping her suspicions to herself, Lori thanked him cordially and asked for the hard drive to be forwarded to her at the FBI as soon as it was available. She waited until she was back on the freeway and well away from the lab to use her cell phone again. "Balver," Connie answered, her voice bright and melodic as it always was.

"Connie, it's Lori. Any luck with the Masonic lodges?"

"Nope," she said quickly. "Dr. Tsien was not a member of any of the local lodges. How was the geek squad?"

"About as chatty as your last boyfriend."

"Yikes!"

"Tell me about it," Lori agreed. "That place gives me the creeps. I'll be back in the office in a little bit. Thanks for checking on that for me."

"Sure."

Lori hung up without saying goodbye. As she reached down to drop her smartphone on the seat, she noticed the plain backside of a white business card sticking out of her notebook. Breaking several laws by multitasking while driving, she read the card and dialed up the number on it. It was picked up on one ring.

"Dansby." The voice was gravelly and distinct.

"Mr. Dansby? This is Special Agent Pars," she began. "You offered to help me with the Tsien case . . ."

"I certainly did."

Lori took a breath, wondering if she was about to make a Faustian pact. "OK then. Tell me everything I don't know about Mars."

9.

"Explain to me how it would be in my best interest to answer that question, Miss Pars." Dansby was trying his best to be coy, but Lori could tell he was anxious to talk, probably just to find out what she knew.

Lori decided not to play. "Don't jack me around, Mr. Dansby. You're the one who gave me your number, remember?"

There was a brief silence. "True enough," he finally said. "Let me start by asking you a question. Is this call on an open line?"

"I suppose. I'm using my FBI cell phone."

There was another pause, longer this time, and Lori wondered for a moment if he had hung up on her. Then she heard the shuffling of papers on a desk. "The first thing you should know is that there are a lot of things about Mars that NASA knows which have never been made public."

"Such as?"

"Such as the sky isn't red, as you see in all the pictures from the surface, it's blue, just like Earth."

"You mean NASA alters the color of the sky in the pictures they release?"

"Yes," he confirmed, "it actually looks very much like Arizona."

"You've been there?" Lori was only half joking. She wouldn't put much of anything past Dansby.

He ignored the insolent tone of her question. "I've seen the unfiltered images from the surface, yes."

"Is that how you know Dr. Tsien?"

"I don't know the good doctor at all. My concern for his case is purely professional."

Lori didn't buy that at all. "Is it? Then in what capacity is your professional concern, Mr. Dansby? What job do you do at DARPA anyway? Your card doesn't say."

"I'm the director of the Information Awareness Office," he said, as if that title should mean something to her.

Lori realized they were off on a tangent, perhaps as he wanted them to be. "What else?"

"I'm afraid I don't understand the question, Special Agent."

"I'm sure you do, Mr. Dansby. What else is there about Mars that NASA doesn't tell us?"

Lori thought she heard a self-satisfied little chuckle under his breath. "Many things. For instance, contrary to what you have been told, there is liquid water on Mars, in some cases in vast amounts."

Lori had watched enough Discovery Channel Mars specials to know what that implied. "So then there is life there as well? NASA has proof of that?"

"They have pictures. Brown and green patches on the rocks that expand and recede seasonally, with the warm spring weather and the melting of the polar ice caps, which puts more water vapor into the air."

Lori considered that for a moment. "Is that why they change the color in the photographs? To keep anyone from noticing the growth of these simple plants, or whatever they are?"

She could almost hear the acknowledging smile in his voice. "Now you're thinking like you need to."

"Like I need to for what, Mr. Dansby?"

"Like you'll need to if you're going to solve this case."

"Oh," Lori said. "I thought you were just worried about closing this case, not solving it."

Dansby took another beat. "That's what I'd like Assistant Director Ruby to think, Special Agent."

Lori let that statement settle into her consciousness before she went on. "So is there anything else?"

"Not that I can discuss over an open line on a cell phone network, my dear."

Lori took that to mean that he *could* have a further discussion -- in private. "Then I just have one more question, Mr. Dansby. . . "

"Certainly, if I can."

Lori went for it: "*Why* haven't they told us about life on Mars?"

He laughed, a bit smugly, she thought. "My dear, I thought you understood. Because it isn't time yet."

Lori was about to hang up when Dansby added one more thing. "Special Agent, you should know, one soldier to another, that pursuing this case, actually trying to solve it, could be detrimental."

"But I thought that's what you want me to do."

"It is. I'm just warning you, it could be detrimental."

She was not intimidated. "To my career?"

"Oh no. To your life, my dear."

Security was dramatically tighter in the Wilshire field office after that morning's incursion, and it took Lori several minutes longer than usual to get through all the extra checks. Marshall was waiting for her when she got to her desk.

"I'll have the flash drive cracked in an hour," he announced. The grin on his face told her that he expected high praise for this accomplishment.

Lori was inclined to oblige him. He had written some of the best decryption code in the Bureau, and he had a right to be proud of it. Besides, she still felt guilty for the way she'd talked to him earlier. "Very well done, Marshall!" she said, letting a broad smile cross her face. "I'm also going to need you to look over a hard drive coming from JPL later."

He nodded. "Yeah, they just called. They're sending it over by courier. We should have it about the same time. What am I looking for?"

"It's a backup of an e-mail server. We're looking for any patterns or anomalies in the data. You know, files sent to outside e-mail addresses, addresses that correspond to odd recipients, that kind of thing."

"And what do you expect to find on the flash drive?"

Lori shook her head. "I don't know. Hopefully the reason Dr. Tsien was killed."

Marshall handed her a printed out e-mail. "I called the Albuquerque field office. The SA in charge recommended we call the local police to conduct our questioning."

Lori had called from her car and asked him to follow up on the identity of Richard Garvin and to see if somebody in New Mexico could question him concerning Dr. Tsien. She took the paper, thanked him and sat down to dial the

Albuquerque Police Department's main office number. A few minutes later, after confirming her identity with the staff sergeant, she was on the line with the deputy chief of police.

"Deputy Chief Castro," he said into the phone.

"Officer Castro, this is Special Agent Lori Pars. I'm with the Los Angeles FBI field office. I was wondering if I could trouble you for a favor."

Castro's voice was warm and friendly. "Certainly, ma'am. How can I help you?'

"Well, I've got a lead on a case out here, and it may involve a person who lives in your area. I was hoping that somebody from your department could go out and perhaps ask him a few questions for me."

There was a slight hesitation on the other end. "What kind of case is it?"

"It's a homicide."

Now his tone became much more serious, and he breathed heavily into the phone. "Well, I don't know. I think I'd prefer the chief to authorize that one. We're a little busy here at the moment."

"I understand. Could I talk to the chief directly, then?"

"Chief Schultz is out in the field. He's personally overseeing a serious case right here."

"If you could give me his number. . ." her voice trailed off.

Castro took a good long moment to think it over. "OK, I'll give you his number. Normally, I'd say yes myself, but I think the chief would want to make this decision." With that, he gave her the number and hung up.

A few minutes later, she had the chief on the phone. "Look, Special Agent, I'd love to help you, but I can't spare the manpower right now. We're investigating a murder of our own that took place last night, and I'm up to my ears in the crime scene." His tone didn't sound as if he were really all that anxious to help her.

"Chief Schultz, I understand your situation and I empathize, but this would only take an hour or so. Just a visit by one of your officers to ask this man a few questions." Lori did her best to sound helpless and needy.

The chief was unimpressed. "Why can't the people in your office here take care of this?"

"They told me you weren't keen on federal interference in your jurisdiction. I figured you'd be more inclined to help if I asked your office first."

He blew some air out between his lips. "OK, lady, I guess I can't complain when you follow protocol. I'll send somebody out. Where does this guy live?"

"In the foothills above the city."

"Excellent. That's where I am now. What's his name?"

"Richard Garvin. His address is—"

Schultz interrupted: "11638 Canyon Peak Drive. Right?"

Lori was stunned. "How did you know that?"

"Because I'm standing outside what's left of his house right now. Somebody put a bullet through his chest last night and burnt his place to the ground."

Lori put her hand over her mouth.

"So if you don't mind telling me," Schultz began, "exactly why did you want to talk to my freshly dead body here?"

After some cajoling, Lori managed to get Schultz to agree to remove the hard drive from Saunders's computer and have it delivered to the Albuquerque field office. Once there, the computer tech could link it up so Marshall could pull the contents for analysis over the closed FBI network. He had already managed to get Saunders's e-mail records off the AOL servers.

Lori felt like drinking. Somehow all these strange events were connected, but she couldn't yet see how. She rubbed her temples, wishing she were on a white, warm, sandy beach somewhere with the FedEx delivery guy. . .

"Hey." Connie's soft, almost caressing voice broke her reverie. "You doing OK?"

Lori looked up. "Not really." She shuffled the papers on her desk and then pulled out the photograph that the intruder had left.

"I can't seem to get my head around this case. I've got two dead guys who may or may not have known each other but at the very least had e-mail contact. One is a respected NASA scientist, the other is a professional conspiracy theorist who specializes in exposing NASA's secrets. I interviewed the scientist's co-workers, and they are definitely hiding something, but I don't know what. My boss . . ." she lowered her voice, "who just happens to be my ex-lover, assigns me to the case even though I've never worked a homicide before. He's being watched closely by a creepy dude from DARPA, which it turns out my dead scientist also works for. Then, I've got someone who apparently knows something about the case and is able to easily penetrate FBI security. Oh, and the only description of the possible killers? Well, they look like ninjas." She threw her arms up in the air. "Have I missed anything?"

"Yeah," Connie said, pointing to the photograph. "The whole thing about the Masons."

Lori rocked her chair back. "Oh yeah. Thanks for reminding me."

Connie's mouth pursed and she crossed her arms as she leaned back on the desk. "A murder case isn't linear. You don't go from point A to point B in a nice, straight line. It's more like a jigsaw puzzle. You take a piece here, a piece from over there, and when you get enough pieces, it starts to form a picture. You just have to be patient until you get enough pieces."

"*If* I get enough pieces," Lori added.

"Sometimes it works better if you simplify things," Connie responded. "What you really have here is two murders, and the victims were passing information back and forth. The behavior of one of the victims' associates indicates that while they may not have done the murder, they have a pretty good idea *why* it may have happened. And you have outsiders who seem to be very interested in the case, for whatever reasons. It's really as simple as that."

Lori frowned. "That doesn't help me any, really. What do I do about any of this? Increase the pressure on the JPL guys? Kick an idea up the line to Ruby and see if that shakes anything out? What?"

Connie shook her head. "Wait for a break. In a case as active as this, something is bound to happen soon."

Just as Lori opened her mouth to respond, Marshall stuck his head over the top of her blue-gray cubicle wall. "Hey, guys," he said excitedly, "I've got a positive ID on our security breach. You're not going to believe who this guy is."

Lori exchanged a glance with Connie. "Yes I will," she said tiredly.

"His name is Trevor Vartan." Marshall was showing them a military ID picture of the same handsome, rugged-looking man they'd seen in the security footage, but perhaps a few years younger. "He's a former Royal Navy staff officer and get this, ex-MI-6!"

Connie spoke for them both. "James Bond, basically," she said.

Marshall nodded. "Even more than you think. He was born in 1968 to a Scottish father, Admiral Sir Edward Boyce, GCB, OBE, DL—former First Sea Lord of the Royal Navy and Chief of Defence Staff, from 1980 to '83. His mother was a Hungarian woman of Armenian descent named Sophie Vartan. He was raised in various naval posts as he followed his family around the world. He spent the longest period of his childhood in Gibraltar, where his father was commander of the British garrison."

"Not exactly from the rough side of town," Lori noted.

"He didn't have it that easy," Marshall said back to her. "He was orphaned at age eleven in 1983 when his father and mother were killed in a small plane accident on a vacation in Monaco." He reached down and picked up a piece of paper from his printer. "After their deaths, he took his mother's maiden name, stating in the court proceeding that quote, 'I wish to do so as a way to honor her memory and because I wish to make my way in the world on my own merits, not my family name,' end quote. This is an eleven-year-old boy, remember."

"What else?" Lori asked anxiously.

"He inherited a trust in the amount of one hundred ten million U.S. dollars, and this was in 1983! He went to live with his aunt on his mother's side, and she sent him to British boarding schools as a teenager, where he graduated a year early and attended Balliol College at the University of Oxford. He majored in ancient history. Graduated with honors in 1991 and joined the Royal Navy with the rank of lieutenant, or 'left-tennant' if you're British, in 1992 and then completed a series of assignments as a staff officer, working as an adjunct to an Admiral Arthur Milner in the Royal Navy. He led a NATO Special Forces squad in Bosnia in 1995 and received several commendations. After attaining the rank of commander in 1996, he left the Royal Navy to assume a post with MI-6, the British Secret Intelligence Service."

"Just as a note, that was a horrible British accent on the left-tennant thing," Connie deadpanned.

"Go on," Lori said, wanting to stick to business.

"There's not much on his MI-6 days, but I found a few references to a case from 1998. Apparently, he was assigned to track a group of American National Security Agency officers who went AWOL from a West German listening post. He later tracked them to Gulf Breeze, Florida, where he led the special tactics group that arrested them. After capturing the officers and debriefing them, he abruptly resigned from MI-6 in 1999. Since then he's apparently been an intelligence source for Richard Garvin, providing him inside information on various space-related activities. Garvin refers—uh, referred—to him as 'Deep Space' in various correspondences."

"How do you know for sure Deep Space is Vartan?" Lori asked.

"It's in Garvin's e-mails from him," Marshall said. "I've recovered most of the data from his hard drive already. It wasn't too badly damaged."

"That NSA case, what was the disposition?" Lori asked.

Marshall shook his head back and forth. "That's the weird part. The army officers that he captured, they were all given honorable discharges in early 1999. It was right after that Vartan resigned from MI-6."

"Why the fuck would he do that?" Connie blurted out. "Oops," she said, raising a hand to her mouth, "Did I say that out loud?"

"No, it's a good question Connie," Lori observed. "This guy was on the fast track to a major career in British intelligence, maybe even a political career. Then these army intelligence officers go AWOL, set off a worldwide manhunt, and then a few weeks after they're caught, they all walk away with honorable discharges and Vartan quits. What's up with that?"

Marshall shrugged his shoulders and pointed back to the picture of Vartan on the screen. "I don't know. But I bet he does."

Lori and Connie were back at Lori's desk when Marshall popped in the cube an hour later. "I've got something," he told them. "I've compared the emails that Garvin got with the ones that Dr. Tsien sent. What I found is that there's one common contact between the two of them."

"Trevor Vartan," Lori said confidently.

"Wrong!" Marshall exclaimed. "I knew you'd guess that. No, it's an email address that pings back to an apartment in Culver City."

"Do you have a name?"

"Uh, it just seems to be registered to somebody named, uh, "Honey.'"

"Hmm," Connie intoned. "Culver City, named Honey. I'm guessing either a stripper or an escort. Or both."

Lori nodded her agreement. "Give me the address, please."

Marshall handed her a printout with the address on it, and Lori rose to leave.

"Need help?" Connie asked.

"No, I think I can handle 'Honey' by myself. Why don't you get Mike Hammer here to run the address and see if it pops out a real name?"

"Hey wait a minute," Marshall protested as Connie took him by the arm, "how do you guys know she's a stripper or something?"

Connie patted him on the shoulder. "That's why we're the detectives, Marshall," she said.

10.

Lori was almost at the address Marshall had given her when Connie called with the ID. 'Honey' was a twenty-six-year-old named Andrea Tully, or at least that was the name of the person on the apartment lease. It turned out to be an average Culver City apartment house with about forty units, a dingy pool and a recent coat of paint. Lori got the manager to let her in, and soon she was standing in front of unit 333, knocking on the dark brown door, her back facing the open central atrium.

"Who is it?" The voice was female and sounded either tired or hung-over.

"It's the manager. I need to do a quick check on the plumbing," Lori lied.

"You don't sound like Teri," the voice shot back quickly.

"Teri's out with the plumbers. The company sent me down to check all the units." Lori thought this new lie was even less convincing than the one before.

"I didn't hear any trucks pull up this morning," the voice protested, sounding more suspicious.

Lori decided to give it one more shot. "They're out back. Now will you please let me in so I can look at the pipes?"

She heard the chain slide over the door. Lori wasn't sure if the girl inside was attaching it, or pulling it off. Then the door opened partway, the tautly drawn chain keeping it from opening completely. Lori stuck her foot in the door to wedge it open and flashed her badge, holding it in her left hand. She never showed her badge with her gun hand, no matter how benign the situation appeared.

"Special Agent Lori Pars, FBI. Are you Andrea Tully?"

The girl squinted at the badge. "Who are you with?"

Lori pondered whether she could possibly be clearer. "The FBI, honey. You know, the Federal Bureau of Investigation?"

"Are you a cop?"

"Something like that. Now open the door. I need to ask you some questions."

Although Lori could only see half of her face, the girl appeared to frown and started to slide the chain off the door. Lori stepped back so she could close it first and remove the chain before opening it back up.

Andrea's place was a bizarre mix of wildly expensive electronics and trash. There was garbage of all sorts strewn about; pizza boxes, dirty paper plates, laundry and even some unopened moving boxes. That contrasted with a sixty-five inch LED TV, Blu-Ray DVD player and a pricey surround sound stereo system. Lori scanned the scene and spotted a bong and some other pot smoking paraphernalia on the coffee table.

"It's my boyfriend's," the girl said, as if she were immune to the possibility of being arrested because of it. "He's such a loser," she added absently.

Lori walked around the apartment, checking the closets and bathroom to make sure they were alone. A little black Scottie terrier came shuffling up to her, his tail wagging as he breathlessly sniffed Lori's hands.

"That's Brutus," the girl said. "He's a sweetie."

"Hi Brutus!" Lori said brightly as she knelt to pet the little black dog. Andrea seemed blissfully oblivious to the fact that she had a federal police officer in her apartment, and that could only mean something serious was going on. Lori elected to play friendly cop with her.

"So you're Andrea Tully?"

"Yeah," the girl said. "Listen, if this is about Jamie, I told him last month he couldn't stay here if he was going to keep selling. He promised me that the only stuff he had was for him. That he wasn't selling anymore."

"Andrea… look, I'm not here about the pot. I need to ask you some questions about a . . . friend of yours."

Lori stood and turned to look her in the eye for the first time. She had long straight black hair with some reddish blond highlights, big brown eyes with thick, perfectly groomed brows, high, sharp cheekbones and full lips. She wore a mint green t-shirt and distressed jeans with several strategically placed tears in them. The top was skin tight around her very full figure and Lori had to admit that although her chest was obviously artificially enhanced, her doctor had done a superb job. It took Lori a moment longer to realize Andrea was stunningly beautiful and not simply stunning.

Andrea noticed the play of this evaluation process across Lori's face. Even though they were only six years apart in age, the look Andrea gave her made it seem like decades. Lori decided to get to the point.

"Are you hooking, Andrea?"

The girl made a disgusted face. "Eeew, no. I wouldn't do anything like that. I'm a dancer. And an actress."

"So how do you know somebody named Xian Tsien?"

A look of confusion crossed her face. Lori realized she might not be pronouncing it correctly. "Dr. Tsien, from JPL?"

Andrea shook her head, "I still don't . . . oh wait! Dr. Zen, from Pasadena?"

She pronounced it in a simplified way that sounded completely different from the way Lori had said it. "That's him," Lori said.

"Oh he's a nice guy. Much cuter without those glasses."

"Where do you know him from?"

"He comes to the club where I work. The Lickety Split, on 9th in Santa Monica."

Lori stifled a grin. What a stupid name. "OK Andrea. Did you know he was dead? Murdered?"

A look of profound horror crossed the girl's face. This time, her voice was serious and measured. "I didn't know that. When did it happen?"

"Last night." Lori decided the girl hadn't known before she was just told. "So tell me why he was sending you emails and calling you on the phone?" The latter assertion was just a calculated guess.

"I give lots of customers my phone number and email. I get asked for them all the time at the club."

"Do you date a lot of your customers?"

A frown crossed her face. "I never date regulars," she said tersely.

"Was Dr. Tsien a regular?"

"Yeah, and he was nice. And smart. He never got the idea that I was his girlfriend or anything. He was happy just to be friends."

"So you didn't kill him?" Lori asked just to see if she could shake her up.

"No! Of course not. That's stupid. I worked last night and then went to dinner in Hollywood. Then I came home."

"And you didn't see Dr. Tsien at the club last night?"

"No."

"Where'd you go to dinner?"

"Toi, up on Sunset Strip. It's a Thai restaurant. I went with Kevin. He's one of the security guys at the club."

Lori tried to ice her down with a stare. Then; "So you've never seen Dr. Tsien outside the club?"

Andrea put her left hand on her right arm, crossing her chest, and turned slightly away from Lori. "I didn't say that." She was tensing up.

"So you do see your clients outside the club? Why did you lie to me?"

"I didn't. I'm not a 'ho,'" she protested. Lori couldn't wait to hear this subtle distinction. She just stared Andrea down.

"Sometimes, if I like a guy, I'll see him for a private dance." Her voice was apologetic, but there was still a hint of defiance in it.

"A private dance?" Lori's tone was mocking. "So I assume this involves an exchange of money, a lack of clothing on your part, and probably some form of sexual release by your . . . friend. But you're not a 'ho,' right?"

"Fuck you lady," Andrea shot back. "I don't have to justify myself to you."

Lori realized from the intensity of Andrea's response that she'd made a mistake in judging her too harshly. It hadn't occurred to her that this slightly vacant girl might have a sense of ethics that was internally consistent, at least to her.

"I'm sorry if my genes didn't come from some Ivy League sperm bank like yours did, lady," Andrea went on. "I do what it takes to get by."

Lori felt genuine sympathy for her. "OK Andrea, you're right. I'm sorry. I know times are tough."

Andrea turned away and dismissed Lori's apology with a wave of her hand. So much for her attempt at being friendly cop. "So how did Dr. Tsien make his appointments with you?" Lori continued.

Andrea crossed both her arms across her chest then and seared Lori with look that made it clear they were through talking.

"OK Honey," Lori said more forcefully, deliberately using the girl's stripper name. "There are two ways we can do this. You can answer my questions here, and then I can leave and you can go on with your life. Or, I can bust you for possession with intent to distribute, and you can answer the same questions from your holding cell downtown. What's it gonna be?"

Andrea looked back and forth between Lori and the bong. "It's not mine," she said, not a hint of defiance in her voice.

"I'm sure the judge will believe you over a federal agent, sweetie. But we won't know for sure for a couple of days, will we?"

She dropped her arms to her sides. "He would email me."

Lori looked around. "Where's your computer?"

"I don't have one. I get all my emails on my Galaxy." She bent down to the coffee table and picked up her smart phone.

Lori reached for her own phone and pulled a data cable from her purse. "Give it to me. I'll upload the memory to the field office." After a moment, she looked up to see Andrea still holding onto her phone.

"Don't you have to get a search warrant or something?"

Lori crossed the room in two quick steps and got right into Andrea's face. She pulled her jacket back so her gun was clearly visible. "Trust me, Honey. You don't want me to have to get a search warrant."

Andrea swallowed once, then she scowled and slapped the phone into Lori's hand and turned away from her. Lori connected the two devices and started scanning the Galaxy's memory. On a hunch, she pulled Trevor Vartan's picture from her bag and showed it to Andrea. "I don't suppose you know this man, do you?"

Andrea turned and looked at the picture, but didn't really study it closely. "Doesn't look familiar."

"You don't know him?"

Andrea shook her head. "No."

After the memory upload was complete, Lori tossed the Galaxy back to Andrea and then took out a card. "Here's my number. Call me if you remember anything else important about Dr. Tsien."

Lori started for the door. Andrea's voice, sounding weak and scared, stopped her. "Ma'am? How did he die?"

Lori looked down. "They beat him to death." She flashed a look at Andrea, and saw a quick glint of fear cross her face. The moment hung between them. Most people who hear this kind of news for the first time ask the police if it is a random act of violence, seeking reassurance that a person they know has not been specifically targeted. Lori knew from her training this was a natural inclination when the victim is known personally to a suspect, because it means that even though their friend or family member may be dead, they are probably not the killer's next target.

But Andrea didn't ask that.

Lori opened the door. "I assume you're working tonight?"

"Yes," Andrea responded quietly.

"Good. Don't leave town." Lori stepped out and closed the door behind her.

Lori was less than three blocks from Andrea's apartment when Marshall called. "I just cross referenced the emails on Saunders' computer with the data from Honey's

Galaxy. There are at least a dozen emails from her to him that weren't sent from the Galaxy."

"What do they contain?" Lori asked.

"Some have image files, a couple of schematics of NASA probes, things like that. The image files match the file names of the emails Tsien sent from his JPL computer, but they aren't the same."

"What do you mean, they aren't the same?"

Marshal was hesitant. "I mean, well, they have the same image numbers, and they are of the same terrain on Mars, but they look different."

Lori pressed him. "Define *different*, Marshall."

He paused. "It'll be easier if I just show you."

Lori's mind flashed to her earlier phone conversation with Prescott Dansby. He had warned her not to dig too deeply into what JPL was looking for on Mars. She was short with him. "Fine. I'll look them over when I get back to the office. Do you have anything else?"

"Yeah, the emails that didn't come from Honey's Galaxy? They were definitely sent from her local area network. From her apartment."

"Thanks Marshall." She snapped her cell phone shut, and hit the steering wheel in frustration.

"The little bitch lied to me!" she fumed out loud.

"OK Honey, where is it?" Lori was on a rampage.

"Where is what?" Andrea was trying her best look innocent and confused.

"Don't give me that shit! The computer. Where is it?" Lori was storming around the apartment now, tossing aside couch cushions and looking in drawers. Brutus was following her and barking.

"Stop it!" Andrea protested. She reached out and grabbed Lori's arm. "You're scaring Brutus! Stop it. It's in my attic."

She pointed to her bedroom closet. Lori crossed over to it and saw the opening in the ceiling, covered with a wooden board. She spotted the stepstool in the closet and set it up and then reached up and lifted the board. Inside, she found a compact Apple laptop. "You don't spare much expense on the electronics, do you?" she asked.

"I like my gadgets." Andrea said defensively. Lori gave her a dirty look and then fired up the laptop. Within a couple of minutes she had the machine up and running and was skimming through the emails.

"Why did you lie to me? Do you have any idea what the penalty is for misleading a federal investigation?" Lori could tell she hadn't thought much about it. "Five years," she told her. "I could send your ass to prison for five years."

Andrea tossed her hands in the air. "For what? Not helping a bitch cop?"

"The thing I don't get," Lori was busy reading the emails and talking to Andrea at the same time, "Is who you were trying to protect? Dr. Tsien is already dead." Then it dawned on her: "Unless you were protecting somebody else."

Andrea tightened up visibly. "I'm not protecting anyone," she said unconvincingly.

Lori stared her down. "On the acting thing? Don't quit your day job." Andrea didn't respond. Lori reached into her purse and pulled the picture of Vartan out again. "So, tell me how you met him."

Andrea folded her arms across her chest and looked away. Lori circled around to face her.

"Andrea Tully, you better listen to me. I'm investigating the murder of a NASA scientist. This man," she flashed the picture in front of her face again, "is a prime suspect. I have you dead to rights on obstructing a federal investigation. Now unless you want to go to jail, and I'm serious about that, then you'd better tell me what you know."

Andrea's head dropped, and she sat on the back of her couch.

"He came to the club one night." Her voice was very quiet. "He said he was a friend of Dr. Zen's. He said that he needed a way to send emails back and forth without getting Dr. Zen in trouble."

"Trouble at work?"

She nodded. "He said those JPL people were pretty bad."

"Did you ask Dr. Tsien about him?"

"Yeah, he said it was OK for me to let him use my computer to pass emails back and forth. Dr. Zen would come and see me, and leave stuff on my laptop. Then Trevor would come by the club or call and make an appointment a couple days later." She looked at Lori, clearly wondering how much more she should tell.

"You mean he would just show up?"

"No. he gave me a number to call whenever there was something new on my computer."

Lori shook her head a couple of times. "And you never looked at what was on your computer?"

"Yeah, but it was just pictures and stuff. Nothing that I thought was especially important."

"It was important enough that Dr. Tsien is dead because of it," Lori reminded her.

"You don't know that!"

Lori took a comforting tone. "I'm pretty sure it's true, Andrea."

Andrea seemed downtrodden. It was hard to stay mad at her. She had a certain kind of innocence, but allowed herself to be used in ways that Lori couldn't fathom. She found herself longing for a good, clean political corruption investigation.

It was time to change tactics: "How did Trevor pay you for your time?"

"Cash. He always had a lot of it."

"And did you do 'private dances' for him?"

"Yeah. He was cute. I didn't mind."

Charming, Lori thought. "Did he ever say anything about who he was sending emails to?"

"No."

"And it never crossed your mind it might be illegal, Andrea?"

"No."

Lori let out a small sigh. "Well, the man they were sending emails to? He's also dead."

Andrea reacted with widening eyes. "Was he…?"

Lori nodded. "Also murdered."

Andrea's face dropped, and her hand went to her head. "Holy fuck I'm in a lot of trouble, aren't I?"

Lori nodded again. "Yes you are. But if you help me, I can get you out of trouble."

Andrea looked at her with a hint of desperation on her face. "What would I have to do?"

Lori reached down for the Galaxy on the coffee table. "Send Trevor a text."

11.

Marshall had finally cracked the encryption on the flash drive recovered from the Tsien crime scene, and he was anxiously waiting to show Lori what he had found when she got back to her desk. It was now well after three P.M., and it had already been a long day. Still, his boyish enthusiasm energized her, especially when she saw what he had found.

His computer monitor was displaying two identical grayscale images of the surface of Mars, side by side. They were dominated by a huge, bulging landform that was commonly known as the Face on Mars. Marshall had rotated the images so that north was in the upward direction, and the Face's vertical axis was offset from that by about twenty degrees.

"OK," Marshall began excitedly. "This image on the left is the one taken from Dr. Tsien's flash drive, and the one on the right is the one that he emailed from his JPL computer to this Garvin guy the night he was killed."

"The night they were both killed," Lori corrected. Was it all just last night?

"Right. Anyway, they are both numbered identically, and they are both in the same format."

"Oh," Lori honestly had no idea what he was talking about and wished he'd get to the point.

"The thing is," Marshall continued, "superficially, they look the same. But actually, they aren't. If you look closely at the one from Garvin's hard drive, you can see that certain features have been airbrushed out."

Lori looked at the area where Marshall was pointing. In the image from Tsien's flash drive, there were a series of regular vertical striations at the base of the Face. They seemed to be imbedded in the ground around the object, and attached somewhere higher up on the Face itself. There were also regularly spaced horizontal bars that seemed to reinforce the structure laterally. On the version that had been emailed to Garvin, these areas were blotted out, as if someone had taken a blur tool to the image and simply removed the detail.

"One of these is a fake," Lori said aloud.

"Exactly!" Marshall was obviously pleased he'd gotten his point across. "Now look at this," he continued. "Look at this circular thing to the north of the Face. Now this looks a lot like a collapsed volcanic dome. But notice again how the Garvin version and the Tsien version are different? See how there is this gray, blurry area all around the base of this dome? On the Tsien version, things are completely different."

Lori looked again at what he was showing her. She could see a series of regularly spaced horizontal spokes emanating from underneath the base of the dome. They looked for all the world like walkways leading into the object. "It looks like a sports arena or something," she said, half whispering to herself.

"That's what I thought," Marshall agreed. "Look Lori, I studied architecture in school, I was considering making it my major before I went with computer science." He hesitated a moment, as if grappling with the gravity of what he was about to say. "This is architecture. From a structural standpoint, these design features make complete sense."

Lori considered this information carefully. "So, if I understand you correctly, you're saying that these objects are artificial? Have I got that right?"

Marshal exhaled loudly. "Yeah, I guess that's what I'm saying. I'm saying that this Garvin guy was right all along about this Face thing. And I'm suggesting Dr. Tsien knew it."

Lori crossed her arms. "Is there a publicly released version of this image?"

"Yeah, it matches the one from Garvin's hard drive. The one with the blurry gray areas on it."

"So then, how do you know which version is the real one, and which is fake?"

Marshall pointed again to the screen, and selected a box shape inside one of the blurry areas. A graph popped up on the screen. "Because when I analyze the histogram for these areas, there is almost a complete lack of detail. There are only about twelve shades of gray in these blurry areas, whereas the rest of the image has the full 256 shades of gray. That's an almost sure tell-tale indication that this part of the image has been 'digitally airbrushed.'" He made little quote signs with both fingers.

"And you'll go on record with that opinion?"

"Absolutely."

Lori's lips pursed. "Marshall, you do realize what this means if you're right?"

He nodded. "Yeah, it means NASA has evidence of life beyond the Earth, that they're covering that information up, and that when they found out Dr. Tsien was trying to pass the real stuff along to Mr. Garvin, they killed him for it."

Lori's eyes met his. "That's certainly one scenario." She shook her head in disbelief. "I don't understand. Why would NASA want to cover this up? Isn't this what they're searching for out there?"

"That's what they say, but this Garvin guy has been claiming all along that it's a scam. He found this document that was commissioned by NASA back when it was first formed that says if they find evidence of a superior civilization, or make alien contact, they should cover it up."

"What?"

"Yeah," Marshall continued. He switched windows on his computer and brought up a .pdf file of an old government study on his screen. It was titled *Proposed Studies on the Implications of Peaceful Space Activities for Human Affairs.* "It's generally called 'The Brookings Report,'" he said. "Because it was commissioned by the Brookings Institute. And it warns NASA that there's a good chance they'll find *artifacts* left behind at some point in time by an alien civilization." He turned around to Lori. "Does that sound anything like what I just showed you?"

She had to admit it did. "Yeah, "she said simply.

"It goes on to say that if they do make such a discovery, that they should seriously consider *withholding* the information from the public. It says that the *War of the Worlds* broadcast in 1939 is proof that we couldn't handle the news without going crazy. Lori, they're saying that if these discoveries were revealed, our society might disintegrate. That's the word they actually used!" Marshall shifted in his chair. "Lori, do you think this is why that DARPA guy is so interested in this case? He's trying to make sure nobody gets a hold of these images of what's really on Mars?"

Lori's expression hardened as she recalled her earlier conversation with Dansby. "I know it is, Marshall."

She sat back down in her chair and chewed the inside of her mouth, a nervous habit she had developed as a teenager. Marshall watched her closely as she mulled things over in her head. "OK, I want you to put the key images together in a presentation, side by side. I'll go back over to JPL tomorrow and confront Dr. Saunders with it."

Marshall was confused. "You aren't going back over there today?"

"No. I have an operation I'm setting up for tonight on our intruder. I think that should be my main focus for the rest of the day."

"Too bad, I'd have liked to have seen their faces when you showed them this evidence."

"You'll get your chance tomorrow, Marshall." She rose again to leave his cube, but he reached out and stopped her.

"OK. There's one more thing though."

Lori turned back wearily. "What?"

"I read your case notes, and I think that Dr. Saunders lied to you."

"About...?"

"Your notes said he claimed he didn't know who Garvin was?"

"That's right."

Marshall pulled up a video on his screen. "I found this on YouTube. It's a debate from a CBS News program called Nightwatch, from back in 1989. It's between Dr. Saunders and Richard Garvin."

"You're telling me that Saunders debated this guy on national television once?"

"Yeah. And he lost. Pretty badly too. Garvin pinned him down and got him to admit he'd never actually seen any pictures of Cydonia or the Face, even though he was on TV claiming there was nothing to it."

Lori sat back down and watched as Marshall played back the video. When it was over, she patted Marshall on the arm. "That's good work. It's pretty hard to believe that Dr. Saunders wouldn't remember that experience."

"Isn't it?" He paused a moment. Then: "Lori, there's something else."

She sighed. "Of course there is. What?"

"That *Mars Observer* probe they were debating on TV? JPL announced it was missing three minutes after this debate was over."

Lori considered the implications of that revelation for a moment. "I don't suppose they ever found it?" she asked.

He shook his head. "Nope."

"Why did I know that was going to be your answer?"

12.

A few minutes later, Connie came into Marshall's cube and pulled up a chair. She sat in it with her arms and legs crossed. Marshall's eyes started darting nervously between her and Lori.

"So, I hear you're going undercover at a strip club tonight," Connie said quickly.

Lori stood up straight from where she had been leaning over Marshall's computer. "Yes," she said simply. Connie made a little "humph" sound, the kind she always made when she had something to say but wanted to be asked first. Lori crossed her arms, matching Connie's closed body language. Marshall looked like he was trying to come up with an excuse to leave the cube.

"Go ahead," Lori said, not too enthusiastically.

Connie looked her up and down. "In *those* clothes?" she said disdainfully.

"Well, yes, actually. What's wrong with my clothes?"

"Nothing, if you're going to church."

Lori frowned at her. "My work clothes are practical!"

"Yeah, if you work in a convent," Connie shot back. "C'mon Lori, you're going out to a strip club in that outfit? You won't exactly blend."

"And what, may I ask, is wrong with my outfit?"

Unwittingly, Lori had taken the bait and Connie jumped in. "Tan skirt below the knee, plain white blouse that's about as see-through as the lead blanket in a dentist's office, a matching tan jacket and shoes with no heels at all. And let's not forget the man-repulsing gold cross necklace."

"It was a gift from my father!"

"When you graduated from an all-girls religious high school?"

"Well, yes."

"Man-deflector!" Connie pointed up at her.

"I am not," Lori protested. "And what's wrong with wearing comfortable shoes? What if I had to chase down a suspect?"

"And that was *so* likely to happen while you were interviewing the scientists over at JPL."

Lori reacted again with a frown. "Oh, and you're just so sexy in your little pin stripped blue pants suit."

Connie stood up and turned around, lifting her jacket as Marshall looked increasingly uncomfortable. "Notice how my suit jacket only comes part of the way down my butt? That's so someone behind me can see that I actually *have* a butt, unlike you. Notice there are no visible panty lines, prompting any male tracking me to ponder whether I actually have underwear on or not. And these little heels on my shoes? Notice how they push my rear end up and accentuate the curvature of it? It's all about geometry with men."

Connie then turned around and buttoned her jacket. "And notice here, with my jacket buttoned, how it's just a bit too small, pulling it tight across my boobs? Guess what? Men like a girl with actual boobs."

Lori was unimpressed. "Men like the way I dress," she protested.

Connie smirked. "Oh yeah, like who?"

Lori turned to Marshall for support, but he was frozen, as if by not moving he could slowly fade into the background and avoid being drawn into the dispute. Once they both made eye contact with him, he looked back and forth between them, his eyes begging not to be asked his opinion.

"Sure," Connie said, pointing to Marshall. "Ask him."

Lori started to ask Marshall a question, but gasped when she saw the look of dread on his face. "Oh my god, you *agree* with her don't you!"

"Well. . ." Marshall stammered, looking like a man trying one last time to avoid the pool of quicksand that was rapidly spreading before him. "I guess you can be a little on the conservative side. . ."

Lori just stared at him, her mouth agape.

Now suddenly he was the enemy. Connie shot him a dirty look and took Lori by the hand. "I'm just trying to help sweetie. You can always charge some new clothes as a 402b expense and get reimbursed."

"A 402b is only for essential expenses required for an undercover operation," Lori argued.

Marshall started to say something, but Connie gave him The Hand. "Believe me, honey, this is essential," she said gently.

Lori's face dropped as she contemplated that perhaps she was more than merely professional, she was downright bland. Connie took out her phone and sent a text message to Lori.

"This is my niece's name and number. She works in the mall at bebe. Go over there on your lunch hour and tell her what you need. She's really into Aunt Connie's FBI stuff and she'll be more than happy to help."

"I never shop there," Lori said dejectedly.

"That's OK, Sears will survive the fiscal quarter without your normal sales numbers." Marshall's attempt at levity fell flat, and both women shot him a seething look. Lori stomped out.

Connie scowled at him. "Didn't your mother teach you anything Marshall? You just don't say things like that to women."

"But *you* did! "

"That's different. I'm a *girl*."

Marshall tried to say something, but Connie was already following Lori out of his cubicle. "No wonder you never get laid," she said, loud enough for others in the office to hear. Marshall sank down into his chair.

Lori opened the door nervously, hiding behind it and checking to see if any of her neighbors were in the hallway. Seeing the coast was clear, she grabbed Connie by the arm and pulled her and Marshall in. Marshall kept moving forward into the apartment, staring at the artwork on her walls and seemingly marveling that he was actually in Lori's Holy of Holies. She had a framed print of Dali's *Crucifixion (Corpus Hypercubus)* over her mantle, and he seemed transfixed by it.

As Connie turned, Lori closed the door behind her and opened her arms at her sides, "Well," she said, "here I am."

"Oh honey that is so much better. You actually look hot."

Connie's words brought Marshall out of his artistic reverie and he turned to look at Lori. She was wearing a tight fitting black cropped tank top over a second white tank. Both just barely came to her waist. As she moved, a brief flash of her midriff would show. "Oh!" Connie squealed, "you even got your belly pierced!"

"Yeah," Lori said, "it hurt like hell."

Connie pointed to the low heeled shoes Lori had purchased to go with the outfit. "Sexy shoes!" She turned and snapped her fingers in Marshall's direction. "What do you think Marshall?"

Marshall appeared catatonic. He just stared for a long moment, then finally nodded and smiled, indicating that he liked the low cut, hip hugging jeans she had bought.

"Apparently, his tongue is in sleep mode," Connie said, crossing the room and nudging him with her elbow.

"Sorry," Marshall responded, flushing red a bit. "You look fabulous Lori."

"Earlier today, he was so excited at the prospect of the new, sexy Lori," Connie said, smirking at him. "Now I think he's not so sure."

Lori pulled them both together. "OK," she said a bit sheepishly. "There's one more aspect to this you should see. I'm a little nervous about it."

"Go for it girl!" Connie said quickly.

Marshall looked worried. "You're not . . . you don't have *any more* piercings, do you?"

Connie smacked him. "Pervert!" she said. Marshall first gave her a confused look before realizing what she was implying. His face went beat red. "Oh, no! That's . . . that's not what I meant!"

Lori deliberately narrowed her eyes at both of them. "Marshall, please. Focus!"

Marshall nodded and Connie gave her a look that said "go ahead."

Lori turned away from them and dropped her watch on the carpet. "Oh look, I dropped my watch!" she said in mock distress. "I guess I'll have to bend over and pick it up."

As she bent down on one knee and picked up the watch, her low slung jeans pulled down, exposing the high-cut thong underwear and a good chunk of her rump. The top pulled up, revealing an Ouroboros, a circular snake consuming its own tail, tattooed on her lower back. She turned and smiled back at them.

Connie was delighted. "Honey, you got a tat! It's very sexy."

Marshall's mouth hung open. He slowly came out of his trance-like state when he saw an expression of worry cross Lori's face. "Don't worry, "she reassured him, "It's only temporary."

"Whew, that's good," Marshall said, concern stressing his voice.

"I don't care if it's only a Henna tat, you look hot babe!" Connie said. Marshall seemed excessively relieved. "Marshall, what's the matter?" Connie asked. Lori started to check her own backside as best she could, worried that more was showing than she wanted.

"Nothing. It's just that . . ." he trailed off.

"Yes?" Connie pressed him, losing her patience. She could tell Lori felt really good about how she looked, and she wasn't about to let Marshall's adolescent jealousies mess that up.

"Well, I've never actually seen a girl's 'whale tail' before."

Lori was confused. "A what?"

Connie had to hold her stomach to keep from giggling. "You know, the little triangle of material that holds the three prongs of the thong together? It's called a 'whale tail."

Lori's face flushed red. "You can see that?"

"Only when you bend over, sweetie. Don't worry. You won't be the only girl at the club tonight with her thong showing a bit." Connie walked over and put her arm around Lori and her eyes narrowed as she considered Marshall. "There's something else, right Marshall?"

"No."

"Yes there is. Don't forget, I'm a detective."

Marshall's face dropped. There was no way he was going to get out of this one, not with Connie on the scent.

"OK," he said haltingly. "It's just that my mom always said to stay away from girls with tattoos."

"Because they're bad?" Connie asked.

Marshall nodded.

"And you don't want other men to think Lori is a bad girl, do you?"

"No." he said quietly, looking away.

Lori's face crumpled up in sympathy and she took his face in her hands. "Oh! That is sooooo sweet!" She pulled him in and gave him a quick kiss on the cheek, her lipstick leaving a mark.

Connie considered him dispassionately, crossing her arms. "I have a tattoo," she told him. "Am I a bad girl?"

"That depends where it is."

"You'd have to see me naked to know that."

"Well, it's not like we're at the office or anything . . ."

Lori smacked him on the shoulder. "Marshall!" she said loudly.

Marshall burst into a big smile. "OK, you got me!" he said to Connie. "Your detection skills are dominant." He pointed to the lipstick. "At least I got a kiss out of it."

At that point, Lori realized he was just playing a game with her. She gave him her best displeased look. "Affection whore," she said to him, smirking. Then she crossed over to her coffee table and picked up a mid-sized gray purse with a faint checkered pattern and put it over her shoulder. "Check this out," she said to Connie.

Connie's eyes lit up. "A Louis Vuitton handbag! And just big enough for everything a girl needs." She went through the purse, calling out the contents. "A smartphone, special agent badge and ID, an emergency torpedo…. and a Glock nine millimeter!" She pulled an extra ammo clip from the purse. "Complete with a spare thirteen-round clip! You go girl!"

Lori smiled, took the purse and checked herself one more time in the mirror. Connie came over and put her hands on her shoulders from behind. "Trust me honey, you're going to distract an awful lot of customers from main stage tonight." Lori brought a hand up to place it over Connie's, and smiled broadly as she grabbed her leather jacket and started to move toward the door. Marshall paused just as she was locking up the deadbolt.

"What's a 'torpedo'?" he asked sincerely. Connie rolled her eyes.

13.

Connie was checking her voicemail as Lori drove the short ten minutes from her apartment to the Lickety Split. Like Lori, she was dressed to go out with a short denim blue coat and a black strapless top tube top and hip hugging jeans. She was also wearing practical shoes with a small heel.

"So," Lori began, making conversation, "I see you're wearing practical pumps tonight too."

"Don't get too full of yourself, dear," Connie warned her. "Tonight we might actually have to chase this guy around and I'm being smart about it." She smirked at her friend as she deleted the last of her messages. "He won't outrun me."

Lori knew Connie had been a sprinter and high jumper in high school, and her athletic prowess was a point of pride for her. "Are you sure? It won't take much to run right out of that top."

"I considered that possibility. Glue is an amazing thing, though."

"You *glued* your top on?"

"An old cop trick. You'd know it if you had worked undercover more often, newbie."

Lori laughed. "I can't wait to see you take it off. Ouch!"

"Nail polish remover does the trick nicely."

"Oh, you just have an answer for everything, don't you?"

Connie smirked at her again, and then looked down at her Blackberry as another voice message alert went off. She frowned.

"Did you hear from Leif again?" Lori asked.

"Yeah, but I'm so over him. He's in love with me and getting all needy."

"It isn't easy being popular."

"Stop it. You know how I feel about him." Connie had a pattern of obsessing over certain men, getting them to pay her all manner of attention, and then losing interest within a few weeks. "It wouldn't kill you to go out with the guy again. He seemed nice." Lori said.

"Yeah he was nice. Now all he needs is a job. If he hasn't made it as movie director by thirty, I'm kinda thinking it won't happen."

"That's not it and you know it, Connie."

Connie raised an eyebrow at her friend. "Hey!" she said. "Only one of us gets to be the psycho-analyst at a time. Today is my day."

Lori smiled and then changed the subject abruptly. "How do you want to handle this?"

Connie went seamlessly into cop mode. "Stay together, act casual. If we spot him, inform the management but not security. Try to take him from two sides at once. And don't waste any time about it."

Lori nodded. She marveled at Connie's ability to switch quickly from talking about personal issues to police business. She was very confident of her talents as police officer and was experienced enough that Lori had no problem following her lead. They both knew the plan now and would follow it wordlessly from here on out.

"I sure hope he makes it easy on us," Lori mused.

"Not likely," Connie said. "He's smart enough to know this could be a trap, so he'll be ready." She looked out the window as they passed neon lit blocks full of adult video and liquor stores. "But I think he'll come. He must want something from us or he wouldn't have shown up at the office today."

That last thought gave Lori a little chill. Vartan had demonstrated earlier that day that he was a highly competent adversary. Add to that his special forces training and taking him down would not be easy. "You realize," she said to Connie "that we can't match up with him physically."

Connie clicked a clip into her gun. "That's why we've got these," she said.

A few minutes later they had found a spot in the crowded Lickety Split parking lot. Once again Lori wondered at how quickly Connie slipped into character, as she started giggling and talking a bit too loudly as soon as she opened the door. She also added a slight stagger to her step and stopped to flirt a bit with the overdressed parking lot security guards. Anyone watching her would have quickly concluded she was tipsy.

All of the security guards were wearing either black suits with white shirts and red ties, or black blazers over dark open collared shirts. It was obvious they were trying to exude an aura of class even as they dealt with one of the less classy sides of urban life. Both girls were surprised to find that female guests weren't charged a cover, so they were passed through security and into the club without having to wait in line.

Lori quickly assessed the layout and all the exits. The club itself was surprisingly plush. There was a thick, soft red carpet all the way around and a pair of backlit, well stocked bars on elevated platforms on either side of the main room. A towering waterfall stretched from floor to ceiling. There was a central stage which jutted out into the main floor, with a row of chairs all around it and the usual brass rail and dancer pole accenting the stage. There was a state of the art light and sound system running at full bore, but the music wasn't as deafening as Lori expected. The main floor was littered with circular tables and deep backed chairs with rollers on them. One entire wall was mirrored from floor to ceiling, making the club look twice as big as it actually was. The only secondary exit was marked by a red sign that was next to the backstage entrance. Two large men with clipboards guarded a very dark backroom area closed off by a velvet rope.

"I wonder what goes on in there?" Lori motioned to Connie, keeping her voice just loud enough for her partner to hear. Connie smiled and got close to Lori's ear.

"Probably stuff we'd have to arrest people for if we saw it." Lori smiled and nodded.

Connie pointed to two open stools at the far end bar. "Let's sit up there. We can see the entire floor area. You want a drink?"

Lori and Connie soon were seated at the bar stools, facing the action on the floor. Connie made her way to an open part of the bar, and within moments the bartender, a very attractive young girl wearing a tight sleeveless vest and a bow tie was poring a Cosmopolitan for Lori and Lemon Drop for Connie. As Connie waited, Lori scanned the scene. On the stage was a tall, athletic black girl, hanging upside down from the stripper pole. She soon removed her bikini top, and there was a hoot from the audience as she slid quickly down the pole, making a loud streaking sound as she did. There were girls circulating throughout the floor, stopping and talking to men at the various tables. A few girls were performing lap dances right at the tables, wearing nothing but flimsy g-strings. As Lori watched, one of the girls, a beautiful young blonde, turned from rubbing her behind in a patron's crotch and leaned forward to shove her bare breasts in his face. Lori wondered if anybody could see her blush in the midst of all the colored lights.

"What did you expect, ballet?" Connie was back with their drinks, and handed the pink glass to Lori as she sipped from her own green-yellow colored concoction. "They don't spare you much around here," she said. "Get used to it."

Lori sipped. The cranberry based drink was sweet and not too strong. "I know but geez . . ." Lori giggled a little and turned her head.

Connie was smiling. "Now aren't you glad you let me back you up on this? You'd better relax or you'll blow our cover."

Lori shook her head. "I wonder what makes a girl do this."

Connie shrugged. "Bad relationship with their dads? Dropped out of school? Who knows?" She scanned the floor again. "But there sure are a lot of guys who are glad they do it."

"I guess."

Connie touched Lori on her arm and pointed. "Is that our girl?"

Lori nodded. Andrea was circulating through the crowd, wearing a catholic school girl uniform with a plaid skirt and thin white shirt that tied off between her breasts. There was no sign of Vartan.

"I guess we'll just watch the show and wait." Lori said.

One hour later, they had seen more than a dozen girls go up on stage to ply their trade and display their charms. Every so often, a man would approach the stage and fling a handful of dollar bills in the air over the girl who was dancing. Lori soon learned that this was known as "making it rain." Finally, Lori saw Andrea head backstage, presumably because it would soon be her turn to dance on the main stage. Connie noticed it too.

"I'm going to head to the ladies room," she said, giving Lori a look that indicated she wasn't coming back right away. If Vartan was coming, it would probably be soon. It was already well past eleven P.M., the time Andrea had said he normally showed up at the club.

As Lori was watching Connie get into position at the far end of the club, she became aware of a tall, thin man in a dark suit next to her. She looked up to see the face of the man who had been at the front desk when she and Connie had first arrived. He was standing uncomfortably close and when his eyes met hers, he got even closer, blocking her view of the stage.

"Do you mind?" she asked, trying to sound as annoyed as possible. "I can't see the show."

The tall man smiled down at her, as if he knew something secret about her that no one else did. He had long straight hair that hung to his shoulders and a thin build. He focused his brown eyes on her intently.

"I know what you're doing here," he said confidently. Lori wasn't sure if it was a fake British accent, but he was desperately trying to sound refined, if not elegant. She could tell he considered himself quite good-looking, although he was a bit stiff and greasy looking for her tastes. She wondered if she had somehow blown their cover. But one look at his expression, a sort of leering, self-satisfied smugness, told her he was clueless.

She straightened up in her seat, and pulled on the bottom of her top to cover up a bit more. "I seriously doubt that," she finally said, trying to look past him to the stage.

"Look, you can't fool me. I've been the manager here too long." He looked over his shoulder at the stage, where Andrea was starting her dance routine to a non-descript blaring hip-hop rhythm. "So, why don't you just tell me where you work now, and we can talk about the terms here."

"What?" Lori was genuinely confused.

"You and your friend. What club do you work at now?"

She finally realized that he thought she and Connie were strippers, here to scope out the scene at the Lickety Split.

"Oh, um… the Jet Strip, over on Hawthorne." It was the only one of the other strip clubs they had passed on the way in that Lori could remember.

He nodded with a closed mouth smile. A self satisfied gesture if there ever was one.

"Well, I dare say you'll find the rules and facilities here much more accommodating. Our dressing rooms are first class and our tip outs are only one percent of gross. And it's only fifty dollars to work." He obviously tried very hard to be precise with his language, and just as obviously thought it gave him an air of sophistication. "We treat our ladies with class and dignity, and we expect them to behave in the same manner in return."

"I'll keep that in mind," Lori said as she strained to look past him to the bar on the other side of the room. Connie had moved to a position that enabled them to make eye contact, and when they connected she made a slight shoulder shrugging gesture, as if to say "What the hell are you doing?"

Lori didn't think making a scene would help their situation. "Look," she finally said. "We just want to take a look around and see what the vibe is here. If we're interested in working here, we'll let you know." Then, she seized on an idea: "Do you have a card?"

"Well yes, I do indeed." He reached into his jacket pocket and handed her a glossy business card.

"Thank you," she said politely, reading the name on the card. "Thank you, James."

She'd hoped that would get rid of him, but as far as he was concerned, the conversation was far from over. "You're quite welcome. Would you like a tour of the facilities? It would be my pleasure to escort you."

"No thank you."

He wasn't taking no for an answer. "Well then, perhaps I can get you something from the kitchen, or buy you another drink. Our food service is excellent."

"I'm sure it is, but no thank you."

Andrea had completed her first dance, which Lori knew by now involved a dance routine fully clothed, if a bikini could be considered "fully clothed" anywhere but at this place. She saw her retreat to the back stage area where she would quickly change into a second outfit, the one that would come off on stage. She caught a glimpse of Connie, who was motioning to her as subtly as she could.

Lori couldn't understand what she was trying to get across to her, until she saw Connie, in exasperation, simply point to her left, toward the back of the main room. Lori leaned to her right, looking around James, so she could see the area Connie was pointing to.

Then she saw him. He was sitting at a table in one of the deep backed chairs against the back wall of the club, next to the roped off VIP area. In the dim light at the back, she could see a well dressed man wearing what appeared to be black blazer and a white open collared shirt. He was sitting in a casual repose, all the way back in his chair, but she could just make out the rugged face and curly dark hair.

Trevor Vartan.

Lori cursed herself for letting this slippery bastard distract her. How long had he been there? Had he had time to scope out her and Connie? Did he recognize them from earlier in the day at the FBI field office? She only knew one thing; she had to get rid of James the slimy club manager quickly.

"Look," she said, not taking her eyes off Vartan. "My friend and I would be glad to take a tour of the club the next time we're here, but right now, we just want to watch the show and see how things work."

"But I insist," James replied, his accent growing ever more formal – and insistent.

By then Andrea had come back out on stage, wearing a skimpy sequined bikini and high platform shoes with flashing lights in them. Someone in the audience hooted as she dashed across the stage and flung herself onto the pole, spinning completely around it and then increasing her momentum by letting one arm reach out away from her body. While it was an impressive demonstration of the law of the conservation of angular momentum, Lori doubted that's what the patrons were appreciating. Many of them had dropped dollar bills on the stage, and as Andrea dropped to her hands and knees and writhed at the front of the stage, several more bills crumpled into tight balls came flying in from the tables around the front of the club.

Once she had made her way to the edge of the stage, Vartan was on the move. He got up from his chair and walked deliberately to the jutting stage front, the red and purple and green lights playing off of Andrea's bikini top and sending rays of color to all corners of the room. How did they arrange that?

Once Vartan passed Connie's position, she began to move slowly down the steps that separated the bars from the lowered main floor. She circled around behind and to his right, trying to get into position to approach him over his right shoulder. Seeing this, Lori knew she needed to get in the same position at his left.

She tried to stand up. James quickly put his hands on both her arms and forced her back down on the barstool.

"Oh come now, have I offended you somehow? Why don't you stay and chat with me a while longer?" He smiled his best salesman's smile, but his thin face looked like it wasn't very comfortable contorting into that position.

Lori had had quite enough. She took her eyes off Vartan and met James' brown eyes with a look of supreme annoyance. As she did so, she pulled her right hand from her handbag with the loaded Glock in it. She lifted it just far enough out so that James could see it, but the security cameras probably couldn't.

His face went white when he looked down and the smile quickly faded. He stepped back and held his hands out in front him. "Whoa, whoa, whoa! There's no need for that!" he said, looking quickly back and forth between her hand and her face.

Lori leaned in and spoke as quietly as she could, considering the environment. "I'm with the FBI. Get your security people out of the way and have them cover the exits."

He gulped and swallowed. "Yes. Yes of course. I'll just do that!" He was already moving away to the left before the words were even out of his mouth.

Lori knew she had just blown Connie's plan, but there had been no choice. She'd have to move quickly now before the security was alerted and their movements tipped Vartan off.

She cautiously stepped down from the bar platform onto the main floor, her purse over her right shoulder. She was acutely aware as she held the cold, heavy gun inside her purse that she'd never actually used her weapon in the line of duty before.

She was already behind and to Vartan's left, but there was still plenty of room between her and the back exit. He could easily beat her out the back door if she didn't take the angle away, which would be tough to do without him noticing.

Fortunately, his attention was focused on Andrea. She smiled as she saw him approach and take a seat right at the tip of the rounded stage extension. As soon as he was seated, she moved to the brass rail and reached behind to remove her top, dropping the sparkling bra off in a flowing gesture. She reached down and pulled her left breast up to her mouth and licked the nipple, all the while smiling and maintaining eye contact with Vartan.

Lori began to step carefully between the tables. She was still at least thirty feet from them. She stayed focused on the back of Vartan's head.

She saw him reach into his left coat pocket and pull out what looked to be a twenty dollar bill. As she moved more to the left, she could see the side of his face and the crinkled muscles of his smile. Andrea was smiling back, her attention totally focused on him. He put the twenty into his mouth about halfway, and she grinned even more. Either Andrea had completely forgotten that she and Lori were there, or she was actually quite the actress.

Lori took another careful step, moving between two more tables and closing to within twenty feet of him. There were two more rows of tables to go. She didn't even look up at Connie. She knew what position she would be in.

Lori tensed up as she saw Vartan get out of his seat and lean forward, extending his head over the rail toward Andrea with the twenty in his mouth. Andrea was on her knees, but elevated slightly above him on the stage. She leaned forward slowly, pushing her chest toward his head and then pushing her breasts together. He stuck his face in between her breasts and she squeezed them together, wrapping his head in them like a vice closing on a piece of woodwork. She let him linger there a minute, then began to slowly pull herself back.

Lori realized they'd never have a better chance to take him than right now, while he was totally distracted and with his face buried in Andrea's boobs. She took two quick steps forward to close to within ten feet and decided now was the time to pull her pistol out of her purse.

Before she could even begin the movement, Andrea finished pulling herself back and released her "grip" on his head. As she did so, she let her hands fall to her sides and Lori could see the twenty stuck to her chest, on the inside of her left breast. She was smiling broadly down at Vartan. Lori couldn't see his face but from her angle she could see that his facial muscles were still crinkled up in a smile, so he apparently hadn't noticed her or Connie approaching from behind.

Just when she thought this might be easy, she caught the faintest glint of a red light off the brass rail in front of Andrea. With all the colored lights swirling around, it could have been anything, but Lori quickly assessed that this one was different; strong, coherent, and narrow.

It was a laser sight.

Her first instinct, in that frozen moment of panic, was to call out a warning. But she also knew that whoever was wielding the weapon attached to the laser sight was probably already about to fire. Vartan too must have seen the glint, because he suddenly dove to left and as he dropped his head and the red light of the laser shone squarely on Andrea's chest.

She was still smiling when Lori heard the crack and saw her chest explode in a rain of blood and tissue, spattering everyone around the stage, including Lori. Andrea's body toppled lifelessly backward. The last thing Lori saw of her was her opened, blankly staring eyes.

Following her training, Lori spun to her right and pulled her weapon to return fire, but the club had exploded into screams and panic, and there were people scattering in every direction in front of her. In her peripheral vision she caught a blur to her left, a large black form mounting one of the tables. The drinks and a plate of nachos scattered everywhere, further distracting her. She heard three loud, quick shots: Pop! Pop! Pop! The crowd cleared just enough for her to see one of the security guards, his head split open, presumably by one of Vartan's shots, crumpling awkwardly to the carpet, a large gun with a laser sight mounted on it in his left hand.

The crowd surged against her, clawing for the backdoor exit and pushing her off balance to her left. She rolled with the surge and turned to see Vartan, chest high above the crowd, leap from one table to the next, firing a hand gun as he did so. He was making his way toward the back door as well, and Lori knew she needed to get there before he did to prevent him from escaping. She took one sideways step to her left and raised her gun, but a panicked young girl in a sliver-blue dress ran right into her, putting her face directly in front of Lori's gun. She heard the crack of five or six more shots, but had no idea which direction they came from.

Shoving the girl out of the way, she kept her eyes on Vartan. The main floor was starting to clear now, and he jumped again to another table and fired several shots toward the bar she had been seated at. Several bottles and the mirrored bar rack shattered and the alcohol spilled down the back panels of the bar and then burst into flames. Lori surmised that Vartan must have had an incendiary round in his clip. It was then that she knew he was prepared for what was happening. He wouldn't have done that if he wasn't planning to shoot up the bar. She caught a glimpse of James the slimy manager frozen in panic on the floor, trying to hide underneath the front of the bar, as if the flimsy bar stools could protect him. He jumped each time a shattered bit of glass cascaded over the front of the bar in front of him. His face was contorted in what Connie would have called a "girly scream." She wished she would be able to see his face when he realized the bar above him was on fire, but it was a fleeting thought and she quickly focused on reacquiring Vartan.

When she turned back, she couldn't see Vartan. Although he was a tall man, the rush of people out the back exit created a pile up at the door, and she realized she'd lost him somewhere in it. Cursing herself inwardly, she took the time to make a quick scan of the floor.

In addition to the burning bar, she could see the bodies of three security guards besides the one that she had seen

Vartan shoot. One of them was still moving, moaning in pain as he clutched his knee. She looked to the left of him, back to the area Connie should have been covering.

Her body was obscured partially by a downed table, but Lori could see a girl lying face down on the carpet, her head turned away from Lori. She instantly recognized Connie's dark blue jacket. Although she couldn't see an obvious wound, there was a puddle of dark blood forming around Connie's head and shoulders, probably from a wound in the forehead.

Before Lori could go to her friend, she heard a scream from over her shoulder. She turned back to the rear door. Vartan had emerged, probably from a hiding place in the backstage area, and a girl who was stumbling over several fallen customers had seen the gun in his hand. Without thinking, Lori turned and fired off a shot at Vartan.

The bullet missed over his head and struck the wall beyond him, sending out a puff of plaster. He flinched from hearing the sound, and instinctively turned to fire back. When he saw the shot came from Lori, he seemed to think better of it and threw the girl back and out of the way. Lori was impressed by his strength. She figured the girl was at least a hundred and thirty pounds, and he tossed her aside like she was table lamp.

There were too many people now between he and Lori for her to attempt another shot, so she ran to the back area, stepping between several fallen customers that she was relieved to notice were simply laying low. She made it to the back wall, just in time to get her gun on Vartan, who had been held up by the panicked crowd filtering through the narrow doorway.

"Freeze! FBI!" she shouted, holding her weapon with both hands. Her own voice sounded shaky and weak to her.

Vartan turned and looked at her, a gravely serious expression on his face. He kept his gun down and raised his left hand, making a calming motion. "You know I didn't kill them!" he shouted over the din of the still blaring music.

She tightened her grip on the gun. Connie was injured, probably dead, and there were four other bodies scattered around the room. She wanted to shoot him. The only thing that held her back was the fact that she was now very sure he hadn't killed Tsien and Garvin.

"Surrender your weapon and hit the floor!" she shouted back.

"That would be a really bad idea," he said, more calmly than she would have expected given the circumstances.

"Why?" she demanded.

"Because they aren't done yet," he shouted back to her over the din.

Before she could answer or react, he was out the door. He'd used the standoff to let the crowd disperse and clear his path of escape. He had created just enough doubt in her mind to buy himself the chance he needed to get out the door.

"Damn!" She cursed again and then followed him out the door.

He was nowhere.

Where had he gone? There were still droves of people scattering around the parking lot, screaming and waving their hands in panic as they ran off in all directions. She looked left and right, then turned to her right and decided to head back around to the front of the club. As she took her first step, three security guards came around the front of the building, spreading out in a line about thirty yards away. They were setting up a perimeter to keep any cars from getting out of the parking lot. She heard the sound of a car starting behind her.

Since she had a gun in her hand, she decided she'd better show some ID. Reaching with her left hand into her purse, she found her badge and held it over her head, so the guards could see. "FBI!" she yelled at the top of her lungs, much more satisfied at the authoritative tone her voice took on this time.

The guards responded by raising their weapons.

If anything else could surprise her about this day, this was it. When she heard the sound of a car screeching through the parking lot behind her, she briefly considered that Vartan was trying to escape in it, and that they were preparing to send some suppression fire his way.

All notions of that dissolved when she heard the crack of a large caliber hand gun and felt the hot breath of a bullet skipping past her right ear. The heat was quick and scorching, like a lighter being held briefly on her skin, and she felt the wind from the projectile brushing her hair back as it passed. A few inches to the right, and she'd be dead.

She fell to the ground, reacting automatically and rolling over as her training demanded, and she raised her weapon to fire back, not noticing the scraping of the hard blacktop on the skin of her back. The guards were already scattering, and she could hear shots coming from behind her and the sound of a car racing toward her.

The car pulled up next to her position and the brakes screamed under the stress of being slammed to the floorboard, the tires screeching as they desperately tried to find enough grip to stop the vehicle. It was so close she was sure the front tire had touched the hair on her head. She looked up to see the open door of sliver-gray car above her.

"Get in!" The voice was commanding; the accent was British.

Vartan.

She got to her hands and knees, and a rain of bullets cracked off the car door in front of her, one of them deflecting off the door and striking the ground inches from her right leg.

That was all the motivation she needed. She dove from her kneeling position and into the passenger's seat, clinging to the center console of the car with her feet still dangling out the door. Vartan hit the gas and the car door swung back as the vehicle lurched forward, but she stopped it with her feet. Given the position of the guard she'd seen and the speed the car was already up to, she decided to take a chance and kicked the door back open as hard as she could, at the same time pulling herself up into the seat and curling into a ball to keep from exposing her legs.

As it turned out, her timing was perfect. She heard a deep thud, like the sound of a watermelon being dropped from five stories up. The door slammed back shut and she knew she'd hit one of the shooters with it.

"Nice," she heard Vartan say.

The car veered sharply to the right, and she felt herself being pushed up against the center console with some significant degree of force. The acceleration of the car was impressive.

Within a couple of seconds, they were up to sixty miles an hour or so and there were no more sounds of gunshots. She pulled herself up into the seat and trained her gun on him. "Pull over!" she commanded.

He smiled and looked at her confidently. "I don't think so."

"I'm FBI," she said again. "Pull over."

He kept glancing over at her as he backed the car's speed down a notch.

"I know who you are," he said calmly, "and surely you know I didn't shoot your partner."

Connie. Lori had completely forgotten her in the last few minutes.

"I know nothing of the kind," Lori said sharply.

He checked his mirrors. "Come on Miss Pars, I just demonstrated I'm a better shot than that, and I had no reason to involve you two. And in case you didn't notice, they were shooting at you, not me."

There was no question he was right about that. "Who are they?"

"You wouldn't believe me if I told you."

"What is this, a movie? What am I now supposed to say now, 'try me'?"

He cracked a smile. She was impressed and revolted at the same time that he could be so cavalier after just shooting four people dead. Her own stomach was churning, but she couldn't afford to start feeling anything right now. She moved over in her seat and put the gun to his temple.

"There are at least six people dead in the last two days, including possibly my partner, and you seem to be at the center of it all." She rotated the gun so he could see the lug that indicated there was a round in the chamber. "So who were they?"

He swallowed, for the first time revealing the slightest hint of fear. Then he seemed to catch himself and turned his face toward her, so that the gun barrel was square in the middle of his forehead. He looked right into her large green eyes.

"Vatican secret police," he said matter-of-factly.

She held the moment for a long time, scanning his impassive face for any hint that he might be lying, then pulled the gun back and relaxed into her seat.

"Son of a bitch," she said, shaking her head. "Why did I know you were going to say something weird like that?"

14.

"Give me your cell phone," Vartan said to Lori as the car sped along the 405, heading north. His voice sounded completely calm and measured. Her hands were still shaking.

"Why?"

"Because any minute now, your FBI friends will learn they have one agent down and another missing, and they'll try to track you by the ping of your cell transponder."

Lori knew he was right, but she still wasn't sure if she should trust him or shoot him. "Maybe I want them to find me."

He gave her a passing glance. "That would be exceedingly foolish. Think about it. Those guards weren't shooting at me, they were shooting at *you*. Do you think that was by accident? You know what these people are capable of. They were trying to wrap this whole thing up in one nice, tidy little package." He turned to look her in the eye. "Who would that benefit?"

She had to admit that if she, Connie, Andrea and Vartan were all dead, that would pretty well wrap up the case. An obsessed former military officer who knows both murder victims is killed in a shootout with police. With the additional benefit of Andrea being gone, there would be no one who knew anything about what was passed between them. All signs would point to Vartan as the killer of Tsien and Garvin, timelines and locations notwithstanding, and the only investigator who suspected something different – her - would be dead. But . . .

"Why would the FBI want me dead?"

"Not the FBI per-se, but someone in it. Who in the Bureau are you a threat to?"

"No one," she said quickly.

He looked at her. "Not your boss, the one with the political ambitions? Not the man from DARPA, who would very much like this case to go away before you ask too many more questions? Admit it; you're a threat to both."

She dismissed him with a negative shake of her head.

He pressed her. "Haven't you wondered why you were transferred to LA from Seattle? Who arranged that? Your boss, didn't he? And then he assigns you to a case outside your area of expertise. A case that just nearly resulted in your death. So I ask you again; who benefits if you're killed?"

She took a deep breath. "Eric Ruby," she said in a quiet voice.

"Exactly."

She mulled that notion for a moment. "I've known him a long time. He's no murderer."

This time Vartan shook his head. "He doesn't have to be. He just assigns you to a risky case and something bad happens. Do you seriously think that someone as calculating as he is, who used you the way he did, is that bloody concerned for your well being? That he's going to spend the next few months mourning you, lamenting what might have been? No. when the news comes, the thing he'll feel the most is . . ."

"Relief," she said distantly, interrupting.

She had to admit it to herself. Their past relationship was a time bomb that could explode at anytime in the course of his political career. Whatever had passed between them before, whether she had imagined his feelings for her or not, they were not a factor now. Getting her out of the way would make it a lot easier for him to continue his ascension in the political world. But again . . .

"Why target me?" she said to Vartan. "There were others."

"Like Special Agent Danielle Woodrow? She was killed in the line of duty two years ago in Denver while under Ruby's command. She was one of his girls too."

Lori looked straight ahead at the winding road. "You've certainly done your homework on me, haven't you?"

"I'd be a fool not to, Special Agent." He looked over, but she didn't meet his gaze. "I took a chance. I concluded you were someone I could trust."

Lori reached down and pulled the back panel off her smartphone. She stared at the battery. "You're asking me to go rogue," she said quietly, the weight of the decision audible in the stress in her voice.

"No I'm not," he said. "I'm asking you to help us stay alive until I can figure out what's going on. Why this is all happening."

Now she looked over at him. "Oh," she said. "I thought you knew." Her tone was scathing, but she didn't care. Connie and Andrea were probably both dead, and for what? Some bizarre UFO conspiracy?

Silently, he turned his attention back to the road. She reached down and pulled the battery out, handing it to him.

He reached over, but instead of taking the battery, he grabbed her cell phone. Before she could react, he smashed it three times against the dash console, until it splintered in to several pieces. "Hey!" she protested, "what did you do that for?"

"All cell phones have a backup battery that can be activated remotely over the network." He sorted through the dismembered circuit boards until he found the one with the spare battery on it and then tossed it out the window. "If your tech guy is any good, he'll be trying that in an hour or two."

Marshall was good, she knew that. She also knew she was essentially a prisoner now. And she'd now lost any chance of finding out if Connie was dead . . . or worse.

Seeing this play of emotions across her face, the worry for Connie, the realization that she was isolated from any support from the FBI, the idea that her former lover may have tried to set her up to be murdered, he saw she needed some reassurance.

"Relax," he said, trying to sound soothing. "You've still got the gun."

She looked up from her reverie and realized he'd gotten off the freeway. "Where are we going now?"

"To change cars. They'll be looking for a sliver BMW 740, heading north. By the time they backtrack and review the position of your transponder, we'll be in a white Mazda, heading east." They pulled into a garage in an industrial looking area of Santa Monica. "Well," she said, "you've thought of everything, haven't you?"

Within minutes, they had changed over to the white Mazda and were soon criss-crossing the surface streets of Los

Angeles. Vartan had changed from his dress shirt and blazer into a simple blue polo shirt, and Lori had noted several scars on his back and arms as he changed. She made a note to ask him about them later. After they had driven silently for a few minutes, he turned and spoke to her while they were stopped at a red light. "Don't blame yourself. It wasn't your fault your partner got shot."

She looked over at him, and tried to convince herself his patronizing tone was all in her head, not in his voice. "Actually, I wasn't even thinking about that. I was wondering how you knew so much about me. About my personal history."

The light turned green. He accelerated. "I didn't," he admitted, keeping his eyes on the road. "But I know pretty well how your boss operates."

"And what he likes?"

He looked her up and down and for the first time in hours she was conscious of just how skimpily she was dressed. "Yes," he said.

She took a moment to absorb that. "How did you get into the FBI databases to steal that crime scene photo?"

"I'm not completely incompetent. I was with MI-6."

"That's not an answer, Vartan."

"Well, the coroner's office computer network isn't as well protected as the FBI's. It wasn't that difficult."

"And the FBI ID badge?"

He scoffed, audibly. "I've been making fake badges since my first job in the Navy."

She silently accepted that answer for what it was. He reached behind her seat and handed her a pink plastic cell phone with a large electronics pack attached to the back of it. She gave him a questioning look.

"So you can call later and check on your friend," he told her. "But not until we get where we're going."

"Where *are* we going?"

"Some place safe."

"Tell me where," she insisted.

He clearly didn't want to. "A place where I've got some weapons and some cash." She watched him chew over whether it was a good idea to tell her more. Then, "It's in an abandoned mine."

She raised an eyebrow at that one. "Oh," she said casually, "that must be some new definition of the term 'safe place' I wasn't aware of."

He ignored her sarcasm. "It'll be a couple of hours. It's been a tough night. You should get some sleep."

Her hands were still trembling. "I'm too wired."

She felt a sharp prick of a needle on her bare shoulder and the tension began to drain from her body. Suddenly, she felt very sleepy.

"Hey. . ." she started to protest, but in the next moment, she was departed from the stresses of the conscious world.

Vartan took the small vial he'd injected into her and tossed it out the open moon roof into the wind. He looked down at her, her chest rising and falling in a slow, rhythmic pattern that indicated a deep state of relaxation, her lips slightly parted and flushed with a kind of pink fullness that indicated she was in another place altogether. For a moment, he allowed himself to think of her as just a beautiful woman, asleep at his side.

Then he reached across her and into her purse. He pulled out the gun and stuck it on the seat next him, at his left hip and away from her reach.

15.

Lori woke up to the sound of the car traveling at high speed over a rough, gravelly road. The car was bouncing along over bumps and potholes, jiggling her up and down and throwing her from her state of peaceful bliss. Outside it was a completely dark, moonless night, and she could not see past the limited illumination of the headlights. Vartan was looking straight ahead, totally focused on the task at hand.

She shook her head to clear it. She felt like she'd been asleep for ten hours, but she knew it had to be far less. "Where are we?" she asked him over the din of the gravel bouncing off the sides of car.

"About seventy miles outside Las Vegas," he said, offering no other information.

"How long was I out?"

"Three hours, I'd say. You needed the rest." It was not expressed as an opinion, but a fact.

"What did you do to me?"

"Your body knew what it needed. I gave it a little chemical incentive to rest."

Then the memories came flooding back. There was still blood on her new tank top from where it had been splattered when Andrea was shot. She thought of the strange way the security guard, if that's what he was, had crumpled to the ground when Vartan shot him. And Connie, lying face down in a pool of her own blood.

"I need to make my phone call now," she said, not offering any room for argument.

"In a few minutes. We need to get to where we're going to first. It's not far now."

She noted that he was negotiating the rough, dark and twisting road at an alarming rate of speed. "What's the hurry?"

"There's a DARPA sat that will be flying over this area in about eight minutes. We need to get out of sight before it takes a picture of us."

She accepted this answer without question. He'd certainly demonstrated a sophisticated knowledge of such things to this point, and she doubted he'd be risking their lives if there wasn't a compelling reason to do so. Fortunately, his driving was up to the task.

A few minutes of twists and turns passed, and soon they were climbing a calmer dirt road up a small hill. She looked back to her right and could see the lights of cars running back and forth on a major freeway of some kind.

"I-15," he offered, anticipating her question.

By the time she turned her attention back, they'd pulled up to what appeared to be a heavy iron door, anchored with several heavy padlocks. He stopped the car and got out, unlocking them and tossing them aside. Then he pulled a remote control from his pocket and pressed down on the button, and a mechanical sound like a super heavy duty garage door opener or a winch started up and the door began to open.

Lori wasn't feeling too good. The combination of worry and stress from the shootout and the rough ride had turned her stomach. As he got back into the car, she stepped out and threw up into the dry, dusty night. When she was done, she returned to the car, her face still pale as she checked it in the passenger side mirror. "What the fuck did you give me? I feel awful."

He remained impassive at her sharp language. "I told you. Something to help you sleep."

"I've just about had it with your bullshit answers, Mr. Vartan. What did you give me?"

He looked across at her from the driver's seat, taking his time, and Lori wondered if he was going to tell her or not. "A Ketamine-Valium injection."

Lori knew her drugs. "That's bullshit. It takes at least four minutes for that to take effect. I was out in 10 seconds. I remember that much."

He smiled. "I used an accelerator. It's my own special blend."

She studied the self satisfied expression on his face, and it made her furious. For all she knew, her best friend was dead, and she was playing semantic lunge and parry with a man she didn't even know she could trust instead of checking up on Connie. "I hope you're as good at chemistry as you seem to think you are, Mr. Vartan," she said mildly.

"I assure you I am." The answer was confident to the point of being smug. Lori's blood boiled and she got back out of the car and stomped off into the night.

Alarmed, Vartan jumped out to follow. "This is no time for an emotional overreaction," he called after her. She ignored him and kept walking back down the road. He ran after her and caught her by the arm. She turned in a sudden rage and started beating him on the chest.

"Get your hands of me you bastard!" she screamed. She tried to kick him, but he side stepped and grabbed her arms, holding her away from his body.

"Special Agent... Lori, this is no time to get emotional. The satellite will be overhead in moments."

She twisted away from him, easier than she expected, and swung at his face, just clipping the tip of his nose. "I don't give a shit!" she screamed again. He seemed surprised at her quickness and strength and she saw him get a very serious look on his face. For a moment, she thought she saw the eyes of an assassin, the eyes of a man who was quite capable of doing anything he felt was necessary at any given moment. He used her momentum against her and clamped down on her right arm, twisting it back behind her shoulder and pressing his weight down on her. He brought her quickly to her knees and torqued her arm even tighter. She let out a small whimper at the pain and felt that her arm might break under the stress.

"I assure you I will break it if necessary," he said coldly. "I understand your concern about your friend and I assure you I will do what I can to get you some information on her condition. But you *will* get back in that car if I have to knock you out cold and drag you back. Do you understand me?" His voice was tense and his lips were tight with anger. At least she now knew he could be angered, she thought to herself.

She let out a guttural growl and he tightened the grip on her arm even more. Feeling completely helpless, she finally felt the stress go and nodded silently. He only slightly eased the pressure on her arm. "Am I to understand you'll get back in the car now?" She nodded again. He released her arm and she fell forward onto her hands and knees. He stood over her and she gave him a scathing look. "Now," he said threateningly. Not wanting another dose of the arm lock, she got up wordlessly and walked briskly back to the car and got in, letting her intensity indicate her displeasure with him. "I could have given you something if I knew you were feeling bad," he said as he also got in.

"I've had quite enough of what you're pushing, thank you very much."

He said nothing, put the car in gear, and inched forward into the mine entrance, or whatever it was. They weren't long inside when she heard the door winch shut behind them. It was pitch black except for the amber running lights, and she could see trestles and supports overhead holding up the narrow, descending shaft.

"Where are we, the Batcave?"

He took no note of her sarcasm. "A safe house. I put this together a few years ago. I was never actually sure if I'd use it." His voice showed no hint of the anger she thought she had detected earlier, and she felt her own intensity easing.

After a few hundred yards, they emerged into a wider, more open space that was the size of a four car garage with a high ceiling. He stopped the car and got out, using a flashlight to navigate, and she heard him fussing with another lock. A few moments later and she heard a generator crank up. A few seconds more, and the lights came on.

The lights were too bright at first, but after her eyes adjusted, she could see a large workroom with supplies, provisions, a computer terminal, a short wave radio and several types of electronic equipment she didn't recognize. In one corner, there were stacked pallets containing jugs of fresh water, dried foodstuffs and medical supplies. She also noted a large weapons locker, closed off by a mesh grate that contained what looked to be automatic weapons and grenade launchers. She got out of the car and looked around. "Prepping for the apocalypse?"

He smirked at her. "I used to be a Boy Scout."

"Not likely," she said. Then, more seriously; "I need to make my phone call."

He nodded and pulled the pink plastic phone from a duffel bag and began hooking it up to some cables connected to a computer terminal. "I just need a few minutes so you can make this phone call off the grid," he told her. "By the way, I'm sorry about the use of force back there, but we had to get out of sight. It was imperative." She nodded, not commenting on his apology, and decided to look around while he worked to make the connections.

She was astonished at the sheer volume of electronic equipment he had stocked his "safe house" with. There were state of the art scanners, color copiers and laser printers, a laminating machine and various kinds of cables and wires running to mysterious electrical boxes in the corners of the room. She assumed this kind of equipment was how he had managed to forge an FBI ID badge. She also found a box full of at least eighty of the pink plastic phones he had handed her. They were clearly disposables with untraceable numbers. "I take it back," she said to him. "This isn't the Batcave, it's a Kinko's franchise."

He said nothing in response. She made her way to the weapons locker. He tossed her the key when she asked for it, and she assumed it was a gesture of faith. She opened it up and saw what amounted to a gun lover's dream collection. "Wow," she said admiringly. "You've got quite the arsenal here."

He looked over from his task. "You can try the Kalashnikov, if you'd like. It's a genuine Russian made piece, not the Cuban knock offs you usually see in the States."

She took out the Russian machine gun and sited down the barrel, just to get a feel for the weapon. She'd never fired a machine gun, not even in FBI training. She replaced the AK-47 in the rack and then examined the hand guns, pulling out a Glock-17 similar to her own. The lightness of her purse hadn't escaped her notice as she exited the car. She reached down and loaded a clip into it. "I have to say, I'm disappointed," she said conversationally.

"Oh?"

"Yes. No Walther PPK."

He smiled at her without taking his eyes off the terminal. "There is a P99. And I choose to be flattered by that little joke."

After a few minutes, he motioned her over to his console. She slipped the gun into her belt, safety off.

"Do you know who you're going to call?'

"Yes," she said. "Marshall Masters. He works as an analyst. He should know the news about Connie."

"Right," he said, for the first time sounding truly British. "You can only talk to him for three minutes. He'll eventually trace the call to Northern California. Tell him you're in Redding. That's not believable, given the time that has elapsed, but maybe it will get them thinking that's where we're headed. It won't be long before they run my records and find out that I own this property."

"Marshall has already run your records," she said.

"Yes, but I doubt he's looked for property purchases in this county. The FBI segregates data by counties. He'll have to run them one by one."

She was impressed by his knowledge of FBI procedures. "Yeah, but he'll start with the neighboring counties."

"Exactly." He checked his watch, a gaudy Brietling. Had he been wearing that before? "We leave in thirty-three minutes."

"Where are we going?" She was getting very tired of being out of the loop.

He reached down and lifted a heavy suitcase, slamming it on the desk in front of her. Then he opened it and showed her it was full of packs of one hundred dollar bills. "Someplace where they don't question somebody who spends large amounts of cash."

Las Vegas. "To buy time?"

He nodded. "By the way, these are all legitimately acquired genuine U.S. dollars."

"Of course," she said dryly.

He nodded at her, then handed her the phone. "You can take this to the other end of the room. The cord will reach that far without a problem. I'll load the car up if you'd like some privacy." He pronounced it "privicy," instead of "pry-vacy," and for just a moment she was reminded again that he was British. She thanked him and moved to the far corner of the bunker, at least thirty feet away and out of earshot.

She took a deep breath and dialed Marshall's number, not sure if she really wanted to hear what he would say about Connie. The phone was answered on the third ring. "Hello?" Marshall sounded confused. He probably didn't get too many calls from outside numbers.

"Marshall, it's Lori."

"What the... Lori! Are you OK?" he spoke excitedly, but in *sotto voce*.

"Yes, I'm fine. Marshall, do you know anything about Connie? Have you heard anything?"

His voice got sad. "Not much. They took her to the hospital with a head wound. She was in surgery last I heard. Things are pretty crazy here. It feels like the whole world is looking for you and Vartan."

"I assumed that much."

"Lori, where the hell are you? Why don't you come in?"

"I can't Marshall. Some of the things that happened . . . I'm not sure who to trust."

His voice became more intense. "Lori, tell me you're not with this guy, with Vartan."

"What if I am?"

"He just shot up a bar, for starters. What the hell are you thinking? We've got six dead people now, four of them cops, and who knows if Connie will come out of this."

Lori thought she must not have heard him correctly. "What did you say?"

"I said we've got six dead people now. Two victims and four Peace officers. Haven't you heard? It was all over the news."

She took a deep, long breath. "What haven't I heard?"

"Those guys he shot up at the Lickety Split. They were Treasury Department. Secret Service. They've been following him for months. He's a counterfeiter. We got in the way of their bust."

Lori's mind boggled and she made a quick, pained little sound. It suddenly all made sense. Tsien was probably using his computer imaging skills to help Vartan create the photographic plates. The money was printed somewhere else, maybe that's how Garvin fit into the scheme, and the money was periodically retrieved by Vartan, laundered through Las Vegas casinos and stored here in the safe house before it was circulated in Los Angeles.

He'd done the Tsien murder, for sure. Garvin must have met his end at the hands of an associate. All the tracks were now covered. And none of the rest of it, the mysterious Mars pictures, the ritualistic nature of the Tsien killing, all of it had been a gigantic distraction to set up the shootout at the Lickety Split and get away with the scam. As soon as she was dead, he'd make himself a new identity and disappear. That had to be it.

"Lori, where are you? We need to get you some help. This guy is really dangerous." She no longer really heard Marshall's voice. She told him she'd call him later and ended the call. She started to make her way back toward the car and Vartan, all the while pretending she was still talking and hoping he would stay distracted.

"No Marshall, I can't tell you where I am. I'm still not sure what I'm going to do. I just called to find out about Connie . . ."

Now she was behind the rear of the car, her back to Vartan as he threw various items into the trunk. Out of the corner of her eye she saw him bend down to stuff a bag further back in the trunk. She turned in one smooth motion and stuck the gun right under his right ear. He backed slowly out of the trunk, straightening up and putting his hands up where she could see them.

"All right you bastard. We're going in," she told him.

He was stiff and tense under the threat of her gun. "Special Agent, I don't know what your friend told you, but I assure you it wasn't the truth. It probably wasn't even a version of the truth."

She kicked him in the shin and he buckled slightly. Painful and effective. She hated him now. She wanted to pull the trigger so badly . . . "I should just shoot you and be done with it."

"Then why haven't you?"

She said nothing. She knew conversing with him was her weakness. She been in this position before, but he had talked her out of it.

"What did they tell you?" he asked urgently. "Did they say I killed your friend? Is that it? Or that I started the whole thing?"

She was furious now. She had so much rage that tears began to well in her eyes and her arms shook from the strain of keeping her finger from pulling the trigger. But she couldn't talk to him. Couldn't answer him. That would only weaken her resolve.

For the first time he looked truly frightened and tried to get her to talk to him. "You were there, remember? You've still got blood on your top from Andrea's wound. They shot at me first. You saw it. Do policemen do that? Is that the way you were trained?"

"Shut up!" there was a torrent of emotion in her voice, and she moved the gun up under his chin.

"I know you're grieving for your friend, but think this through. What kind of police officer shoots an innocent girl in public? And if I was the killer you think I am, why haven't I killed you when I had the chance? The only reason to keep you alive is if I'm in the dark as well."

She saw his eyes dart back and forth between her hand on the gun and her angry, tear filled face. He tried one last admonition. "You must doubt what you've been told, or I'd already be dead. Don't make a mistake here."

"You shot Connie you *bastard!*" she shouted the last word, her finger tightening on the trigger.

She could almost see him making the calculations now, asking the questions. Could he slap the gun out of her hand before she squeezed off the shot? Could she be talked down from this emotional precipice? Which tack was his best chance at saving his own skin? She got madder and madder as she watched this play across his face. He was so much less cool under fire with a gun at his throat.

She was breathing short and quick now, her rage rising with her pulse, her fingers twitching at the pressure of not doing what her heart wanted to do. Then the image of Connie flashed into her mind again, and she screamed at him in a fit of rage . . .

At the last split second, she pulled the gun away, even as she fired. He anticipated her move and dropped to the ground, spinning away from her as the gun went off. The bullet missed him by inches and pinged loudly as it skipped off the surface of the raised trunk lid and embedded itself in the far concrete wall.

He tried to kick out at her, but she was too quick and stepped back, the gun still aimed squarely at him. He made no further moves and simply stayed in the down position, his arms raised in surrender.

"OK. OK," her breathing was fast and labored, even faster than her words. "Maybe those guys weren't Treasury Department. Maybe those aren't counterfeit hundreds in your suitcase. Maybe Connie just got caught in the crossfire." Her breathing slowed, just a bit. "But I swear to *God* if you don't start coming up with some answers I will put a bullet in your head so fast you won't have time for your life to flash in front of your eyes."

He made a small gesture with his hands, a careful "calm down" motion. "OK," he said, letting out a breath. "What would you like to know?"

She wiped her eyes with her left hand, and lowered the gun just a hair. "Tell me what this is really all about. Starting with the Vatican Police."

16.

"The Vatican has always had a secret police force, at least since the end of World War Two. These stories you've heard, about these 'Men in Black,' that's who they are." He seemed very uncomfortable with her gun pointed at his face, and Lori kept a safe distance between them. Vartan was seated at his terminal, hands still raised where she could see them.

"You mean 'Men in Black,' like in the movies? The guys that go around wiping the memories of people that see UFO's?"

"Something like that." She could sense tension in his body. "I'm serious," he offered, seeing her skepticism.

"Why would the Catholic church be involved with intimidating UFO witnesses, Mr. Vartan?"

"Think about it, Miss Pars. If the truth about extraterrestrial life were revealed, who stands to lose the most? Governments? Corporations? Or the traditional religious institutions?"

She shook her head doubtfully. "My mother was raised Catholic. You're telling me that her church has a secret police force? One that does murders and intimidation? Over what? What could Dr. Tsien and Garvin have known?"

"I won't know that until I see what's on the flash drive that you recovered from the murder scene. It could be anything. Internal memos. Secret reports . . ."

"Images of ruins on Mars?"

He acknowledged her idea. "Perhaps. The point is, there are a great many powers within the hierarchies of governments, corporations and yes, even churches that you don't know about. Governments within governments, special boards within the corporate boardrooms, police forces within churches."

"That still doesn't explain why all those people are dead, and how they got that way."

He looked her in the eye, his courage returning. "I can give you an answer, but I'm not sure you'll believe what I tell you."

"Try me," she said coldly, aiming the gun right between his eyes. Maybe that movie dialog was cliché for a reason.

"This would be a bit more comfortable if you'd stop pointing that thing at my face."

She sighted down the barrel. "Maybe I don't want you to be more comfortable."

The corner of his mouth turned just slightly upward and he lowered his hands to place them on the desk in front of him. "When I was at MI-6, I was given some assignments that I felt were strange. One of them involved infiltrating the Catholic Church. As part of my briefing for the assignment, I was given a report to read that implied that the previous Pope, John Paul the First, had been murdered."

She smirked. "By who?"

"That was unclear. What was mentioned in the report was that John Paul the First had undertaken something of a grand crusade behind the scenes almost as soon as he took office. According to Vatican documents I read, he had issued Papal Bulls authorizing the formation of a secret committee to 'expose and expunge' what he called the 'Freemasonic pestilence' infecting the body of the Church. He evidently felt that Freemasons had infiltrated the hierarchy to the point that they had become a serious threat to the stability and even existence of the Church."

"OK . . ." she said, going along with him. "So what makes you think he was murdered?"

"I don't say that, necessarily, the report did. The biggest clue was that he died exactly thirty-three days after taking office. Thirty-three is a crucially important number to the Masons. The highest degree one can obtain in the Scottish Rite of the Craft is the thirty-third. The death, on the thirty-third day, was a message. A Masonic warning to anyone who dared oppose the movement within the Church. It said loud and clear that they can get to anyone."

She lowered the gun slightly. "What about Dr. Tsien's death? The ritualistic way his body was placed and the way his clothes were set up?"

Vartan nodded. "A similar warning. A message to anyone inside NASA or JPL who might be considering following in his footsteps and feeding information to outsiders, like Richard Garvin."

Lori took a breath. "Now I suppose you're going to tell me that the Masons have infiltrated NASA in the same way?"

He looked at her silently for a moment. "Most of the astronauts who walked on the Moon were Freemasons. The director of NASA in the Apollo era was a Freemason. The man who ran the Mercury, Gemini and Apollo programs at NASA was a Freemason. His brother later became the titular head of the Scottish Rite itself. The second man to walk on the Moon took a Scottish Rite thirty-third degree ceremonial apron with him and performed a Masonic ceremony with it in the Lunar Module. The Apollo program patch features the constellation of Orion, which represents the ancient Egyptian god Osiris, who is the preeminent god in the Masonic religion." He opened his hands wide. "Shall I go on?"

"I think you've made your point, actually." Then she shook her head. "All this doesn't add up to anything. You've got nothing. This is just a bunch of paranoid conspiracy crap."

"Perhaps. But if I were to tell you that all of these same people were Catholics, for instance, and they all attended the same church in Washington D.C. or Florida, and that the astronauts performed a communion ceremony on the Moon before the first Moonwalk, would you be so skeptical?" He studied her face for a moment. "Of course you wouldn't. But that's only because the Catholic Church is such a public organization, and its rituals and sacraments seem harmless and acceptable."

"Or maybe I'm just skeptical because this sounds like a bunch of BS from a guy with a gun pointed at him."

He smiled with one half of his mouth. "I can understand why you think that. But please, you've got to give me a chance. Just another day to try and figure out what it was that Tsien was trying to get to me and Garvin. What they had reason to kill him for."

She tried to think of a reason not to give him that chance, but her rage was fading. She knew full well that he was right about one thing; no legitimate police officers would have opened fire the way the men in the club had, nor would they have brazenly fired at her when she was standing in the parking lot. It came down to a matter of who she trusted more, Vartan, or Ruby.

Truthfully, she trusted neither. But Ruby was a snake, and Vartan was no simple counterfeiter, she could see that much. She reached into her pants pocket and pulled out the tiny silver flash drive she'd taken from Marshall's computer. She let him see it, then tossed it to him. "Try looking over what's on here," she told him. "Maybe it has all our answers."

He looked at the drive in his hand, and started to smile. She raised the gun again. "But first, I want to know why you resigned from MI-6." She flexed the trigger again, but he didn't flinch.

"Oh that," he said casually. "I had my reasons."

"I'm sure you did. I would like to know what they were."

He looked down the barrel of her gun again, this time a bit less confidently. "Let's just say I had something of a crisis of faith."

Lori lowered the gun. "Haven't we all," she said.

"While I worked for Admiral Milner at the Admiralty, I was given a number of assignments I thought were strange." Vartan had relaxed visibly once she had lowered the gun and the information was now flowing out. "Among them was to attend a lecture at the U.N. by Richard Garvin concerning the existence of extraterrestrial artifacts on Mars."

"So that's when you first met him?"

Vartan nodded. "Yes, but I was less intrigued by him at the time than I was by another man I met at the speech. He was an American intelligence operative named Prescott Dansby."

Lori swallowed. "You know Dansby?"

Vartan was cautious "Let's just say we're acquainted. He was working for the National Reconnaissance Office then. He was not nearly as important as he is now."

"What the hell is the National Reconnaissance Office?"

"A very specialized unit connected to the United States Department of Defense. They design, build, launch and operate all of your U.S. spy satellites. They are rumored to have their own launch facility somewhere in the mountains of Utah, and their own fleet of advanced space shuttles. At any rate, Mr. Dansby was quite interested in what Mr. Garvin had to say at the U.N., and wanted to know what I thought about it."

Lori put her hand under her chin. "That's interesting. Why would a U.S. spy agency be interested in what NASA might have found on Mars?"

"That was my question," Vartan acknowledged. "Of course, one might ask the same of my presence there as well. As it turned out, Mr. Dansby was investigating what he called the 'Masonic infiltration' of NASA, and he suggested that because of my assignment to look into the same thing inside the Church, we might find it mutually beneficial to exchange ideas and information from time to time."

"And did you do this?"

"Yes. He never quite told me what it was he was after by following Mr. Garvin, but I know he did keep tabs on him for some years afterwards."

Lori didn't react beyond taking a deep breath. "OK, so you know Dansby from your military days," she said to him. "And his interest in this case is obviously a lot greater and more personal than he made it out to be. But none of this explains why you resigned from MI-6, which is what I asked you in the first place."

He nodded. "I was getting to that. As I'm sure you know, when I was with MI-6 back in 1998 I was assigned to track down some NSA military personnel who had gone AWOL from an intelligence listening post in Germany. I tracked them to Gulf Breeze, Florida, were there had been a rash of UFO sightings at that time. They were headed to Cape Canaveral. When I debriefed them, they said they had been fooling around with an Ouija board, and they had made contact with a spirit which had told them to go to Cape Canaveral and wait for his sign."

Lori knew she would hate the next answer. "Who was the spirit?"

"They said it was an Egyptian god named Osiris. The god of the Freemasons."

"And you believed that answer?" Lori scoffed. "Oh come on!"

He leveled his gaze at her. "By that time I had encountered so many strange things in my career that I had basically stopped asking questions."

"Not exactly Carl Sagan in the skepticism department, are you Vartan?"

"Dr. Sagan was an intelligence operative who reported to Mr. Dansby. His skepticism was a cover for his real activities as a government UFO case analyst." His expression was unwavering, and she could see that he was firmly convinced of the veracity of his own work.

But they were off the subject. "You're ducking the question," she said. "Again, what prompted you to resign?"

"Instead of prosecuting them, your President Clinton gave them all honorable discharges. At that point I knew that my work wasn't being taken seriously at all. They didn't even care that one of the soldiers wrote a book about the whole affair. So I quit. I decided I needed to learn the truth of all this. And I'd learned all I could on the inside."

"So the fact that the U.S. government didn't take your pet project seriously anymore led you to resign? To walk away from everything. Even your career?"

He stood and turned away from her and walked to the car. "Not entirely," he said. He opened the trunk and reached into his briefcase, the one with all the money in it. She raised the weapon again, but this time with very little sincerity. He saw this and moved slowly, always keeping his hands visible. She saw him reach in and pull a rolled up parchment out. He walked toward her deliberately.

"This is an ancient Masonic document I obtained from inside the order itself. It has been confirmed to date from the fourteenth century, but was probably copied from an earlier document that goes go back much, much further. It contains a series of prophecies about future events. All of them save two have already come to pass." He saw her start to react, but held out his hand to hold her from speaking. "Think of it as a sort of Masonic version of the Book of Revelations. It says, among other things, that *this* civilization, which the Freemasons refer to as the Fourth World, will end just as the first three worlds did, in some sort of global cataclysm."

She rolled her eyes. "What is it this time? Fire, floods? Asteroids? Every ancient culture has some sort of apocalyptic eschatology."

He gave her an admiring smile. "My dad was an Episcopal preacher," she explained. "Very much into the end times stuff. But my point is that every culture has these kinds of prophecies and predictions. So what?"

"Well, these had a habit of coming true. Specific dates of earthquakes, natural disasters, wars. All happening as this document predicts. But it also contains two predictions which haven't come true yet, at least as far as I can tell."

She gave him a "do tell" look and waited. "It says that one day man will journey to the Moon, and bring back something from it. It does not say what, exactly. It says that this must not happen, because it will throw the world into imbalance, and hasten the coming of the final prophecy and what it calls the next world, the Fifth World."

"And the catastrophe that precedes it," Lori added.

He nodded. "After the Gulf Breeze incident, I decided to try and gain access to records inside NASA, to see if anything other than rocks had indeed been brought back. I was told in no uncertain terms that I would cease this line of inquiry immediately. The next day, a man who worked in my office was found dead, hanging from a bridge over the river Thames, his clothes arranged exactly as your Dr. Tsien. The police ruled it a suicide."

Lori was impassive. "If they were going to kill someone, why not just kill you? Why bring someone who wasn't directly connected into it?"

"I assume because I was from a prominent family. My death would have been harder to smooth over. To cover up. Either that or . . ." he trailed off.

"Or what?" she pressed him.

"Or, I'm more valuable to someone alive."

Her eyes narrowed. "Because?"

"Because I found this." He bent down clicked on a file on his computer, and an image came up on the screen. It showed a barren, gray landscape and two astronauts in white spacesuits. One of them was standing next to the Lunar Rover. He clicked again, and the color in the scene dramatically changed. The barren, magnificent desolation transformed to deep blacks, dark browns, and a patch of brilliantly orange soil. In the distance, the rocks and hills and mountains were sprinkled with pink and blue and purple tones.

"This is what the surface of the Moon really looks like," he told her. As he spoke, he clicked and slowly zoomed in on the interior of a crater in the foreground. As he panned and zoomed, a small object came into focus. The closer he got, the more it became obvious that it did not belong there amongst the plain rocks and glittering soil. When he got in tight enough, she could clearly make out what it appeared to be-- a human skull. In a crater. On the Moon.

A wry smile of disbelief crossed her lips. "Bullshit," she said, almost under her breath.

"I've been studying this picture for years," he responded, not impressed by her disdain. "It is the right size for a human head. It has two eye sockets of the same size in precisely the right locations. It has a nasal protuberance, and the upper part of a jaw or mouth. And it is not isolated. There are other artifacts strewn all over this picture."

"You expect me to believe that there are humanoid skulls on the Moon?"

"Not at all."

"That's a relief," she said sarcastically.

"It's a robot's head."

"Of course." She turned away. "That's ridiculous."

"Is it? No flesh or bone could have survived eons exposed to the micro meteorite bombardment or the cosmic background radiation. But a machine could. A machine built to withstand the lunar environment."

She turned back. "Then who built it? Aliens? Oh come on!"

He was unmoved by her intensity. "You're missing the point. It doesn't matter who built this. It doesn't matter if it was aliens or some prior advanced human civilization, like Atlantis. The only thing that matters is if they brought it back. And if certain people in possession of it are exploiting it to extract its advanced technology."

"Please . . ."

He looked at his watch. "We're running out of time. We have to get out of here. I realize what I've told you sounds crazy..."

"Do 'ya think . . .?"

". . . but I'm convinced both our answers may lay in what's on that flash drive. If we're going to find out why two men are dead . . ."

"Six," she corrected him.

". . . and why someone seems to want you and me to join them," he continued. "I have to get to a place where I can think and work without a gun on me." He turned from the computer, and went back to the car and closed up the trunk. "I'm leaving. You can either come with me and help me solve this crime, Special Agent, or you can shoot me. But I'm leaving."

She watched him get in the car and start it up. He backed it up and turned it around so it was facing back up the gravel path to the door. He stopped and waited for her. "Well?"

She paused a moment, then walked slowly up to the passenger side door. She stood there, contemplating the decision. Then: "I'm not saying I believe a word if this, Mr. Vartan. But you tell a good enough story that I'm willing to give you one more day. Besides, you don't behave like a guilty man."

A slightly cocky smile crossed his face, and Lori realized for the first time that he was actually handsome. "Oh? What do I behave like?"

His attitude angered her and she pierced him with an angry glare. "Like someone who's obsessed with confirming his own version of the truth. And who doesn't care who dies trying to find it." She pulled her blood soiled tank top out and away from her body so he could see it more clearly. "This is Andrea's blood on my shirt. You slept with her more than once. Do you even care?"

"Of course I do," he said somberly, "but I didn't kill her." Then he got out of the car, leaving it running. He went to a locker and pulled out a dark blue cotton shirt. He helped her put it on over the blood stained tank and button it up. His manner was gentle, even compassionate. They got back into the car, and she put the gun away in the glove compartment. She'd decided she had to trust him.

"Do you think they'll kill us if they find us?" she asked softly.

He nodded. "They'll say we were killed in a shootout, or something like that. Our biggest problem will be the local police if they spot us."

She nodded grimly. "They'll probably tell them we're terrorists."

"That would do it."

He started to put the car in drive, but she put her hand on his to stop him. "Vartan, one more thing. You said the Masonic document said there were two prophecies that haven't come true yet. One might be that thing they brought back from the Moon. You haven't told me what the second one is."

"It hasn't happened yet," he said, just a bit too quickly.

She studied him closely. "Look Vartan, if we're going to make it out of this alive, we need to start trusting each other, at least a little bit. How about if you start right now?"

He looked down, then back into her deep green eyes. He clearly did not want to tell her. She kept eye contact with him and did not relent. "It said that a great abode in the sky would fall from the heavens in a great crash. There would be fire and death, and it would appear as a blue star in the sky as it came down."

Lori didn't understand. "A great abode in the sky . . .?"

"Yes," he said. "The International Space Station, I assume. Or ISIS, as we like to call it."

Lori broke eye contact and sat back in her seat, and a worried expression crossed her face. "How do you know that any of what you've learned is the truth? That you haven't been lied to?"

"I don't," he said simply. "The worst thing you can do in intelligence is to believe anything you've been told without corroboration. That's how they keep everybody in line, how they keep all of these secrets from leaking out. They tell everybody, at all different levels of security, a different version of the truth."

She nodded. "The lie is different at every level."

"Exactly."

17.

"Nice to see you again, Mr. Atherton," the hotel doorman said to Vartan as they passed through the sliding glass doors. Vartan acknowledged him with a nod and kept walking toward the check-in desk.

"Mr. Atherton?" Lori asked as she looked around the opulent lobby of the hotel.

"Yes, I got tired of being 'Ozzie Osborne' everywhere I went," Vartan said dryly.

Lori was impressed by the sheer opulence of the hotel. She'd never been to Las Vegas, and while she'd heard that the new generation of resort hotels were impressively opulent, she had no idea what that meant until she saw it with her own eyes. The Venetian hotel lobby was an enormous expanse of golden brown marble, renaissance style artwork and highly detailed stone work and frescos meant to represent the architecture of the palaces of Leonardo's era.

A well dressed black man in a dark suit approached them with a broad smile crossing his face, his highly polished dress shoes clacking on the marble floor, and stuck out his hand to Vartan. "Mr. Atherton, it's been too long. Will you be staying with us a while?"

"Just two nights, I'm afraid." There was not a hint of the British accent in his response.

The young man's smile faded just a bit. "Very well. Will you be requiring your usual room, sir?"

"Of course."

"Very well. Right this way."

He motioned them to a more private area where there was no one standing in line. Lori was surprised that even though it was past three A.M., there were a number of people waiting in the regular check-in line. Vartan moved to the side desk area and handed the man a black credit card and Florida driver's license. She could just make out the name on both items, "Joseph Atherton." The man accepted the two cards and began typing into a computer terminal. Lori took the time to spin around and take in the expansive lobby. There was a fountain just inside the door, intricate lattice work on all the walls and ceilings, and glittering light fixtures everywhere. Just the chandeliers must have cost fifty thousand dollars apiece. She turned around and the casino host had handed Vartan back his credit card and fake ID and then gave him an envelope with two card keys in it.

"Shall I make your usual reservation at Bouchon for this evening?"

"No, we'll be dining in," Vartan said quickly.

"Very well. Will you require any casino credit?"

Vartan turned to Lori, then back to the casino host. "Yes, twenty-five thousand dollars will be enough."

"Certainly sir." He made a few more entries into the computer, and then reached out to hand Lori a pass for the spa. "Is this Mrs. Atherton?" he asked brightly.

"Yes it is," Vartan answered before Lori could react.

"Excellent. Here's a pass for a massage at the spa, if you'd like one. They open promptly at nine A.M. I can schedule it for you right now if you'd like."

Lori took the pass. "Thank you," she said. "I'll call down later when I'm ready."

He smiled and nodded. "My number is right on the pass."

A few minutes later they were in the elevator alone. Vartan had elected to carry the case full of cash himself.

"Mrs. Atherton?" she asked, just a hint of teasing in her voice.

He raised his eyebrows at her. "You should always answer a question like that quickly, so it doesn't look weird."

"Yeah, but no one will believe it."

"Why?"

She held up her ringless left hand. "Oh," he said, "I suppose we'll have to correct that."

"I should think."

A few minutes later and they were in the room. It was every bit as lavish as the lobby. The room was dominated by a massive four poster bed with a wooden canopy and sheer drapes hanging from it. There was a separate sunken living area separated by a wrought-iron railing with a dining table, sofa, entertainment center and work desk. The view looked out over the Las Vegas strip. It was spectacular.

"I'll be sleeping on the couch of course," he said, sounding a bit anxious about the arrangements. She said nothing and went into the massive, ornate bathroom to wash her face. He went to the room safe and began stuffing wads of cash from the suitcase into it.

She closed the door and undressed, trying not to think about the events of the night as she peeled off the white tank top stained with Andrea's blood. She threw it under the sink and made a note to herself to dispose of it later. She picked up a luxuriously soft washcloth and ran hot water over it for a few minutes, then lifted it to her face. The hot, damp cloth felt wonderful on her skin.

For the first time in hours, she noticed her own appearance. Her face was drawn and tired, her eyes droopy and bloodshot. She wondered if she'd ever get back the innocence that these last few hours had stolen from her.

There was a knock on the door. "Yes?"

"I just wanted you to know, I've got the files on the flash drive decrypted."

"That's good," she said, trying not to sound surprised. He had done that much faster than Marshall. She was impressed. "I'm going to take a shower," she told him through the door.

"Why don't you take a bath? It'll be much more soothing." His voice was somewhat muffled through the door.

"That's a good idea, I think I will."

"Would you like anything from room service?"

Her stomach was still in knots. "No."

"All right. I'm going to start going over the files then."

She appreciated his efforts to comfort her, to suggest ways she might recover emotionally from the disturbing events of the night. She drew the bath and spent a good long hour in it. About thirty minutes in, just as she was drifting off, a flash of the image of Connie lying on the dirty, gooey floor of the Lickety Split flashed into her head. She felt a surge of emotion flowing up from her midriff, much as the tingling vibration of the Angels did in her dream, and she felt her face contort into an agonized, wrenching mask. She heard herself make a soft whimpering noise first, then a much stronger and audible cry of anguish. Embarrassed, she quickly turned on the faucet to mask the noises of her pain and let go. She felt certain Vartan must have heard her, but if he did, he made no attempt to intrude. Connie was the closest thing she'd had to a sister since Melissa's murder. The thought of losing her too was unbearable. After the initial burst of emotion, she quietly sobbed her hurt away.

When she was done, she barely had the energy to lift herself from the tub, dry off and put on one of the plush white robes that was hanging in the bathroom. When she came out, Vartan was working at his computer screen in the dark.

"I'm going to try to get some sleep," she told him.

"I'll see you tomorrow."

She said nothing more, got onto the bed and was asleep in moments.

Lori woke with a start, and thought she had cried out. The dream of the shootout came flooding back to her as she returned to consciousness. She saw it all so clearly. Andrea falling backwards, the heat of the bullet zipping past her head, Connie lying on the floor and the pool of blood around her.

She was in a clammy sweat, cold but at the same time overheated. She'd slept on top of the bed in the soft, comfortable robe. The sun was up and bright, pouring through the sheer draped windows. She looked down into the living area to see Vartan asleep at the work desk, his head arced over the chair back and his mouth wide open. He was snoring like a chainsaw.

"Vartan," she said in her normal volume. He did not respond at all. "Vartan!" This time she shouted it, and he jumped back to consciousness, looking both ways and then focusing on her.

"Atherton," he corrected her.

"I need to call Marshall again."

He rubbed his eyes, and then rose from the desk and handed her a paper print out. "That won't be necessary. I tapped into the hospital records. Your friend is out of surgery and her signs are stable. It appears that the bullet hit her at an angle and deflected off. She has a skull fracture in her forehead and a deep cut, but there doesn't appear to be any brain damage. They're keeping her sedated until later today, at the least."

Lori felt the weight drain off of her, like stepping from a hot humid day into an air conditioned room. She tried to read the chart but didn't understand most of the terms. "There are no guarantees, but it looks like she has good chance to make a full recovery," he continued.

She dropped the paper and put her head in her hand. She thought perhaps she should say something, maybe a grateful "thank god." But if she did that it would be all for him, and in truth she didn't care much about him at that moment.

He sat next to her on the bed, and put his hands on her shoulders. It was a careful, considerate gesture, and she appreciated it. After a long while staying in that position, he rose and went back to the work desk.

"We'll need to get you some clothes, and a ring, right away. What size are you?"

"Two," she said distractedly. The memory of the horrible dream and the feelings of dread were slowly fading. "But I'll go myself. The inner tank top I was wearing should be clean and dry. I washed it and hung it up last night before I went to bed," she told him.

"Very well. Are you hungry?"

That's what that horrible, gnawing feeling was in her stomach. "Yes I am."

"I'll order us some breakfast."

She nodded and got out of the bed. "I'll be getting ready. Did you make any progress?"

He turned to her. "Some. But I need time to go through all the files. The images are impressive, but I'm more concerned with some of the other files. Schematics and such.

I can't figure out why Tsien would be sending them to Garvin."

She turned to go into the bathroom, but he stopped her with a hand gesture. He went to the safe and pulled out a brick of one hundred dollar bills. He pulled off the tape holding it together and handed it to her. She looked at him blankly, still half asleep.

"For your shopping," he said. She took the money and put it in her purse. It made her think about how much simpler life had been before yesterday.

Lori returned from her shopping spree to find Vartan showered and shaved, and hunched over his laptop in an intense study of the documents in front of him. The breakfast tray was completely askew on the dining table, and he had evidently devoured its leftover contents after she had eaten and left.

"Honey, I'm home!" she said brightly, dropping a pile of shopping bags on the floor by the bed. For the first time in days, she felt mildly optimistic and refreshed. The news of Connie's recovery had buoyed her immensely, and she'd actually had fun shopping for the new clothes in the expensive boutiques on the Venetian's mezzanine level.

"How much did you spend, dear?" Vartan said dryly, not looking up from his screen.

She tried to keep her tone playful and bright. "I saved over fourteen hundred dollars!"

"Oh, thank god. I was afraid you'd spent the entire twenty-five hundred I gave you."

"Well, I did, but I saved over fourteen hundred dollars! I got it all on sale."

He turned from his computer to look at her. "You could be getting used to this illicit lifestyle, Special Agent."

"Illicit?" She raised a brow in an exaggerated gesture. "I thought all this cash was 'legitimately acquired.'"

"It was. But we're still on the run."

She frowned. "As if I had forgotten that."

He looked at the bags, with logos of various designer brands on them. "You didn't have to go to the most expensive boutiques, did you?"

She smiled. "Just trying to keep up appearances, 'Mr. Atherton.'"

"And you're doing such a good job of it."

She put her hands on her hips. "So I had a little fun with the cash you gave me. You didn't give me any guidelines. Besides, after the last few days, you owe me."

He looked her right in the eyes for the first time in a while. "Fair enough," he said quietly. He did not divert his gaze, and she became a bit uncomfortable.

"Of course, there's still the little matter of my hand," she said.

He picked up on the light tone in her voice. "Your hand, my dear?"

"Yeah," she said, holding up her left hand and showing him both sides. "It feels a little light."

He smiled, warmly. "Yeah, the ring. It does seem to be missing."

"That's what I noticed."

"Well, I suppose we'll have to correct that oversight this afternoon."

"How about one O'clock?"

He laughed. "OK. One O'clock."

She smiled. "This will be fun." She reached down and started to pile the shopping bags up on the bed.

"Of course," he said conspiratorially, stepping up from the living area to join her. "Such a gift would normally be expected to come with certain . . . privileges."

"Don't even go there," she said sharply. She was smirking, because she could tell his tone wasn't serious. He backed away, holding his hands up in the surrender position.

"You bring a girl to Vegas, buy her expensive gifts. . ." he let his voice trail off.

She turned and crossed her arms in mock displeasure. "Look at it this way; I haven't shot you yet. That has to count for something."

He broke into a broad smile, and she shared it with him. "Again, fair enough."

She'd had enough of the flirting and banter. She pointed to the computer. "What have you found?"

He put his hands in the pockets of the white robe he was wearing. "Not much. The images are impressive, but by themselves they aren't enough to justify all that's happened."

"Not enough? Marshall said he thinks they're pictures of actual ancient ruins. On *Mars*."

"True, but we've had lots of those over the years. You've heard of the Face on Mars, I assume? The arguments continue to rage about their legitimacy on blogs and bulletin boards all over the internet. The press mostly doesn't care. Even the revelation that NASA has been doctoring the photos to hide the evidence isn't enough to go on a killing spree."

She sat on the bed. "There's got to be something in those files that would be worth killing for."

"I agree. But I'm not sure what." He started to pace, slowly. "There is one other item."

She lifted her hands, palms open. "Yes?"

He took a breath. "There are some schematics in with the picture files. They're of a new NASA probe that JPL was building, called *Prometheus*. It's designed to study the moons of Jupiter for several years, beginning in 2015. It launches in a few days."

She jumped up. "That's got to be it. If the pictures aren't what got him killed, then it has to be these files."

"That's what I thought initially. But they just turned out to be routine diagrams of the fuel systems and power lines. Nothing particularly fascinating."

"No," she insisted, "I'm telling you, there's something in there you're not seeing. Something we're missing."

"Perhaps. But I'm at a loss as to what that might be."

He rubbed his eyes and she could see he was tired. "Let's take a break," she said, reaching out for his hand. "We've both been at this too long, especially you. Why don't you go get dressed and we can go down and buy me a ring. We'll take a gondola ride or something. Play the happy newlyweds for a while."

"That is an appealing idea." He still seemed hesitant.

"C'mon. We can take a break for a few hours, at least. I didn't see anybody eyeballing me while I was shopping. I don't think they've figured out where we are yet."

"I agree. But they will."

She indicated the bathroom. "Get dressed." Her tone was insistent.

He did as she asked, and headed to the bathroom to change. She looked around the room once, and then flopped down on the bed, stretching her arms out. "You know, it's too bad there are people trying to kill us. A girl could get used to this."

"I'm sure," he called back from the bathroom.

18.

The gondolier was singing a romantic, operatic song at the height of his lungs, obviously enamored with the sound of his own voice. Beautiful though it was, Lori could do without it just then. The warm sun and the gently lapping waves had put her in a state of quiet relaxation. She actually resented the intrusion.

"Hey Pavarotti," she called out. He looked down from his perch at the back of the little boat, stopping in mid song. "Thank you," she said with a smile. "We'd like it a bit quieter, please."

He bowed formally. "Certainly ma'am," he said politely. She was seated close to Vartan, leaning back against him, playing the married couple on a romantic vacation. He held her hand. It was rougher and his grip was far stronger than she'd expected. Her gaze drifted up to the replica of the famous Venezia clock tower that stood over the property.

"I imagine you've been to the real Venice," she said conversationally. "It's probably different."

He nodded and looked around at the lavish confines of the hotel grounds, "Yes. This is . . . an unreasonable facsimile."

She smiled up at him. "I'm sure."

He picked up on her attempt to make conversation. "Things must have been very different where you grew up." It was not a question.

"Different from Vegas, or different from Venice?"

"Either way."

"Yeah they were," she told him. "My dad was an Episcopal preacher. We lived in a small town in eastern Washington State."

"So your father has passed away?"

Interesting he would assume that, she thought. "No, just retired. My mom and he still live in the house I grew up in."

"Any brothers or sisters?"

She flashed to her persistent dream of Melissa. "Not anymore." She was immediately unhappy with herself. She had no reason to be so open with him. "I had a sister once," she said too quickly.

"Did something happen to her?" He tried to make his question seem like harmless conversation, but he was probing.

"I don't want to talk about it."

"Fair enough." He turned his head to glance up at the hotel veranda as they passed underneath the main walkways.

She kept looking straight ahead, and not at him. Maybe it was time to trust him, at least a bit. There really wasn't anyone else on the planet she could trust at the moment. "I'm sorry. I don't like to talk about it. She was murdered when I was twelve."

He jumped right in. "Was she older than you or younger at the time?"

She thought that an odd question. "Older. She was fifteen."

He nodded. "So it's been some time now since it happened."

"Yes."

"Is that why you're a policeman?"

The directness of the question caught her off-guard and she took her hand out of his. He'd skillfully jumped from one subject to another and surprised her. He was quite the talented interrogator. "I suppose," she said. "I never thought about it like that."

"Really?" His tone indicated his disbelief, not his sympathy. "It's well known that having a violent criminal event in one's childhood can impel a person to make a career out of law enforcement."

"Really?" She mocked his tone. "And tell me, what kind of childhood event leads someone to scrap a fast tracked political career to spend ten years skulking around the fringes of the UFO movement?"

He smiled at her. She'd caught him at his game. "Sorry," he said earnestly. "It seemed as though you wanted to talk about it."

"Maybe I did," she said back sharply. "But you were interrogating me. That's not the same thing as lending a sympathetic ear."

"Sorry," he said again. "My old training must have kicked in."

"Right." She turned back and leaned against him again. She could feel his muscular physique. After a few moments he spoke again.

"You don't have to do this, you know. This is my fight, not yours. I'm the one that those men are really after. You're just a target of opportunity. I can deliver you safely to the FBI field office before I move on."

Her lip curled up, a gesture he couldn't see because she had her back to him. Was he trying to get rid of her? Would she wake up tomorrow to find him and the flash drive she'd trusted to him long gone? "No, I don't think so. I don't quit on things."

"Or let the bad guys get away with trying to kill you?"

She pulled away again and faced him. "Nice insight. Something like that." She thought about it a bit more. "I'm in this until the end now. I'm not quitting."

He gave a silent and short nod. "Very well then," he said, accepting her answer.

The ride was over and the gondola had pulled back to the dock. The gondolier jumped to the dock and held his hand out to Lori. "Be sure and tip him good. He had a very nice voice," she said to Vartan.

"Yes dear," he said, playing the hen-pecked husband with a bit more enthusiasm than she felt the situation merited.

As they rode the elevator back up to their floor, Lori couldn't stop admiring the ring. It was a two-plus carat VS-2 clarity round cut diamond in a simple platinum setting. Vartan had bought a wide, flat matching platinum band encrusted with dozens of smaller diamonds. He didn't bat an eye when the whole thing had come to more than thirty-five thousand dollars at a jeweler so exclusive she'd never even heard of it. He simply handed a black American Express card to the cashier and took her to the chocolatier next door for a box of truffles.

"I think," she said, still gazing at the ring with envious eyes, "that this is the most beautiful thing I've ever seen."

"I know what you mean," he said, after just a moment.

She looked up to see his eyes fixed on hers, and with a certain intensity that she wasn't very comfortable with. They had gone to separate corners of the elevator, leaving plenty of space between them, and in that moment, she was glad of it. She had to admit he was very handsome, not to mention rich, and under any other circumstances she might be interested. But she was hardly unaware of the danger they were both in, despite the innumerable enticements of their present oasis. She would not allow either of them to lose focus on that. "I don't know what *you* mean," she said carefully.

"I think you do. That ring suits you very well."

That response surprised her. Was he really about to make a pass at her? "Flattery . . ." she said, her voice trailing off. He continued to stare intently at her, but didn't move toward her. "Look Vartan, this . . . playful banter is fun, and under completely different circumstances, I might be tempted, but . . ."

"You assume too much," he said quickly back to her. "I wasn't making a play for you. I was merely making an observation."

"Oh. Well . . ." She stumbled for words. For the second time, that wasn't the response she had expected. He saved her by intervening.

"Look, you're not crazy. I am attracted to you. But if anything, I'm more aware than you are of the danger we're in. We can't linger here much longer, and I can't allow either of us to get distracted. I was just enjoying the moment."

She nodded. "OK," she said. After that, there was an uncomfortable silence until they reached the room. When they got in, he went straight for the laptop.

"Vartan," she said after him, softness creeping into her voice. She was immediately embarrassed by the tenor of it, and flushed slightly. He certainly must have noticed.

"Forget it," he said. "It's normal for two people under stress to bond a bit, as we have. Let's just get back to it."

She nodded silently. He sat down and began to work. With nothing to do but watch him, she soon began to pace. She didn't even have a trashy romance novel to pass the time.

After about ten minutes, he rose from the computer. "Lori?" he said, his voice full of frustration. It was the first time he had called her by her first name.

"Yes?"

"Why don't you find something to do? Maybe go get that massage?"

She shook her head. "I couldn't sit still, I'm too agitated."

"I noticed," he deadpanned. She started to bite her thumbnail.

"Do you gamble?" he asked.

"I've played some blackjack before but I'm not very good at it. . ."

"Excellent!" he interrupted. He went directly to the safe and handed her another brick of hundreds. "Take these to the casino cashier and have him match the amount from my credit line. Go find a fifty-dollar table and play."

"But that'll be thousands of dollars! It will take me forever, even if I lose it all."

"Precisely!" he said with a pleased-but-desperate smile. "I need you out of here so I can work."

She looked at the wad of money. "So, you don't care if I lose it all?"

"I've got more."

"Evidently." She was a bit frosted that he wanted to get rid of her, but if it meant getting somewhere on the case . . .

She took the money and grabbed her key card. "I'm keeping what I win, just FYI."

"Enjoy the tables dear!" he called after her. She wanted to scowl, but she knew he was right. She needed to get out of his hair for awhile.

She made her way down to the casino and turned her cash into chips at the cashier, then inquired about the credit line. After a phone call up to the room to confirm with Vartan, they issued her the credit in the form of more chips. She lingered briefly at a boisterous craps table, but the game had always been incomprehensible to her, even if Marshall had once accused her of being a math geek. She decided against trying to play. It was midday and the casino was relatively quiet, but as she made her way around the vast space she eventually spotted a table with a fifty dollar minimum. Fortunately for her, it was a non-smoking table in a secondary area of the casino. She was allergic to cigarette smoke and was grateful for the efficient ventilation. There was a table full of smokers just twenty feet away, yet she couldn't smell anything.

There were two other people already playing. One was an overweight, balding, middle-aged man in a white polo shirt and the other was younger male wearing a baseball cap, football team jersey and casual jeans. Neither looked like they had slept much.

She sat at one end of the semi-circular table and began to pull the chips out of her bag and place them on the green felt game top. As she stacked her chips up, she looked around and was impressed at the style and elegance of the casino. There were games of all types being played, even though it was surely a slow time of the day. Large forty-two inch flat screen TV's hung above many of the gaming tables and the roulette wheel, all showing different live sporting events or horse races. Cocktail waitresses in very short but reasonably classy dark dresses milled in and around the patrons, bringing drinks back and forth to the tables on what looked like a regular schedule. As she always did, Lori checked for her best exit routes so she knew how to get out in a hurry if she needed to.

The middle aged man looked up from his hand and smiled at her. The younger man didn't even seem to notice her existence.

As she waited for them to finish their hands, this bothered her ever so slightly. Had she really reached an age where she had become invisible to younger men? She did realize that she was dressed a bit more conservatively than before in her black slacks, low heeled pumps and a sleeveless white top, but she thought she looked good enough to at least draw a glance. Her concerns were allayed when, after finishing his hand, the younger man looked up and gave her a quick smile. It faded quickly as his eyes were drawn to her enormous wedding ring.

Now that the hand was done, Lori pushed two green chips onto the betting circle and waited. They had reached the end of the deck and the dealer, a red headed woman in her mid-fifties, was using a machine to reshuffle the deck. After it was done she pulled the cards out, placed them on the table and handed the yellow card cutting insert to the balding man. He shook her off.

"My luck's been bad all day," he said. "Let the lady cut it."

The dealer handed the cutter to Lori and she placed it toward the rear third of the deck. The dealer then swapped the two blocks of cards around and placed the deck into the dealing shoe. She pulled the first card in the deck out and discarded it. She looked around the table and made sure everyone had placed a bet. When she came to Lori and her sizable stack of chips, her eyes went up in a quick gesture.

"Starting out slow ma'am?" she said conversationally.

Lori looked up at her. "I've got some time to kill, Susan," she said as she read the woman's name tag. "I'm waiting on my husband."

Susan smirked. "I know what that's like," she said as she started dealing the cards. "Slots or horses?"

"What?" Lori said, not getting the question.

"What's he off playing? Slots or horses?"

"Oh. Golf actually."

"We're getting more and more of that here," Susan said. "Nobody wants to spend money anymore unless they're sure to get something out of it."

"I don't blame them," said the balding man. "Especially after the way you've treated me today."

"It's your own fault," Susan said back to him good-naturedly. "I keep telling 'ya not to stand on fifteen."

"Yeah, yeah," he said. "You're killing me."

"You're killing yourself darling."

Susan finished dealing the cards and showed her top card, an eight.

Lori knew the basic rules to some extent. Marshall had showed her once. She had a six of hearts and a five of clubs. The bald man stood on eighteen and the capped young man took a hit. Unwisely, he took another hit and busted when he got a King to go with the seventeen he already had. Susan then came to her.

"Double down," Lori said, placing a second fifty dollar bet next to the primary one.

"One card," Susan said, holding up a single finger and dealing Lori a nine of spades.

"Nice call," the bald man said.

She then watched as the dealer flipped her hidden card over and revealed a nine of Hearts. Seventeen. She would have to take another hit. It was a ten.

"Whoo-hoo!" the bald man called out. "Lady, you may be just the luck I've been hoping for."

Four hours later, Lori was up more than a thousand dollars, and the bald man had caught up to nearly even. Susan had gone on a horrible losing streak, busting on about three out of every five hands, and winning only a small portion of the other hands. Lori had been at it so long that her rump was getting tired from the chair, but she realized she hadn't thought about Vartan or Connie in hours. She leaned back and stretched, much to the delight of the bald man, who had been stealing glimpses of her chest all day.

"Well," she said, "I think that's about enough for me."

"No, stay!" the bald man protested.

"No, I really need to go. This has been fun though."

"C'mon," he said, "play it all on one hand."

She looked at the table and all her chips stacked on it. She really couldn't bring herself to risk all of Vartan's money in one shot like that. The bald man saw her hesitation. "At least bet what you're up," he suggested.

She considered it. Why not? In a sense, it was "her" money anyway. "Oh, all right," she said. She took two black chips and placed them in the betting circle on the table in front of her.

"Betting one thousand," Susan called out to the pit boss. The burly, mustachioed man in a gray suit came over and looked the table over carefully, then OK'd the bet. He stayed to watch the outcome of the hand. Lori watched as Susan dealt up a five to the bald man, a queen to the younger man, and a six to the chunky Latina girl who had joined the game about thirty minutes earlier. Lori got a nine of spades. The pit boss was training a keen eye on Lori's hand as Susan dealt her an ace of diamonds.

"Twenty," Susan called out to the table. "Not bad sweetie." The pit boss looked unimpressed. Susan herself was showing a seven of clubs.

As she went around the table, the bald man hit and stood on nineteen. The young man hit on his fourteen and was rewarded with a jack of clubs, busting him out. The Latina girl hit on her hand and got a deuce, leaving her in no man's land with sixteen. She took another hit and busted on a ten of spades.

Now it was all down to Lori. She made a back and forth slashing gesture, indicating she was standing on her soft twenty. Susan flipped her hole card to reveal a four of spades. She then began to deal herself more cards until she had fifteen.

Susan paused as they all waited. "I've got a bad feeling about this," the bald man said dejectedly, giving up before he even saw the card. Susan pulled the last card and looked at it a moment before she placed it on the table. It was a six. She had twenty-one.

"Oh!" Lori exclaimed. "Damn it! I can't believe I lost on a twenty!"

The bald man leaned forward and dropped his head on the table and made a low groaning sound. Lori, despite her disappointment, didn't feel too bad. After all, it wasn't real money to her anyway.

"I'm sorry," she said to the bald man. "My luck ran dry on you."

He looked up at her. "Not as sorry as I am."

They started to share a laugh, but Lori stopped as soon as she looked up at Susan. Not only wasn't she collecting the chips from the table, she was frozen and staring off in the distance. So was the pit boss. Lori looked to her left, over the pit bosses' shoulder, and she could see people at the other tables getting up and clumping together in packs. At first, she had no idea what they were looking at, but as she scanned back to her right to see what Susan and the pit boss were fixated on, she could see that people were gathering around the TV sets that were scattered throughout the casino. There was a general buzz in the room that was quite different than the background buzz of the casino that she had been listening to for hours.

As she turned to look at the TV, she could see that there was a reporter on the screen talking urgently about something. In the background of the picture there was an enormous digital clock counting upward in hours, minutes and seconds, and a flag pole with a huge American flag flying in the wind. She had no idea what the casino goers could have seen on the TV that would have been so fascinating.

She got up and stepped away from the table, leaving her chips and backing up a few steps to look at the TV that had been almost right over their heads as they played, facing outward. She watched, but it was still showing a college basketball game. Then, before she could ask anyone what was going on, the picture suddenly changed to a black screen with huge white block letters on it that read "Special Report." She reached up and turned up the sound.

"We interrupt our regularly scheduled programming to bring you this special report from the Fox News studios in Washington," the announcer's voice said. The picture was suddenly replaced with a standard talking head anchor shot with the U.S. capitol in the background. The anchorman's expression was grave.

"Good afternoon ladies and gentlemen, I'm Wilson Parker reporting from Washington D.C. About five minutes ago we got word from NASA that all communication with the International Space Station and the Russian Shuttle *Kirov*, which had been attached to it, has been lost. According to NASA, about forty-five minutes ago they began to get reports that the shuttle's maneuvering thrusters had started misfiring. NASA says that very quickly after that, the station and the shuttle began tumbling out of control. NASA spokesmen say that for the next ten to fifteen minutes, they were in communication with the station and the shuttle and were attempting to initiate an emergency undocking of the shuttle *Kirov*. As they were in the midst of that process, all contact was lost with the shuttle and the station simultaneously. Shortly after that, NASA says that telemetry from both vehicles also ceased, but according to a NASA spokesman, the last telemetry they did have indicated that the orbit of the station and the shuttle had, quote 'dramatically decayed' end quote. NASA is still attempting to re-establish communication with the station, but all attempts to do so have failed to this point. Just a few minutes ago, French television began broadcasting images of what appeared to be debris re-entering the atmosphere over Paris. We're going to take you there live right now to get the latest."

Lori stood, frozen in time, as the images from French television came on the screen. It showed the Eiffel Tower in the foreground, with blue-white streaks visible criss-crossing the night sky above the city. As the cameras strained to zoom in and focus on the streaks, she saw what appeared to be large chunks of something tumbling and falling from the sky at tremendous speed.

They looked like stars. Brilliant, blue-white stars.

And Lori gasped.

19.

Lori had ascended the twenty-eight floors to their suite in a haze. As she robotically inserted the key card into the door lock, she was vaguely aware that she hadn't even remembered the walk up to the elevators, or what she had been doing for the last few minutes. Absently, she checked her purse and realized she'd left the chips at the blackjack table. As she entered the room, Vartan rose from the desk and smiled at her, a smile that quickly faded when he saw her pale complexion and the look of horror on her face.

"Lori, what is it? What happened? Did you lose all the money? That's OK . . ."

"No," she sharply interrupted him. "That's not it. It's . . ." she trailed off, finding it too hard to even speak the words.

He crossed the room quickly and took her hand. "Then what is it?"

She found it difficult to even look at him. "Just turn on the TV."

"I don't understand . . ."

"Vartan please! Just turn on the TV!" Her emotions; fear, anger and sadness came welling up to the point she could hardly choke out the words. He was confused but sensed her intensity and went to turn on the flat screen TV in their living area. The TV took a maddeningly long few moments to flicker and come to life, and when it did, it was showing the hotels' generic welcoming screen. Vartan, now looking a bit shaken himself, fumbled for the remote as the female voice on the channel encouraged him to try a wide variety of entertainment choices. Eventually, he found the channel selector and began scrolling through the channels. CNN was the third channel after ESPN and the Las Vegas history channel.

When he saw it, Vartan's body became rigid and he froze up. CNN was showing more video of the blue-white chunks of debris falling over both London and Paris. The new shots of Paris showed fires illuminating the night sky where chunks had apparently struck the city itself.

"I don't understand," he said, his voice betraying a hint of uncertainty – or was it dread? He turned to her. "What's happened?"

She suddenly flashed back to where she'd been on the morning of September 11ᵗʰ, 2001. She remembered customers watching the events on live TV in the coffee shop completely bewildered, not comprehending what was happening.

"Vartan," she began softly. "It's the space station. It's been lost."

"What . . ." He started to speak, then broke off and turned back to the TV. The news crawl at the bottom of the screen stated that NASA had issued a general warning and an emergency alert for southern England, France, the Mediterranean, and parts of northern Morocco and Algeria. His eyes narrowed with recognition of what he'd just seen. His face went pale.

They just stood there, motionless, for the next few minutes, not saying a word. It was as if they both understood the implications of what was happening, but dared not speak of it for fear it would become real. Finally, after nearly thirty minutes, Lori felt light headed from the adrenaline running through her bloodstream and had to sit down. She placed her head in her hand, trying to stop the room from reeling about. After a few moments, she felt better, and decided to try her voice again. "Vartan," she said gently. He did not respond.

"Vartan," she said again, more forcefully. This time he turned and sat down on the couch next to her, his eyes never leaving the screen. "Vartan, does this mean what I think it means?"

He turned away from the TV and nodded. "I think so," he said. Although neither had stated it, they both knew what the subject at hand was.

"That parchment that you got from the Masonic archives, the one with all the predictions for the future?"

"Yes," he said. His voice was very flat.

"And the things it said about a great abode in the sky, falling like a blue star?"

"Yes."

She took a deep breath. "Is that what we're seeing now?"

He looked back at the screen, then to her. "Yes, I think so. I think this is the prophecy that the document spoke of."

She took a beat to let that sink in. "So then, the other things, the things it said about the other prophecies, about the end of time, and the great catastrophe, or whatever he called it. Those might be true too?"

He looked at her, ashen faced. He swallowed, hard, and then nodded. "Yes . . . I should think so."

Her mind raced with possibilities. She wanted to believe anything else, anything except that what she was seeing on TV had been foretold hundreds of years before by an ancient and secret society.

She argued with herself internally. She reminded herself she was a practical, modern woman. She wasn't taken to believing in ancient prophecies or conspiracy theories. The idea that this world could actually end, that there wasn't anything special or fated about it or the people on it went against all that she'd learned in church as a little girl, all that she'd believed. It couldn't be. This couldn't be happening.

Maybe this was all a complex ruse. Maybe Vartan was still working for MI-6, and he was undercover on some special assignment. Maybe he'd caught word of plans to sabotage the station and bring it down for some unknown reason, and he'd made the whole story of the parchment up . . .

He was still looking at her, right into her eyes, and he seemed to sense what was running through her thoughts. "I didn't make it up," he said, his tone final and forceful.

She studied his face for any hint of deception, any strand of hope that he was lying to cover up some mundane explanation for these events, but she could find none. In his face she was confronted with a shattering reality she wanted desperately not to accept: He had told her the truth.

She put her hands over her nose and mouth. Her pulse was racing in her ears. She was scared.

After a few moments of silence, watching the situation in Europe go from bad to worse, she got off the couch and stood at the window, taking one last look at the sprawling desert playground that now seemed so fragile and transient. The lights of the Paris hotel, with its chintzy half-scale Eifel Tower glittered in the distance. Beyond that was the Luxor, with its guardian Sphinx at the base and the brilliant spotlight shining out from the tip of the pyramid, a beacon visible from space. She watched all the bustle and activity below her dispassionately, if not contemptuously. She was becoming more and more convinced that there was some much bigger plan in place, some profound battle being played out all around these people. But they remained blissfully ignorant of it.

"One thing," she said to him then. He stood and turned. "Was this an accident? Was it just random, or . . ."

His face darkened, and he looked again at the TV. It showed images of a horrific inferno engulfing a portion of the Louvre, and the glass pyramid that adorned the courtyard of the museum had been shattered by debris. "No, I don't think so," he said. "Somebody planned this."

That made her even more frightened, yet at the same time, more inquisitive. "So then, this has something to do with why Garvin and Dr. Tsien were murdered? This has something to do with what they were digging into?"

"Yes, I imagine so. And we'd better find out what it is, and quickly." His voice had just the faintest quaver in it, and she realized that for the first time since she'd met him, he was well and truly scared. Not even her gun at his head had frightened him this much.

"We should go," she said, admitting the truth to herself.

"I agree," Vartan said quietly. He got up and began to pack his belongings. She did the same.

20.

As the lights of Las Vegas dimmed in the distance, Lori's thoughts turned to the epic scale of the tragedy that had just unfolded. There were nine astronauts between the shuttle and the station crew, six of them Americans, and they were all certainly dead now. In addition, the radio news services were reporting that there had been at least forty deaths when the debris hit an apartment complex in London, and perhaps hundreds more in the fires that were now raging around Paris. The Parisian emergency response teams were pressed to the limit trying to contain the fires caused by white-hot pieces of the wreckage striking older wooden buildings. One elderly man in London said the fires there reminded him of the buzz bomb attacks he'd seen in the city as a child. "Something I never wanted to experience again," he lamented.

Lori reached out and turned off the radio. "I think it's time you tell me what you know," she said to Vartan strongly. "Everything."

He did not react, instead keeping his eyes fixed firmly on the road ahead. He seemed dazed. "You must have some ideas about what's going on here. Why this is all happening," she pressed him.

"I'm afraid you've overestimated me. I'm as much in the dark about all this as you are."

"Bullshit," she said sharply. "I know you know more than you've told me about who these people are and why they're doing this."

"I do, but . . ." he trailed off. "Again, I don't think you'll be inclined to believe me."

She turned to gaze at the desert vista stretching out in front of them as the sun began to recede over the horizon. "Frankly, after what's happened the last few days, I think you'd be surprised by what I'm inclined to believe."

"All right," he said, sounding resigned. "I'll tell you. I'll tell you what I think." He took his eyes off the road for just a moment. "You know something about the Freemasons, correct? Do you remember the way that Dr. Tsien's body was positioned? They way he was dressed?"

"I wish I didn't remember."

"I'm sorry, but it's important. His clothing was arranged in the manner of an initiate to the First Degree of Freemasonry."

Lori nodded. "Entered Apprentice. That's why you wrote those words on the back of the crime scene photo."

"Yes. And to make a point. Remember that I told you about what I found out about the Masonic influence inside NASA? About how everybody who was anybody at NASA during the moon programs was a Freemason in some capacity?"

"Yes," Lori said tiredly, "but so what?"

He changed lanes. "To start with, NASA is not civilian science agency, as most people think. It's a subordinate agency of the United States Department of Defense."

"DOD? I didn't realize that."

"Most people don't. The congressional act that created it explicitly states that NASA must report to the DOD any discoveries it might make in the course of space exploration. And it authorizes the office of the president to classify any part of this information he deems to fall under the purview of 'national security.'"

Lori considered this. "That would explain a lot."

"Yes it would," he agreed. "If Dr. Tsien was leaking out the real pictures of Mars to Richard Garvin, ones that could prove that there were artificial ruins there, then very likely, under that definition, he would have been leaking actual classified military secrets to him, not just proprietary JPL data."

"And that might be enough reason to kill him, is that what you're saying?"

Vartan was hesitant. "Perhaps," he said cautiously. "There was a government report, commissioned by NASA at the dawn of the space age . . ."

"The Brookings Report," she cut-in. "I know all about it. They were afraid of another panic. Like after the War of the Worlds broadcast in 1939."

"Very good," he said admiringly. "That became the official policy behind the scenes; if you find anything out there, cover it up."

"But again, that isn't enough reason to kill two prominent men," she countered. "We've had forty years of Star Trek, Star Wars and stuff like that. Most of us are very comfortable with the idea that we're not alone."

He shook his head, negatively. "You're not thinking this through." She frowned at him.

"Think about it," he said. "Imagine a press conference. NASA officials get up there and tell us that they've discovered ancient, advanced artificial ruins on Mars or the Moon. Now, imagine you get to ask the first question at that press conference. What are you going to ask?"

She thought for a moment, and understood. "I'm going ask them if this is true, and there was once a civilization on Mars more advanced than we are now, then what happened to them? Why is their superior civilization in ruins?"

Vartan smiled at her. "That's the one question they can't allow to be asked. The one answer they can't possibly give. Because the answer itself would destroy all that exists today. Once people realized that something terrible had destroyed a culture far in advance of our own, then they might easily conclude that our own civilization was far from safe. That we're certainly not immune to whatever catastrophe devastated them."

She took that in for a moment. "And then there'd be chaos."

"Probably. People stop caring about going to work, paying bills. Having children. They start living for the day. They give up on the future."

"And preventing that might be reason enough to kill them over."

"Exactly."

They drove on in silence for a while. She looked out the window at the constellation of Orion, rising slowly in the west. "I asked you what you *know*. This is all conjecture and supposition. It doesn't tell us anything more about why this is all happening. And who's trying to kill us."

"The same people who killed Dr. Tsien and Richard Garvin, obviously. People who are good at keeping secrets. And people who are willing to risk an awful lot to keep whatever is on that flash drive secret."

His evasiveness was starting to grate on her. "Another non-answer answer, Vartan. I need something I can use."

He considered her for a moment, taking his eyes off the road. She wasn't trying to hide her frustration. "OK . . . he said seriously, "but you won't believe me."

"I can't tell you how tired I am of hearing that from you."

If he was bothered by her reaction, he didn't indicate it. "During my assignment to Admiral Milner in the Royal Navy, I was given several high security clearances, far above the Top Secret clearance you have."

"*Above* Top Secret? There are levels above the top?"

He nodded. "Far beyond. I had clearances even some of your presidents haven't had."

"I find that hard to believe," she scoffed.

"As I predicted. Why do you persist in asking me questions you don't want the answer to?"

"Sorry," she said simply. He gave her a small nod before continuing.

"At any rate, after I was reassigned to MI-6, I was given access to certain highly classified documents. I was only allowed to read them inside a secured room with an armed guard present. One of them was quite special. It was titled 'The Assessment.' I was told to go into this room several times a week until I had read and absorbed all the material. Given that the document was eight inches thick, that took a while."

"I can imagine. What was it a report on?"

"It was a history of the most highly classified secrets the government knew. Secrets that had been kept, in some cases, for more than a century." He paused there.

"Like . . .?" she asked.

"Like the fact that the two atomic bombs that were dropped on Japan weren't American. They were German. Captured by the Americans from the Nazis. They had the bomb before we did, but their regime fell before they could be used in the field."

"I suppose we should be thankful for that. That's wild."

"Yes, but there was more. The German rocket scientists that were captured also tried to bargain for their freedom. But they had something far more interesting to offer." Again he paused somewhat dramatically.

"Such as?"

He blew some air out of his mouth, as if he knew his answer would only enhance her disbelief. "Such as the exact date of the end of the world."

"Jesus." Lori didn't like to curse, but it was not the answer she was hoping for. "Now I see why you didn't want to tell me."

He nodded again, and checked his mirrors once more. "The scientists told the Allies that they had been ordered to decipher a number of ancient calendars, the Aztec, the Mayan, the Egyptian, even the Babylonian, and that they had come to the conclusion that they all had the same end date; December 21st, 2012. This corresponded with a celestial alignment that they said would cause the Earth's magnetic poles to flip, which would cause an environmental catastrophe."

"Swing and miss on that one," Lori said. Then she held out her hand. "Wait a minute, I don't get it. How can a calendar 'end?' Calendars don't have an end."

"Most ancient cultures didn't view time as a straight line as we do," he said. "They viewed it as a great circle. A cycle that repeated again and again. It was linked to the twenty-six thousand year precessional cycle. Their calendars are like precessional clocks ticking down."

"Like a countdown for a rocket launch?"

"Yes. Exactly."

She considered this a moment. "And what happens when the countdown ends?"

"I thought you knew," he said, stealing a glance at her. "Time's up."

She looked out her side window. "And our government bought into all this? Based on what, exactly?"

He shook his head. "The Assessment says that our respective governments didn't believe them at first. But it soon became clear that the Nazis had been doing a great deal of highly advanced astrophysics research, far beyond even what even Einstein had accomplished. The Assessment said that right after the war, the United States military began to conduct research into the possibility that the Earth's magnetic poles might be drifting. They sent expeditions to the north and south poles to take measurements. The consensus among our scientific teams was that the poles were indeed slipping, and that a rollover, a polar realignment, was inevitable."

Lori could feel her throat tightening up. "Did it say anything about when this might occur?"

"That part of the report was useless. It set the time frame as anywhere from seventeen years from the time of the scientific studies to one thousand years. The studies were published in 1947."

"So these calendars were in the ballpark, give or take a thousand years?" she asked.

"Yes, which isn't bad considering they were all supposedly backward, savage sun-worshipers."

"OK," Lori said, going along with him. "What was our response to this information?"

"The Assessment laid out three options: Accept the inevitable and begin preparations to save as many of the elite populace as possible; try to find new technologies to reverse the slippage; and third to find somewhere else to go to ride out the storm."

Lori voice was very quiet. "Somewhere else to go?"

"Yes," he said firmly, indicating upwards, "space."

She closed her eyes and rubbed her temples. "Did the Assessment say which one of the options had been chosen?"

"Yes. All three."

She chuckled softly to herself. "That's what I figured."

If he noticed the tone of sarcasm in her voice, he didn't seem fazed by it. He was on a roll now. "An immediate crash program of building underground bases was commenced. New Mexico, Australia, places like Area 51 in Nevada, and massive undersea complexes."

"You've actually seen these bases? You've been inside them yourself?"

"Yes I have, actually. But unless you're cleared to read the Assessment, you have no clue what the real purpose of them is."

She nodded. "So this is all pretty far along then?"

"Truly, you have no idea. What happened was that these three alternative responses factionalized. They each came to believe that the solution they had been tasked with executing was the only viable one. Behind the scenes, they began to vie for power, money and control. Over the decades they began to chart their own courses and follow their own agendas. And they each tried to undermine the others."

She understood. Even the FBI was in constant rivalry with other government agencies to remain relevant. "Not a cold war. A silent, unseen war."

"Yes," he said simply. Garvin and I first became aware of it when we discovered the extent of the Masonic infiltration of NASA. At first, NASA was staffed with representatives from all three factions. The Freemasons were the group that was tasked with getting us into space, to the Moon and Mars and beyond, in the hope we might find a suitable place to relocate."

"And were they able to find one?"

"Not according to the Assessment. All they found was a civilization in ruins. An incredibly advanced, incredibly ancient civilization, but one that had been utterly devastated."

"So there's no hope of getting out of Dodge City. No place to go?"

He seemed to understand the cinematic reference. "No, but NASA was also tasked with going to the Moon to see if there was anything that could be retrieved that might be of value. Possibly technologies that could be exploited to prevent the pole shift."

"You mean like that head thing you showed me in the Apollo photograph?"

"Right." He swallowed. She could see he was nervous, but was determined to press him.

"What happened after that?"

"The Nazi elements were forced out of NASA after the Apollo program. The Masons needed them initially to exploit the knowledge of the German rocket engineers to get to the Moon. Once they had that, Von Braun and the other Germans were swept aside. But they had allies and advocates inside the government by then, even amongst the Masonic elements in NASA, and they regrouped and began to concentrate on the underground bases. On surviving the next cataclysm here on Earth somehow."

That seemed plausible to her. "What about the other group?"

"The assessment doesn't say much about them. They're even more secretive than the other two. They are the ones tasked with developing advanced technologies that might prevent the pole shift."

"And . . ." she tried not to sound too hopeful, "did they have any success?"

He nodded. "The Assessment said as much. By the time I left MI-6, the consensus was that our new technologies would enable us to stabilize the poles and keep them from flipping over."

"What kind of technologies could do that? I mean, what are we talking about here? Atomic power? Lasers? What?"

"Far beyond those kinds of things," he said dismissively. "Spin generators that produce power on the terawatt scale. Spacecraft that can travel from Earth to Mars in 15 minutes, magnetic field generators that cancel out the effects of gravity."

"That sounds like flying saucers," she observed. Then: "Did the Assessment say anything about aliens?"

"Yes it did. But none of this technology came from extraterrestrial sources."

He looked uncomfortable. "Care to elaborate on that?" she asked him.

"No." Then there was a long pause. She simply waited for him to go on. Finally, he did. "We've had flying saucer technology since the 50's. The government is quite happy to let people think they are all driven by aliens, since it gives them cover to develop our own craft. The truth is, some

UFO's are extraterrestrial. Some of them are also simply mistaken natural objects. But a lot of them are ours." He paused again and turned to her. "The point is, we've found ways to stabilize the poles and keep them from slipping."

She turned away from him and looked out the window. "So the world's not going to end after all."

"Apparently not."

She listened intently to his tone. "OK", she said. "But you don't believe that."

"Our stack of dead bodies would seem to argue against the conclusion that all is well."

"Yes, they would," she agreed. "And the Masonic prophecies and what we've just seen on TV."

"Yes."

She let him drive several minutes further before speaking again. She could see tension in his body, as much as he was trying to hide it and assume a relaxed posture. There was something more.

"Now the rest," she said finally.

"What?"

"The rest of it. The part you're still not telling me."

"There isn't . . ."

"Don't insult me," she said before he could finish. "I'd be a pretty crappy cop if I couldn't tell when someone was holding something back."

He tightened his grip on the steering wheel. "Lori, from my run-ins with these three factions, they argued their positions with an almost religious fervor. I don't think that the side that was preparing for the apocalypse was gong to just pack up and give in because the technological guys said they had a solution."

"What alternatives did they have?"

"More than you'd think. After fifty years of working on a plan, operating outside the normal checks and balances of government and public oversight, I think they've gotten quite accustomed to the trappings and delights of privilege."

"And you don't think they're going to give those up easily." It was not a question.

"I don't think they have any intention of giving them up at all. I think some on the inside are intent on seeing their agenda through to the end."

Her eyes narrowed. "Exactly what is that statement supposed to mean?"

"It means they are willing to go to extreme lengths to ensure that their agenda and all their work in preparing for the end isn't discarded."

"To the point of killing Dr. Tsien and Richard Garvin?"

He took a deep breath. "To the point of creating an apocalyptic event if one doesn't happen on its own."

Lori blinked. "Oh my god," she said, putting her hand over her mouth. "That's what you think is happening. That's why you think the space station disaster was arranged."

"Yes," he said, shifting his focus back to the road ahead. "I think somebody is playing out an Armageddon script, and I think Dr. Tsien and Richard Garvin got mixed up in it somehow."

"So the world was supposed to end on December 21st, 2012, when the Mayan calendar ran out. But it didn't," Lori observed.

"And that made some very powerful people very, very angry," he said.

Lori leaned back in her seat and closed her eyes. She'd been listening to him for almost thirty minutes. He turned to her sympathetically. "I know all this new information is a bit much to believe under the circumstances."

She couldn't help herself and smiled, her eyes still closed. "Under the circumstances? Hardly. But don't kid yourself. That sounds only slightly more insane than everything else you've told me in the last two days."

This time he noted the teasing tone in her voice, and they were so caught up in the moment, sharing a small laugh at his expense, that neither of them noticed the dark windowed SUV speeding up from behind them.

21.

Vartan's first inkling of trouble was when the SUV slammed into the left rear quarter of the tiny two-seater Mercedes they had switched out in Vegas. He was barely able to control the car as it swerved across the lanes, but a combination of his driving skills, the various traction control devices and the steering assistance built into the little roadster saved them. After flat spotting at least two tires as they skidded sideways down the freeway at nearly 80 miles per hour, he jerked the wheel back to the right all the way to positive lock and hit the gas. The 350 horsepower engine kicked in almost immediately, and he regained the balance of the car as they straightened out and shot back up the road. Luckily, they were on a wide, flat, straight section of asphalt, with no other cars around. Lori had been completely silent during the three or four seconds it had taken for the whole sequence to play out, and that told Vartan that she either wasn't in sufficient command of her faculties to make so much as a noise, or she had been expecting something like this and wasn't particularly surprised by it.

He was, and he cursed himself inwardly for getting so sloppy. They'd lingered too long in Las Vegas, especially after the station had come down, and they'd allowed their pursuers to catch up to them. A quick glance in the rear view mirror and he could see the headlights of the SUV receding in the distance as the powerful engine of the Mercedes hit maximum revs.

He took a brief moment to consider just who was chasing them. He'd caught a quick glance at the vehicle, and it didn't seem to have any white panels or a light rack on the roof. Unless it was a chance encounter with an unmarked police vehicle, which he doubted, he was virtually certain that they were in a conflict with the same group that had probably killed Tsien and Garvin. It certainly wasn't typical law enforcement procedure to try and wreck a car you're pursuing without trying to stop it peaceably first. Whoever they were, they evidently intended to wreck them as opposed to making sure they killed them, since they could have waited for a

more treacherous stretch of road to hit them with their much
larger vehicle.

"He's coming again," Lori warned, a remarkable calm
in her voice given the situation.

"I see it," Vartan said back, checking his side mirrors.
A quick glance down at his speedometer told him they were
doing better than an hundred and sixty, a speed at which no
normal SUV or police cruiser should be able to overtake
them. But yet, there were the approaching headlights getting
larger and larger.

OK, he thought to himself, in some ways that would
make it easier. There wouldn't be any additional police
brought into the fray, no back-up units or road blocks to
complicate the chase. He need only rely on his skills and
training to get him out of a tough spot once again, as it had
many times before. Seeing the SUV now within about ten
seconds of overtaking them, he started to look for an
opportunity on the road ahead to make a move.

He could see the road swing to the right in the dim light
of the falling dusk, maybe a half mile ahead. The turn was
blind and it looked like the road dropped in elevation after
that, but he couldn't be sure. The SUV wouldn't be able to
take the turn nearly as fast as they could, and so would have
to bleed off considerable speed as they both went through the
narrowing section of roadway.

The driver of the SUV must have seen this as well,
because the truck lurched forward as he apparently shifted
into a lower gear to get more torque. It had gobbled up a huge
amount of the gap between the cars with that one surge and
Vartan could tell he needed to coax some more speed out of
his own vehicle if he was going to even make it to the turn.
He slammed his foot down on the accelerator, even though he
was already beyond a speed he felt he could safely handle,
and the little Mercedes surged ahead just in time to avoid the
attempted rear bumper hit by the SUV.

He moved into the left lane to set up for the sweeping
right hand turn, and the SUV followed, now maybe fifty feet
behind them and closing fast. His mind jumped to a scene he
remembered from a movie once, and he resolved on a course

of action. But, he'd have to sell it to the driver behind them. He kept his foot on the gas and the sliver Mercedes kept accelerating.

There were less than a hundred yards to the turn now.

The driver of the SUV must have decided to make one last run before the turn, because he took the bait and accelerated even faster. Vartan watched as it swiftly consumed the pavement between them, closing fast on his rear bumper again. They were closing far too fast, and he'd have to time this just right . . .

With the SUV literally just inches behind them, Vartan jammed the wheel to the right and slammed his brakes. There was a horrifically loud screeching sound, undoubtedly the tires leaving layers of rubber on the asphalt and the carbon fiber breaks burning at high temperature. The car fishtailed wildly, and as he fought for control amidst the screaming brakes and gray black smoke that started filling the cabin, he expected the hit from behind at any second.

He waited for it, but it didn't come.

They were into the turn now, and he could see the metal glint of the guard rail outside Lori's window, inches from her head. She was frozen in place, forcing herself back into the cushioned seat while pushing her feet against the floor boards and her hands against the dash in a reflexive attempt to brake the car herself. Her eyes were fixed straight ahead, and she didn't even notice the proximity of the guardrail outside her passenger window. Vartan made a quick, short turn of the steering wheel back to the left, and there was finally some separation from the metal barrier on the cars' right side.

Before he could cast his eyes out the front windshield, he felt the powerful thud of a high speed impact in his left. He looked up to see the black sidewall of the SUV right on top of them, but slipping away as it spiraled outward. His maneuver had worked, as his sudden application of the breaks had caused the SUV to overshoot them, if only for the moment. He felt the car shudder and strain beneath him as the frame twisted and wrenched, trying to follow the commands given to it by his steering input. The turn was long and had a narrowing radius that would soon bring the SUV back into their lane.

But the SUV had a higher center of gravity and far more weight, and try as he might, the driver could not match Vartan's quick maneuvers and the Mercedes' steering response. The SUV had gone into the turn far too fast, and it was a testament to its driver's skill that he had made it this far through the turn without wrecking. Vartan had slowed the Mercedes fishtailing now, and their speed had dropped below one hundred, but the SUV was sliding nearly sideways down the road, just as their own car had done moments before. The driver tried to steer back onto the roadway, but in what must have been a moment of panic he over corrected and the SUV came out of the turn angling leftward.

Without the sideswiping contact, he might have made it, but the additional sideways momentum from brushing their Mercedes pushed his left side over the yellow line and onto the rumble strip. Again, he tried to turn back to his right, but the left rear tire just barely clipped the guardrail run-out, sending the tire off the vehicle and sailing into the air. The left side of the SUV collapsed, and it quickly flipped into the air, bouncing off the road and careening off the embankment.

Vartan had now regained control, but just barely, and he eased up on the brakes as the car began to slow. The turn did drop off into a slight depression, and the SUV began to bounce across the dirt divider and into the oncoming lanes. Fortunately, there were no cars coming in either direction and the SUV left shattered glass and metal bits all along the highway as it bounced and bounced and bounced. It made at least eight full revolutions before it skidded along the asphalt and came to rest up against the guardrail on the far side of the deserted road.

Vartan watched the SUV out of the side window as their car went whizzing past the crash site. He contemplated just hitting the gas again, but instead he applied the brakes, this time far more gently, and brought the car to a halt a little farther up the road. He looked over to Lori, who was panting and holding her chest. He was glad she had no idea how close he'd come to hitting the rail on her side of the car. She looked over to him, still breathless, and he felt a sudden rage wash over him, something he'd never felt before, not even in the club with all of the security guards shooting at them.

Without a word, he put the car in reverse and started backing it down the road.

"Vartan, what . . . what the hell are you doing?" Lori was looking back now at the crash. "Vartan stop it! Let's just get out of here."

He ignored her, and continued to back up until he could spin the car around and cross over the dirt divider. He drove right up to where the SUV lay in a crumpled, upside down heap facing in the wrong direction.

"Vartan, god damn it this isn't necessary!" Lori was clearly alarmed now, and she reached out for him but he was already getting out of the car. He left the door open and she tried to exit on her side, but her door was jammed, probably because the metal frame had been slightly bent, and he could hear her cursing behind him.

He pulled out a clip and loaded his gun as he walked purposefully across the dirt divider and up to the steaming hulk. He quickly assessed that there was no fire and therefore no danger of an explosion. Bending down, he peered inside the wreck. The driver and the front seat passenger were jammed up against the dash and hanging upside down in their seat belts, which had held through the horrifically violent crash. They had been crushed as the engine compartment had collapsed inward when the truck hit the railing head on. He looked in the back seat and saw a third body, twisted and mangled almost as bad as the SUV was. Vartan reached in and yanked the back of the man's head, which was covered in what looked to be a ski mask.

He had no face.

Where it should have been there was just a red, bloody mass of skull and tissue encrusted with dirt and grime. Vartan looked back up the road and could see a streak of blood and goo on it where the SUV must have slid along the pavement as it slowed to a stop. It was obviously the missing part of the man's face.

He looked across to the Mercedes, and saw that Lori had given up trying to open her jammed door and was now crawling across the center console to get out on his side. Then he heard it; a low, desperate, painful moan. He walked deliberately around to the other side of the wrecked SUV.

There was a man crawling along the road on his belly, just a few feet from the wreck. Like the others he was dressed all in black. Vartan could see a trail of blood behind him, coming from his pelvic area. Both his legs looked to be broken, one of them with bone protruding through the material of his tattered black outfit. Vartan reached down and grabbed his right shoulder, turning him over violently. The man screamed.

"Vartan don't," Lori called out, rushing up from the Mercedes. She got there just in time to see him remove the mask that the man was wearing. Lori looked away as he screamed again, the mask pulling layers of skin from his face and scalp as Vartan yanked it off him. She turned her attention to Vartan, putting her hand on his right arm.

"Vartan don't," she said again. "This doesn't help us."

He ignored her. He stared down at the man, who he knew to be a well practiced killer, someone completely without feeling or compassion. He looked into the man's eyes. They were bloodied but he could see that they were green, and he had tufts of reddish brown hair still left on his head. His features were Caucasian, and Vartan could see that he was suffering, but still conscious.

Good.

Without a word to Lori, he lifted the gun and fired three times into the man's head. Crack! Crack! Crack! Lori jumped each time from the sound, but he didn't care at this point and she did nothing to stop him. He held the gun out for a few moments, contemplating what he'd just done, and then bent down and began tearing at the man's clothing. Since the black outfit was already torn up, it came apart readily.

"What are you doing?" Lori asked, raising her voice.

When he was done, the man's body was stripped of the left sleeve and the pants legs were rolled up, just as Dr.

Tsien's had been. He then stood up to his full height, towering over her, and looked right down into her eyes.

"Sending a message," he said. Then he turned and went back to the car.

It was several hours before Lori could bring herself to speak to Vartan again, much less look at him.

"I hope you enjoyed that," she said to him, her voice harsh and judging.

"I did, actually," he shot back. It seemed to her that he was relieved to finally be speaking to her again.

"So you enjoyed killing that man in cold blood?"

"Given what he or his associates have done to my friends and yours, yes. I'll not apologize for it."

His accent was far stronger than before, and his diction was precise. It sounded to her as if he had retreated to a familiar place emotionally, to some past mindset or time in his life. Conceivably, it was his way of coping with the feelings he was having. At least, she hoped that was it. Because that might mean he actually had feelings of some kind. "You didn't need to shoot him. He was already going to die. And in agony," she said.

His tone was unyielding. "Then consider it an act of mercy."

"That's not the point. It was a murder. You've murdered at least five people in the last two days."

"That's a matter of perspective. It was self defense from where I stand."

"It's not self defense to shoot a mortally wounded man who's defenseless."

He seemed unimpressed. "These people have killed two others, and tried to kill us and your friend. I wanted them to know we could get to them, too."

"And that was worth having more blood on your hands?" She was still looking straight ahead. "Worth what it costs you?" She knew he understood that she wasn't talking about costs in terms of money or time, but in terms of the spirit.

He was silent for a long while. "You need to accept the fact that it's us or them. We don't have the luxury of making moral judgments just at the moment."

She made a quick, dismissing sound. "We always have that luxury," she said. Now she was angry with him; angry that he was not the man she wanted him to be. She looked out the window again at the stars. "They say that once you've killed for the first time, it gets easier after that. Is that true Vartan?"

"Perhaps you should ask yourself that question," he said sharply. "You don't think that man in the parking lot you hit with the door survived, do you? You may not have seen it, but the door hit his head as he tried to duck under. It's relatively certain he's dead."

She felt the blood drain from her face as she remembered the dull thud and the limp form under the door. He was probably right. She fought hard not to think about what killing him meant, what her father and mother would have thought of that had they known. "You're a bastard," she said angrily to him.

"Only when I have to be."

His responses were quick and defiant. He wasn't even going to consider her argument. As far as he was concerned, the black clad men were the enemy, period. They would get no quarter. But then he seemed to soften to her emotional turmoil. "We both did what we had to do," her offered, a hint of sympathy in his voice.

"No," she said back quickly, "one of us did more." He did not respond, and she let her statement hang in the air between them for a long few moments. "Well, at least you finally admitted that much," she finally said.

"Does that make you feel any better, thinking that?" He was really pushing her now.

"Do I feel better that I'm forced to help a murderer who seems to enjoy killing? Or at least doesn't seem to mind it too much? Not really."

"I saved your life back there," he pointed out. "I'll have no problems sleeping tonight."

"That's too bad. I will."

"Your compassion for those who are trying to end your life would be enviable, if it weren't so foolish."

She shook her head slowly. "You're not getting it Vartan. I don't have any compassion for them," she said. "It's you I feel sorry for. If we come out of this alive, you'll never be the same. Never be what you could have been."

He looked over at her for the first time in hours. "You don't know me. You don't know this is the first time I've had to kill."

"I don't need to know you any better, Vartan. Your hands have been shaking ever since we got back on the road." He did not respond or look at her again. He just kept driving.

After a few more miles of silence, he pulled off the highway and began following a dark, desolate road into the hills. Eventually, he found an empty campground that looked to have been abandoned for several years, at least. He parked the car and retrieved his laptop from the trunk and plugged it into the cigarette lighter outlet. The Milky Way was brilliant in the sky above them. "We'd best be off the road for a while," he said to her, his formal accent still stronger than usual. "They'll be finding the wreck soon enough, if they haven't already, and we have some crash damage on our bumper."

She didn't respond. She leaned her seat back and rolled away from him, shutting her eyes to try and get some sleep while he worked. She couldn't sleep.

"Vartan," she said softly after about fifteen minutes.

"Um-hmm?" The sound he made seemed calmer and less defiant to her.

"Tell me the truth. Did you enjoy killing that man?"

She heard him slap the laptop lid shut. A frustrated sound. "Why is this important to you?"

She thought about all the reasons why, about all the lessons in Sunday school that warned her that no one got into God's kingdom without a pure heart. About the times when she was a little girl and her father had read to her from the Bible, and about how he'd told her that we all sinned, but what mattered the most was if we truly regretted it. And she thought about the fact that they might not make it out of this alive. And that she wanted to see him again in the next life, the one that Melissa had shown her so many times when she despaired.

But she couldn't tell him any of that. "I don't know. It just is."

She heard the regression in her voice. She sounded very much like that little girl on her daddy's lap, trying to read long with him. Thankfully, she was still turned away from him, and he could not see how she flushed with embarrassment.

If he noticed the tenor of her voice, he gave no hint of it. "No Lori. I didn't enjoy killing that man. I did what I thought I had to do at the time."

His voice sounded sincere enough, but he took too long to answer.

She didn't believe him.

Lori was awakened by the sounds of the gravel pinging off the exterior panels of the car. They were moving again, and she'd fallen asleep after all.

"What's going on? I thought we were going to stay put."

He looked over from the driver's side. "I've been monitoring the police communications. They've found the wreck but don't seem to realize it wasn't an accident yet. They may not realize that until they do an autopsy. The whole thing was pretty gruesome."

She couldn't argue with that. "How long was I out?"

"About an hour. I buffed out the marks on the car as best I could. They'll probably assume the silver marks on the SUV are from the guardrail."

"So we have some time?"

He nodded. "Time enough, I suppose. We can be almost out of the state before they figure out the one man died from gunshot wounds."

"So you're admitting that shooting that man was a mistake? They probably wouldn't even be looking for us at all if you hadn't shot him."

His answer was short and sharp. "That's correct. It was probably a mistake."

She took a certain pleasure in that acknowledgement. "At least I lived long enough to hear that."

She looked up to see them passing a road sign just at that moment. It said "Flagstaff 233."

"Where are we going?" she asked.

"Albuquerque."

"Won't that be one of the places they'll be looking for us?"

"One of the places, yes," he said.

"Then why are we going there?"

"While you were sleeping, I did some more work on the files you gave me. It turns out there's a reason that the schematic files are incomplete on the flash drive you gave me."

She sat up straighter in her seat.

"They aren't the original files," he continued. "They've been tampered with somehow."

She wasn't buying that. "Marshall gave me those files. There's no way he tampered with them."

"Not at your end. They were altered before they were sent from Albuquerque."

"What? By who?"

He shook his head. "I don't know. I just know that the files you received over the FBI secure network were not the original files from Garvin's computer hard drive."

Her eyes narrowed. "Explain to me how you know that."

"Every computer file has a special identifier. It's called a UUID, or Universal Unique Identifier. That means every file that is created on every computer the world over has a special, unique signature that can be read by any other computer. It crosses operating system lines and is a one hundred twenty-eight bit number, meaning it can never be duplicated."

"That sounds like wishful thinking," she scoffed.

"Actually, I suppose it is. The numbers actually can eventually be duplicated."

"I thought so," she said.

"Of course, there would have to be ten trillion UUID's created every nanosecond for ten billion years to have that first duplication, but it is possible." He smiled over at her. "That's ten trillion UUID's every one billionth of a second, by the way."

She wasn't amused by him. There were still too many harsh memories from just a few hours ago. "Well," she said flatly. "I guess we can rule out any possible random duplication then."

He agreed with a nod.

"So you can use this 'UUID' how?" she asked.

"What I found was that when I compared the UUID's from the files off your flash drive to the ones on some files I had that Garvin sent me before, the computer ID was wrong."

"So what does that tell you?"

"It tells me that two of the files – specifically the two Prometheus probe schematics I told you about – aren't the same ones that Dr. Tsien sent to Garvin via email. They're altered copies."

"Maybe Garvin altered them himself."

He was shaking his head. "No. These files were created on a UNIX workstation, a Sun UNIX workstation to be precise, and Garvin didn't have any computers like that."

She wasn't sure she wanted to know the answer to her next question. "Who does?"

"The government still has lots of them. Especially NASA, JPL, DARPA, and…" he paused, "the FBI."

"Great," was all she could muster in response. "So what do you think happened?"

"The most likely scenario is that the Albuquerque police sent an image of the hard drive over to the local FBI field office, and somebody there intercepted it and made the changes before making another image file and sending it to your friend Marshall."

She put her hand to her mouth. "Shit," she said, cursing for one of the few times in her life. "This means we can't trust anything we think we know."

"Maybe. Or maybe it just means that somebody was in a rush to cover up Tsien's tracks, and went about it in a clumsy way."

That didn't add up for her. "Then why not just delete those files from the image they sent to us?"

He shrugged. "Probably because they were worried we'd notice the discrepancy, the missing files. Eventually, we would have."

"Marshall would have," she agreed. "So, what are we doing?"

"Going to get the real hard drive and pull those files ourselves."

"Oh. Is that all. We don't even know where it is."

He smiled again, the James Bond smile. "I know exactly where it is."

She waited, trying her best to look unmoved. He didn't budge. "OK Vartan, I'll bite. Where is it?"

He indicated the road ahead. "Albuquerque," he said lightly. "Or more precisely, the Albuquerque Sherriff's department evidence room."

"Vartan, I hate to break this to you, but they aren't just going to give it to us if we ask nicely."

"Of course they're not," he agreed. "We're going to steal it."

22.

It was past ten A.M. when they finally pulled into the outskirts of Albuquerque, New Mexico. It was a dry and desolate place, with as much sand and dust by the side of the road as there was vegetation and scrub brush. Fortunately, it was still Fall and relatively cool, but she knew that by summer it would be an unbearably hellish environment, hot as the sun and dry as the Moon. She wondered what could have possessed people to settle in such a place, especially back in the old west in the days before air conditioning and modern aqueducts. It wasn't that far from the Rio Grande River, but still . . .

They drove through a series of suburban communities that ranged from broken down trailer parks to exclusive housing developments sporting towering split level mansions and sprawling rambler style homes. Eventually, they found a cheap motel off the main roads that seemed like a good place to settle in because they operated on cash exclusively. After the long drive, they both tried to catch some sleep, but it was impossible in a motel that advertised "hourly rates" and had a constant influx of prostitutes and drug users utilizing the adjoining rooms. Lori laid on her side on the rock hard bed with an extra pillow between her legs and tried to ignore the obviously phony screams of passion coming from a young American Indian girl in the next room. She had been running at least one client an hour in and out of the room since they had arrived. After several hours of this, Lori began to giggle almost involuntarily, and when she heard Vartan, who was camped out on the floor with a blanket and pillow, start to chuckle as well she decided it was time to give up the ruse and just get up.

"Not exactly the Venetian, is it?" he said ruefully.

She rolled her eyes. "Not quite."

They showered and dressed again in some of the new clothes they had bought in Las Vegas the day before. Lori waited until they were both ready to go to ask him the obvious question at hand. "So, I assume you have a plan for getting the hard drive from the local police?"

He couldn't seem to resist the opportunity to make another joke. "Actually, I thought I'd just drive a truck through the front entrance, shoot the place up, and take it," he said dryly. She gave him her best "not amused" look. "I assume you still have your FBI identification, correct?"

"Sure," she said, reaching into her handbag and pulling out her laminated ID badge to show him.

"Good then. We can work with this," he said, taking it and looking it over.

"Don't you still have the one you used to get into the Wilshire field office?"

"Of course but that name will be on a watch list by now, I assume."

"You assume correctly," she said, wishing that she had not made sure it could not be used again.

"That's OK. We can give me a new name. I was thinking of your friend Marshall."

She was quick on the response to that idea. "No way. I'm not dragging him into this. You'll have to pick another name."

"So give me another male co-worker of yours, then."

She considered that a moment. There was Jim Weston in finance, she hated how picky he was with her expense reports, and then there was the annoying guy from tech support, what was his name? Bill Anders? She could use him, but then she thought of the perfect candidate. "Eric Ruby," she said, unable to stop a wicked smile from crossing her face.

He raised a single eyebrow. "OK," he said without much more animation.

She resisted the temptation to ask him what he knew about Ruby. He'd certainly indicated he knew about her history with him. Instead; "So how do you plan to fix us new ID's? Lori Pars is going to be a name they're looking for."

He walked over to the lamp table and opened the drawer underneath. He pulled out the yellow pages phone book and began to rifle through it. When he found the page he was looking for, he held it up to her and tapped an ad with his right index finger. "Kinko's," he said.

"You can do it there?"

He nodded. "It'll be good enough for what we need it for. If you needed a real ID with a magnetic strip to get into an actual FBI office, we'd be screwed."

She was a bit surprised by his choice of phrase. She'd not yet heard him use such a casual and American colloquialism.

"You're forgetting one thing though," she told him.

"What's that?"

She reached in her purse and pulled out her metal FBI badge with the golden eagle on top and the shield with the Department of Justice logo below. "This will be a little harder to duplicate."

He frowned. "They'll ask for that?"

"Possibly. You'd better be able to show it if they do."

He took it from her hand and looked at it closely. "Well, then I guess you'll have to go in alone."

She took the badge back from him, a little miffed at his casual attitude. "I'm trying hard to fight the impression that you're just using me."

He turned from the bag he had started packing up. "For what?"

"I don't know," she said, studying his deep brown, almost black, eyes. "Something you're after that doesn't have anything to do with keeping me alive or getting us out of this."

"That's simply not true," he said, the quickness of the denial revealing its inherent dishonesty. "I'm totally focused on the task at hand, which in my mind is finding out who killed Richard and Dr. Tsien and finding a way to get you your life back."

"My," she said, "that's downright altruistic of you."

He looked away, seemingly a bit miffed. "Don't mock me," he said quietly. Was he actually a little hurt by her sarcastic tone? "I am a man of my word."

Lori looked at him, and found herself desperately wanting to believe him. *This guy has killed five people right in front of me*, she thought. *Why do I feel so damn safe with him?* "Nevertheless, Mr. Vartan, I get the feeling that it's the words you don't speak that are the most important." She continued to study his face, and she thought he was struggling with the idea of telling her something. He sat on the bed, locking his eyes on hers.

"You're right," he said, surprising her with his candid response. "I've been chasing this for more than a decade. I've had a lot of leads, and a lot of promises from a lot of very well connected people. A few times, I've been very close to something I thought was the truth. To finding out what this whole bizarre game was actually all about. But the problem is that what I always find is that the people I think should know everything, the big picture, they've been lied to in order to keep them in line. That's how control is maintained. Every player thinks he's in on the biggest secret ever. But he's just been let in on a version of the truth. A convenient story that plays to his ego."

"The lie is different at every level," Lori observed.

He nodded. "But I've never been this close before. I've never been close enough to look in the eyes of my adversary."

"Like you did last night," she interrupted him.

He looked away, briefly, then back. "Exactly," he said. So he *was* using her, or at least her case, in a way.

"So that . . ." she searched for an appropriate word. "That event last night. That was about more than sending a message. That was fifteen years of frustration and pent-up anger coming out."

He exhaled, loud enough to be audible, and looked away from her gaze. "No, it's not that simple. There's more to it than that."

She shrugged. "What? You want me to believe you didn't kill simply for pleasure or revenge? Then tell me."

He stood up. "I will not." Again, the formal British accent. He tried to turn away, but she grabbed his arm and held him as best she could. She was acutely aware of how strong he was compared to her.

"What's the matter Vartan? Are we getting to something that's too close to real for you? Are you afraid I'll find the thing that makes you who you are? What your big dark secret is?"

He tried to pull his arm from her, but she tightened her grip. "Why is this so important to you?" he snapped.

She shook her head. "Uh-uh. We're not changing the subject back to me this time, no matter how angry you pretend to be. Tell me."

He broke away from her, forcefully but carefully. "This is waste of time. We've got to go get the drive in any event, if we have any hope of getting out of this alive."

She clearly saw it, his desperation to move away from this issue, to not examine his own belly button. Only one thing she knew about him could have tweaked a nerve so raw, only one event in his past had the gravity to still haunt him at this point in his life. "This is about being an orphan, isn't it?"

His back was to her, but as he looked back over his shoulder at her she could see the almost imperceptible flexing of facial muscles that told her she was right. "What is it Trevor?" She deliberately used his first name in a caressing, gentle tone, the way his mother might have. He turned on her, smoldering inside. She tried to smile as cruel a smile as she could. "Did they kill your parents? Is that what this is all about? Is that why you resigned? Did one of your contacts tell you that their plane crash wasn't an accident?"

He clenched his fist, but that was as close as he got to a genuine reaction.

"Tell me!" she said, her voice harsh and commanding this time.

His eye twitched, and then he slowly exhaled and seemed to get a grip on his emotions. "MI-6 has a very special breed of agents. Call them the 'double O's,' if you like. And yes, they are all orphans. They don't find these men by accident. They create them."

He said nothing more, but he didn't need to. In that moment, he seemed truly vulnerable for the first time since she'd met him. She fought the urge to reach out and hold him, and found that her own anger was dissipated. "I'm sorry," she said after a beat. "But I needed to know."

He continued to glare at her, and she wondered if he might actually strike her. After a long, tense pause, he spoke in a slow and still deeply angry voice. "I'm not clear why," he said to her.

She broke the eye contact and sat down on the bed in a relaxed movement.

"Because now I can trust you," she said earnestly.

23.

Lori pulled up to the Albuquerque Sherriff's headquarters in the used gray Toyota that Vartan had purchased for eighty-five hundred dollars from a run down, low priced used car lot. After that, they'd left the Mercedes on a mountain road and stripped the plates and VIN tags from it before ramming the front of the Toyota into the hind quarters in an effort to cover-up the black paint from the SUV impacts. All this was merely designed to buy time; any competent law enforcement jurisdiction would be able to match the paint from the two vehicles in a matter of a few hours, at most. But they would have to wait a few days at least for detailed test results if the black was obscured by the gray paint from the Toyota.

As she parked the car she couldn't help but notice the moldy, sour smell coming from the air conditioning. It was just past eleven-thirty in the morning and the temperature was already in the low eighties. It was going to be a scorcher by the late afternoon and she needed the cooling to keep from sweating too much. She didn't want to look untidy as she tried to bluff her way past the administrative clerks in the Sheriffs' department. After all, she was supposed to be button down Federal Agent Connie Balver from the big bad Los Angeles FBI office.

The building was a fairly unexceptional one level red brick structure, with several thin branched and almost leafless trees out front. She imagined that they looked a bit healthier during the cooler winter months. Lori got out of the car and gathered her things, including a large purse with a false bottom in it that Vartan had fashioned for her. It contained the dummy hard drive she hoped to exchange for the real one, assuming she made it past the first level of security. There was no telling whether the Albuquerque PD would even give her access to the evidence room. It all depended on the personality of the clerk who handled the evidence. If they were the casual and trusting type, she had a chance to slip through. If she encountered a serious, officious bureaucrat, she'd never make it beyond the initial layer of checks.

She reached up and pulled the clip out of her hair, letting it flow down over her shoulders for maximum effect. Then she straightened her sleeveless white blouse, which was just translucent enough to cause a second glance but opaque enough to look professional. She didn't have a bra on underneath, only a lacy camisole. This had been Vartan's suggestion on the assumption that most of the officers were likely to be male. She wasn't used to being quite so free and walked carefully and deliberately to avoid any excessive jiggle. It seemed there was no limit to the amount of personal discomfort this adventure would make her endure.

She stepped up to the clear glass door, pulled it aside and stepped in.

To her surprise, the office was clean, new and fairly modern. There was a main desk, several uniformed clerks behind that and numerous computers and consoles set up in the back room. A number of other officers worked at desks shuffling paperwork and taking information from phone calls down on notepads. There was a distinct low pitched hubbub of conversation and background noise. A telephone dispatcher monitored radio activity in the Command and was giving audible instructions into a telephone headset. Most of the light was provided by big glass windows and additional overhead fluorescent light fixtures. When she approached the front counter, her shoes made a distinct clacking sound on the linoleum floor. Something about the sound and rhythm of her steps must have tipped the men in the office off, because several of them looked up from their administrative tasks to check her out.

She got to the counter and waited as one of the uniformed male officers got to his feet and met her there. He was a dark haired, mustachioed and fairly athletic looking man in his late thirties, she guessed. He walked to the desk with a manner of confident self importance.

"Good afternoon ma'am. What can I help you with?"

Lori realized she was exceedingly nervous. She was well and truly in the belly of the beast now and this was as close as she could get to actually being caught since she decided to throw in with Vartan. She was acutely aware of the fact that he wasn't in a position to help her with this task. Not this time.

She smiled her best relaxed, friendly girl smile and told herself that this was no different than dealing with a man at a bar. Just use your charms, she thought to herself, trying to forget the fact that Connie had chided her so recently for not having any.

"Hello," she said brightly, choosing not to correct him on the fact that it was still morning. "I'm here to see Captain Castillo. I had an appointment with him at noon?"

The man's face dropped for a second when he realized she was there to see someone else, but then he seemed to rally at the thought that he could spend more time with her by helping her himself. Just what she had hoped for.

"I'm afraid Captain Castillo isn't here at the moment," he said politely. "He's out working a case in the field. We had a murder here a few days ago, you know."

She flashed a look of disappointment. "Oh, yes I know. That's why I'm here actually."

The officer was easy to read. He suddenly got anxious. "Well maybe I can help. I'm Deputy Robbins."

Lori lifted her purse onto the counter and reached in. "That would be really nice of you, Deputy." She deliberately did not use his name. She'd save that level of praise for later.

She reached in the bag and pulled out her ID and badge and flashed it. "I'm Special Agent Balver, out from the Wilshire, California FBI field office? Captain Castillo was supposed to have an evidence package ready for me to pick up."

Deputy Robbins did his level best to hide that he had no idea what she was talking about.

"Oh yeah, you're the FBI girl. Captain Castillo mentioned that you were coming." His air of self-assurance was fading.

Lori smiled again. "Yes that's right. I'm the FBI girl," she agreed happily. Then she went for the advantage. "So where's the package? I assume he left it with you?" *Because you're so important* was the implication behind her words.

Robbins looked around at the desk that she presumed was normally manned by Castillo. It was exceedingly neat and organized and there certainly wasn't an evidence box or sealed envelope on it. Robbins leaned on the counter casually, but she could see he was scrambling to find something to say to her. She waited until he made eye contact with her again, then she quickly looked past him to Castillo's desk.

"It isn't there?" she said, letting a hint of displeasure raise the pitch of her voice just slightly.

"It doesn't look like it ma'am," he said quickly.

Lori gave him a disappointed look. "Well, is there any chance I can go through the evidence myself? I have a plane to catch."

That seemed to stir Robbins a bit. "We can't let you take evidence out of state, ma'am."

Lori knew she needed to disarm his suspicions. "Oh no, it's not going on the plane with me. It's just going over to the local field office for some additional tests."

He seemed satisfied with this answer. He then reached over the counter to touch her right arm while he turned away to a portly Hispanic woman with short graying hair who was banging away on a keyboard and completely ignoring them. "Martha, you want to get me a day badge for our guest here? She needs to get some evidence for the Saunders case."

"Badge number," Martha said back in a staccato delivery, never looking up from the keyboard or breaking her typing cadence.

"D six, forty-two, thirty-nine," Lori responded, glad she had all of her closest co-workers badge numbers memorized.

"Full name," Martha said with the same mechanical delivery.

"Constance Maria Balver," Lori said as Robbins turned back to her with a smile.

"Printer," Martha said next as the laser printer spit out a temporary ID badge with Connie's name on it. Robbins took it out, folded it over and slipped it into a plastic holder. He handed it to Lori and she pinned it into her blouse while Robbins watched the process with far too much interest.

When she was done she smiled up at him and he buzzed her through, moving to meet her behind the little divider door.

"Got a guest going back," he announced, to zero reaction from anyone in the office. Martha continued to type without looking up at them.

Bowing slightly, Robbins pointed the way back into the bowels of the building with his left hand and then slipped in behind her, probably so he could get a good look at her ass, Lori surmised. She walked carefully into the back area, taking her time so he could get an eyeful. She had to admit she found the whole thing kind of fun, and wondered if that was a stress reaction to the acute danger she was in.

Robbins put his hand in the small of her back as he led her up to a clerk's window and knocked on the wall next to it. Lori looked into the window to see a young man in his early twenties seated at a desk strewn with files and paperwork. There were racks of shelves with evidence boxes and file folders in a large storage area behind him. He had a set of earphones in his ears, a chunk of gum in his mouth that he was working feverishly and his feet were up on the desk.

Perfect, she thought. *A slacker.*

The young man took a moment to notice them before casually removing his headphones and coming to the window. He did not wear a police uniform and was obviously a civilian city employee.

"Yeah?" he said, noticeably displeased that his musical interlude had been interrupted.

"This is FBI Special Agent Balver. She needs to inspect some evidence for the Garvin case." Robbins did his best to sound commanding, as if he was in charge, but the clerk gave him a look of irritation that bordered on blatant disrespect. "Dude, I've told you a million times, I can't do anything without a case number. Why can't you get that through your head?"

Robbins face got very red very quickly, and she could see that the young man had embarrassed him with his flippant and defiant attitude. Not the best way to impress a lady, he must have been thinking.

"Listen son, I've told you the case number over and over. It's twenty-seven, seventeen, oh-three. Now let's get this process moving."

The young man gave Robbins a disdainful glance and then popped a few numbers into a computer terminal keyboard and asked for Lori's ID. He noted the badge number and then handed it back, all the while chewing loudly on his gum. "Bag please," he said to her.

"Oh," Lori said, handing him her purse. If he noticed the extra weight of the bag, he didn't say anything.

He took the bag into the office area and then hit a buzzer which was below the window opening and out of sight. The door to the office buzzed and popped open, and Lori went in with Robbins right behind her.

The man handed Lori her bag without a word and started to go back to his chair when Robbins stopped him. "Wait a minute," he said sharply. "That's no way to do your job, son. You're supposed to inspect that bag."

Lori cringed. Of course he would have to pick this moment to try and impress her. The younger man just looked at him as if he hated Robbins and couldn't wait to get rid of him. Robbins opened his mouth to say something more, but Lori cut him off.

"Deputy Robbins," she said, using his name and putting as pleasant a tone in her voice as she could, "I really need to get on with this. My plane leaves in an hour and I really need to make sure this gets over to the field office."

"I know Miss Balver, but I can't let this kind of attitude pervade amongst the civilian staff. I'm sure you understand that our procedures are in place for a reason."

"Of course," Lori said, trying to think of a way to dissuade him from an attempt to regain his pride.

"Now Hansen you know how to inspect a visitors bag. Get on with it." Robbins scolded the younger man.

The slacker, 'Hansen' Robbins had called him, just stared at Robbins and chewed his gum for a good ten seconds. Then he opened her bag, looked inside it with little genuine interest and handed it to her. "Correct me if I'm wrong Mr. Robbins but isn't she a cop? Do you always treat cops like they're the criminals?"

Robbins had trouble containing himself this time. These two obviously had a history of run-ins and disliked each other immensely. "It's not your job to judge whether someone's trustworthy enough to pass through here, Hansen. Your only job is to follow the procedures of this evidence room as I've written them up."

He stepped close to the other man and got even closer to his face. Hansen just smirked at him. "I always wondered what you did sitting at that desk all day, Officer Robbins. Thanks for telling me."

"Now you listen to me you insubordinate little . . ."

"Gentlemen!" Lori cut in forcefully. "If you'll excuse me, I have an investigation to conduct . . ?"

Robbins was clearly steamed as he turned away from Hansen, who just looked over at Lori. "Rack eighteen, shelves four and five. It's all there," he said.

"Thank you," Lori said back, heading into the storehouse and looking for the correct location. Robbins stayed behind and kept arguing with Hansen.

Lori quickly found her way back to rack eighteen and pulled several boxes down off the shelves. She kneeled down on the floor and checked to see that the two men were still arguing before opening the first box. She found candles, several art pieces and some blackened clothing in the first one, all labeled and neatly packed in clear plastic bags, but not the hard drive. She opened the second one and began to rifle through it. This one was packed with more technical gear, a cell phone, a melted cordless home phone, a small crystal clock and a number of other office knickknacks. There were still a lot of bags piled up in the bottom when she reached into the pile and went all the way down with her hand. Then she felt it; a cold, metal rectangle. The hard drive.

She pulled the bag out and quickly popped the seal on it. Then she went to the bottom of her purse and lifted the false bottom. Both drives were the same three and a half inch profile, but the one from Saunders's home computer was in considerably better shape than she expected and it would be obvious that the one she and Vartan had torched wasn't the same drive. Hopefully by the time they discovered it they'd be in another state altogether. She placed the dummy hard drive in the evidence bag and put the real one in her purse, re-closing the false bottom panel. Then she took the evidence bag and started to put it back into the box.

Robbins voice stopped her.

"I'm afraid we can't let you remove any items unless an ASD officer accompanies the evidence offsite," Robbins said. He was standing behind her. How long had he been there, and how much had he seen?

She turned to look up at him. "Oh, I thought I could take it over to the field office."

"I'm afraid not," he said, firmness in his voice. "Computer hardware is not on our allowed distribution list."

Damn! Lori had initially thought that Hansen's insolence would be an asset in getting her close to the evidence pile. Now, she realized it had just wounded Robbins' pride and made him more rigid than he might otherwise have been. She quickly stuffed the dummy hard drive back in the box, hoping he didn't notice how burned it was.

"Oh that's all right," she said, thinking quickly. "I just needed to pull it out to get to what I was after." She searched the floor in front of her, then picked up a bag. "This clock."

"That's odd," Robbins said, leaning down to look into the box. "I could have sworn that hard drive was at the bottom of that box. I packed it myself."

Lori leaned in front of him to pick up the other items, exposing a bit more cleavage as she did so. She smiled and quickly re-packed the box, then handed the clock to Robbins. He stooped to help her as she lifted the evidence box.

"No Miss Balver, you'd better let me do that. I need to recalibrate the box before I put it back on the shelf."

Lori sucked in a quick breath. She hadn't noticed the flat platforms adorning the bottom of each evidence shelf. They were scales. If the dummy hard drive didn't weigh within a few ounces of the real one, an alarm would sound and she'd be locked inside here with Robbins.

Robbins went over to a smaller scale at the head of the aisle and placed the evidence bag containing the clock on it. Then he beeped a few buttons and set it aside on a separate table top tray. She assumed the weight of the clock was now subtracted from the total weight of the box. He nodded to her and she stooped to pick up the evidence box, but pretended to struggle with it. He was quick to come around and lift it for her, giving her an opportunity to reach into her handbag and find the handle of her gun. Her grip tightened on it as he lifted the box, and she released the safety on it as he plopped the box back down on the upper shelf.

She waited, her hand on the pistol as the little yellow lights ran back and forth on the scale monitor while it calculated the new weight. After a few seconds, the lights stood still, turned green, and a beeping tone was emitted. The weight was close enough. She could breathe again.

"OK, I guess I can let you have the clock, at least," Robbins said conversationally. Technically, it doesn't fall into the category of an electronic device, at least not in the sense that I meant it when I wrote the evidence room rules."

"How lucky for me that I got the guy who set those rules up to help me out," she said, smiling up at him while she walked back to the evidence room door.

"Yep," he agreed.

After a few minutes of paperwork, Lori was out the door and walking across the parking lot to the little gray Toyota. She was just reaching out for the door handle when she heard Robbins voice behind her. "Miss Balver." He had an urgent tone to his voice.

"Yes?" she said, turning.

Robbins was trotting across the parking lot, trailing after her and holding out his right hand and flicking his fingers in a demanding gesture. Over his shoulder, she could see Vartan emerging from around the side of the building. He had gone to acquire them yet another car, and had apparently decided to check on her progress. She assumed he had become alarmed at the sight of the police officer chasing after her and holding out his hand. He was walking briskly across the parking lot and looking all around him, the way undercover police did when they thought they might have to use a gun in public.

"I'm afraid I can't let you take that," Robbins said.

Lori tensed. She started to reach into her purse for her own gun, just as she saw Vartan go under his loose fitting white shirt to his hip pocket for his.

"Excuse me?" she said, hoping her voice did not betray her concern.

Robbins stopped just short of her bumper, and once again indicated with a gesture that he wanted something from her.

"Your temporary badge," he said, pointing to her chest. "I need it back."

"Oh," Lori said, cracking her widest smile. "I did almost run off with that, didn't I?"

She kept one eye on Vartan as she took her time unpinning the badge and handing it back to Robbins. He had stopped about twenty feet behind them, watching. Before he turned to go back into the office, Robbins evidently decided to make one last impression on her. "I certainly want to say it was a real treat having you here. I hope you make it back here soon."

She cocked her head slightly to the side and then slipped her sun glasses down on her nose and looked at him over them.

"Well, I've got to catch a plane now, but if you ever make it out to LA, I'd be glad to show you around a bit," she said, just the slightest flirtation in her voice. "You know, one officer to another?"

He broke into a wide grin. "I'd like that," he said far too quickly.

"Good. You can get my number from the directory at the field office."

"I sure will!"

"OK," she said, turning and getting into her car. "Bye."

"Bye-bye," he said back, still beaming. He watched her back out, put the car in gear and drive away, and she waved to him from the window. Vartan had retreated to a far parking lot, started his car and also waved at Robbins as he drove past slowly. Robbins tipped his hat to Vartan as he walked back to the police station. *He never knew how close he was to dying,* Lori thought.

Maybe none of them did.

24.

They met, as had been prearranged, in the parking lot of an abandoned electronics store in Bernalillo. Lori parked the Toyota close to the building where it couldn't be seen from the street easily. She left the keys and stood up as Vartan pulled up in the latest vehicle he had procured, a red wine colored 2004 Dodge Intrepid SXT. She hoped it would be the last one for a while.

"I assume you got it?" he asked impatiently. She smiled and pulled up the false bottom in her bag and handed him the drive. "Good," he said. "Did you have any trouble?"

"Almost," she said, "but I handled it."

"I was concerned there at the end."

She nodded. "I noticed that. You weren't supposed to be anywhere near the area."

"I found a car quicker than I expected, and I knew you were nervous about getting caught, so I decided to see if you needed any help."

"Now you need to work on trusting me," she said firmly.

"I suppose. It's hard for me to allow myself to be dependent on others. I assumed you understood that."

"Knowing it and accommodating it are two different things, Vartan. You could have blown it for us."

He used his eyebrows to give a quick acknowledgement of her point. "So they didn't check with the field office on your ID?"

"No. They didn't seem to be all that concerned about who I was."

He nodded again. "That tells us something."

"Yeah, that they haven't told anybody that you might be traveling with an FBI agent." She sighed, just slightly. "I wish I could access the police bulletin services. That way we'd know what they had put out on us."

"It's way too dangerous. Besides, I'm beginning to think they didn't put anything out on us at all."

This was an idea she hadn't considered. Might it be to the advantage of whoever was pursuing them not to have the police involved. "Even Ruby would have a hard time stopping that one," she disagreed. "How would he keep Marshall and everybody else from looking for me? For all they know, you've kidnapped me."

"True, but what if he's assigned someone to the case specifically? Someone he can trust to do nothing? Couldn't he then refer all inquiries to that officer?"

She nodded. "Theoretically. But he'd have to convince Marshall and Ron Harmon that he was following up on leads. Not to mention Connie when she gets up and around."

"Maybe he's convinced them they're better off leaving it to others. Maybe he convinced them they're too close to the problem. Too emotionally invested."

She had to admit that was a possibility. "But, why would Ruby, or whoever is behind him, not want law enforcement help?"

He opened his palms and shrugged again. "Maybe they're freer to deal with us in their own way without law enforcement. No warrants and procedures and Miranda rights. Just find us and kill us."

She looked around the deserted back lot of computer store. "Maybe we should consider trying to make the police our friends."

He appeared to mull that idea for just a bit. "I don't think so. Possibly if things were different. But right now we can't trust them."

Lori held her breath as a police cruiser passed them in the opposite direction and kept going.

"All we've got is each other," he reminded her.

Lori was about to say something when she heard the screech of car tires closing quickly behind her. Shocked, she turned to see an Albuquerque police cruiser pull up next to her Toyota while the two officers quickly exited the vehicle and trained their guns on her. "Freeze!" the policeman yelled in unison. They were both white and slightly overweight, and she wondered how easily Vartan would handle them when he got close enough to disarm them. She turned, expecting to see him getting out of the Dodge, but instead he threw the car into reverse and also screeched his tires as he laid rubber down on the asphalt.

Lori's heart raced as she watched him expertly spin the bulky American mid-size around and power off into the distance, turning a sharp left and disappearing behind the carcass of the abandoned warehouse.

He had been using her all along. Now that he had the hard drive, he was abandoning her, leaving her to the local cops to fend for herself. She stood frozen.

"Hands in the air lady!" the fatter cop shouted. Snapping herself out of her unmoving state, she turned and complied, letting her purse slide down to her elbow. Now her heart sank. She never truly trusted Vartan, but she never thought he'd leave her hanging at his first opportunity.

"Tim, call that car in. We got us a couple 'a looters," the fatter cop said, seemingly quite self-satisfied with his catch. As the second cop lowered his head to get into the cruiser, Lori again heard a sudden screech of tires straining to gain grip on asphalt. It was a red wine colored Dodge coming around the corner from behind the police officers.

Vartan.

He revved the car engine as best he could – it was clearly no Mercedes – and aimed right for the standing police cruiser. The smaller police officer looked over his shoulder to see Vartan coming back; he must have circled all around the abandoned building. He panicked and jumped away, but Vartan swerved at the last minute to avoid hitting him and the man stumbled backwards out of the car and fell sharply on his back, his unprotected head hitting the pavement with a resounding "crack!"

"Tim!" the fatter officer exclaimed, turning and lowering his gun just slightly. It was all the opening Lori needed.

She crossed quickly to the other side of the Toyota while the fat cop was fixated on Vartan and the other officer. Swinging her heavy purse as hard as she could, she clubbed him on the right side of the head with it and he went down in a heap, his gun clattering away. As he tried to regain his feet, Lori kicked him swiftly under the chin with her heel and his eyes rolled up as he went swiftly unconscious. She turned to see Vartan had pulled the Intrepid up to the scene and was ready to get out and finish them off, but they were both dead to the world. "Sorry I was late getting back. I assumed you needed help," he deadpanned.

She wasn't about to smile. "All we have is each other, huh? For a minute there I was pretty sure you were going to take what you needed and ditch me."

He straightened up in the driver's seat of the Intrepid and hit the unlock button for the passenger side. "For a moment there, I considered it."

Vartan drove them around for almost an hour before he was satisfied they weren't being followed and then pulled into another cheap motel. It took them only a few minutes to get situated and get the laptop plugged into the drive and whirring to life. Within a minute or so, it was obvious from his expression that there was something wrong.

"What's the matter?" she asked, trying to prevent the deep concern she was feeling from creeping into her tone.

After a few moments of silence, he cursed under his breath and slammed his fist on the table, though not as forcefully as he could have. "This isn't the real hard drive," he lamented. "It's a fake."

"What?"

"Yeah. Somebody got to that evidence room before we did."

"Are you sure?"

He got a bit irritated with her at that moment, she thought. "Yes, I'm sure. I should have noticed the serial number on this drive doesn't even match the configuration on Richard's computer."

He put his hand over his mouth. She sat dejectedly on the bed. "So what do we do now?"

He shook his head. "I don't know. I should have anticipated this. They've been a step ahead of us the entire way."

"Except they don't know where we are," she reminded him. The look he gave convinced her that he knew they'd be hunted down sooner or later. She had not seen him this down before, and this was the first time she thought he might not have a plan in mind. They were going to have to scramble now.

"Where could they have taken it?" She asked the question knowing there was no good answer. She just couldn't let him give up. If he did, they were as good as dead.

He leaned forward and closed his hands over his nose and mouth. "No telling. Probably just destroyed it. We'll never get it back."

She could see the fight draining from him moment by moment. She couldn't let that happen. She hit him on the shoulder, more than a play tap but not hard enough to really hurt him. She just wanted his attention. "God damn it Vartan, we have to do something! We can't let these bastards win this easily."

He completely ignored the fact that she had just struck him. "Please don't use pop psychology on me, Lori. If I could think of anything useful to do, I'd be doing it. But the truth is they've out maneuvered us." He looked out at the late afternoon sun. "We're done."

She tightened her lips. "No we're not. We have to keep going. There has to be a clue somewhere."

He threw his left hand up. "All right. Where?"

She didn't know. "I don't know. Maybe we should go to Garvin's house? Maybe the police missed something important."

He chuckled slightly, disdainfully, and rubbed his temples. "OK Lori. Fine. We'll go to Garvin's house. Fine."

She started to grab her things, but he held her arm. "But not until after dark," he told her. She nodded in acknowledgement, studying his face. He seemed quietly resolved to defeat. "Do you think they'll be waiting for us there?"

"Possibly," he said. Then he took out his gun and began to clean it.

"I'm getting the impression you wouldn't mind that very much," she said. He gave her a look indicating his disagreement, but she wasn't buying it. "I think you wouldn't mind a straight up fight to all this skulking around."

He kept cleaning. "Again, spare me the pop psychology. I'm just trying to stay alive at the moment. Like you are."

Lori didn't say another word. She decided maybe she'd better clean her gun too.

25.

It was just after dusk when they pulled up to Garvin's house, running on the Intrepid's fog lights. It was easy to spot which house had been his, since there was only a charred pile of charcoal-black embers where there should be a sprawling rambler. All of the other houses in the area were equally spaced on large plots, with brush and cacti and long gravel driveways up to the homes.

Lori was surprised by the amount of destruction the fire had caused. She didn't realize that a stucco home could burn so completely to the ground. Vartan exited the car and closed the door quietly and she did the same. A Border collie in a neighboring backyard began to bark softly at them from behind a chain link fence, but he quieted down when he saw they weren't coming toward his territory.

It was very dark in the foothills, with the Milky Way arcing out across the sky and partially blotted out by the nearby Sandia Mountains. Lori could see the dim light of the Sandia tramway as it ran up the thin cable to the top of the ten-thousand foot high mountain peak. Looking around she found the constellation Sagittarius and the dense galactic core, visible against the faintly glittering sky as huge black serpent about to consume its own tail. She instantly recognized the symbol of the ouroboros from the henna tattoo she had gotten just a few days before.

"At least we'll be able to see anyone coming," Vartan said sardonically.

Lori nodded, and then realized he probably could not see the gesture in the gauzy light of the night sky and simply murmured a tone of agreement. Vartan's white long sleeved shirt stood out, even in the low light, and she followed his ghostly form as he walked over to where the police had erected a line of evidence tape. He surprised her when he cut it with a pocket knife he pulled from inside his lower left pant leg. She hadn't even been aware that he carried a knife. She stole one last glimpse of the stars and followed him into what was left of the house.

Vartan made his way to the back of the lot, to just past where it looked like the garage had been, judging from the sooty concrete slab. He kicked at a few piles of cinders and debris until he seemed satisfied with his understanding of the layout.

"This is where his office would have been," he said to her, holding out his arms to indicate the basic parameters of a room. She stepped over some burned planks and charred boxes to join him there. "Do your policeman's instincts tell you anything?" She was surprised not so much by the question, but by the defeatist - if not outright derisive -tone of it.

"What do you expect me to do Vartan, channel a clue out of this pile of rubbish? We have to look around, and be systematic about it. That's how we find something useful."

"Very well, but I still think this is a waste of time."

So did Lori actually, but she couldn't think of anything else to do, either. She stooped down and began to sift through the charred remains of Garvin's life. Amazingly, she almost immediately found a small wooden pyramid with a gold medallion on one face, a raised sculpture of the Face on Mars on another, and an emblem of Mars itself on the third face. The bottom was covered with black felt. She surmised it must have been a gift or award of some kind.

It was always surprising to her the kinds of things that survived fires. As a little girl, her neighbor's house had burnt substantially when a space heater caught the curtains on fire, and her best friend Jessie had lost nearly everything, including her beloved teddy bear, Lizzie. But somehow, a picture of she and Lori at Disneyland the summer before had gone almost unscorched, expect for a bit of browning at the edges. It became a prized possession of Jessie's. She carried it to school for months in her backpack, hanging on to a crucial if not solitary link to the past. She'd kept it with her for at least a year like that, until well after their house had been rebuilt and their belongings replaced. She remembered how violated Jessie had felt as the whole neighborhood had come out to watch their house burn down. She wondered if somewhere Richard Garvin was feeling the same way about them sorting through the remnants of his life.

She held the little wooden pyramid up to Vartan, who didn't notice it until a glint of light caught the metal medallion just right. He took it from her and examined it incredulously. "I remember when he got this. A fan that was also a sculptor made it for him. A tetrahedral pyramid with the Face on Mars on it. She gave it to him at a lecture in Phoenix. It must have been 1999 or so."

Lori could see a hint of emotion on his face, even in the dim star light. He'd cared about Garvin, that much was obvious to her. "It's strange what survives," she said, trying to sound sympathetic, "and what doesn't."

He looked around again, acknowledged her with a nod and then went to the car to put the little pyramid away. Lori went back to sifting. She got down on her knees to go though some of the papers from the office, occasionally using a pen light to read those that weren't too badly burned. She found several letters from fans, a patent for a water powered hydraulic engine, and bits of what looked like a contract for a TV appearance on a cable TV channel. There were so many fragments it was hard to tell what was what.

"I'm going to try looking in another part of the house," Vartan told her when he returned. She didn't answer. He walked to the other end of the ruined house, presumably toward the bedroom, and begin to work his way though chunks of rubble there. They worked separately for the next fifteen minutes or so, not finding anything of significance.

She was beginning to agree with Vartan that this was all waste of their time. If Garvin had received the schematics they were looking for, they were probably on the stolen hard drive or burned along with the rest of his papers. Maybe it was time to give in to Vartan and abandon the search before their pursuers decided to stake out the place looking for them.

"We should go," she called out to him from across the burned slab of concrete that once held Garvin's house. "This is pointless."

He reached out and kicked over another piece of debris. "I suppose you're right," he said dejectedly. "But we could go through what's left of the boxes in the garage."

She felt herself shiver. The night air was getting cooler. "I don't want to. I just want to get out of here. This has been the weirdest couple nights of my life. And lately, that's saying something."

He could see her crossed arms as she tried to warm herself. "All right. Let's get you out of here." He looked left and right, as if he too was worried that they had lingered too long. He crossed to her side of the house and reached out and took her arm to guide her back to the car.

Before they got a step, they were surprised as they were bathed in light from headlights coming up the driveway. They both froze momentarily. Vartan took his hand from her arm and started to fumble for his gun. Lori took a second longer to react, and by then a truck had stopped at the end of the driveway and the door was being opened up. They were both nearly blinded, their eyes having become so used to the deep black mountain night that they were overwhelmed. Vartan jumped to his left and out of the beam, finally getting his gun up to his hip. For some reason, he held back from firing.

Out of the beam, a smallish man walked deliberately toward them. He held his own hand in front of his eyes. "Trev?" It was the voice of an older man, at least sixty, Lori thought. "Trevor Vartan?"

Vartan squinted against the light and then came forward, lowering his gun. "Ken? Ken Marsden is that you?"

The man let out a jovial chuckle. "It is you! I'd recognize that homo British accent anywhere."

Now the man had stepped into the light and Lori could see he was slightly built and in his early sixties, just as she had suspected. He wore a faded tan windbreaker and loose fitting blue jeans. He had a nice smile, a head full of gray hair and a playful demeanor. She noted that he would have been quite handsome when he was younger.

Vartan smiled and reached out his hand. "Ken, you're the last person on Earth I would have expected to run into."

Marsden took his hand and shook it vigorously, putting his thumb oddly on top of Vartan's hand. Then the smile on his face faded. "I heard about Richard on *Nationwide AM* coming up here. I guess you'd know better than anybody. Is it true?"

Vartan nodded solemnly. "Yes Ken, I'm afraid it is. He's gone."

"Thought so," he said quickly, "but I'd hoped . . ." He looked around the burned out hulk of the house. "Never thought it could happen. Guess I was wrong."

Vartan looked to Lori. "This is Ken Marsden. He's a friend of Richard's." Then he turned back to Ken. "This is Special Agent Pars from the FBI. She's investigating the case."

"Well, well," Ken said, a knowing tone in his voice, "and here I thought she was just another one of your honeys." Lori smiled at him. She could see that he had the potential to be charming. She took his hand, and he shook it normally, without the raised thumb movement.

"I'm very sorry about your friend," she said sincerely.

He tipped his head to her. "Well ma'am, I always told him he was messing with the wrong people. But I never thought he was really in this much danger."

Vartan looked slightly uncomfortable as he addressed Marsden. "None of us did, Ken."

Lori reached out to Ken. "Mr. Marsden, if you don't mind my asking, what exactly are you doing here?"

"Well, one thing is I just wanted to see for myself if the stories were true or not." He looked around. "I guess I have my answer on that one." Then he went back over to the passenger side door of his truck and opened it, reaching in to retrieve a thick, soft cover package. He brought it around to the front of the truck and handed it to Vartan. "The other reason is this."

Vartan took the package and examined it. It was still sealed but had no return address or postage on it. The only thing written on it was the name "Richard Garvin" printed on a plain white mailing label. Ken pointed to it. "I found it in my mailbox this morning. I hadn't heard any of the news reports on Richard's murder, so when I tried to call and got no answer, I figured I'd better head up here and give it to him. It seemed like it was important."

Vartan looked at Lori and then tore the seal on the package, pulling out the heavily bubble wrapped contents and then cutting through the wrap with his knife. Inside the bubble wrap was a simple black velvet bag. Vartan opened the rope tie on it and reached in. When his hand came out, Lori saw a flash of light off a bright aluminum panel.

It was a three and half inch computer hard drive.

She reached out and took it from him, his eyes wide and her mouth agape. It was charred and discolored, evidently from being exposed to intense heat, but it was otherwise intact. Neither of them could think of anything to say. "Vartan . . ." she trailed off.

"Don't question it," he said sharply, "just take it."

"I'm guessin' you two think this is important?" Ken drawled.

Vartan nodded. "It's what we came here looking for, Ken." He looked back over his shoulder at the road. "But we need to get away from here and examine it more closely."

Marsden took the cue. "I suppose we'd best be on our way then. Do you need a place to stay?"

Lori and Vartan exchanged glances. He opened his mouth to say something, but Lori beat him to it. "Actually we do," she said.

"Great. Come on down to my ranch. You can stay there as long as you like."

"That'd be good Ken. Thank you," Vartan said, staring Lori down the whole time. They went to their car and got in. Once the doors were shut, it was obvious Vartan was intensely unhappy with her. "You shouldn't have done that. I didn't want to involve him. He's got a wife and about a dozen grand kids."

"I thought it was something like that, but we need a place to go and I doubt the bad guys will think to look for us there, at least not right away." She reached over and picked up the hard drive. "Besides, it seems like somebody else has already involved him."

Lori and Vartan got belted in and were following Marsden out of the development before she spoke again. "Do you ever get the feeling somebody's trying to tell you something?" she asked him earnestly. "Is somebody trying to tell us we have allies?"

He shrugged. "I honestly have no idea," he said to her, his unhappiness dissipated. "But someone's helping us."

As the two vehicles moved slowly down the gravel driveway, a figure stood alone in the darkness and watched them leave, waiting until they were out of sight before venturing from his hiding place behind a neighbor's shed. As he walked to his own vehicle, the man straightened his charcoal colored suit and the Border collie made a nervous sound at him. The figure turned and looked back but continued on his way, ignoring the dog as he quietly dropped his paper coffee cup into a green plastic garbage bin.

26.

It was nearly three hours down to Ken's ranch, an isolated homestead in the hills about twenty-five miles from Roswell. As few as three days ago, the mythical home of the world's first flying saucer crash would have been the last place on earth Lori would have expected to find herself. Now it seemed to align perfectly with her present circumstances and coming here seemed natural.

She and Vartan got out of the Dodge and Vartan went to the trunk to retrieve his laptop. They followed Ken up the gravel walkway to his house silently. Ken opened his unlocked front door and excused himself, disappearing into a back room. Lori and Vartan turned to their right to head into the front room. There were toys and baby bottles scattered everywhere, along with children's clothing of various sizes and both genders, and Wal-Mart bags filled with board games, stuffed animals and bags of candy.

"They babysit the grand kids a lot," Vartan said to her under his breath.

"I guess," she whispered back to him. She could hear the low rumblings of Ken speaking quietly in a back room somewhere.

Vartan pointed to a space on the couch, which was a hideous broken down red-brown settee, and she put her bag on it. She pulled out the hard drive and handed it to him, and then he made his way through the litter on the floor and began to set up his equipment on the dining room table. He had to clear a pile of shopping bags off one of the folding metal chairs just to create a place to sit. Lori was aware of a shuffling sound coming from the back of the house and turned just as Marsden emerged from the darkened hallway with a very petite woman in a pale blue bathrobe and slippers. He stood aside to let her go into the front room first, and she gave him a little look indicating that she was unhappy he hadn't made way for her sooner. "Lori, I'd like you to meet my wife Fran," Ken said formally. The lady bowed a quick nod in Lori's direction, not cracking even the slightest of smiles.

"Hello ma'am, I'm Special Agent Lori Pars of the F.B.I. Thank you for having us in your home." Lori was polite, but made no extra effort to be nicer than Fran was being.

Fran sized her up carefully and then spoke loudly, in Vartan's direction. "Well, you've managed to improve the quality of your company," she said with just a hint of teasing in her voice. Vartan looked up from his makeshift desk at the kitchen table and smiled. It was a relaxed, disarming, handsome smile, one that Lori had never seen from him before.

"That's what happens when you hang around with women that carry guns," he said playfully. "It can't help but improve the quality of your company."

Fran smirked and made a little grunting sound, then put her eyes back on Lori. "The last time this big secret agent showed up here he brought along a belly dancer," she said very loudly.

"She was a ballroom dancing instructor," Vartan protested.

"Hmmpf," Fran made the little sound again. "Ballroom dancer my ass," she said back to him. "She had a tattoo of a snake on her . . ."

"Now momma . . ." Ken cut in, his tone cautionary. A little smile creased his face. Fran considered her husband just briefly before she decided to drop it. She turned her attention back to Lori. "It's late ma'am. Can I get you some coffee or tea?"

Lori caught Vartan's eye and smiled wryly. "Tea would be wonderful, thank you," Lori said. Fran began to make her way toward the kitchen and Lori followed after her, keeping her eyes on Vartan. "I'll come in and help you. That'll give us a chance to discuss that belly dancer," Lori said. She found it more than mildly amusing that Fran evidently thought she was Vartan's girlfriend.

A few minutes later, she sat with Ken and Fran in the living room while Vartan worked at the dining room table, within earshot.

"I worked at NASA nearly thirty-five years," he was telling Lori. Fran sat calmly sipping her coffee, her expression indicating she'd heard this all many times before.

"First Apollo, then later Skylab and then the Shuttle." He shook his head then, ruefully.

"And in all that time, I never really suspected anything wasn't right. Not until I met Richard. Then a whole bunch of things started to make sense. A bunch of weird experiences started to add up."

"Weird experiences?" Lori wasn't just being polite, she wanted to know.

Ken sat up in his seat. "Things I saw. Things people said."

"Like when they told you to destroy the photographs?"

"Oh, you know about that?" He seemed genuinely pleased.

Lori nodded. "Trevor . . . Trev and I have had a lot of time to talk on the way down here," she said.

Fran smirked again. "I thought you were just working together." Lori could tell she thought she was really on the scent of some big scoop.

"We are," Lori said, smiling. "He's helping me on the case. We drove down here from Nevada."

Abruptly Fran got mad, her cheeks reddening. "Well I sure as hell hope you get the bastards that did this," she said sharply. "Richard was a good friend. He didn't deserve what happened to him."

No one ever does, Lori thought to herself. "We're trying," she said, hoping she sounded sympathetic enough.

There was an awkward silence as Fran's eyes welled up. Ken put his arm around her to comfort her. "I'm sorry sweetie," she said to Ken.

"Now that's OK," he said gently back to her. "That's OK." He pulled her a little tighter, and Lori gave them a few moments to work though it all. She realized she'd never been close enough to a man to have ever been comforted like that. Watching them, with so much obvious history and shared experience between them, she actually felt a little jealous.

After a bit, Fran excused herself and returned to the bedroom. Lori turned her attention back to Ken.

"Tell me your stories," she said. "Please."

Ken leaned forward, his intensity clearly picking up.

"I used to be a fighter pilot back in Vietnam. After my tour, I went to NASA through the Grumman Corporation. I got assigned to astronaut flight training for the Lunar Module. I spent a lot of time at the Cape and also in Houston, at the Manned Spacecraft Center. Anyway, I used to train the astronauts to fly the Lunar Module, and I got to be good friends with a lot of them. Dave Erving, he was the commander of Apollo 15, we used to lead bible study together. But my best friend was probably Dan Alden. He was the second man to walk on the Moon. He and I used to go out quite a bit. Dan wasn't much of a drinker, but he was a real friendly, philosophical guy."

"Was he also a Freemason?" Lori asked, knowing it might be a touchy subject. Ken got an amused expression on his face.

"I see you and Trev have been talking about a lot of things. Yes he was. He even sponsored me into the Freemasons back in the day." He held out his left hand for her so she could inspect the ornate gold and diamond encrusted Masonic ring that he wore on his ring finger in place of his wedding band. She resisted the temptation to ask him how Fran felt about that.

"Wow, that's really . . . blingy," she said, hiding the big ring that Vartan had bought for her in Las Vegas.

Ken smiled at her. "Anyways, after Apollo, he and I stayed in touch. Even though we lived in separate states, we'd get together two or three times a year for a round of golf or some poker. One time, I guess this was 1983 or so, I decided to ask him about some of the rumors I'd heard. That he'd taken the Scottish Rite flag to the Moon and that he'd performed a ceremony with it, and that the mission had been paced by UFO's the whole time. Well, he was fine talking about the flag, but he got real uncomfortable when I started asking about the ceremony, questioning whether it was really a Christian ceremony or a Masonic one. Then he just flat blew up when I asked him about the UFO's. He just threw his clubs down, gave me a dirty look and stomped off the green. I haven't spoken to him or heard from him since."

Lori could see the regret in his eyes, that he hadn't known that his questions would cost him the friendship. "I'm sorry," was all she could think of to say. She seemed to be doing that a lot around these people.

"It's OK ma'am. I should have thought better of it and not done it." He leaned back on the sofa, his eyes welling up a bit.

"What else?" Lori asked him, wanting to shift away from his lost friendship with Tyrol.

"Oh. I'm sorry," Ken said apologetically. He'd clearly lost his way thinking about the last exchange with Alden.

"Well, they used to have these steel trailers at the MSC in Houston out in back of the LEM training facility. That was where the landing site selection committees would meet. I used to watch Dr. Sadat . . ."

"Farouk Sadat?" Lori cut in.

"Yeah," Ken said. "The Pharaoh himself. And Dr. Pace, Dr. Tessers, I used to watch all those guys come through our building on the way to their meetings. I could never figure out why those meetings were closed, why nobody could find out what was discussed. It didn't make any sense to me. Now of course, I know what they were hiding. Anyway, one day after they're done with their meeting, I wander back there 'cause I'm curious why it's all so hush-hush. So I try the trailer door and it's unlocked. I go in there, and there are all these big blue three-ring binders full of papers and stuff. So I start to leaf through them, and I come across this picture of Mare Crisium, that's a big dark sea area in the north. And I'm looking at it, and I swear if it doesn't show these big clear domes over some of the craters on the floor of Crisium. And right in the middle of the picture is this big, glowing tower, like some kind of glass skyscraper or something. So I start to get freaked out. I quickly memorize the frame number, it was an Apollo ten picture, and just as I set the book down I hear this voice from behind me that tells me to freeze. One of the security guys is standing there pointing his gun at me! So I freak out and put my hands up, and the guy searches me and takes me away. They put me in this detention cell and they interview me for like three hours. I almost got fired. I just could never figure out why they were so pissed off if there was nothing to all this."

"Did you say anything about the picture?"

Marsden shook his head. "No way. But later I looked it up in the Apollo 10 catalog, and it was there, but none of the weird structures were on it. It was whitewashed."

"And this didn't arouse your suspicions?"

Ken smiled a quick, pedantic little smile. "Ma'am, I didn't have time to be suspicious. We were all so busy, it was all we could do keep our heads above water. Remember, we all thought we were in a race to beat the Russians to the Moon."

Lori felt properly put in her place, and nodded her acknowledgement. Satisfied that he had regained her attention, Marsden went on.

"Then one other time I was taking a shortcut through the photo lab to get to a meeting, and I saw these young kids, interns I guess they were, airbrushing all these pictures of the Moon taken on the Apollo missions. I talked to one of them, and he said they were told to clean up defects on the negatives so they could use them for press kits. Now, airbrushing prints to clean them up for a press release, that's one thing, but these kids were airbrushing *negatives*, which you never do because you want to preserve your originals in case you need to do a photography study later."

She nodded again. "But maybe you do it if you want to cover things up. Make sure nobody can get their hands on the real stuff?"

"But that's not the best story."

She sipped her tea, eyebrows raised.

"Well, on that particular case, this was Apollo fourteen. After we had received the film, right after the astronauts had returned to the Earth, it had been processed in the NASA photo lab. It was my responsibility to put together a private viewing for the chief astronomer, that was Dr. Terry Pace and his associates and contributing scientists. I took the film over and set it up into what is called a sequence projector. It's kind of like one of the gun cameras they use in the military where you can stop, freeze frame, go forward, back up and zoom in.

"And we were viewing the Apollo fourteen footage, coming around the backside of the Moon as we were approaching a large crater. Now this particularly large crater showed a cluster of about five or six lights down inside the rim. And this column or plume, or out-gassing or something, was coming up above the rim of the crater. At that point Dr. Pace had me stop and freeze and back up; and go back and forth several times. And each time, he'd pause a second and look, and he finally turned to his associates and said: 'Well, isn't *that* interesting!' And they all chuckled and laughed, and Dr. Pace said 'Continue.'"

"Well, I finished up that viewing and I was told to check the sequence camera film back into NASA bonded storage in the photo lab. The next day, I was to check it back out and show it to the rank-and-file engineers and scientists at the Center. I was pretty freaked out, but I did what I was told."

"While we were viewing it the second time and several of my friends were sitting next to me, I was telling them: 'You can't believe what we saw on the backside of the Moon! Wait until you see this view.'

"And, as we were approaching the same crater and we went past the crater, there was nothing there! I stopped the camera, took the film out to examine it to see if anything had been cut out and there was no evidence of anything being cut out. I told the audience that we were having 'technical difficulties,' put it back in and finished. That afternoon, I ran into Dr. Pace over at the Lunar Receiving Laboratory and asked him what had happened to the lights and the out-gassing or steam we saw, and he kind of grinned and gave me a little twinkle and a chuckle and said: 'There were no lights. There is nothing there.' And he walked away. And, we were so busy, I didn't get a chance to question him again."

Lori realized she'd been sitting there almost frozen, listening to his stories. "Did you ever find out anything else about the film? What happened to it?"

Ken shook his head. "No. The only way they could have done it was to take it out overnight, cut it, splice it, then make a copy of the spliced version and put that one back in the bonded storage. I think that's what they must have done. Years later, I just kind of forgot about all this. Until I met Richard . . ." he trailed off, sadness in his eyes again.

The moment lingered, and then they were both distracted when Vartan suddenly stood bolt-upright. Lori and Ken could both see immediately something was very wrong.

"What is it?" Lori called from her seat. When Vartan didn't respond, she looked at Ken and then they both got up and went over to the computer to look at the screen. All it showed were two windows, one with the schematics Lori had seen before and one with a series of tables full of numbers. Vartan didn't acknowledge either of them at first.

"I think I know what they're going to do," he finally said. Lori put her hand on his right forearm, and Ken studied the screen for some hint of what he was talking about. Vartan just continued to stare at the screen, barely acknowledging either of them. Lori caught Ken's eye, a worried look on her face. She'd never seen Vartan like this.

Ken put his hand on Vartan's left shoulder and nudged him just a bit. "C'mon buddy, talk to us. You're scaring the young lady here," he said.

Vartan turned to him and then back to Lori, seeming to come out of his state of shock. "They're going to blow it up," he said to her simply, as if it was self-evident what he was talking about.

She made a motion with her mouth, as if she was going to speak, then thought better of it. She reached down and took his hand. It was rougher and more calloused than she expected. "I don't understand," she said softly. "What are you talking about?"

He looked again at Ken and her, in sequence, his face ashen. "Jupiter," he said. "They're going to blow up Jupiter."

27.

Lori got Vartan some tea and she and Ken cleared two chairs and pulled them up next to the kitchen table where Vartan had the laptop laid out. After a few sips, he seemed calmer and clearer and started to explain himself to them.

"These files, these schematics and tables, they're the reason Dr. Tsien and Richard were killed," he told them flatly. "This is what Tsien was trying to get Saunders to look at more closely. He slipped them in with some of the MRO pictures of Martian ruins hoping that anybody monitoring him would be more concerned about pictures. But he was wrong. They realized what he was trying to do."

"I don't get it," Lori offered. "What's so important about the satellite specifications?"

Vartan shot a glance at Ken and then addressed Lori. "Back in the nineties, NASA sent a probe to Jupiter called *Galileo*. It spent years orbiting and taking pictures and measurements of Jupiter and its moons. When they were through with it, they plunged it into the planet's atmosphere, supposedly to avoid contaminating the moon Europa. Before they did this, a NASA engineer put up a web site under a pseudonym where he warned that the plutonium pellets in Galileo's reactor could potentially go super-critical under the tremendous speed and compression of the plunge. His warnings were ignored and *Galileo* was destroyed apparently without incident."

"Super critical?" Lori was a little fuzzy on the physics of anything other than a nine-millimeter slug.

"It means that the plutonium-238 in the reactor could detonate, like a nuclear bomb," Ken told her.

"And that could have potentially started a nuclear chain reaction that would have ignited Jupiter," Vartan added, "into a second sun."

"But it wasn't a big enough load," Ken added quickly, as if to comfort her.

Vartan nodded in agreement. "But Richard found a black spot in Jupiter's clouds, almost a month later. It was identical to similar black spots caused by the Shoemaker-Levy-9 comet when it broke apart and plunged into Jupiter's atmosphere back in 1994. He calculated that it would have taken about that long from the destruction of *Galileo* for the carbon plasma cloud generated by the detonation to reach the surface and be visible."

"How does this relate to the schematics?" Ken asked.

Vartan pointed to the screen. "*Prometheus* uses a new ion propulsion system to get to Jupiter more than twice as fast as it normally takes. You could get there in two and a half years, as opposed to five. Previous versions were solar-electric, but they don't generate enough power. So the decision was made on *Prometheus* to use a plutonium fueled reactor, like the one on *Galileo*."

"But bigger, I assume?" Ken said.

Vartan nodded. "Much bigger. It's carrying almost two hundred pounds of plutonium-238."

"That seems like a lot," Lori said.

"Not really, not for a twenty year mission, which this was originally scheduled to be."

Lori could see where this was headed. "Originally scheduled . . . ?"

"Yes. After some budget cuts, the *Prometheus* mission was scaled back to only seven years. But there was one thing they didn't change."

Ken turned to him and Vartan looked him right in the eye. "They cut back the mission, but *they didn't cut back the fuel*. They left the two hundred pounds of plutonium-238 in the design all the way through."

Ken got it: "It's a giant atomic bomb," he said.

Vartan nodded again. "And one that will almost certainly finish the job that *Galileo* was sent to test out."

"You're saying that the *Galileo* destruction was a test? To see if the idea could work?" Lori asked.

"Yes. And this time, it *will* work. Unless we stop it."

Lori stood straight up and her chair fell backwards. "Whoa, whoa, whoa, stop what? What are you talking about?"

"*Prometheus* hasn't left yet. It launches from the Cape in three days," Ken told her.

"You're not suggesting . . ."

"That we go to the Cape and figure out some way to stop the launch? Yes, I am." Vartan spoke the words sharply to her. She could see that he was reinvigorated, that simply having a goal had energized him again.

Marsden could see it too. "Trev's right," Ken said to her. We've been expecting them to try to something sooner or later, but not something this big. We thought maybe we had run out the clock."

"OK," Lori said wearily, tired of always feeling like the only person in the room who didn't know what they were actually talking about. "Clue me in. Run out the clock on what?"

"The end game," Vartan. "The Masonic 'final solution,' if you will."

"Oh, fuck Vartan we're not back on that Masonic-Nazi crap again are we?" Even Lori was surprised by the intensity of her own response. She could feel her heart racing. This was beginning to sound more than simply crazy; it was scary.

Ken put a calming hand on her shoulder. "OK Miss, just calm down a bit. We've been at this so long together that sometimes we forget that you don't know everything we've found out." He motioned for her to sit down. When she didn't budge, he pressed down on her shoulder and guided her back into the chair. Reluctantly, she gave in to him.

"Now then," Ken began, his voice as soft and grandfatherly as he could make it, "we've been tracking NASA on this stuff for years, since just after we realized how many astronauts and NASA lifers were Freemasons. We believed they were operating on some kind of ritual calendar, that they were gearing up for something around 2012. But we had no idea what. The Masonic infiltration of NASA is pretty extensive."

"The Masonic infiltration of my family is pretty extensive too," Lori shot back. "What has that got to do with blowing up planets?"

Ken and Vartan exchanged a concerned look. "Young lady, I've been working for NASA since before you were a dirty thought in your daddy's mind. Besides the stories I told you, there was a whole lot more going on. Most all of my bosses were Masons. The higher you got in NASA, the more of them there were. Six of the twelve men who walked on the Moon were Masons. So were their program managers, the head of NASA itself, and so on. We found that NASA operated on a ritual calendar. That certain dates were sacred, and that they kept landing on the Moon and Mars on these dates and at specific times, with the stars all lined up according to ancient Masonic astrological charts."

"Again," Lori said brusquely, her frustration showing, "so what?"

"So we found out that many ancient calendars, the Mayan, the Aztec, the Babylonian, predict that the current cycle of time, the current epoch of human civilization, ended on December 21st, 2012. This just happens to coincide with a very significant stellar alignment of the Earth, the Sun, and the galactic center, and a major total solar eclipse."

"I've already discussed this with her," Vartan interjected.

"Well," Ken said, "that's fine. Have you also told her that a couple of Masonic scholars concluded that the Masonic calendar, the *Anno Lucis* calendar, recycles on the same day? That it in fact recycles at the exact same moment: 11:11 A.M. GMT?"

"We hadn't gotten to that part yet," Vartan admitted.

Lori suddenly realized that he must have known all along that their pursuers were some Masonic faction. The Catholic Church had nothing to do with it. Her eyes seared him. "You bastard. You've been holding back on me this whole time!"

"I've not," Vartan told her. "I only had suspicions. Nothing I didn't share with you."

"You knew all along that we were going to end up in Florida, to try and stop the launch, didn't you? What was I Vartan? A cover? A decoy for them to shoot at while you slipped out the back door?" He kept his eyes locked on hers, but she didn't waver. "I knew you were using me."

Vartan looked furious. "Lori, I'm only going to say this once, so you'd better get it. I had no idea what was happening, how this all fit together. Not until this very moment."

His stare was intense, and Lori wanted to believe him, but she just couldn't let go of the doubt. She got up from the chair and started to head for the door.

"Sit down!" Ken boomed at her. Lori was shocked by the force of his words, and she stopped. "Young lady, I have known this man for a long time, far longer than you have, and if he says he didn't know what they were planning before just now, well, then you can bank on that." He took two quick steps toward her, and she backed up. "Now sit down!"

Lori looked at Vartan again, and he simply stood his ground, looking right into her eyes.

She sat back down.

"*Anno-Lucis* means 'year of the light.'" Vartan stated, as if nothing had happened. "We always assumed that was symbolic, that some sort of event which prompted enlightenment or new knowledge would take place. That maybe the Masons were going to reveal what had been found on the Moon, or on Mars. Or maybe there would be some culture changing event, a true Harmonic Convergence or something."

He stopped there for a moment, and looked directly into her eyes again. "But now I think it's this. I think 'year of the light' means after Jupiter ignites. It means the light from a second sun."

"Even the name *Prometheus* is connected to the symbolism," Ken added. "Prometheus is the Greek god that gave the knowledge of fire to Man. The *Anno Lucis* calendar begins from the date that the Masons believe that we were given this gift by the gods. But unlike most calendars, it doesn't count up from some past event, like the *Anno Domini* calendar. It counts *down* to an event; the 'year of the light.' 2012."

Vartan stepped forward. "And of course it has a double meaning, as most Masonic references do. *Prometheus* is interchangeable with another ancient figure, the fallen angel who supposedly turned against god and tried to seduce Man."

"Satan," Lori interjected.

Ken shook his head. "No. The Masons believe that Satan is the Devil, yes. But they believe that the god who gave us the fire is another entity altogether and that his purpose was to enlighten us, rather than seduce or enslave us. That entities name wasn't Satan, it was Lucifer. We don't view him as evil. We view him by a literal interpretation of his name . . ."

"The Light Bringer," Lori said distantly, remembering her Bible studies.

"Exactly. In the Masonic view, Yahweh, the god of the Hebrew Bible, isn't the same being as the all knowing, all loving spirit that we call God. He's a separate and lower entity, one that seeks to enslave us here on this planet and keep us from connecting with the one true God. Prometheus, or Lucifer the Light Bringer, he was an opponent of Yahweh, and he didn't agree with that. He felt Man deserved to know the truth, and have the same powers that the gods did. And Yahweh punished him for that, and smeared his name, and tried to keep Man from truly using the gift of knowledge that he had given us. Secret societies, like the Knights Templar and the Freemasons, were set up to preserve the knowledge that the Light Bringer had given us."

Vartan took over from there. "But somewhere along the way, they lost sight of their original mission. A few inside the organization hijacked it for their own benefit. And now they're trying to literally bring fire to man. To make themselves the Light Bringers." He looked at Ken, as if he just had a sudden realization. "To make *themselves* our gods." Ken nodded silently. They both looked to Lori.

She tried to give them her best skeptical "I'm not buying it" look. "But this 2012 thing has come and gone. The world didn't end."

"Yes," Ken said measuredly. "And I'm sure that left some people very, very disappointed."

"So they decided to take matters into their own hands," Vartan added.

Lori was still skeptical. "You're asking me to believe that all this, these murders, the people that are chasing us, all has something to do with carrying out some ancient ritual?

To make sure the lights go on at the right time? Wouldn't the pictures of Mars be enough reason to go after Tsien and Garvin? Why does it have to be this?" She knew she sounded scared, and she was. It had been hard enough to go along when it was all about pictures and ruins, but this . . . Hollywood conspiracy; this was just too much.

She saw Vartan follow this play of emotion on her face, but he seemed unmoved by it. "They always had plausible deniability on artifacts. No matter how good the pictures are, they can always say they were Photoshopped. But this . . . keeping this quiet was worth killing for."

She stood and turned from him slightly but he reached out for her. "Lori, I've already done the preliminary calculations. If they're able to launch *Prometheus* as planned in three days, it will arrive in Jupiter orbit on or around mid-to-late December, 2017. If the orbital insertion burn goes wrong, if it's off by just a fraction of a second, *Prometheus* will fly at high velocity right into Jupiter's atmosphere, and this time with enough fissile material to turn the planet into a new sun. To change our world and the solar system we live in forever."

"Change isn't necessarily a bad thing," she offered weakly. "Is it?"

"It would be in this case," he said calmly.

Ken stepped in for Vartan. "The light and heat we'd feel right away, maybe an hour after the detonation, because radiant heat travels at or near the speed of light. A few hours after that, traveling much more slowly, would be the radioactive shockwave. The blast wave would be spherical, and it would dissipate somewhat over the millions of miles to the Earth. But it would hit us with searing heat and radiation, like a giant solar flare. Basically, it would sterilize the half of the planet that was facing the wave. Maybe even boil the oceans and set fire to the vegetation."

"And the shock wave would also pass through the asteroid belt between Mars and Jupiter, pushing thousands of asteroids into the interior of the solar system from their current stable orbits," Vartan warned. "The odds are pretty long, but it's a reasonable bet that we'd get hit with at least one or more of those objects at some point in the aftermath of the shock wave."

"An apocalypse," Lori said disdainfully. "You're asking me to believe that these people – NASA, are trying to create a man-made apocalypse?"

"Not NASA," Vartan argued. "A very small group at the top, inside of NASA. A rogue group of very powerful, very elite men who don't live by the same laws you do, hold the same values you do, or worship the same God you do."

"Vartan . . ."

He cut in before she could argue with him. "And yes, you could describe it as an apocalypse. About three-to-four billion people would die in the blast, another one and a half to two billion would die in the aftermath. Wars, famine, the competition for what was left of the available natural resources. Maybe one in five of us would be left after all that."

Lori shook her head skeptically. "But why would they do that? Why would they want to kill most of the world off and leave only a few of us left? What would there be left to rule over?"

Vartan looked at her with an expression that exuded compassion for her. "Have you ever read Milton, Lori?" She shook her head, not certain of the reference.

"Paradise Lost," Ken said solemnly. "Satan's last words to God as he was cast into the pit of Hell. 'It is better to reign in Hell than to serve in Heaven.'"

"And they'd be safe and comfortable, miles underground in their bases," Ken reminded her. "It wouldn't be so bad for them."

Lori turned away from them, still not ready to believe this bizarre scenario. This time Vartan did not attempt to stop her.

"I know this is hard for you," he said gently. "I know this isn't the world you've lived in up to now. But you have to trust me. I have. There's a war going on out there. A war between . . . "

"Good and evil?"

"No," he said earnestly. "Between those who want to keep us from our true heritage and those who want to wake us up to it."

"And which side are you on, Commander?" She deliberately used his military rank. "Because with all the dead bodies lying around, I'm really having a hard time figuring that out."

Ken could see Lori was getting angry and stepped between them. "Hey!" he said loudly. "That was uncalled for. I've known this man for fifteen years."

"No Ken, it's a fair question," Vartan said, staring her down intently. "She deserves an answer."

She looked back and forth between them, waiting.

"Lori, have you ever heard the terms Owls and Roosters?" he asked.

"If it will mean you'll actually answer my question, then I'll tell you the truth. No," she snapped tiredly.

Ken chimed in. "Those are intelligence terms for internal factions that have different viewpoints on whether something secret should be disclosed. Usually it just refers to a specific piece of intelligence, something like whether a given country has WMD, or maybe if there's a specific threat of a terrorist attack. The Owls feel that it is always better to be silent, to operate behind the scenes to affect the problem and not alarm the public. The Roosters feel that the question should be brought into the open, that the agenda is better served if the public knows the facts about whatever the threat is. That's what we've stumbled into. We're in the middle of war between those who want to keep silent, and those want to see *Prometheus* and this whole plan exposed."

She kept her eyes locked on Vartan's. "Do you guys have a genetic incapacity to answer a straight question or something?"

"You already know the answer," Vartan asserted. "The people that are after us aren't trying to help us hold a press conference."

Lori had to admit that was true enough. "Then why aren't your friends helping us more, Vartan? Why are we the only ones doing anything to stop this? Where are all your friends on the inside?"

"There's always been a religious component to this, Lori. Maybe it's a question of respecting our free will."

"Free will? As in controlling our own destiny? So this is some kind of test of our worthiness to survive? To create a disaster in order to sort out the worthy from the unworthy? Is that what you're saying?"

"Something like that."

"Oh, Jesus Christ . . ." she said.

"What are the Freemasons, if not a religion?" Vartan responded. "And the Catholic Church? And what is the one thing all of our religions have in common? It's that we have a choice, a say in our own destiny. That's why people like Mr. Dansby can only help us indirectly." He saw Lori react to his mention of Dansby.

"Yes," he said, "I'm well aware you've been in touch with him. It seems I'm not the only one holding something back."

She broke off from his gaze and turned to Ken. "You really believe all of this stuff too?"

He nodded. "I've just seen too many weird things over the years to *not* believe it, Special Agent."

"So all of this," she swept her arms out. "Everything. The murders, the car chases, Connie. It's all because some people who think they're special, who think they're above the rest of us, aren't willing to accept that catastrophe has been avoided. They're so invested in Armageddon that they're willing to create it themselves if it doesn't happen on its own?"

"Yes," Vartan said. "But some of them are trying to warn us. To give us a chance to avert Armageddon."

"The Roosters, as you call them. But why would they do that?"

Vartan shrugged "Maybe to make sure that if something does in fact happen, they wouldn't be held accountable for not warning us."

Lori eyes narrowed. "And who exactly would they be accountable to?" she asked.

Vartan and Ken exchanged a glance. "I'm afraid only they know that," Vartan responded.

28.

Lori walked out the front door to find Vartan standing alone and facing west, staring into the night sky. It was even darker here than it had been in Albuquerque, and the Milky Way spanned the horizon like a great glittering serpent snaking across the heavens. She stopped a few paces behind him, and he didn't turn as she approached. Was he that well trained that he could tell it was her from the mere sound of her footsteps?

The night was warm and the air was thick, but she still felt a mild chill and crossed her arms to warm herself. "I'm sorry I'm being such a bitch," she offered. "I'm sure this wasn't the life you had in mind for yourself, either."

He continued to face away from her. "It's understandable. Ken and I have had a lot of years to get used to the idea of all this. You'd never even heard of it until a few days ago. Don't be too hard on yourself."

She smiled, a useless gesture with him still facing away from her. "I should have learned to trust you by now," she said. "You've had plenty of chances to show me you were serious about all this. It's just hard. It's hard to have to deal with a different reality. To choose to live with the burden of it. It must have been difficult for you. Not really being able to enjoy life the way the rest of us can."

He didn't respond to her for several moments. Then he turned just slightly in her direction, speaking over his shoulder to her. "Lori, I don't want you to feel obligated here. Ken and I have to do this. You don't. This is our fight, not yours. You just got caught up in it."

"No, I didn't," she disagreed quickly. "I dove head first into it. I could have let this case go a couple of times, but I chose to go forward. I chose to be here."

"You can still go back. Get your old life back. Drop the case."

She smiled again. "We haven't been at this very long," she said, "but I thought you knew me better than that by now." She looked up at the stars. "Ken shouldn't be involved. He has a wife. A family. Grandchildren. He has a life. I'm the one who doesn't have anything to lose. He should stay here. Stay here and be with his wife."

"I agree," Vartan said softly. Once again he had surprised her. There were no more words for a bit. As she turned to go back inside, his voice stopped her.

"That's Sirius," he said, pointing upwards at the brightest star in the sky. "And Orion. To the Egyptians, they were Isis and Osiris. The goddess of life and god of death, judgment and resurrection. The gods of the Masons. I wonder if we're somehow doing this all for them. If this all has something to do with them." He turned to her. "In their minds, of course."

She looked at him. He seemed tired. God knew she was. "What difference does it make?" she said to him. "Either way, if we don't stop them, we'll all be dead anyway. Or wish we were." She stuck her hand out to him. "C'mon Vartan. Let's try and get some rest. I've got a feeling we have a couple busy days ahead of us."

He walked over and took her hand, the one with ring on it, and walked back with her inside the house as Isis and Osiris watched over them in silence.

"They're holding a memorial service at the Cape on Saturday, the afternoon before the launch. It'll be open to the public. That's the perfect chance," Ken was saying.

Lori had tried to lie down while Vartan and Marsden formulated a plan. She hoped to clear her head and get some rest, but she couldn't help overhearing the discussion and finally decided to get up and join in.

"Perfect chance for what?" she said from her position on the couch. They both looked up at the sound of Lori's voice and Vartan at least seemed glad to have her involved.

"A chance to slip through security and get to the *Prometheus* launch facility," he told her.

"They're going up on a Delta five rocket, from launch complex seventeen. We'll have to enter through gate two, here at the south end of the facility," Ken said, pointing to a location on the map.

This already sounded like a shootout to Lori, and she'd had it with gunplay over the course of the last few days. "What are we gonna do when we get in?" she asked facetiously, "shoot it with our guns?"

"If we have to," Vartan responded with all seriousness.

She was taken aback by that answer, not really expecting him to even consider a direct assault on the rocket. "Somehow I don't think we'll be able to get that close to it. NASA must have some security people."

Ken nodded. "NASA has their own security guards from a private company that's owned by one of the Germans who came over after the war, and they're pretty damn good," he said. "Believe me, I've run across them myself."

"I can handle them," Vartan said quickly, leaving no doubt by the tone of his voice that he could.

Lori was growing tired of doing things Vartan's way. "Regardless," she objected, "Shooting our way in there isn't the best option. And it shouldn't be our first choice."

Ken watched this exchange between them with some curiosity. "Agreed," he said, siding with Lori. "So what do we do?"

It took her a moment to gather her thoughts; she hadn't actually thought about it that much. "We get on the premises for the memorial ceremony, and then try to slip away at some point. We hide out overnight in the bushes there and then head to the launch facility in the morning. We try to disable the rocket somehow, keep it from launching. You said they had a very tight launch window, right?"

Ken nodded. "Even if you can delay the launch by ten or fifteen minutes, it will mess up the celestial mechanics to the point that they might miss the chance to get to close enough to Jupiter. And that might be enough to stop the plan altogether."

Vartan shook his head. "That's not good enough. We have to kill it. We have to make sure it never gets to Jupiter. We can't take the chance that they'll settle for 2018 to set off their fireworks."

Lori sat down on the couch next to him, looking at the map of the facility. "What will happen if we get close enough to actually shoot at the rocket? Will it just punch a hole in it, or will it explode?"

"It'll explode," Ken said quickly. "As long as you hit the center main stage tank. When that much pressurized liquid hydrogen is sparked by a high-velocity projectile, like a nine millimeter slug, oh yeah, it'll definitely explode." He pulled a picture of a fearsome looking rocket on the launch pad from under the map. "Aim here, just below the white band around the middle. That's where the main stage hydrogen tank is. One good shot and it will go up like the Hindenburg."

"Killing whoever was close enough to fire the bullet in the first place," Lori added. "And spreading radioactive plutonium all over the Florida coast. Thousands of people will die."

"Probably tens of thousands," Ken agreed.

"Better than four billion," Vartan interjected. His tone was pointed, cold, and indifferent. For just a moment, she saw what he was capable of. Strangely, this made her feel less rather than more frightened of him.

"It's a last resort," she said firmly. "We have to find a better way. There has to be a way to take it out after launch, so the debris gets spread over the ocean."

"Not ideal," Ken said, nodding. "But preferable to the alternatives. The environmental damage would be minimal."

"But the direct approach is more certain," Vartan said. "And we can't afford not to be certain."

Now Lori felt angry at him. "Why are you so damn anxious to die over this? Is there some inner demon that drives you to confrontation? Knock it off. Just let go of the James Bond complex. You're not Superman. We'll try to do this in a way that doesn't get anybody killed." He started to argue with her, but she cut him off. "I don't want to hear it. I'm not planning on dying over this, and I'm not letting you die over it either. No matter how much you might want to martyr yourself."

He seemed to get mad at her then, and she could tell her last rebuke had stung a bit. But she had no time or inclination to deal with his unfulfilled death wish, or the psychological scars behind it. She turned to Ken. "You worked at the Cape. What can you tell us about how to get in?"

Ken pointed again at the map, ignoring the uncomfortable tension between Lori and Vartan.

"If you can get into the public service, they'll probably bus you from the visitor's center over to launch complex 39B, where the American astronauts trained. That's just north of pad seventeen, where the Delta rockets launch from. You can try and slip into the bushes here." He pointed to a spot on the map. "They'll have security, but it won't be that tight for something like this. Wear dark clothes and you should be able to get behind the rope lines and into the swampy areas without being noticed."

"Which only solves the first problem," Lori noted.

"Right. The next day, you'll want to follow the brush along this shallow lake for about two miles until you reach the security fence behind gate two. If you can get through the fence, you can get access to the launching pad and block house about a quarter mile away."

"The blockhouse?" Vartan said, sounding alarmed "Why are we going there?"

"Well, you wondered about how to destroy the rocket over the ocean, and I've got an idea about that," Ken responded. Then he rose and went over to a kitchen drawer, fumbled through it and came to them with a small plastic ID badge, which he tossed on the table in front of them. Lori picked it up and looked it over, then handed it to Vartan.

"I used to work for the ULA," he informed them. "The United Launch Alliance. I kept my ID. I always keep my ID badges."

"But won't this have been deactivated?" Lori asked, taking it back from Vartan.

"Sure. But with wizard boy here, he should be able to crack the code on the magnetic stripe and make you two fakes ID's. Right Trev?"

"Theoretically," Vartan intoned, examining the badge again. "It's probably 128-bit encryption, so it will take some time. A few hours at least." He looked up at Ken. "But that still doesn't get us close enough to the rocket to shoot it up."

"You're still on that? You won't have to," Ken said, a satisfied grin spreading across his face. "I worked in the blockhouse on the pre-launch check outs. You'll be able to get right to the main override board down there."

"And do what, exactly?" Vartan asked skeptically.

"Get to the main under bus panel and clip the primary clamp timer wire under panel B. When Mission Control sees that they're not getting a signal, they'll have to go to a manual override. All you have to do then is set the clamp release mechanism to fire a quarter second late. The torque from the engines will crimp the superstructure of the main stage monocoque. By the time the rocket is one hundred seconds into the flight, the torsional stresses and the G forces will cause a crack in the frame, and within a few seconds the SRB's attached to the outside shell will pivot into the structure. It'll cause a rupture of the primary propellant tank."

"And then what happens?" Lori hated how ignorant she felt.

"Poof," Ken said, pulling his hands apart in an expansive motion. "Just like Challenger." A broad grin began to cross his face.

"Won't somebody question why you're pulling apart the, what was it, the main under bus panel?" Lori asked.

Ken shook his head. "Nope. I used to do it all the time. You're just checking the connections, right?"

Lori nodded. It seemed logical enough to her

Vartan tapped the ID badge against his thumbnail, thinking. "That just might work," he said distantly, apparently visualizing it in his head. "It just might work."

"And the best part is, nobody has to die," Lori added with a smirk. Vartan reacted to her statement with his now typical coolness.

"No they don't," he said.

Lori turned to Ken. "How do we get out?"

He shrugged. "That's your problem."

"I'll get us out," Vartan said flatly. Ken and Lori exchanged a glance, neither wanting to ask how he planed to do it.

Ken looked at Vartan until he caught his eye. "You'll have to head straight to the assembly area for the pad workers two hours before launch time. I can show you which building it is on the map. There's a dressing facility where you change into the whites you wear for the blockhouse crew. But you'll have to find one particular guy, the guy who took over for me when I retired. You'll have to keep him from getting on the bus to the pad."

"That's not a problem," Vartan said.

Ken didn't seem impressed by Vartan's response. "I'll bet it's not bud, but he's my friend. I'm not helping you if you hurt him."

Vartan gave Ken a small, quick smile. "All right, Ken. I'll make sure he gets out of the way, but only for a little while. Just long enough to miss the launch."

"What about me?" Lori asked.

"You're his intern," Ken said. "A trainee." He pointed to Vartan. "And you're substituting for Jerry Flynn, my buddy. The bosses never even care who you are as long as you have the right ID. We subbed in contract workers all the time."

"That's fine," Lori said, "but how will he know which panel is which?"

"No problem," Ken said. "I've still got my training manuals for the classes. I used to teach the new pad workers for the ULA. And I'm pack rat, remember?"

Vartan joined him in a smile.

"And thank god for that," he said happily.

29.

They were just leaving Mobile, Alabama when Lori noticed the sign that said "Atlanta 330." She looked up to see that they were on I-65, heading north towards Montgomery and then on to Atlanta. "Hey, shouldn't we be heading south on the I-10?" she asked Vartan, trying not to betray the concern she was holding inside.

"There's something I want to show you," he said back, his voice casual and not at all like the formal tone he had taken with her back at Ken's ranch.

"We have to be there by one in the afternoon on Saturday," she pointed out to him, her suspicions eased.

"Yes, I know that. We've got time. And I think you need to see this."

"See what?"

He gave her a quick, disarming smile. "You'll see what."

It was nearly seven hours later when the red wine colored Intrepid pulled off the freeway and headed slowly up a twisty dirt road. When they got to the top of a small hill, the tree lined pathway opened up to a small clearing. In the center of the clearing was an odd looking granite structure. Lori could see from the car that it had a central rectangular block column and an overhanging rectangular capstone that gave the central core a "T" configuration. Four slab-like legs emanated from each corner of the capstone arrayed in an "X" formation and looked like huge gray-granite versions of the famous monolith from *2001 – A Space Odyssey*. The entire structure was probably about twenty feet tall. There were four crooked concrete walkways emanating from the central structure, apparently lined up to north, south, east and west. At the end of each pathway was a shorter marble wall with a mural painted on it. They were too far from the murals for her to see much detail.

She was incredulous. "This is what we drove seven hours out of our way to visit?" Had Vartan wasted nearly a day's travel just to show her a carved rock slab and some paintings?

He started to get out of the car. "Let me show you up close," he said cryptically. Confused and a bit frustrated, she followed him. They walked up the slight rise to the base of the main structure as the sun began to set in the west. The dimming sunlight cast long and ominous shadows across the concrete floor underneath the slabs and onto the adjoining grass.

As they got closer, she could see there were symbols or writing of some kind on all the faces of the granite slabs, and the finish was rough and rugged, as if to suggest it was very, very old.

"It's commonly called the 'Guidestone Monument.' It just suddenly appeared here in 1980," Vartan informed her, as if to answer her unspoken question. "No one knows who built it for certain. The name on the permit was 'R.C. Christian.'"

As Lori got closer, she could see there was a dedication stone buried in the ground next to the structure. On it were carved various bits of information, including the height of the monument, astronomical alignments and the name of the builder. The rest of the dedication stone showed a number of symbols, including a rising sun, a Masonic square and compass, and a Star of David with a swastika inside it.

"R.C. Christian, a pseudonym," Lori said aloud, reading the inscription. "What does it mean?"

"R.C. Christian is a pseudonym for Christian Rosenkreuz. In English, it translates as 'Christian Rose Cross.' Or the Order of the Rose Cross, or the Rosicrucian Order."

"So the Rosicrucian's built this?"

"Presumably," Vartan told her. "Or the Hermetic Order of the Golden Dawn. Or the Freemasons. Or the Nazis . . ." He trailed off, having made his point. "But we later found out that all the money to build it came from the local Masonic temple. And they own the land."

She looked around the marble base of the monument, noting that the likenesses of a number of fish, plants and odd looking animals were carved into it. "All extinct species," Vartan said. Then he pointed to the dedication date. "July

20th, 1980. The eleventh anniversary of the first lunar landing, and the date of the helical rising of Sirius in ancient Egypt. And the birth date of Osiris, according to some texts."

Lori had long since ceased questioning Vartan on this kind of thing. Instead, she just began to pace around the dedication stone. "It says there's a time capsule buried under here," she noted.

He acknowledged her with a nod. "But we don't have time to dig it up just now."

She went then to the monument itself and began to examine it. On each face of it were symbols and words, some recognizable, some not. She pointed to one set of symbols.

"Egyptian hieroglyphs?" she asked.

He nodded. "Demotic, technically." Then he pointed to the other faces of the monolith stones. "And Greek, and Sanskrit, and Babylonian cuneiform. All tongues of the ancient world. Some of them living, some of them dead. But all saying the same thing."

"Which is . . . what?"

"That the planet's population should be reduced to five hundred million, to better live in harmony with the Earth. That we should be careful who we breed with, in order to keep the genetic pool clean. A bunch of Darwinian-Nazi nonsense, basically."

She finally had come to the English translated slab. The words were organized in ten separate lines. "The ten commandments of the New World Order?" she asked him.

He shrugged. "Something like that I suppose."

"I don't understand. What's the point of all this? Why build something like this and call for the extermination of most of the human race? Why telegraph what your plans are?"

He pointed to one of the walls erected further up the field and connected to the monument by a twisting concrete path. "This will tell you."

He took her hand, and she flushed slightly at the force with which he touched her. He wasn't giving her the option of not going. He led her to the westernmost mural wall, directly into the setting sun.

"This path is exactly thirty-three yards in length," he told her. "And this site is exactly at thirty-three degrees latitude. You can check the GPS on your phone if you'd like." She opted not to.

As they got closer to the wall at the far end of the clearing, she could see shapes and figures painted on the wall. It was a four foot tall mural of some kind. In the center was a large gold encrusted symbol laid out in a rough cross shape. It was noting compared to the mural.

It was a horror show of violent, war-like images. The central figure was a monstrous, Nazi like creature wearing an olive green cape, a Darth Vader-like mask – perhaps a gas mask - and Nazi era military hat. On the hat was the same golden symbol that was in the center of the mural. The figure held a machine gun in its left hand and an Arabic sword in its right. Impaled on the tip of the sword was a white dove of peace. The figure stood amid the burning ruins of a modern city. At its feet were the bodies of hundreds of dead children. To the left were the mourning figures of their grieving mothers. In the sky above him were a series of bright blue streaks which looked exactly like the debris from the space station they had seen on the TV coverage.

It was something like what Lori had always imagined the Anti-Christ might look like.

Vartan then directed her to each of the murals in succession. The next one had an image of a burning forest in the background, filling the sky with a choking smoke. In the foreground were frightened and abandoned children, carrying teddy bears and wandering through the forest, their feet cut and bloody. In the foreground were three coffins, in each was a dead child's body. One was an American Indian, the next a Negro child, and the third appeared to be a Jewish child. Above them, encased in a plastic sphere was a double headed eagle – the symbol of the thirty-third degree of the Masonic Scottish Rite, seemingly trapped and unable to fly away. The third mural showed a second sun rising over some distant mountains. In the still darkened sky above it was the constellation of Orion and its companion star Sirius. The fourth mural showed children carrying swords all lining up to have them beaten into plowshares by a handsome Aryan boy. All of the children were Caucasian. In the background were two bright suns, birds chirping and dolphins and whales pirouetting in the air above a crystal clear ocean.

"So this is the plan?" she asked, not really sure she believed what her own eyes had seen. "Everything is here. The fall of the space station. The birth of the second sun. The wars and the famine that will presumably follow?"

"And the extermination of the lesser races. A genetic purification, as they see it." Wordlessly, Vartan helped her to mount the last mural and stand atop it, so she could see the entire layout of the area. The central core and its four satellite murals were laid out in a distinct swastika formation.

"Keep in mind the swastika is an ancient Hindi symbol. It means 'vortex' or doorway," he told her. "It was only with the Nazi regime that it gained a negative connotation."

He pointed back to the golden symbol, a stylized Maltese Cross "This symbol is also nearly identical to the Hopi symbol for the Mayan calendar. It's meant to be read as a clock. A clock that ran out in 2012. That's when this cycle of renewal was supposed to begin. The double headed eagle back there? It's actually a Phoenix bird. That which rises from the ashes."

"But in order to rise from the ashes, you have to burn everything to the ground first." She was not really questioning him any longer. This place was just too weird for her to ignore. But . . . "I still don't get it. Why build this at all? Why even take the risk of revealing your plans, even symbolically?"

He shrugged. "In all religions, even the ancient lost ones, there's always an aspect of accountability. Whoever these people think they will ultimately be accountable to, I think this is their 'get out of jail free card,' as you Americans like to say. They can face their gods and say that they warned us of everything that was going to happen. We just didn't listen."

She conceded his point silently, taking one last look around the bizarre landscape. She could sense him becoming more formal again with her, the way he did when he had to withdraw emotionally before taking action. She knew this meant that the Cape was their last destination. There was nowhere else to run, nothing else to stop, no other way out of the situation they were in.

Lori knew instinctively this was the end. Vartan had opened a window to a larger world, and there was no going back. She'd never look at a church icon or a movie or even the presidential seal in the same way again. Now she was like him, noticing everything, suspecting everyone, and trusting in nothing but herself. She knew she would go to Florida with him and finish the job, not because she necessarily believed his stories or shared any of his suspicions, but because she could see no other way out, no other way for the danger and constant state of awareness she'd been in to stop. And she wanted it to stop.

"Thank you for showing me this," she said aloud.

Vartan seemed to understand. "It's time to go," he said simply.

30.

It was mid-morning on Friday when they checked into a dingy Cocoa Beach Motel. Vartan brought in the suitcases, one of which she knew to be filled with weapons and ammo. Once they were secured away in the room he checked each of the weapons, making sure they were clean and that they had plenty of loaded cartridges for each one. He didn't even seem to notice her as he worked, methodically priming each weapon and double checking the bolt action.

"I presume you'll want the Glock 17?" he finally said to her after nearly an hour.

"That's the one I'm most comfortable with, yes," she responded. He loaded the gun and handed it to her.

"California cartridge, I'm afraid," he said apologetically. "Only ten rounds."

"It'll do," she replied, not really caring. It was becoming more and more evident to her as the hours passed that Vartan had little faith in the success of their plan to disable the rocket. He seemed grimly determined to shoot it up rather than rely on Ken's idea to work.

They went to a local diner and had a non-descript coffee shop meal. Lori ate the hot turkey sandwich and skipped desert. Vartan ordered a grilled cheese sandwich and a hot fudge sundae for himself. They ate silently, paralleling the behavior of an older couple that had eaten without a word to each other in the next booth. Lori hoped she'd never be in a marriage like that, where there was just nothing left to say. She kept quiet until the elderly couple had paid their bill and walked out. Vartan took little notice of them, or of her.

"You're eating like condemned man having his last meal," she observed, speaking softly and trying to inject a little levity into his somber mood.

"Not at all," he responded, not picking up on her teasing tone of voice. "I think this has an excellent chance of working, provided we can slip behind the security."

"Is that why you loaded about eighteen guns back there? Because you think Ken's plan will work?"

"I'm preparing for the worst Lori, not expecting it."

His lie was transparent, and it made her angry. "Excuse me for having just a bit of difficulty believing that."

"Why should that be difficult for you to believe? I have no wish to die."

She pushed a little breath out of her mouth. "That's contrary to my experience of you, Vartan." She deliberately used a careful, almost British style of speech and intonation. Why was she so anxious to get under his skin?

He brushed it off. "I defy you to name one reckless thing I've done during this whole affair."

She rolled her eyes. "Um, shooting up a strip club . . ."

"They fired first."

"Stopping to go back and kill that man at the crash scene . . ."

"It bought us some time."

"Breaking into the FBI field office . . ."

He leveled his eyes at hers. "I had to get in contact with you somehow."

"Ever heard of email, Vartan? A cell phone? Or couldn't you find my records when you infiltrated the FBI security mainframe?"

He threw his hand up, in a scoffing gesture. She *was* getting to him. "Is there some point to this?"

"Yes, Vartan, there is. Before I risk my life – again, I have to know that you'll give Ken's plan a real chance. If you shoot this thing at the first opportunity, we'll both die and so will thousands of other people. It isn't too tough to figure out that you'd prefer to just do that. Now I don't know and I don't care at this point why you're so anxious to die over this. I only care that you'll help me try and disable the rocket first."

His expression hardened. "If what you were saying was true, I wouldn't have even brought you along. I wouldn't have even included you in this."

"Yes you damn well would have," she snapped, "because you owe me after all we've been through, and you know it. That's the only reason you're letting me tag along. You feel guilty about dragging me into this."

"Not true."

"Bullshit," she said, her voice almost a whisper.

There was a long silence, which she took as a concession of her point. He gently stirred some sugar into his cup of coffee, not meeting her eyes, which had not wavered. Then: "I'm just not sure I can trust *you*."

"What?"

He looked around from side-to-side, making sure no one was listening in. "I'm not sure I can trust you to take out the rocket if something happens to me," he said. "I have to know that you'll follow through. That you'll do what you have to do to stop the launch."

"Stop the launch? You mean shoot the rocket from close range and kill myself?" There was no point in pretending they were talking about anything else.

"Yes."

She considered it. "I promise you that on one condition."

"Which is?"

"Tell me why you really resigned from MI-6." She was as surprised as he was by her own question. "The truth this time."

He looked acutely uncomfortable. "Not here," was all he said, dropping a twenty on the table and rising from his seat.

It took about twenty minutes to pay up and get back to the privacy of their motel room, a trip that they took in absolute silence. Vartan pulled his gun from inside his coat and threw it on the bed in what seemed like an angry gesture even before Lori had closed the door behind them. When he turned, his eyes were red and furious.

"When I arrested the Army officers who had abandoned their posts in Germany, I spent several days questioning and debriefing them." He blurted the words out without pausing to address the initial question, as if he had been holding his tongue the entire time. "They told me things. Among them was that they had been in contact with an extra-terrestrial deity that instructed them to run away to Gulf Breeze. They told me that they had done so specifically to meet with me.

They always knew they'd be captured, and that I was the one that would interrogate them."

Lori held her hand up. "Wait a minute, an 'extraterrestrial deity' . . .?"

He nodded. "Yes. Osiris, specifically. The leader told me that Osiris had a message to deliver to me. They offered up a series of predictions as proof that they were in contact with a god. The predictions matched the Masonic prophecies exactly."

"They could have read about those," Lori offered.

Vartan shook his head in disagreement. "No. Those were never published anywhere else or spoken of publically by the Masonic elders who gave them to me."

"Still . . ." Lori mused.

"No. There was more. They also told me a member of the British Royal family would die within weeks. At first, I thought that maybe they had been in on the plot, but we quickly established that was not the case."

"OK," Lori said. "I can buy that. But you said they had a message for you. A message from this deity. What was it?"

"Two words," Vartan said. "'Echelon,' and 'Monaco.'"

"What does that mean? Echelon?" Lori asked.

"It's a NATO communications monitoring system. Basically, it records every cell phone call, every radio broadcast, every microwave transmission, every form of communication in the world," Vartan told her. "And I knew Monaco was a reference to my parent's plane crash. But I only had access to certain levels of the Echelon database. I had some assistance; I'm not sure from whom to this day. I suspect my old friend Mr. Dansby, but I can't be sure. Whoever it was pointed me to some files that indicated my father was making inquires about the American space program when he died. He was really pressing."

"And you think they killed him for it?"

Vartan nodded. "Whoever 'they' are."

"But that's not why you resigned," Lori said, not allowing any room for debate.

"No," he admitted. "While I was poking around the database, I came across some chatter, some MI-6 communications about someone they were tracking in Paris. I didn't know who until the next night, when Princess Diana was killed. Then I knew it was her they were tracking."

Lori was incredulous. "So that's why you quit? You think MI-6 had something to do with her death?"

"No, no, no, no. They were just following her because of what the leader had told them. I quit because what he told me had come true. And that's when I knew that I had to find out what was really going on."

He reached down and picked up one of the guns, cocking the firing chamber to put a live round in it. "And that I had to stop it."

31.

The next day dawned bright and sunny over Cocoa Beach, the exact opposite of the mood of the town and the entire space coast of Florida. As they made the trek up the beach cities to the NASA compound, town after town had a pall over it; flags at half mast, murals depicting the lost astronauts as heroes, and makeshift memorials of flowers, balloons and candles all along the crowded road. Vartan seemed hyper aware but strangely composed at the same time, as if he was operating in a conflicting duality; his mind racing but his body relaxed as if he was conserving his energy for what was to come.

They had a good plan. The biggest obstacle would be slipping undetected behind the security lines at the memorial service. Vartan was more than prepared to arrange an escape by force, but they both knew this would make their chances of surviving the night or getting to the distant launch pad highly unlikely. But, if they could slip into the glades and get through the night, Lori was relatively certain that their manufactured ULA badges could get them close to the launch pad. Then it was simply a matter of either shooting the rocket or disabling it. It was really up to them once they got close.

"I can't believe I'm actually doing this," Lori said, rechecking the secreted holster on her thigh under her tan skirt. "I'm not exactly the type of person who goes in for conspiracy theories."

"So what changed things for you?" Vartan was sounding casual as his eyes darted from side to side, looking for any signs they were being pursued.

"You know what changed for me," she said, "ISIS."

Vartan nodded. "Now every one of the prophecies on the Masonic parchment has come true."

"Not every one," Lori said, rolling down the window and letting the wind brush across her face and push back her red-blonde hair. "Not the second sun."

She felt so far removed from the spiritual place in her heart, the place that she always went to for guidance in the difficult moments in her life. She hoped that somehow the sun and the wind could restore her. Could make her feel one again with the spirit that she felt so much more rarely now than when she was a little girl. She closed her eyes and felt the warmth of Sol. The touch of God.

"Vartan . . .?" she said sadly.

"Yes?"

"Will we die tomorrow?"

She never opened her eyes to see if her question surprised him. The tone of his voice was what she wanted to hear anyway. After a beat, he responded.

"Nobody knows what's going to happen tomorrow," he said. There was no deception in his tone. He just didn't know.

Ninety minutes later, they boarded busses at the main assembly lots and began the long drive to the pad. Lori had never been to the Cape before, much less Florida, and she was fascinated by the strange flora and fauna and the many distant buildings where they assembled the launch vehicles. From the approach road to pad 39A, they could see the *Prometheus* Delta rocket on its own pad, the launch gantry enclosing it and white suited workers scurrying about. She hadn't even noticed when, but Vartan had taken her hand as they sat together, and had begun to absently toy with the diamond in the ring he had bought for her. He was playing the loving husband again. She turned and their eyes met, and for a brief second she felt like there could be some actual closeness between them. Something deeper than just the natural attraction brought on by the stress of their circumstances. She had no idea why. Maybe it was the black suit and tie he wore, and how handsome he looked in it. Or maybe it was just that they were in great danger, and she wanted to be close to a powerful, strong man.

The moment made her uncomfortable. "If we make it through this, remind me to give this back," she whispered, lifting her hand to indicate the ring.

He made a displeased face, but when he spoke, it was with a tone of amusement. "If we make it through this, you're keeping it," he whispered back.

Soon, they had arrived at the launch pad and waited until the security indicated it was OK to depart the buses. It quickly got uncomfortably hot in the humid Florida sun, and Lori took off her jacket top to try and cool down a bit. Finally, after nearly thirty minutes, they were cleared and began departing the buses.

The crowd was huge, much larger than she'd expected. There had to be at least twenty thousand people gathering. Vartan loosened his tie and scanned the crowd, looking for the security personnel as they'd arranged beforehand. She held her jacket over one arm and his hand in hers, walking slowly and casually to the assembly area. A makeshift stage and public address system had been set up at the base of the old Space Shuttle launching pad. They drifted to the back of the crowd, finding a spot in the shade of some of the taller trees and reeds along the paved pad area. It was a good excuse to be in the back.

There was a thin line of yellow rope indicating the security line. Along it, dark suited security personnel were spaced about every one-hundred feet.

"Treasury?" Lori asked him. Vartan shook his head and leaned in to speak in her ear.

"I don't think so. They look like simple rent-a-cops to me. They aren't very observant. We might have found some luck here."

Lori scanned the area again and agreed. "If only we can get a distraction."

Vartan's expression hardened. "I'll provide one if I have to."

"Please don't," she said quietly. "Let me." Inwardly, she knew her words were selfish. The last thing she wanted was for this operation to fall entirely on her shoulders. He didn't respond, and she couldn't see his eyes behind his dark Ferrari sunglasses.

There were no more words between them until the ceremony began, with a somber invocation by a Catholic priest, followed by prayers from a Rabbi and a taped message of condolence by the President that was played on the large LED screens that bracketed the stage. He'd have the toughest job the next day, presiding over the public funerals at Arlington National Cemetery. Soon they had moved to the opening remarks by the NASA administrator. He was a tall, thin man with white hair and a reddish complexion. His eyes were heavy with the sadness and regret of a dead man walking. He surely knew this kind of calamity was something that few men in politics could survive. He was known as an efficient bureaucrat, nothing more, and the truth was that nobody inside or outside of Washington liked him well enough to save his job for him. This would surely be one of his last official duties. He cleared his throat before beginning.

"To leave behind Earth and air and gravity is an ancient dream of humanity. For these eleven brave men and women, it was a dream fulfilled. Each of these astronauts had the daring and discipline required of their calling. Each of them knew that great endeavors are inseparable from great risks. And each of them accepted those risks willingly, even joyfully, in the cause of discovery."

He went on to sing the praises of the shuttle and station crew, of the men and women who had put them into space, and to insist, without much enthusiasm Lori noted, that the space program would continue. His final remarks were greeted with polite applause, and then it was time for the Senator from Florida, Rick Nielsen, to address the crowd. He got as enthusiastic a reception as one could get under the circumstances, being well known for his advocacy of NASA and for the space program that was crucial to the state's economy.

He had just begun his remarks when Lori noticed a stirring in the crowd up front.

It started as just a few sharp, quick movements that seemed out of place. Then she could see that there was actually a surge of people moving forward, toward the center of the disturbance. Next came the sounds of chanting. Incomprehensible at first, then more clear as it picked up in volume. She could see that the movement she noticed was from people trying to raise signs in front of the platform that held the TV cameras for all the major news networks. As more people moved up to see what was happening, the chant picked up in intensity just enough for her to make it out.

"No nukes in space! No nukes in space! No nukes in space!"

Environmental protesters no doubt, trying to make their point about *Prometheus'* nuclear payload in front of a captive national TV audience. Vartan was scanning the crowd now, watching the security guards. They all started placing their hands to their ears in an effort to hear the instructions they were no doubt being given as the chanting got louder and louder. She exchanged a look with Vartan, who had removed his sunglasses and was slowly backing up toward the glades and the yellow rope line. She followed suit.

Moving slowly, she saw Vartan inching closer to one of the guards, whose attention was still on the protestors. She circled around in his direction, not moving too quickly. She looked back over her shoulder to see if the next guard in the line was watching her. He wasn't. He was also focused firmly on the developing situation in the middle of the crowd.

Now the chanting grew ever louder, as more people planted in the crowd started joining in. Many of them started shedding over shirts to reveal underlying tie-die t-shirts with peace symbols or nuclear radiation symbols with a red circle and slash over them. More of them began to raise signs that called for Nielsen's impeachment for polluting outer space with nukes. Lori, as tense as she was, couldn't help but laugh at them. How idiotic was it to worry about radioactive contamination of *space?*

She was closing on Vartan now, who was still cautiously approaching one of the guards from behind. The guard was a husky, dark skinned man well over six feet tall, and his muscles rippled under his navy blue suit. She wondered if Vartan could take him, elite Special Forces training or not.

As it turned out, she would never know. As Vartan moved to within a few feet of him, the Senator had become frustrated and began to shout back at the protestors over the PA system. Soon, angry members of the crowd began to join in, trying to shout down the protesters. This led to an escalating level of intensity, topped off when one of the small group of protesters closest to them pulled a megaphone from a back pack and began shouting more slogans into it. *Typical hippie protester*, Lori thought to herself. They'd made their point, but just didn't know when to quit. A huge, overweight man in a light blue NASA logo t-shirt and dark blue shorts that were way too small for him stepped forward. He had so much back hair that some of it poked through his shirt. One of the protesters, who looked like the slacker kid in the MAC vs. PC commercials, saw him approaching and turned the megaphone on him, blaring it right into the large man's face. Lori cringed. It was Bubba vs. Bambi. This would not be pretty.

The large man grabbed the megaphone and twisted it effortlessly out of the protester's hand. Another protester with a full hippie beard and long, light-brown hair tried to grab Bubba's left arm. He was tossed aside. The slacker kid took the opportunity to charge the large man, who fired off a straight right hand punch that splattered the young kids face with blood. It sounded like a watermelon dropped from ten stories up.

With that, the whole area exploded. More members of the crowd jumped on the protesters, and soon they were on the ground, getting the shit kicked out of them. There were hoots and hollers of approval from the mostly pro-NASA crowd. Lori shot a quick glance back at the guards. They were gone.

She looked up to see them running into the crowd, trying to break up the fights that were breaking out all over the place. Bubba stood at the center of the maelstrom, like the Dark Knight from opening scenes of the Lord of the Rings movies, towering over the warring crowd. She looked to Vartan, who was already moving toward the tree line. She followed.

They both tried to make their movements as smooth as possible to avoid attracting attention. In just a few seconds, they were deep into the woods, well back from the ongoing commotion, which sounded like it was escalating into a full scale riot. They trudged their way through the first set of woods and emerged on a gravel road which was completely empty. They crossed it quickly, and within a few more minutes were a good half mile away from the commotion. Vartan checked the sun. "We'd better start heading south," he pointed the direction. He pulled up a Google map image from his cell phone and checked their position before leading her south. "I don't think anybody saw us, do you?"

Lori was stepping carefully around the branches and fallen trees, and his tone surprised her. She'd never heard him sound insecure before. "I doubt it," she said to him.

It was getting harder and harder to find their way in the swampy foliage as the night grew darker. At one point she put her foot into what looked to be solid ground only to have it sink in almost six inches and muddy her shoe. She began to wonder if there was any quicksand on the complex. Finally, after a few more minutes of trudging through the slop, Vartan reached out and grabbed her by the arm, silently as they'd agreed, and pulled her down.

"I think this is close enough," he whispered, "and it's getting too dark. We should bed down here." He checked the firmness of the soil with his foot and draped his coat on the ground, waving her over. She did likewise.

They settled in and she found the soft ground reasonably comfortable. After a few minutes though, she got cold, and moved closer to him. He rolled over from lying on his back to snuggle in a bit, spooning her. After a few minutes, she began to drift off.

She awoke with his hand firmly over her mouth. It was very dark, save a sliver of moonlight. "Stay quiet," he whispered. She could hear the distant sound of a truck engine, or maybe a jeep. It was getting closer. She heard the distinct creek of breaks as a truck stopped along the road just outside their swampy enclave. She could hear the sounds of military police radio chatter, but the specific words were indistinct.

The trees above them brightened as the MP's used a searchlight to scan the undergrowth. An intense white beam passed right over them, but they were sufficiently down in the brush that they evidently escaped notice. After a few more passes, the vehicle went into gear and proceeded slowly up the road, stopping and scanning every few hundred feet.

"We should move," Lori whispered, "they're looking for us."

"No," Vartan whispered back. "More likely they're just making sure all the protesters are off the base. Ken said there might be some extra nighttime security the night before the launch."

"But if they start searching back in these wooded areas . . ."

"They won't come in here on foot," he said confidently.

"How can you be so sure?"

"Well . . . because if the alligators."

Her head snapped around. "The *what!?*" She was trying desperately to keep quiet.

"The alligators," he clarified, looking somewhat amused by her discomfort. "Surely you knew this whole area was wild game preserve."

"I most certainly did not!"

He smiled at her, which was barely perceptible in the dim light as her head swiveled from side to side, looking for any sign of large, hungry reptiles. "Well, now you know," he said, not a hint of worry in his voice.

"Great," she said, spooning up to him even more. "As if I didn't have enough to worry about." She stayed in that position for a few minutes, burrowing into him and unable to sleep. Soon, she felt something firm pressed against her buttocks and turned again, more slowly, to look him in the eye. "Please tell me that's not what I think it is." Again, she could see a smile crease his face.

"Well," he said, showing no sign of embarrassment. "You are rather close to me. And I am a normal, healthy male."

"Great," she said again, exasperated. She turned away from him and placed her hands under her cheek for a pillow, but did not move away. "Just stay awake and make sure I don't get eaten by a gator."

"I'm not having a problem with that just at the moment."

He couldn't see it of course, but her eyes narrowed just a bit in an expression of suspicion. "I think you're actually enjoying this."

He didn't answer, and she made a little muffled sound of frustration. He put one arm over hers.

"This was your idea," he reminded her. "I was just going to walk up and shoot the bloody thing."

Tired and worried, Lori couldn't wait for morning.

32.

Lori woke up alone. The sun had come up, and various birds, insects and other creatures were singing its praises. Her right arm and shoulder were stiff from spending too much time in one position. She rolled over and spotted Vartan a few feet away, kneeling on his sports coat and quietly folding up his more formal clothes in a pile. Like her, he had worn a second set of more casual dress underneath. He was now dressed in a plain blue t-shirt and his slacks from the day before. He looked over when he heard her stirring, and ran his hands through his hair. "How do I look?" he asked her.

She studied him. Like all men, he looked rumpled and cute in the morning. She, on the other hand, always felt like she looked like Medusa if she didn't spend an hour putting on makeup and fixing her hair. "Presentable," she told him. He seemed not entirely pleased with her answer, and he ran his hands through his hair again. Of course he hadn't thought to bring a mirror.

She did, and dutifully pulled it out of her purse, checking herself first before she handed it to him. She wasn't too unhappy with her looks, considering the situation. Other than the bags under her eyes from the strain of fitful, reptilian laden nightmares, she didn't seem too bad off. Vartan took the mirror, checked himself briefly, and then went back to his tasks, double checking his side arm. Lori sat up and started to rotate her right shoulder joint in an effort to loosen it up. He was over to her immediately, positioning himself behind her and reaching out to massage her shoulder.

Lori flashed back to the night before, and got a little flushed when she recalled that he had been aroused as they drifted off to sleep. "That won't be necessary . . . ooh," she said, resisting at first and then giving in to his firm touch. He was soon expertly working out the knot in her neck.

"I had the same problem," he informed her, not hinting that he recalled anything about their closeness the night before. She dropped her resistance and forgot for a few moments the danger they were in. Her shoulder felt rejuvenated in a very short time. "You're good at that," she told him when he was done.

"Thank you," he said simply, checking his watch. He'd long since discarded the cell phone, out of fear that base security could hone in on its transponder. "It's seven forty-five. The workers will be coming in now. We should go." Lori got up and checked her own weapon. Satisfied, she nodded to him and they began to move without any further words between them. They made their way through the brush, careful not to make too much noise as they did so. In about twenty minutes, they had made their way to the fence line at a curve in the road just up from the Gate Two entrance. They settled down about fifteen feet from the fence, which was an eight-foot tall light chain link design. It was meant to keep unwanted critters off the road, not prevent a break-in. They waited and observed for a good ten minutes as groups of workers straggled past. They could not see the gate, the pad or the locker room bunker from their position, as there was too much foliage and brush in the way. This was the perfect place to break the fence line. They could not be seen from the security gate or by the workers heading to the blockhouse or assembly areas. As another group went by, it became silent.

"We'll have to get over the fence quickly," she said quietly to him.

"We don't have to," he said back, reaching down to his left sock and pulling out a pair of folding metal clippers.

She smiled, even though he was still intently watching the fence line and the road beyond for any sign of another group of workers coming up the road. "You've thought of everything, haven't you?"

"Yes," he said dryly. "I'm a secret agent, remember?" He went quickly to the fence, crouching for a moment to listen again before clipping several links. He then scurried back, and they waited as another group went by. Then he was back to the fence to finish the job. He had cut the fence along a four foot section, enough to slip through but hard to spot from the road. He came back and joined her in the brushy cover.

"Now we wait," he said, dropping the clippers.

She nodded. "I hope he didn't decide to come in early for once. Ken said he always shows up at the last minute."

Vartan looked at his watch. "Shift change is in forty-five minutes," he informed her. "He should be coming along at any time."

Lori felt butterflies in her lower back. "Let's hope so," she said.

Almost twenty minutes had gone by when Vartan finally spotted Jerry Flynn, Ken Marsden's friend, sauntering casually up the road past their position. He was wearing a dark blue windbreaker and Lori recognized him from the photographs Ken had given them, even if he was a little grayer and paunchier.

Vartan didn't speak, he just got up from their hiding place and she followed. Flynn was late enough that when they got through the fence, there was no one else visible for the entire stretch of road that they could see in either direction. Vartan took out his ID badge and clipped it to the collar of his t-shirt, and she put hers on the middle seam of her dark blouse. Vartan kept pace with Flynn just about fifty feet behind as they all rounded the corner and the pad came into view.

Prometheus.

Even in the light of early morning, it looked ominous to her. The central liquid fueled rocket was painted a dark NASA blue, and the white nose shroud had a NASA "meatball" logo and *Prometheus* mission patch painted on it. Around the base were strapped eight solid rocket boosters, all designed to help the rocket achieve liftoff and accelerate as quickly as possible early in the launch phase. Steam and gases vented from several places along the height of the rocket assembly, which looked more and more like a towering monster to her they got closer. They were still a good two miles from the pad, but she could see ice and condensation had formed along the super cooled central core.

She looked up and they were almost to the worker's locker room and assembly area. Flynn was angling toward the right, with Vartan following him casually. She wondered if she looked as relaxed as he did as she split off toward the left side and the ladies locker room. Vartan gave her a quick, serious glance and then bowed his head and followed Flynn in. Lori continued to the left of the concrete bunker-like building and came to the door. Next to it was badge reader, similar to the ones she used to get into various areas of the FBI field office back at Wilshire. She pulled her badge off and swiped it through, praying to god that Vartan was as good with breaking the encryption codes as she thought he was.

The light stayed red.

Trying not to react, she swiped it again. The light stayed red again.

"Having a problem Miss?" The voice behind her was deep and resonant, with a military tenor. She tensed and swallowed, but did not turn around. She tried to swipe it again. It stayed red.

"I don't know," she tried hard not to sound too nervous. She turned and saw a muscular black man about thirty years old, with a NASA security uniform and sunglasses on. "It's supposed to work on this door," she said haltingly. "It's my first day."

His face was impassive, but he stepped forward and reached for the badge. He had a kind face. She didn't want to shoot him.

Where the hell was Vartan? She suddenly realized that if her badge didn't work, his wouldn't either, and he should be coming around to check on her any second. Even if she didn't want to hurt this man, there was no telling what Vartan would do. Unable to decide what to do, she let him take the badge from her hand. She stepped back as he flipped it over, and reached into her bag for the Glock she had put in it. Her hand slipped around the grip and onto the trigger.

"Looks OK to me," the guard said, swiping the badge through the reader much faster than she had. It still stayed red. She started to raise her purse to level it with his stomach.

"Maybe I should take it back to the gate," she offered, trying to buy some time.

"The gate? You mean badging don't you?"

Shit. "Yeah, the badging office. That's what I meant. I'm supposed to get up there." She dipped her head toward the pad. "Maybe I have a bad badge."

He looked up at her. "We don't have any bad badges, but they might have programmed it wrong."

"That must be it," she said, too quickly, reaching for the badge. "I'll go have them reset it."

He waved her off. "Now calm down there, Miss. There's no hurry. We've had problems with this reader before. Sometimes this works." He took the badge and ran it through the reader in the reverse direction, and much more slowly. She heard a beep, and then the light went green.

He reached for the door handle and pulled it open and held it for her. She smiled stiffly and took it from him. "Thanks so much," she said.

"No problem Miss. I saw you struggling and didn't want you miss your first day."

"Thank you again," she said. He smiled and nodded as she entered the bunker, then passed the badge through the inner door using the same technique. It lit up green. He dipped his head again and let the outer door close. When she was inside and alone, she let out a deep breath. How many more of those scares would there be today?

Vartan followed Flynn into the men's locker room at the staging bunker, about thirty seconds in arrears. His badge worked flawlessly and granted him access to both the inner and outer doors without incident. He could only hope that Lori had gotten in as easily. When he got into the locker room, he quickly scanned the area. There were two rows of lockers with benches in front of them, and a bathroom and shower facility separated them in the middle of the building. Flynn had gone to the back of the bunker, up against the far wall, and was absently whistling to himself as he peeled off his jacket and placed it on a locker hanger. Vartan's eyes went to the upper part of the building, where the wall met the ceiling, and he saw no windows. That was good. No one would hear anything if his attempts to incapacitate Flynn got noisy.

Vartan busied himself with finding a white jumpsuit which fit him from a rack on one side of the room. From there, he could watch Flynn and make sure there was no one else around when he made his move. He grabbed a large sized jumpsuit with the United Launch Alliance logo on the left breast and got into it very quickly. He watched Flynn casually putting on his boots and hat, and gathered up his own accessories from the fully stocked racks of pad worker's gear. Flynn took no notice of him as he stepped away from his locker and headed to the bathroom, leaving the locker open. Vartan followed him to the urinal and took up the spot next to him, between Flynn and the exit. He pretended to relieve himself as Flynn continued to whistle a nondescript tune. Soon, Flynn finished and went behind Vartan to a sink and began to wash his hands. Vartan spun and approached him from behind, just as Flynn straightened up from bending over the sink.

"What the . . .?" Flynn didn't have time finish his sentence before Vartan was on him, wrapping his left arm around the older man's neck and spinning him clockwise to the ground. He was careful not to restrict Flynn's airway with his tight grip. Flynn tried to fight, but he was no match for Vartan physically and Vartan quickly placed him in a choke hold, pinning him in a defenseless position from which he had no leverage. He kicked and scratched at Vartan, but the younger, bigger man applied even pressure to both carotid arteries and within five seconds Flynn's body went limp. Vartan lifted him then and dragged him efficiently to the handicapped bathroom stall by his feet, then hoisted him to the seat just as he began to come around. As Flynn mumbled and tried to focus, Vartan bent him forward and hit him with single quick chop to the occipital ridge at the base of the neck, just below where the skull attached to the spine. Flynn went limp immediately and Vartan leaned him gently against the back of the toilet. He checked and found Flynn's breathing to be very shallow. There was no way of knowing if the blow had been a fatal one or not, as it was always a tricky proposition when using this technique to induce a blackout, especially in an older man like Flynn. It would be a shame if he died but Vartan knew he had no choice. He'd tried to keep his promise to Ken Marsden as best he could. He closed and locked the door from the inside and then slid underneath it. He made one last round of the locker facility to make sure they were alone, then he slipped out the door, his gun stowed firmly in a holster inside his right leg.

Lori was waiting for him in her own white coveralls when he emerged from the men's locker room. Vartan quickly scanned the area and then headed for an electric golf cart with ULA logos on it that was waiting next to the bunker. She followed.

"Any problems?" he asked as he started the cart and backed it out of its position against a railroad tie retaining wall.

"None worth mentioning."

"Try me," Vartan said as he swung the cart around and headed it up the road toward the launch pad.

"I had a problem with my badge. A security guard helped me out."

"I assume you got rid of him?" Vartan said, not taking his eyes off the rocket ahead.

"Yeah I guess. Did you have any trouble with Mr. Flynn?"

"I had to strike him, unfortunately. Hopefully he'll live." Vartan's tone was so cold and businesslike that it chillingly reminded her of who he was, and what he'd already done to get to this point.

"Hopefully we all will," Lori said as her eyes drifted up the length of the rocket.

It took less than five minutes to run up the road to the base of the pad where the blockhouse was located. As they approached, she was surprised at how small the launch complex was compared to the shuttle pad they had been at the day before. The pad itself was a simple rectangular concrete block, with squared concrete exhaust vents jutting out from underneath it in three directions. Their target, the launch complex control room and blockhouse, occupied the fourth side of the pad and was built into a depression underneath the rocket and pad itself. The launch gantry was a towering concrete block, quite unlike the steel-iron rigging structures she was used to seeing in all the archival NASA footage. The pad and vent assemblies were criss-crossed with stairways with brightly painted yellow guardrails. They arrived just as the supervisor was getting on the phone to inquire about the whereabouts of his last worker. Vartan jumped from the cart and flashed his badge to the supervisor, who took down the number on the back and entered it by hand into a paper log book he held.

"Sorry I'm late," Vartan said in a flawless American accent. "Somebody didn't show up and they called me in at the last minute."

The supervisor, wearing a white jumpsuit that matched Vartan and Lori's but with a red hardhat that covered his graying hair, simply grunted. Then he looked down his call sheet and a perplexed look crossed his face. "I don't have any sick calls on my roster," he said to no one in particular.

"All I know is they called me this morning and told me I was backup on the Main B bus sequencer panel." Vartan informed him.

"Hmm," the supervisor said skeptically. Then he looked at Lori. "Who's she?"

"Karen Halliwell, an intern," Vartan said. The supervisor looked them both over once and then pulled a portable badge reader from his belt.

"OK," he said indifferently, "scan in."

Vartan took his badge and passed it through, getting a green light almost immediately. Lori passed her badge through the reader backwards, as she'd seen the guard do at the locker room trailer, and after a second it too glowed green. The supervisor just looked at them like they should know what to do next, so Vartan pretended to be instructing Lori.

"OK, you always have that last check before you go in. Follow me." He started for the blockhouse door, and she followed. The supervisor had already turned away and was busying himself with some other tasks. As they descended the concrete ramp that led under the launch pad to the blockhouse, Lori stole one last glance at the towering rocket above her. The sky had grown a bit overcast and there was a cloudy shadow crossing the NASA logo on the white shroud at the top. She couldn't help thinking that maybe Vartan was right; they should just shoot the main fuel tank now and get it over with. She was still considering that proposition when she lost sight of it above her as she walked the last few steps down the ramp to the blockhouse entrance.

33.

When they entered through the main doors, Lori was surprised at how 20th century the control room felt. There were analog switches, dials, buttons and valves everywhere, with only a scattering of computerized or digital equipment. The light overhead was fairly dim and yellow from low hanging fixtures, and clusters of pipes and vents ran along the walls and ceiling and into the some of the consoles that were spaced along the walls or isolated in rows in the center of the room. There were several rows of these terminals and consoles, but they headed straight for the back of the room and the main control panels. They were huge, stretching from the floor to about six feet high and covered with switches and dials. There were at least twenty-five technicians and workers in the room all milling about, talking back and forth and double checking data. They each wore white jumpsuits like she and Vartan had on, but they were in various states of cleanliness. Lori surmised that many of the workers had their own favorite smocks and work clothes.

Lori was relieved when Vartan walked confidently to an unmanned panel on the left side of the main rear control panel and pulled a checklist from the wall. He looked at her, and his eyes made it clear he wasn't ready to move yet; they would pretend to be real technicians for a while.

Over the next fifteen minutes, they busied themselves with various tasks from the checklist, going through it methodically. Vartan had seemingly retained everything Ken had taught him from the text books and class materials he had been shown. Lori was impressed.

By that time, some of the workers had completed their tasks and had begun checking out of the blockhouse. After about ten more minutes, there were only a handful of workers left along with Lori and Vartan. So far, no one had questioned them or even taken much notice of them. Lori jumped as a loud school bell rang out without warning. Then she heard a quiet chuckle from behind her.

She turned to see a disheveled middle-aged man with shoulder length hair and a scruffy two day beard laughing at her. From a style standpoint, he looked like the decade of the nineties had never happened to him. Or the eighties, for that matter. His laugh was full of chauvinism and disdain. She fought the urge to shoot him in the knee cap.

"Well there little lady," he chuckled again, probably just for effect. "Haven't heard the ten minute bell before, huh?"

She smirked at him, pretending to laugh at herself.

Vartan intervened. "She's my intern. She's never worked a launch before."

"Is that so? I would never have guessed." He smiled, and his teeth were yellow from too many years of cigarette smoking. "Welcome to the club honey."

She decided it was not a good time to piss him off or put him down. "Thanks very much," she said, choking down her desire to show off her martial arts training.

Another man, apparently his boss and a slightly older and more professional looking engineering type, noticed the exchange and was quickly between him and Lori. "Knock it off Ryan. You're done here. Check out." The man chuckled again and then turned and left through the main doors. "Sorry about that," the boss said. "You don't need to worry about him. Several women employees have quit because of him in the past. He's on his last warning."

Lori just smiled and turned back to the panel she and Vartan were working. She heard the boss shuffle away.

"You handled that well," Vartan whispered to her.

"I know," she said back. "I wish I could have let him know I was armed."

"No you don't."

"I do."

He looked at her. She dropped it.

"OK it's time," he told her, stealing a glance over his shoulder. There were only three other men in the room with them now.

He reached up and started twisting the quick release fasteners around the top of the panel.

"Hey." It was the engineer man's voice again. "You don't need to do an inspection on that panel. Flynn cleared it yesterday."

Vartan stopped and then turned. "It's on my checklist," he countered.

"Yeah but I told you, Flynn checked it yesterday. You don't need to re-check it."

"And I told you if it's on my checklist, I'm doing it. What Flynn did or didn't do isn't my responsibility. This panel is."

The engineer man took a step back. "Fine," he said looking up at the mission countdown clock. "But hurry up. We've got five to clear the pad."

"Fine," Vartan said back to him, turning back and resuming his task. "We'll be right out." He unfastened the rest of the quick release screws and pulled the panel off. He pretended to be examining its connections until they both heard the door click shut behind them.

"Are we clear?" Vartan asked. Lori checked over her shoulder.

"Clear," she said. He started to pull at various wires, moving them out of the way and looking for the right connection.

"Five minutes . . ." she started to say.

"More like four," he interjected.

"Can you do it?"

"I think so." He was speaking to her but totally focused on following the wire bundles to their root connections. He couldn't seem to find the right one and kept rechecking connections. Lori had begun to sweat from her forehead as he worked. They had to be down to less than two minutes at this point.

"Vartan . . ."

"I know," he said, still pulling at some of the wires. Then he found a green wire and traced it back into a gray instrument box on a rack inside the panel assembly. "That's it," he said. With one quick motion, he pulled on it and it snapped out.

He looked to her. "Quickly," he said.

She helped him lift the panel back into place and to reconnect all of the twist-on fasteners. Once the panel was secure, he dashed back to one of the standalone terminals in the middle of the control room. She followed and they both bent down over the computer console. There was a red light flashing on the screen. Vartan took the mouse and clicked on it and then began to search the console for the right switch. There was a dizzying number of dials and switches to choose from.

"Clamp delay manual override," he said aloud. "He said it was on this side." Although his voice was completely calm, he, like her, had begun to sweat. After what seemed an interminable search but was more likely no more than ten seconds, she found it. A raised black knob that looked like the temperature dial on an old fashioned electric stove.

She pointed. "There it is. Clamp delay manual override," she told him. He jumped across to her side of the console and found the right dial. After a few seconds of studying it, he reached out and clicked it one setting to the right.

"That should do it," he said, sounding relieved.

"Do not move," said a deep voice from the back of the room, "either of you."

Disobeying the voice, Lori turned. It was the husky black security guard from the locker bunker badge reader. He was pointing a gun at her, holding it tightly and tensely in both hands, his feet spread and square. He was alone. Vartan turned more slowly. There was at least fifteen feet between them and the guard. Too great a distance to charge him against a gun. On the other hand, he couldn't shoot them both at the same time, and didn't seem to want to do so at all. Looking at his face, Lori thought him to be terrified. Vartan must have seen it too, because he raised his hands just above his waist and began circling to his left, creating more space between them. If the guard was going to shoot, he'd have a more difficult time as the spacing between he and Lori grew.

"I said hold it mister," the guard said, aiming his gun more at Vartan. Vartan just kept circling slowly to his left. Lori took a step forward. He snapped the gun back on her. "You'd better freeze lady." His voice sounded shaky.

"Myron, do not approach. Repeat. Do not approach. M.P.'s are on the way." The voice had come over his security

walkie-talkie. They only had a few minutes now, at best.
"Myron," Lori said haltingly. He flashed a look at Vartan,
and his finger flexed on the trigger. "What are you doing?
We have to fix this panel and get out of here. We're getting
close to the launch window."

"You ain't here to fix anything," he said back, pointing
the gun back at Vartan. "I ran your I.D. through the database.
You ain't Karen Halliwell."

Lori, still holding her hands out where he could see
them, took another step toward him.

"Of course I am," she said gently. "Look Myron, I don't
know what this is all about, but you've made a mistake."

"No I haven't ma'am. Karen Halliwell is in the database
all right, but you ain't her."

"But my picture . . ."

"Damn your picture! I checked. It says Karen Halliwell
is five feet four, two hundred ten pounds. And you ain't no
two hundred ten pounds!" Sweat was now visible on his
brow, and his hands were visibly shaking. Vartan had
completed his slow circle to the left and managed to close the
distance between them at the same time. He was now within
ten feet of the guard. Myron tried to step back, but he was
already almost up against the door.

"Myron, listen to me." Lori tried to make her voice
sound soothing. He was getting more and more agitated by
the moment. "I had lap band surgery last year. I've lost over
seventy pounds." She reached out and unzipped the front of
her jumpsuit, past the belly button, exposing a cropped gray
t-shirt over her chest and a bare lower abdomen. Her
movement was swift and sharp, and he jumped the gun back
on her.

"What the hell are you doing?" he demanded.

"I was just going to show you the surgery scar," she
said, acting as nonchalant as she could. Watching him
closely, she tried to calculate if she could reach the gun
holstered on the inside of her thigh and dodge at the same
time. She wouldn't make it, not before he got a shot off.

"Lady I don't want to see no scar. Y'all are terrorists
and I'm gonna take you down." His voice had lost the polite

character it had held back at the locker shack and he was regressing into a rural southern dialect.

Vartan took another step forward and Myron snapped the gun back on him. "Don't you take one more step mister or I'll blowed you away!" Lori noted the misuse of the word tense and watched the finger flexing again on the trigger. They didn't have much time left before he lost it and started shooting. Lori kept her eyes fixed on his face.

"All right Myron," she said. "We're not terrorists. I'm a federal agent. I can prove it. My I.D. is right in here." She started reaching into the opening in her jumpsuit.

"You ain't no federal agent," he argued.

"Yes I am. I'm here investigating possible terrorist sabotage of the *Prometheus* rocket. This man is my assistant from NATO." She stepped forward again. Myron was now sweating profusely and it was beginning to run into his eyes.

"Bullshit!" he said, motioning with the gun as he said the words. Thankfully, it did not go off.

"What she says is true Myron," Vartan offered, his formal British accent having returned. "We're here *tracking* terrorists. If you just let her show you her I.D. . . ."

"Shut up motherfucker! I found the body. You killed Mr. Flynn!"

That was bad. He must have started searching around after he became suspicious of Lori and found Flynn's body. For a brief second, Lori was sorry. But she had other problems.

"Myron we did not hurt Mr. Flynn. We found him too. We think he was helping the terrorists." Her voice was formal, like Vartan's, and authoritative. "And *they* killed him." She saw Vartan steal a glance at the clock. The launch window would be opening in less than two minutes. They were almost out of time.

Myron turned his head, but kept his gun trained on Vartan's face. "I checked the FBI database, bitch. They is looking for two Russian terrorists, a red headed girl and a dark haired older guy." He looked back and forth. "What am I looking at here?"

She knew she needed a distraction. Looking down, she saw a metal tool box with an opened lid on the floor just to her left. A quick kick and it would fly into the metal computer terminal and make an awful metal on metal racket.

"I'm reddish blonde, Myron, not a red head. And I have green eyes. Did the description say what color the woman's eyes were?"

"What?! No it didn't say what color 'yo eyes were bitch!" He was on the brink now, his fingers and arms so tense he could barely keep still. But for the first time, the gun was not on either of them, but had drifted to point at the empty space between them.

"Let me show you my I.D.," Lori said. She lowered her right hand and in the same motion kicked the toolbox as hard as she could. It was light and almost empty, and it flew the four feet across the room and crashed into the console with an echoing bang. Myron jumped at the first sound of her foot hitting the box and his gun went off, sending a bullet zinging around the room, sparking as it deflected off a metal pipe and shot into a far wall.

That was all the time Vartan needed.

He closed the eight feet between he and Myron in a flashing motion, chopping down on his right arm and sending the gun spiraling across the room. Myron yelled and swung his left fist in a hooking punch, but Vartan ducked it and came up with a counter right to his stomach. Lori had heard and felt the bullet pass right over her head and strike the wall behind her, and had ducked instinctively. Finding herself on the floor, she set got up on all fours and lunged into the melee, landing with her full weight on Myron's left knee. She heard the distinct sound of ligaments and tissue popping and tearing, and Myron let out another scream that reverberated around the walls of the room. He was hurt, but still engaged in a strength-on-strength dual with Vartan. They were evenly matched, which surprised her considering how much bulkier Myron's build was. Now flat on her belly at their feet, she rolled to her right and put herself upright in one smooth motion, those years of ballet classes finally paying off in the real world. Without setting herself first – her balance was excellent - she swung her right foot again and delivered a sharp, angry kick right between Myron's legs and deep into his groin. There was split second delay, but then the pain hit him and he began to buckle at the left knee. Vartan stopped pushing against Myron's weight and instead let it fall upon him. Dropping, he swung Myron over his right shoulder and then came up underneath, his open palm striking him flat and directly under the chin. It was a knockout blow. Myron heaped forward and Vartan turned and watched him fall, making sure he was out.

Lori thought that this was the point in the movie where the hero made some clever comment, but Vartan just pulled his gun from inside the jumpsuit and put a round into the chamber. She knew what he was planning to do.

She reached out and grabbed his arm. "Vartan no!" she shouted. "If we can just hold them off for a few minutes . . ."

He yanked his arm away. "There's no time!"

As if to emphasize the point, the room exploded in an ear splitting wave of sound as red alarm sirens started going off, filling the room with noise and color. She had no idea if this was for them or just the final warning before the launch window opened.

She pointed to some tools that had spilled out of the toolbox, a metal hammer and a couple of thick screwdrivers. "We can barricade the door!" she offered. "Jam it shut."

"They'll launch anyway," he shouted over the din.

"Even with people on the pad?"

"What do you think?"

"But the clamp . . ."

He shook his head. "They might figure it out and override the manual settings." He turned away from her. "This is the only way."

Before he got a step, they were blasted back by a shot of something coming through the door. It was a tear gas canister. The room started filling with white smoky gas almost immediately. As they got to their feet, three dark suited figures with gas masks came though the door, holding small automatic weapons at the ready. At first, Lori thought they were more of the "ninjas" that had been pursuing them since Las Vegas, but she saw that their movements were stiff and mechanical, and they wore bullet proof vests with police insignia on their uniforms. They were most likely military police or base security.

Vartan swung out a leg, kick boxing style, and felled the first one through the door with a brutal kick to the face. But before he could raise his gun, the second man knocked it from his hand and the third man slammed his weapon butt into his stomach. Vartan clutched his ribs with his left hand but then swung with his right, landing a blow to the second man's midsection. Lori took a deep breath, probably the last batch of clean air she would get for a while, and dashed for the door.

The M.P. that had taken the kick from Vartan had gotten to his knees, and shook his head to clear it. He spotted Lori heading for the door and jumped up to cut her off. His gas mask was slightly ajar from the blow Vartan had given him, and he overran Lori as he tried to reach out for her at the bunker entrance. She sidestepped and clawed at his mask, successfully pulling it completely off as he struggled to maintain his balance. She could feel the strength in his arms as she scrapped with him and knew she was no match, but he seemed disoriented from the blow he had taken and she got underneath him and slammed him back against the wall. She heard the air push out of his compressed diaphragm, and a second later he was gasping for air, the wind knocked out of him, and sucking in the tear gas. He started coughing and retching uncontrollably, and she easily escaped his grip as he tried to find the exit through red, bleeding eyes. She could feel her own exposed skin, both on her face and stomach, blistering from the noxious gas. What ever they were using, it wasn't run-of-the-mill tear gas.

She burst through the double doors of the bunker then, trying desperately not to inhale the gas, and took a few steps up the ramp to get some clean air. The third guard had gone limp, apparently passed out from gas inhalation. After a few breaths, she looked back into the blockhouse. Vartan was still fighting with the two other M.P.'s amidst the swirling gas, but he was losing. They were both younger and quicker than he, and his eyes were blood red. Obviously, he'd received a large dose of the gas. One of the M.P.'s was holding his hands behind his back and the other was swinging punches into his stomach. She reached down between her legs and pulled out the Glock. She already knew there was a load in the chamber. Vartan took another blow to the face and blood spattered across the room. As his head recoiled, he caught her eye, and the M.P. that was punching him turned to look in her direction. She had her gun sighted right between his eyes.

Lori knew all she had to do was pull the trigger. There was plenty of room between Vartan and the MP, and at this range and with this weapon, she wouldn't miss. But she also knew that she had a more important task now than saving Vartan. Behind her, she could hear the approaching sirens of more police and security vehicles.

She had to get to the rocket.

Vartan took the opportunity to buy her some time. Bloodied and beaten down, he threw his weight forward and tossed the MP that was holding his arms over his back, and then they both stumbled forward and into the second MP, who had frozen while staring down the barrel of Lori's gun. All three men collapsed into a mangled pile of arms and legs. "Go!" Vartan shouted at her.

She didn't think, she simply obeyed his orders, almost as if she were under a spell. She turned and ran up the ramp to the base of the launch pad. The sirens were much louder by now, and she could see three more police vehicles racing up the approach road. Before she heard the shot, a bullet had zipped past her head and struck the railing behind her, pinging and sparking off the iron bar. She jumped and rolled to her right, got to her feet and sprinted back toward the front of the pad, toward the oncoming jeeps. When she got to the base of the stairs leading onto the pad, they were still a good fifty yards from the area, and she jumped up and over the chain that was drawn across the rails and scrambled up the concrete stairs, slipping once and cutting her shin on the stair edge even through the cloth of the jumpsuit.

By the time she got to the top of the stairs, the police vehicles had screeched to halt and at least a dozen officers and M.P.'s leapt out of the trucks, their weapons drawn. She ran to the right, positioning herself so that she was inline with the rocket from their perspective below. She trained her gun on the center tank of the rocket.

All she had to do now was squeeze her finger.

She knew of course that doing so would end her life and Vartan's, and all the guards who were just doing their jobs. The poisonous fallout from the explosion would probably pollute the Florida coast for miles around, maybe hundreds of miles, depending on the winds. Thousands, possibly tens of thousands, would die a horrible, hemorrhaging death, and the poison would show no discretion in its selection of victims. Grandmothers and fathers, children, newborn babies, young mothers and dads, black and white, dogs, cats and birds, they'd all be dead in a few days. The ocean in the area would be a dead zone for a decade, at least.

And all because of her.

She heard the distinct clack-clack sound of a bolt being pulled back, and wondered if it would be the last sound she would ever hear.

"Stand down!" a commanding male voice shouted from below. "If you miss, you'll hit the rocket tank and we'll all be dead!"

"I won't miss sir." The new voice was young and full of bravado.

"But she might not either, corporal! Stand down!"

Lori kept her gun pointed at the rocket, right below the blue NASA "meatball logo," as Ken had told her to.

"Ma'am, drop your weapon. We have you covered. You will not escape." The commander of the unit didn't even consider that she might not care to escape. "Ma'am, I'm ordering you to drop that weapon or we *will* have to shoot."

She knew that was a bluff, but Lori also knew she couldn't start talking. If she did, he'd talk her down off the pad. She just kept staring at the rocket. She turned her body just slightly, showing more of a profile to them. It would be harder to hit her with a bullet from this angle, and easier to hit the rocket beyond.

She heard a commotion from down below, but did not avert her eyes from the steaming, super cooled Delta-five. A loud siren, like an air raid siren from an old war movie, started to sound off in the distance. Ken had told her that when she heard that, it meant they were just seconds away from arming the rocket and opening the launch window.

"Bring him up here," the commander shouted down to the blockhouse. She heard the scraping sounds of a man being dragged up the concrete ramp, not entirely under his own power. Keeping her gun in the same position, pointed at the *Prometheus* rocket, she turned her head to the right. Vartan was being held up by two armed guards, his hands in plastic handcuffs. His face was bloody and battered, with cuts and lumps that he'd not had a few minutes ago. He looked up at her with hopeful, bloodied eyes.

"Lieutenant," the commander said.

"Yes sir!" came the barked response.

"Give me your side arm."

"Yes sir!"

The younger officer stowed his rifle and pulled his gun out from a hip holster and handed it to the commanding officer. He released the safety and cocked the bolt, putting a round in the chamber. Then he stuck it against Vartan's left temple.

"Ma'am, you will drop your weapon and surrender or I will shoot your friend. You have five seconds."

Lori looked into Vartan's eyes, and then the squad leaders. He looked to be in his late thirties. She wondered if he lived nearby, if he had a wife and family. Maybe a dog. She understood that if she were in his position, she'd probably resort to the same tactic. In his eyes, she was a murder, or a terrorist, or worse. She was a threat to his family, his country, his whole world. There were a lot of other people out there too, so many others who lived in different countries and different states, and who had their own little worlds; the people they loved and tried to protect.

And they were all threatened by that dark, cold, venting monster on the launch pad.

"Shoot it!" Vartan screamed at her, desperation in his voice. One of the guards slammed a rifle butt into his lower back, and he groaned in pain and dropped to his knees, the commander keeping the gun barrel to his head.

"Five," the commander said.

Lori knew SWAT tactics. The countdown wasn't really about Vartan. They knew if the threat to him was keeping her from firing, she'd have no reason to live if they killed him. The countdown was actually for one of the other police gunners, who probably had his sights trained on her right now. She assumed he had circled around to another position, so his shot wasn't lined up with the Delta II rocket. When the countdown reached zero, it would be for the gunner to shoot her, not for the commander to kill Vartan.

"Four."

Lori's thoughts drifted back to Melissa. It had been so long since she tried to talk to her, tried to reach her in her mind or her soul. She remembered the dream, her sister's house in the world beyond this one, and the sound and the vibration of the angels singing. And then it was as if she found clarity. As if the pulse pounding in her ears had cleared them, and she finally could hear and remember the last thing her sister had said to her before she sent Lori back to wakefulness, and the heavy burdens of this world . . .

"Three."

"Remember Lori; there's truth here, and beauty; but there's no justice. If you come with me, all I can promise you is the truth." Those were Melissa's last words to her little sister. The ones she'd heard over and over again in her dreams, but could never quite make out.

"Two."

Justice. That was what she'd been seeking all along. Since that one horrible moment when she heard the policeman whispering under his breath to her father, and her mother's horrified cries of pain. Justice for all she'd lost, for all that Melissa had lost, for all that the world had lost by not having Melissa in it. And she knew one more thing; if she pulled the trigger, she would never have justice for herself . . . and neither would any of these other innocent people. And it would be she who would have taken their chance at justice, and their hope, from them.

"One."

She lowered the gun.

She opened her palms and raised her hands, taking her fingers off the weapon and holding it out away from her body. She heard a cry - was it of anguish, or frustration? - from Vartan. There were tears in her eyes, and it was not from the gas she'd inhaled. She knew she'd just let down so many people, perhaps even the whole world. But there had to be another way, another path to justice for her and revenge for Vartan, and one that still allowed them a chance at salvation. She wished she could explain it to him; explain that she had to take this one last chance, for both of them.

She was surprised by how quickly they were on her. One guard snatched the gun from her hand while two others dropped her to the ground and lay on top of her with their full weight. Her cheek scraped on the coarse concrete, but she didn't care. She was beyond caring about much of anything.

She could just see over the edge of the pad as they dragged Vartan away to a waiting security van. His head was slumped down and his body limp. She knew he was defeated, broken at the last minute because she'd failed him. He must have been counting on the blissful relief that death would have brought him.

In just seconds, they had her hands cuffed behind her back and she was on her feet, literally lifted and carried down the twenty five steps she'd run up just a few minutes before. At that time, it had been her intent to shoot the rocket and kill all of them, even herself. Now all she felt was shame that she didn't have the strength to pull the trigger.

The men were in a panic to secure the area and get her in a van. The van that Vartan was in was already speeding away with its siren blaring. They tossed her unceremoniously into the back and without the use of her hands she hit hard, face first, on the cold metal floor. Before she could try to scramble to her feet, they clamped her ankles in chains and once again sat on her, one at her knees and one on her back.

She found it very difficult to breathe. The van doors were slammed shut and clamped. Then two quick knocks on the side of the van and the driver put it into motion, speeding away and likewise blasting his siren.

She had no idea where they were taking her, but the drive seemed to go on at high speed for more than five minutes. She made no attempt to speak to her captors, and she still had no idea if she would even live out the day. She thought herself a coward and a fool as she laid there. She and Vartan would not see another day, and because she lacked courage, his death would be pointless. She'd robbed him of the one thing that would have made his time on Earth meaningful.

The van lurched as it came to a halt, and the back doors were opened again in short order. Her feet were unclamped from the chains and quickly placed in a set of walking chains. Then they shoved her roughly out the back of the van and into the bright glaring daylight of the Florida morning. She was facing the coast, and in the distance the launch pad. They were several miles away from the pad now, and she could see the gantry arms swinging away from the rocket and knew that this was one of the last procedures before launch. Then they turned her to her left and dragged her, too quick for her to keep up with the leg irons on, to a blank brown metal door at the corner of a white three story building. They brought her right up to the door, but did not open it. She turned her head back to her left, and she realized they were all gazing off into the distance. She tried to crane her neck around for a look, but one of the guards restrained her head, and then she heard the deep rolling thunder, like a train or an earthquake coming, Doppler shifting in the distance and growing nearer. Then, the sound wave hit her like a physical force, rumbling the ground and shaking the windows of the van and the building.

So this was the sound of a rocket launching, of a technological wonder, perhaps of a herald of doom. It sounded so different than the angels singing . . .

She felt a sharp pin prick in her hip, and she could feel her muscles begin to relax almost immediately. The feeling rose through her like a slow rolling wave, and she felt a loss of control of her body section by section. Stomach, chest, arms, shoulders, neck. And then a curtain of blackness came over her eyes, and she heard nothing more.

34.

Lori came to slowly over several hours. Her mind was foggy, and she remembered only snippets of time from the last few hours. Or had it been days?

Eventually, she realized that she must have actually been awake for several hours, but was only now coherent enough to recall the last few minutes with any clarity. She wanted to move, to open her eyes, but the very idea of it seemed like an effort far beyond her physical limits. More time passed. She drifted in and out of sleep, each time remembering more of the last time she'd woken up, and more of what had happened at the Cape. After a while, she realized that she was hot and sweaty, and that wherever she was, it was stuffy and the bed she lay on was unpleasantly hard. Finally, she managed the strength to open her eyes. As bad as she felt physically and emotionally, what she saw made it even worse.

She was in a tiny concrete cell, with concrete bricks for walls and no visible windows or air vents. The walls, floor and ceiling were painted a bright sky blue. She was lying on a simple slab with a thin mattress under her. There was a stainless steel sink and a toilet with no seat. At least from where she lay they appeared to be reasonably clean.

Another fifteen minutes passed before she gathered the momentum to prop herself up on one arm and look back over her shoulder at the door. It was tall and black and metal, with what looked like mail slot doors at waist level and at the floor. The slots were closed tight. Eventually, she was able to first sit up on the bed and then stand as she continued to come out of her fog. She was still wearing the white jumpsuit and it was still unzipped to the waist. She had the cropped t-shirt on underneath and was still wearing the boots and socks, although the laces on the boots were gone, as was the belt for the jumpsuit. Barely alert, she became aware of a horrible, bitter taste in her mouth and dryness in her throat. She wanted water. After a time she was able to rise and walk the few steps to the sink and turn on the faucet. The water she got was cool but loaded with chlorine. She drank and drank.

Lori spent the next three days in this tiny cell, assuming her sleep cycle was normal of course, which was no small assumption since she couldn't see the sun at all. Twice a day food would be slid under the door slot at the bottom. She ate, but not enthusiastically. The fare was completely bland. Vegetable soup in a bowl, but no spoon. Plain French bread with a tab of butter, and either carrots or a banana. That was it. At one point, she was awaked by an odd sound which seemed very distant, as if coming from down an unimaginably long hallway. Ultimately she decided that it sounded like a man screaming. Possibly Vartan, but she couldn't be sure. She wasn't even sure if she was in the United States any longer. Vartan could be somewhere on the other side of the world by now - if he was even still alive.

Lori was asleep when she heard the metal on metal sound of the door slots being opened.

"Stand up, walk to the door, turn your back and place your hands on the door ledge." The voice was young, military, and disciplined. She complied. As soon as her hands were resting on the ledge, the middle door slot opened and her hands were pulled back, plastic handcuffs applied to them.

"Step away from the door," the same voice commanded. Lori did so, standing back several steps.

The door opened so rapidly that it surprised her, and three men in dark blue uniforms with no insignia on them came through. Two of them grabbed her arms on either side while the third put a black hood over her face and tied it off. Before it was slipped over her head, she caught a glimpse of the hallway beyond. It was as long as she'd speculated, maybe more so, and dimly lit. It was also completely empty.

They half dragged and half walked her down the hallway for what seemed to be at least ten minutes. They made no turns and did not deviate from their brisk pace. How big must this place have been?

Finally they stopped abruptly, and she heard a door latch being unhinged, then the mechanism unlatching and cranking over. A few more steps and she felt the warmth of the sun and a gentle breeze. It was her first taste of fresh air in days, and even through the hood it exhilarated her.

"Step," a voice commanded, and she lifted her right leg to ninety degrees and set of male hands grabbed her around the lower thigh area, directing her foot to a firm raised surface. Two more steps and then she was being pushed into a seated position and clamped once again in leg irons. She was driven somewhere, she didn't know where, and then made to disembark the van. She was taken up a ramp and squeezed through several narrow corridors, two guards at all times holding her by the arms. She was placed in a seat, strapped in, and then she heard some odd movements around her. She had no clue where she was until she heard the sound of a turbojet engine whining to life.

No one spoke to her for over two hours as the plane made its way to whatever destination they had decreed for her. It was hot in the hood and she tried not to let it get to her. She wasn't claustrophobic, not even a little bit, but much more time in this hood and she would be. Not knowing where she was being taken; to freedom, to another prison or even to her doom, she began to get agitated and sweat ran from the top of her head down her neck. If this was a psychological tactic, it was certainly working. She would tell them anything to get out of the hood at this point.

If only they would ask her a question.

Just as her breathing got labored and her anxiety began to rise, she felt the plane roll over and begin a steep descent. The thought that she would soon discover her fate, at the least her fate for the time being, comforted her. At the rate the plane was dropping, they would soon be on the ground and presumably she would then be out of the hood one way or another. And that was the thing she cared the most about right now.

Ten minutes later the plane was on the tarmac of some unseen air strip, rolling along at a brisk pace that indicated they were at a military base rather than a civilian airport. No pilot could get away with taxiing at this pace around a public airfield. As soon as the plane was stopped she heard the sounds of others unbuckling themselves and then her own belts were unbuckled and she was hauled to her feet. Then it was back through the narrow corridors and out through what she guessed were air stairs at the back of the plane. The air was hot and humid, but far fresher than the recycled air on the plane, and she relished the brief chance to get some oxygen through the hood. A moment later she was back in a van and bouncing up the road, the top of her head occasionally hitting the roof of the compartment as they went over the biggest bumps. Then the van came to a complete stop, and Lori heard the squeaky sounds of a gate being opened. The van started moving again, but much more slowly now, and she could feel it creep occasionally over speed bumps. She had no idea where she was going or what fate awaited her, but it seemed she would soon find out.

Again she heard an odd sound, like a large heavy mechanized door being opened, and the van proceeded slowly again and down an incline. She wondered if she was being taken to a missile silo somewhere. After a bit more movement, the van came to another halt and she had the distinct impression this was their final destination. That was confirmed a moment later when she heard the van doors opening and she was once again hauled out and walked across a smooth concrete floor. She could hear the clacking of dress shoes on the floor coming from the other direction and getting closer. Then she was stopped dead and the guards on both sides of her tightened their grip on her arms just above the elbows.

She could look down and just see a sliver of light through the bottom of the hood. Before she could make anything out, a third set of hands reached under her chin and loosened the rope ties, then reached around and pulled the hood straight off. Lori's hair, by now matted and sweat soaked, fell into her eyes and she involuntarily shook her head and tried to focus. When she did, Lori immediately recognized the woman standing in front of her.

She wore a dark blue business suit with an American flag pin on the lapel and a white blouse. She was tall and had a trim, tight figure for a woman approaching middle age. Her long dark hair was worn up and out of her face, and her countenance was dominated by pale pink lipstick and the black, squared "smart girl" glasses which were her signature accessory.

Her name was Diana Vaughn. She was the Vice President of the United States.

35.

Lori was literally agape at the sight of the woman who was standing in front of her. Of all the things she had expected to see when they took the hood off, the face of the Vice President was easily the last possibility in her mind.

Vaughn's expression contorted quickly into a look of angry displeasure. "Jesus Christ, I told you boys to clean her up before you brought her here," she fumed, her voice heavy with a Midwestern twang. Then she turned to a slight, petite young brunette who wore the same dark blue business attire and wore the same style glasses as her boss. "Emily, get back to my office and get my make-up kit."

The young girl, possibly an intern, looked Lori over once and then nodded to Vaughn and skipped quickly away. Lori took a moment to look around. She was in the garage of underground bunker of some kind, with high ceilings and white lights embedded in the concrete roof. There were pillars painted red, white and blue with signs like "G2" and "G3"on them and a few government vehicles were parked in a circle around them. Besides that, the huge garage was empty.

Vice President Vaughn was far from happy. "At least tell me you geniuses brought her a change of clothes like I told you?"

Lori looked over to the man who held her left arm, and was surprised to find that he was dressed in a gray civilian business suit. He looked like FBI, or maybe CIA, but not military. He was younger than she would have expected and had a look of abject terror on his face.

"Um, well ma'am . . ."

"Forget it," Vaughn snapped. She got quickly on a phone she was carrying and made a call. After a moment she got her intern on the line. "Emily, like we thought, they didn't bring the clothes either. Pull the casual stuff from my closet and bring her some jeans and a sweater. You're a size two, I'd guess?"

Still stunned, Lori just nodded without a word. Vaughn finished her call and then took Lori by the arm. "C'mon honey, let's get you presentable." The two guards tried to intervene, but Vaughn froze them with a fierce look. It was then that Lori remembered something she'd read the previous year. The Vice President's Secret Service nickname was said to be "Sib," which she heard actually stood for the letters C.I.B.; Cast Iron Bitch.

The guards gave no further resistance as the Vice President led her away across the garage to a woman's restroom. They tried to follow the women in, but Vaughn put a hand out and held them off. "That's far enough boys. This is the only way out. She's not going anywhere." She looked at Lori and then back at the guards, who just stood there stiffly and tried not to look her in the eyes. "I can't believe you guys, bringing her here like this," she said disgustedly. With that, she led Lori by the hand into the ladies room. One of the plain clothes guards stepped bravely forward.

"Ma'am, the cuffs have to stay on."

"Fine," the Vice President said, not looking back at them.

Lori was led to a sink and the Vice President helped her out of her jumpsuit as best she could, asking for a pair of scissors at one point to cut the sleeves off. Stripped down to her bra and panties, Vaughn used paper towels and soap to help Lori wash her face and under her arms. During this process the young girl came back with some clothes and a pair of converse sneakers, explaining she got Lori's shoe size from her FBI file. Vaughn then bent her over the sink and washed Lori's hair with warm water and the pink liquid hand soap from the dispenser. Lori remembered as her scalp was being gently massaged by the Vice President that she'd had three children, and Lori felt a degree of nurturing in the way she went about the task. She then used a towel Emily had brought down and the warm air from the hand drier to dry her off. Then Emily brushed Lori's hair while Vaughn applied some makeup.

Lori hadn't spoken at all during the twenty minutes it had taken to complete the task at hand.

"You're a quiet one," Vaughn noted, applying the last touches of eyeliner to Lori. "That's good. It might keep you alive. You've got some friends here. Don't fuck this up for them."

Lori couldn't bring herself to speak. She was still reeling from the experiences of the last few days.

"Hey," Vaughn said sharply, grabbing Lori's chin. "You listening to me?"

Lori nodded. "Yes Ma'am."

"That's good. Emily, go get the key for these cuffs. We need to get her sweater on her."

The young girl nodded and went out of the restroom. There was an exchange of dialog that Lori couldn't quite hear, and then the petite girl came bouncing back with the plastic key in her hand. A few minutes later they had Lori dressed in a black sweater and jeans and then they reattached the plastic cuffs to her hands. Wordlessly, Vaughn went to the door, and then the guards came in and took Lori away, with Vaughn and Emily following. They marched through the garage to a large freight elevator. As they got in, Vaughn hit the button and the doors closed. Lori couldn't see the control panel, but it seemed to her that they ascended at least six floors. When the doors opened, the guards exited first, checking the area while the Vice President and her party waited. Then they came back for Lori and Vaughn led them through a narrow corridor and some tightly packed offices and desks, all of which were unoccupied. Emily peeled off in another direction just as they came to a tall, wide, white door. There was a quick knock from the Vice President, and then she opened the door and waved to the guards. They held Lori's head down as they marched her in and placed her in an overstuffed reading chair. Then they exited the room back the way they had come in. Lifting her head, Lori's eyes traced the elliptical lines of the room, passing by book cases and paintings of famous Americans like Franklin D. Roosevelt, President Truman and President Washington. The Vice President had moved to another part of the room and sat on one of two opposing couches. On the opposite couch were Eric Ruby and a man in a military uniform she recognized from the news. He was the Chairman of the Joint Chiefs of Staff. At the far end of the room was a large wooden desk with a salt and pepper haired man seated behind it, in quiet discussion with another man in a charcoal suit who was facing away from the rest of them. It was then, when she recognized the man behind the desk, that Lori finally realized where she was.

In the Oval Office.

Ruby and the Chairman regarded her with clear contempt. After a quick glance in her direction, the Chairman reached forward and lifted a manila file from the coffee table and compared her to a picture he had pulled from the folder. Ruby made scowling eye contact with her and then turned his attention to the President of the United States, who was still quietly discussing something with the man who had his back to the proceedings. Even from across the large room, Lori could recognize the President and his signature Caesar style haircut and smart, athletically tailored black suit. Behind him were the framed photos of his family and the familiar white paned windows she had seen so often in his addresses from this very office. He wore brass colored wire framed glasses, which he removed when he was done speaking with the other man. He looked across the room at each of the people seated at the couches in turn, but did not pause to consider Lori. He dropped the glasses on the desk in front of him, letting them clatter as they came to rest. "Deputy Director," he said in a flat, emotionless voice.

Ruby stood up. "Thank you Mr. President," he said, sounding nervous. Lori was puzzled. Had he just called Eric Ruby Deputy Director? Of the FBI?

"Sir, it is our position that this problem can be made to go away quietly. The subject can be closed in a matter of minutes with little collateral harm."

The Vice President intervened. "Little collateral harm? Is that what you actually said? You call fifteen million pissed off voters 'little collateral harm?' I'd hate to see your idea of a lot of collateral harm."

"With respect, Madame Vice President," Ruby said, in a tone that displayed none, "we've been monitoring the situation and we agree that the subject will not expose this administration or its constituent interests to undue risk or irreparable harm."

"You're on crack," Vaughn shot back. She turned from him to address the President. "Mr. President, we've already got a huge audience putting pressure on the Justice Department and the Senator from Florida demanding a Congressional investigation."

Ruby ignored her taunt. "The Senator from Florida . . ."

"You mean the Senator from NASA," Vaughn corrected him. Irritated by the interruption, Ruby turned back to the President.

"Sir, the Senator from Florida is in the wrong party to make a stink about this. And the mid-term elections are still several months away. By the time he mustered up the support, the issue would be old news."

The President looked to his right, to a middle aged man in a brown suit seated next to his desk in a folding chair. The man stood and addressed the President. "That's true, Mr. President. But Senator Neilson is also talking about going on the air over this. That's a distraction we can't afford. The polls show an evenly spilt electorate at the moment."

"This isn't even the issue sir," Ruby objected. "The subject represents an ongoing danger to our preparations over the next two years."

The Vice President fired back. "The subject wouldn't even be an issue if it wasn't for your desire to clear another skeleton from your crowded little closet, Mr. Deputy."

Lori had no idea what they were talking about. She still wasn't that far removed from the confusion and claustrophobia caused by the black hood.

"Sir, our position is the subject remains a liability as long as she remains active," Ruby said to the President.

As long as "she" remained "active?" Lori was finally starting to understand. *She* was the "subject" they were discussing, and Ruby's efforts to render her "inactive" were a nice way of suggesting they kill her. Now she knew what the Vice President was telling her in the ladies room, and what she had to do; stay silent.

She watched then as Ruby spent the next several minutes discussing her possible demise in the most distant, bureaucratic language imaginable. How anyone could be so coldly ambitious as to argue for the murder of someone he'd once at least pretended to care for astonished her. Even now, after all the years of regret she'd felt over him and hearing the way he was arguing for her execution, she knew she could never do the same thing to him, no matter the price she might pay. She understood then a truth she should have known all along – the opposite of love wasn't hate, it was indifference. And Ruby could not have been more coldly indifferent to the prospect of her demise if she had been a bug on his wall.

After he had finished making his case, the President thought for a moment before responding. "So that is the unanimous view of the Council then?"

Ruby wavered a bit. "No sir. The Owls at Langley are of the opinion that deactivation is not justified . . ." he trailed off., ". . . at this time."

The President nodded and then turned to the man in the brown suit again. He seemed to know what to say without being asked. "The Rooster faction is divided on this, sir. They concede that deactivation is a viable course, but insist that the subject could be turned to our advantage under the right circumstances."

The President rubbed his left index finger across his lips. "Mr. Chairman?"

Lori studied the Army General as he stood to address his Commander in Chief. This was the man who had turned things around in Iraq and led the way in Iran. He had sent tens of thousands of insurgents and radicals to their God, and his opinion would carry a great deal of weight. He was even more popular than the President right now.

"I agree with the Deputy, Mr. President," he said with the voice of man who had seen plenty of bloodshed in his life, and who seemed to place little value on a single individual soul. "The subject nearly killed thousands of our citizens and almost ruined our plans. If she had succeeded, we would be in a very difficult position."

Lori's heart sank. He wanted her dead too.

The Vice President jumped in again. "Without her, we'd be in an even worse position. At least now we know what the plan is. We can prepare." She looked at Lori, and indicated in her direction. "And we can still use her."

The President nodded and steepled both hands over his mouth, thinking. Lori raised her head and looked at him, hoping he would look back at her, or that she'd see one ounce of consideration for her as human being. He leaned back in his leather desk chair for a moment and then to his left and he spoke quietly again to the charcoal suited man standing over him. Now she knew how the fallen gladiators in the Roman arena must have felt, watching the Emperor consider their fate and extending his hand with the thumb in a neutral position. Would he raise it, and grant her amnesty? Or would he turn it down and seal her fate, sending her soul home to her cat Peeve and to Melissa -- and to the House of the Singing Angels.

After several back and forth exchanges, the President nodded his ascension and placed his hands squarely on the desk in front of him. "It's decided," he said simply. Then he put his glasses back on and picked up a pen and began to write on piece of paper in front of him. Was he signing her death warrant?

She heard a door unbolt and then the dress suited security men were in the room again. Fearing the worst, she tried to stand and find an exit, but it was difficult with her hands cuffed behind her back and they took her, forcing her to kneel and then putting the black hood over her face again. The last thing she saw was the Presidential seal on the blue carpet before her.

35.

Moments later Lori was back in the van, which was bumping along and racing through the streets of Washington at high speed. There was the clack, clack, clacking sound of heavy rain on the roof of the van, and she could hear the whooshing sounds of water being pushed out of the van's path as it plowed through the puddles to whatever destination they had decreed for her. This time, they had bolted her hands to the floor of the van, which forced her into a kneeling position. She was certain this was an indication that they meant to kill her, and she began to silently contemplate the last minutes of her life. She found her thoughts drifting to Dr. Tsien, and what he must have gone through in those last painful moments, of Richard Garvin, and whether he had any idea how or why his life had been taken. And then there was Trevor Vartan. She had, by her cowardice, taken everything from him, even his desperate kind of dignity. He had spent the last decade of his life trying to expose and defeat the plot that had culminated in the launch of *Prometheus*, and he'd had a clear path and a clear chance to fulfill that purpose. He made only one mistake. He had trusted her. He had put aside his better instincts because she convinced him that her way could be better; and that she'd finish the job for him if she had to.

She thought again about Melissa's words to her in the dream, and knew that her purpose here on Earth had been to act as an instrument of justice, to do for those in the next world that which they could no longer do for themselves. And she had failed them. All of them. She was a disgrace.

Faced with this, with the awful truth of who she really was and how weak she had become, she felt the weight of it all descend on her in one brief moment. Quietly at first, but then louder and louder, she began to cry. She cried like the weak, scared, pathetic little girl she really was, the girl who wasn't even strong enough to protect her own sister. The wailing sounds of her own failings and vulnerability filled the van, and she felt a shame she hadn't felt in a long time. The shame of a little girl that had been caught stealing candy. But this time, she had done something far worse, and there were likely to be a great many more people who would be hurt by the duty she'd failed to fulfill.

The end could not come soon enough.

If there was anyone in the van with her, she couldn't tell, not that it mattered. When a soul is stripped bare the way hers was, there were precious few greater indignities to suffer. She assumed that if they were there, listening to her pathetic sobs, they would probably be as relieved to end her existence as she would be.

She felt the van slowing again, and knew this must be the end of the line in the most literal sense. She waited, and then the van was stopped and she heard the scuffling of movement in the cabin and the barking voices of orders that were being given. Then the rear doors swung open, and she felt heat and light from the sun on her skin, even through the material of the hood. Soon there were men in the van beside her, and she felt her hands being unclamped from the floor fixture and she was pulled forcibly to her feet. They lifted her from the van and dropped her roughly on to the pavement. She found herself hoping that they would leave the hood on, but to her astonishment, they did not. In one quick, sharp movement, the hood was off and she was blasted with the bright yellow light of the sun. As she adjusted to the light, she could see that they sky had cleared from what must have simply been an October squall. The asphalt at her feet was drenched and black. As soon as she was standing upright, two of the plain clothes officers took her arms and escorted her around the back of the van. What she saw next astounded her.

She was walking with them across an airport tarmac and toward a brightly painted red, white and blue commercial jetliner. Portions of the wings were polished to a mirror finish, and she could see her reflection and the eyeliner running down her face from her tears. Without a word, they directed her to a set of white air stairs on the left side of the aircraft and forced her up to the top. At the airplane door the guard on her right pounded on it with his palm, and a few seconds later a flight attendant opened it from the inside. The guard handed her what looked to be a ticket voucher, which was examined and stamped. Then they took her inside the airplane and placed her in a first class seat on the far aisle against the bulkhead. The rest of the plane was empty. They belted her into the seat and then did an astonishing thing; they reached down, unlocked her plastic handcuffs, and then left the airplane, the attendant closing the door behind them. She watched open mouthed from across the aisle as they crossed the tarmac back to the waiting van and sped away. Still dazed and emotional, she sat in silence as the plane began to fill with business travelers and families, some of them dressed for California and Disneyland. The attendant brought her water and a hot towel to clean up, but it was not until the plane backed away from the gate that she actually believed she was on a plane bound for Los Angeles.

The flight home was horrific. Not only was it rough and bumpy, but, thoroughly convinced she was going to die in an arranged plane crash, Lori jumped at every routine noise and cranking airfoil adjustment. She spent most of the trip trying to understand what had happened to her, and why they had let her go. Halfway through, she gave into the physical and emotional exhaustion and fell asleep.

She did not dream.

When the plane landed in LA, it was after dark. As she disembarked the plane and exited the gate, she saw a limo driver with a huge sign with her name on it. On automatic pilot much like the plane she had just flown in on, she went to him and he dutifully put her in the back seat and drove her to her apartment, without any instruction from her as to where it was. Digging for the spare key behind her mailbox, she found it and let herself in. Cleo came screeching out of the bedroom, meowing up at her incessantly and mixing in a number of less distinct sounds of displeasure, but belying her true feelings by rubbing her forehead affectionately on her mommy's hands and purring up a storm. Lori went to the kitchen to find Cleo's food bowl full and fresh water in her dish. Even the little motorized faux fountain that she liked to drink from was full of fresh water. Marshall had a spare key and must have come over to see to Cleo's needs while Lori had been gone.

She looked around the apartment, half expecting to find an assassin in the bathtub or a closet, but there was none. She found a large white envelope on her kitchen table that was from the FBI. She opened it. Inside was a replacement Special Agent ID card and the big diamond ring Vartan had bought for her in Las Vegas. She hadn't even noticed it was missing.

The phone rang and startled her. Almost dreading it, she went to the cordless and picked it up.

"Hello?" she said haltingly.

"Hey girl!" It was Connie's bright, feminine voice.

"Connie . . .?"

"Yeah. I guess you are back after all."

Lori flashed back to the shootout at the strip club, and the last time she had seen Connie, laying a pool of blood on the floor. Unable to hold back any longer, she started crying uncontrollably into the phone.

Connie let her cry for a few minutes, and then spoke to her in as soothing a tone as she could muster. "Hey, hey! It's OK honey. You're home safe."

"I know but . . ." Lori trailed off.

"But what?"

"The last time I saw you . . ." Another surge of emotion came out in a heaving sob.

"I'm fine, honey. Come on now, calm down. I know it's been rough for you, but I'm OK. Really."

"But the bullet . . ." Lori sounded like a fussy seven year old, even to her own ears.

"The bullet just grazed my forehead. I'll be wearing bangs for the rest of my life though," Connie said, with her typically inappropriate humor.

Lori laughed just a bit. "That's not funny."

"I know. But I'm the one with the Frankenstein scar," Connie reminded her.

"I want to see you."

Connie's tone grew immediately more serious. "That's not a good idea right now. A lot of things have changed in the last ten days."

Ten days? "I don't care. I just want to see you with my own eyes."

"I know you do honey, but there's time for that. It's Friday. Take the weekend to yourself and we'll talk in the office on Monday."

"Monday?"

"Yeah. Ron Harmon is the new A.D. He wants to see you first thing."

Lori longed for a time when such a prospect would have frightened her to her bones. Now, the idea of dealing with a new boss seemed almost laughable after what she'd gone though.

"Hey," Connie continued, "take a couple of days, pet your kitty, and we'll talk at lunch next week, OK?"

"OK," Lori said in a small voice.

"All right then. I'll take care of telling Marshall you're back. Get some rest. Bye-bye."

"Bye."

Lori put the phone down and turned to Cleo, who was still giving Lori her rapt attention. Connie was right. Sometimes the best thing in the world was just spending time petting your kitty.

36.

The weekend had done little to change Lori's feeling that she was on autopilot. Although she went through the usual routines of life, shopping for groceries, brushing and petting Cleo, even catching up on some TV shows, she found it did nothing to restore an air of normalcy. She got no sense – none at all – that she was being followed or watched in any way.

She could not shake the overwhelming sense of sadness and disinterest she felt. Nothing really mattered to her now. All she could think about was all the people she had failed, and the chance she would never get again. She had even seriously spent some time on the idea of leaving the FBI, which until two weeks before had been her life's calling. Combined with her feelings of guilt was an overwhelming sense of futility. The Brookings people had been right. Once you know that the end may be coming, you stop caring about doing any of the things that keep society moving forward.

She returned to the office the following Monday to find a note affixed to her computer's flat screen. It told her to check in with Assistant Director Harmon as soon as she got in.

She went to Connie's blue-grey cubicle, but it was empty and obviously hadn't been used for a while. There were flowers on the desk and get well cards pinned up on all the walls. She knew she should be grateful that her friend was still alive, but the happy mood of the cubicle made her feel even more detached from reality. What had Connie really won by surviving? A chance to live a few years longer, with the promise of an unimaginable hell to confront after that? Lori wondered if her silent prayers for Connie's recovery had been a good idea at all.

"Hey, welcome back!"

Lori turned to see Marshall, his dark blue windbreaker still on and his sack lunch in hand, standing behind her. Lori flashed him a tiny smile, the best she could muster at that point, and put a hand on his shoulder. He set the lunch down on Connie's desk and turned to give her a big hug. She didn't resist him at all. She was glad to see him, too.

He finally let her down after practically lifting her off her feet, and pulled back to look into her eyes. Marshall didn't often do that. She half expected a pronouncement of his love for her. Instead, he grew stern. "You should have called me more. You should have trusted me."

Lori understood. "Marshall, I can't . . . I couldn't trust anyone. You have to understand that. It wasn't that I didn't trust you. I just didn't know who might be watching you. Using you . . ." Lori knew in her depths that was no excuse. Marshall was another person she had failed, as a friend if nothing more.

"And who could you trust Lori? This Vartan guy? This counterfeiter?"

"He's not a counterfeiter."

"So you say. The point is, he's not a better friend than I am. He's not a better man. I would have found a way to protect you. To help you. A way that wouldn't have left so many people dead."

Lori was sincerely touched by Marshall's words. This was not grandstanding on his part. He really meant it, and it was coming from an adult place in his heart, not out of some adolescent fantasy about her. For the first time, he really did seem like a man to her.

"Marshall, I . . ."

"Don't say it, don't say anything. Just tell me that you heard me. Tell me that you believe me."

That she could do. "I believe you."

"Good. Now you'd better get upstairs. Harmon is already on a rampage around here, and he's only been on the job a week."

"OK."

He gathered up his lunch and turned to go to his own cube. She took one last look at Connie's desk before she headed to the elevator. Back to the same office so much of this had started in.

Harmon had completely redone Ruby's office, and it barely reminded her of the place she'd had the first confrontation with he and the mysterious Mr. Dansby just two weeks before. Harmon was scribbling onto a notepad as she walked in, his glasses slung low over his nose. He took no notice of her as she walked in and sat in one of the two guest chairs facing his dark wooden desk. She crossed one leg of her gray pantsuit over the other as she waited. She knew this was just his way, the grumpy, scruff manner he always used, but for the first time she could remember, it did not annoy her. After about two minutes, he finished his notes and dropped the glasses loudly on the desk.

"Special Agent," he said, reaching into a desk drawer and pulling out a badge and gun. "I believe these are yours." He handed them across the desk to her. She took them, examining the badge carefully. It was the same one she'd had with her almost the whole of the last two weeks.

"I'm not sure I want this anymore, Chief," she said, rubbing across the pressed metal design with her thumb. "I'm not sure I deserve it."

He snorted. "I'm sure you do, Special Agent. But as you say, do you still want it?"

She continued to rub it absently. "Maybe not." She'd been so proud of herself when she'd first earned this badge. Now it seemed so unimportant.

"Well, you should think about it. Lori, I've never told you this, but I think you're the best field agent in this office. I mean that. Whatever happened out there, I'd still like you on my staff."

She shook her head. "I wish *I* knew what happened out there, Chief."

He rocked back in his leather chair. "I think it would be best if neither of us asked too many questions about that."

She shifted her attention from the badge to him. "That's not in my nature, Chief."

"I know it's not. That's why I'd still like you on my staff."

She considered it. "What would I do?"

"What you've been doing. Look, I know this has been a difficult ordeal for you. You almost lost your partner out there. Why don't you take a couple of weeks with pay and sort things out. When you're ready to come back, there's plenty for you to do here. There's no shortage of bad guys in this town."

If you only knew the half of it, Lori thought to herself. "I'm just not sure more time at home is the right thing, Chief. I'd feel better doing something, frankly. Anything."

"But . . .?"

"But just not here. Not anymore." She knew then that she would always feel Ruby's shadow over this office.

"Is this a transfer request or a resignation?"

Lori thought about that. She felt drawn back home now more than ever. She wanted to spend as much time near her parents as she could, especially if Vartan had been right about what was to come. But she couldn't effect any change or make any kind of a difference as a private citizen.

"A transfer request, I think."

"Granted," Harmon said immediately. He pulled a paper from his top desk drawer that he'd obviously had at the ready and stamped it.

"Seattle," he said. "Good luck, Special Agent."

Lori was past being surprised by anything anymore. She took the transfer notice and rose from the chair, gathering up her badge and gun along the way. She turned just as she got to the door. Harmon had already gone back to his notes and the glasses were back in place.

"Sir," she used the proper term instead of the more familiar "Chief."

"Uh-huh?"

"About my case . . ."

"Closed," he said brusquely. "It was an Asian gang initiation killing. It's been turned back over to the Pasadena police. You and agent Balver did a fine job on it."

She nodded, but he wasn't even looking at her. So that was that.

"Thank you, sir," she said as she spun and headed back to the elevator. She assumed this was the last time she would ever speak to Harmon in person.

37.

Cleo was meowing loudly as Connie lifted the cat carrier through the sun roof and into her Volkswagen. "Don't worry pussycat. You're not going to the vet. You're just going to stay with Aunt Connie for a week or so."

Lori loved the caressing, sing-song quality of Connie's voice, especially when she talked to Cleo. She'd be a good mom someday. Cleo continued to meow, and looked at Lori with a worried expression. It broke Lori's heart. "Aww, sweetie!" Lori reached into the cat carrier and stroked her favorite feline's head. "Things will be just fine."

Lori looked up to see Connie giving her a stern look, the kind of look she always had when there was something serious to say. "If you're about to say something profound about things being fine, save it," Lori said to her. "I already know."

Connie smirked. "You take all the fun out of being a girl. Have I ever told you that?"

Lori knew Connie was only partially joking with her. "Sorry. Say what you have to say."

"OK, since you asked. It's nice to see you caring about something again. I was worried you know."

Lori smiled at her. "I know. So was I."

"Yeah, this is me not believing you."

A gust of wind caught Connie's long dark hair and brushed it aside just enough for Lori to see the reddish-purple scar on her forehead. Lori reached out to touch it, but Connie recoiled. "Now who's taking the fun out of being a girl?" Lori said to her.

Connie let out an exaggerated sigh. "Fine," she said, dutifully offering up her forehead to Lori.

Lori reached under her bangs and felt along the scar. It was raised but not too much. It would heal up pretty well in the end. "Poor baby," she said to Connie.

"Not really feeling the love here," Connie said sarcastically. Then she smiled. "I'll be fine."

"I know you will," Lori told her friend. Then she gave her a quick hug and looked around the parking lot of her apartment building one last time. Marshall had done a superior job of packing Lori's whole life into one U-Haul trailer. It was hard to believe she wasn't going to see him and Connie on a day to day basis anymore. She started to feel sad again. "I guess it's time to go," she said wistfully.

Connie, who had been overprotective and hyper vigilant since Lori had returned, noticed immediately. "Hey," she said gently, "this was your idea, remember?"

"Yeah, I know. But it isn't easy."

"Why should it be? It wouldn't mean anything if it was too easy."

Lori nodded. "Are you coming up for Thanksgiving for sure?"

"Absolutely." Lori was glad of that. Connie's mom and she didn't get along, and she hadn't seen her father since she was a little girl. She deserved to have something of a family at this stage of her life. And at this time in history.

Neither of them had noticed the dark Mercury sedan that had been parked across the lot in a visitor's spot until the door opened and a tall, well-dressed man emerged, Starbuck's coffee cup in hand. The loud slam of the door caught their attention, and the man smiled as he sauntered across the parking lot in his fine woven charcoal-colored suit. The ensemble was offset by a white shirt and a thin, black tie, like something out of the 1980's – or even the early 1960's. As he got closer and closer, Lori recognized the wrinkled, craggy face and the self satisfied expression. It was Prescott Dansby.

"Well," he said, sounding overly polite. "I see you're all packed up for your move. Congratulations on your reassignment."

"I asked for the transfer," Lori pointed out.

"Yes, of course. I just wanted to come by and thank you for your work on the Dr. Tsien case, and to wish you luck on your next assignment."

He sipped from his paper cup again. Despite his polite, refined manner, his phony smile made him look more like a reptile than the trustworthy, harmless grandpa he was trying to evoke. Lori instinctively stepped back from him. "I'd say 'thank you,' but I'm not sure what I have to thank you *for*."

"Quite a bit more than you know, I suspect."

Lori was mildly surprised by the candor of his response. "That's not exactly an answer, Mr. Dansby."

He sipped again. "That wasn't exactly a question, Special Agent."

Lori studied his face, trying to get a read on him, but he was implacable. An uncomfortable silence hung in the air like the stale smell of his coffee cup. Was he trying to goad her into asking the wrong question, or leading her to the right question?

"All right," she said finally. "Tell me about my friends. Tell me who saved me from deactivation."

"That should be obvious. The Vice President, among others. Didn't she tell you?"

How would he have known *that*, unless . . . "That was you in the Oval Office, wasn't it, Mr. Dansby?"

He smiled. "Perhaps. But as I said, you have a great many friends. A number of them hoped you would succeed in your quest."

"I wouldn't call it a quest. It was more like playing a hunch."

"In any event, your instincts were correct. There were those that sought to use the *Prometheus* probe for their own purposes."

"Who?" she demanded.

"My dear, I can't make it quite that easy on you."

"Actually, you can."

Again, he betrayed no visible reaction. "You assume too much, Special Agent. I'm not as influential as you suspect. And even I'm not certain that I'm anywhere near the top of the food chain in all this."

Lori nodded. "So everything you tell me could be a lie."

He smiled. The self satisfaction again. "Exactly." He raised his cup to her and sipped.

"But if you knew what these people were trying to do, why didn't your group try to stop them? Why did you leave it to us?"

"We could have. But that wouldn't have been very sporting, would it?"

Lori couldn't decide if his indifference was an act or not. "This is a game to you?"

He shook his head. "Hardly. But even we have certain . . . limitations. And you should resist the temptation to think in black and white terms. It's not as clear cut as you imagine. There are factions on both sides who favored eliminating you, and those that preferred seeing how far you could get."

"And which side were you on, Mr. Dansby? Should I look at you as a good guy, or a bad guy?"

"I should think that would be obvious."

Lori shook her head slowly. "No. It isn't."

He raised the coffee cup again, and then retracted it before taking a sip. "Perhaps if you thought of it in another way. Not good and bad, but . . . Owl's, and Roosters."

That again. "Owl's and Roosters? In the eschatological sense?"

He tipped his cup to her. "Roosters crow to the imminent dawn. They want to rouse the farm, to stir the other animals into action, to shatter the quiet complacency of the barnyard. Owls are night animals. They dislike both the noise and the light. They want to hush the roosters, insisting that it's still night, that the dawn is far away." He tipped his cup again. "Very good, Special Agent."

Connie was in full mother hen protective mode now and was looking at Dansby like she wanted to shoot him right there in the parking lot. If he noticed the hostility emanating from her, he gave no indication of it. Lori stepped between them as a precaution. "That still doesn't tell me what I need to know, Mr. Dansby. Are you an Owl, or a Rooster?"

He smiled again. "I have been known to crow from time to time, Miss Pars."

So, it *was* him in the oval office. He *was* the dark suited man with his back to the proceedings that had intervened on her behalf. "Who are you, exactly, Mr. Dansby? And what sway do you have over people like the President?"

He was obviously pleased that she had finally asked him the question he had come there to answer. "Sway? Why

none at all, my dear. Besides my public duties at DARPA,
I'm also a member of several private consulting firms. It's in
that capacity that I can be most useful to you."

"And what exactly do these 'private consulting firms'
advise the President on, Mr. Dansby?"

Simply for dramatic effect she thought, he sipped again
from his paper coffee cup before responding. "Think of us as
an organization that predicts the future. And we've found that
the best way to predict the future . . . is to create it."

Lori let an acid expression cross her face. "I'd
appreciate it if you'd stop answering me in riddles."

"You're getting impatient, Special Agent. Everything
will become clear in time."

"We don't have much time."

Connie physically reacted to this statement. Lori hadn't
told her anything detailed about all the conversations she and
Vartan had during their cross country trek, and what he
suspected was the real purpose of *Prometheus'* mission. And
she certainly hadn't mentioned anything about the possible
end of the world. Poor Connie had carried enough of her
burdens. Lori could see her tensing, and she reached out a
hand to calm her.

Lori saw Dansby notice the way Connie tensed up, and
he looked back and forth between her and Lori. "I see you
haven't shared a great deal of your experiences with your
friend, Special Agent. Perhaps we should discuss this some
other time." He started to step away, but Lori got angry and
reached across to grab his arm.

"Not until you tell me what happened to Vartan," she
said sharply. Dansby looked down at her grip on his arm and
actually seemed amused by it. Lori wasn't fazed by his effort
to appear confident. She was certain she could take him down
in a second if she needed to. He stopped, then pulled his arm
from her grip and straightened his suit.

"Mr. Vartan is in good health. And I'm sure you'll be
hearing from him quite soon."

"The last time I saw him he wasn't in particularly good
health."

Dansby let one corner of his mouth creep up in half-smile. "I assure you things are much better now. Like you, he's been released. He's free to go about his business."

"Really? And why would you do that? You know he'll come after you and your friends directly now."

"I doubt that, Special Agent."

Lori just looked at him. "I wouldn't, if I were you."

He smiled again, the same arrogant, infuriating smile. "Surely it must have occurred to you that he cut a deal for your release?"

"Actually, I had assumed he was dead."

Dansby turned and slowly began to walk away from them. "Well, he isn't," he said.

"That won't matter," she called after him. "That won't stop him. He thinks you killed his parents," she told him.

Dansby paused and looked back. "Did we? Are you quite certain of that, Special Agent?"

"He is."

"Well then, it seems to me he's already forgotten the most important lesson he taught you in all of this."

Lori knew it was a setup for a straight line, but she said it anyway. "Which is . . .?"

He smirked. "The lie is different at every level."

He gave them both a quick look, deep into their eyes, then turned again and casually returned to his car, started it, and drove away.

Connie watched until his car was well out of sight. "That dude is seriously creepy," she observed.

"Tell me about it," Lori said.

37.

Lori was hard on the breaks as her white Honda descended the last few miles out of the Siskiyou Mountains. She had crossed the state border into Oregon now, near Ashland, and was more than halfway home. It had been a clear sunny drive from Los Angeles, and even though night was falling she decided to make for Eugene, another four hours up the road at the rate she was driving.

Just outside of Eugene, a text message from Marshall came in. Breaking several laws, she picked up her phone to read it. The message told her to tune to a specific A.M. radio frequency. Dutifully, she ejected the CD she was listening to and tuned to the station Marshall had texted her: 1440 A.M. The signal came through loud and clear, and she chuckled to herself over Marshall's techno-geekiness. She suspected he had tracked her progress from the GPS transponder in the trailer, and found just the right station along the way so she could listen in. The program was in a commercial, but a few minutes later she heard a lightening bolt sound effect and the deep, resonant baritone voice of the host.

"Welcome back to *Nationwide AM*," he said. "I'm George Kalb, your host. Let's get right back to our guest. I'm speaking tonight with a man I will only call 'Deep Space.' Most of you have heard of him over the years as a source of information for the late Richard Garvin. Well, tonight he's making the first of what I hope will be many appearances on this program, following as best he can in Richard's footsteps. Deep Space, are you still there?"

"Yes I am, George." The voice was formal, polite, British, and unmistakably that of Trevor Vartan. Lori felt a little surge of excitement up her spine. So he was alive after all, just as Dansby had promised her.

"All right. So let's go back over what we've already covered. You have provided to me, and we have posted on our website, what you say are the real, unaltered, authentic images of Cydonia and the Face on Mars that were given to you by an inside source at NASA. What they show, undeniably, is the smoking gun for proof of artificiality of the Face and other monuments on Mars, is that correct?"

"Yes it is, George."

She could hear Kalb shuffling papers in the background. "OK, fine. How do we prove that? How do we know these aren't just from some slick work you did with Photoshop?"

Vartan cleared his throat. "Honestly, George, we don't. I can't prove that. What I can prove is that the original source data came from a government UNIX based machine, and that it has an earlier date stamp than the official versions released on the MRO HiRise camera web site."

"So you are admitting that as long as NASA denies that these are real MRO images, which they have so far, you can't prove that they're authentic?"

"Unfortunately that's correct," Vartan said. "Even though I was allowed to obtain these images legally, NASA and JPL are under no legal constraints to admit to their authenticity."

Lori tried to contain her excitement at hearing Vartan's voice again and she couldn't keep a broad smile from crossing her face. Not only was he seemingly alive and well, but he had been given the images that Marshall had secured from Dr. Tsien's secreted flash drive. She rolled over the implications of this in her head. What had Vartan given them in return?

Kalb audibly shuffled the papers again. "OK, now I want to ask you something else. Do you think this leak could be a precursor to some kind of official government disclosure? Do you think we can expect more releases like this in the future, or will the president just come out and admit that we've been lied to for decades?"

Again Vartan was silent and Lori could feel herself tensing up. "No I don't think it is part of some broader policy of government disclosure," he said haltingly. "And in fact I hope it's just the opposite."

"Really?" Kalb said, surprise in his voice. "Why is that?"

"Well, I think that all these UFO researchers who are always pining for some sort of official disclosure haven't really thought through the implications of it. If and when the government ever officially admits that they've lied to us about what's on Mars or what the Apollo astronauts found, I'm heading for the hills, personally."

"Because?"

"Well George, why would the powers that be want to upset the status quo? They're already at the top, already holding the reins of power. If they make an official disclosure, not only is the public reaction unpredictable, but the consequences to them are implicitly negative. They don't have anywhere to go but down."

Kalb made a low grunting sound of agreement. "I guess that makes sense."

"Yes," Vartan agreed. "And if they are making an official disclosure of that type, it can only mean one thing." He paused again. "That we are very near the end."

This statement brought Lori back down to Earth and she lost just a bit of her grin.

"Then why would they bother to give you these photos at all, Deep Space?"

"Well, one thing you can never underestimate with these clandestine groups is their adherence to religious principals. The one thing that most of our major religions teach us is the concept of free will. So, in that sense, they can impel events, but they can't *compel* them. If we rise up and demand the truth, they'll give it to us. But they are under no obligation to go beyond that. We simply have to ask the right questions."

"So, you have to be in the game, to be in the game," Kalb said.

"Exactly."

"All right, Deep Space. We can all go to the *Nationwide AM* web site and decide for ourselves, I guess. I've only got you for the rest of this segment so I want to move on."

From her radio, she heard Kalb drum his fingers on the table as he continued. "I have been told by sources at the Cape that there was an attempted terrorist incursion last week before the launch of the new Jupiter probe called *Prometheus*. Can you illuminate us on that?"

"Yes, I certainly can George. My understanding is that there was no terrorist attack on the rocket at all. Rather, I'm told that what happened is that a couple of the anti-nuclear protesters from the memorial services the day before tried to rush the launch pad to force NASA to cancel the launch. If they hadn't been apprehended, NASA would have lost the launch window and it would have been another two years before they could try again."

"OK," Kalb said, "how close did these two get?"

"Fairly close, I'm told." Vartan said in response. "As I understand it they attacked a pad worker and stole worker's smocks. Fortunately, the pad worker, an elderly gentlemen, recovered. There had been erroneous reports that he was killed."

"Well, that's good news at least."

"Yes it is."

This was the first Lori had heard of the fate of Ken's friend Jerry Flynn, and she wondered if Vartan had brought it up hoping she'd be listening in. She was glad to hear he was going to be all right.

Kalb was beginning to sound impatient. "Do you know what happened to these protesters?"

"What I've heard is that Senator Neilson . . ."

"Excuse me Deep Space, but that would be Senator Rick Neilson from Florida?"

"Yes, that's who I'm speaking of," Vartan said. "I'm told that Senator Nielson intervened on their behalf with the President himself."

"Really? Now why would he do that?"

"My understanding is the Senator doesn't want any adverse publicity right now because the NASA budget proposal for the next five years is being debated in a Senate committee just at the moment."

"Oh I see. So his objective is to make sure NASA looks as good as possible to the public during the budget review process?"

"Yes," Vartan responded cordially. Lori wondered where Vartan had gotten his information, and if he knew that it was actually the Vice President and Prescott Dansby that had arranged their release.

"OK, one last thing before I let you go," Kalb was saying. "Many, many of my listeners are more and more focused on rumors that the Sun is growing increasingly unstable. That we might get hit with a big solar flare sometime in the next few years. Do you know anything about that?"

"No George. My information is that the Sun is quite calm at the moment."

"So, if that's the case, then are you saying we have nothing to worry about over the next few years?" Kalb asked.

Lori's could feel tension building in her neck and shoulders. Idly, she wished that Vartan was there to help her work it out.

Vartan was quiet once again. Then: "Not by any means."

"Would you care to elaborate on that? I mean, what is your personal belief about the next couple years?"

Lori felt a chill go up her spine, quite unlike the excited feeling she'd experienced minutes before.

Vartan cleared his throat again nervously. "Personally, I think something terrible is going to happen," he said.

"So you're not optimistic?"

"Hardly."

Kalb grew more forceful. "I really think you owe it to this audience to share what you personally suspect."

Vartan was quiet again for a moment or two. "My biggest concern is that if absolutely nothing happens, a few very powerful people on the inside may take it into their own hands to ensure that *something*, some major event, does in fact take place."

"And I take it you're saying that this 'something' isn't going to be pleasant for the rest of the human race?"

"Yes. It would not be pleasant."

Now it was Kalb who took his time responding. "Wow. That's not exactly the answer I hoped to hear."

"I know, George. And I'm sorry. But it's what I've come to believe after all the things I've seen and all the things I've uncovered."

"Is there a chance you could be wrong?" Kalb sounded anxious to move the show on a positive direction, Lori thought.

"Oh, most certainly I could be wrong," Vartan admitted. "After all, there's no guarantee that what I've been told is at all accurate. As I've said to Richard many times over the years, the lie is different at every level. Even mine."

"Well, let's hope they've lied to you about the future then, Deep Space."

"Yes. Let's hope."

Lori could hear the bumper music start to rise softly in the background. "OK, well that about wraps up our time tonight. Do you have anything you'd like to add?"

"Actually I do," Vartan said, sounding pleased at the question. "I'd like to address this to your audience in general, but also to one person in particular who I hope is listening." Lori knew he meant her. Had he somehow arranged with Marshall for her to listen in?

"It is important for us all to remember a few things as these end dates approach," Vartan continued. "Nothing is pre-determined. Even our own secret documents and studies admit that. We do matter, each of us. And it only takes one of us to make a difference. Yes, it is still night, and the new dawn approaches. But it only takes one stirring rooster to rouse the barnyard. And there is still time before that dawn."

"Well said," Kalb added. Then he thanked Vartan and went into his closing monologue.

As the dark road stretched out before her, Lori smiled again, feeling somewhat lifted in spirit simply from hearing Vartan's voice. She remembered something her father, who had been a boxer in his youth, had once told her when she was little girl and came home scraped up and crying from an altercation with another girl; "Fighting is rounds, Lori."

This, she now hoped, had been only round one.

Made in the USA
Columbia, SC
21 December 2017